SHROUD
OF NIGHT

SHROUD OF NIGHT

ANDY CLARK

BLACK LIBRARY

*Dedicated to Phil, Mat, Jerm and Nick K for being
the best mentors a new writer could ever have.*

A BLACK LIBRARY PUBLICATION

First published in Great Britain in 2017 by
Black Library,
Games Workshop Ltd.,
Nottingham, NG7 2WS, UK.

10 9 8 7 6 5 4 3 2 1

Produced by Games Workshop in Nottingham.
Cover illustration by Akim Kaliberda.

See Black Library on the internet at
blacklibrary.com

Find out more about Games Workshop
and the world of Warhammer 40,000 at
games-workshop.com

Printed and bound in China.

It is the 41st millennium. For more than a hundred
centuries the Emperor has sat immobile on the Golden Throne of Earth.
He is the Master of Mankind by the will of the gods, and master of a
million worlds by the might of his inexhaustible armies. He is a rotting
carcass writhing invisibly with power from the Dark Age of Technology.
He is the Carrion Lord of the Imperium for whom a thousand souls are
sacrificed every day, so that he may never truly die.

Yet even in his deathless state, the Emperor continues his eternal
vigilance. Mighty battlefleets cross the daemon-infested miasma of
the warp, the only route between distant stars, their way lit by the
Astronomican, the psychic manifestation of the Emperor's will. Vast
armies give battle in his name on uncounted worlds. Greatest amongst
his soldiers are the Adeptus Astartes, the Space Marines, bio-engineered
super-warriors. Their comrades in arms are legion: the Astra Militarum
and countless planetary defence forces, the ever-vigilant Inquisition and
the tech-priests of the Adeptus Mechanicus to name only a few. But for
all their multitudes, they are barely enough to hold off the ever-present
threat from aliens, heretics, mutants – and worse.

To be a man in such times is to be one amongst untold billions. It is to
live in the cruellest and most bloody regime imaginable. These are the
tales of those times. Forget the power of technology and science, for
so much has been forgotten, never to be re-learned. Forget the promise
of progress and understanding, for in the grim dark future there is only
war. There is no peace amongst the stars, only an eternity of carnage and
slaughter, and the laughter of thirsting gods.

PROLOGUE

The warp churned. It raged and roiled.

Storms of wrath tore through tattered veils of fate and falsehood, splitting the skin of reality. Ethereal abominations howled their hunger to the void, twining their kaleidoscopic tendrils between the stars. Real space met the immaterium along interstitial fault lines, convulsing with a violence that shattered time and set reason ablaze from one end of the galaxy to the other.

Somewhere amidst the madness hung a world. Above it, in orbit, a fleet. The spacecraft were ornate, buttressed gothic monsters whose hulls flowed and twisted in shapes both elegant and hideous. One amongst them was larger than the rest, a grotesquery of burnished gold and fleshy purple. Upon its flanks the battleship bore the taloned wing of the Emperor's Children. Below the emblem was a name.

Herald of Pain.

On the warship's twisted bridge, its master of auguries knelt in supplication before his lord. He had been borne from the chamber of silvered mirrors upon an ornate walking-carriage, but though slaves and champions alike had cleared his path with their eyes downcast, still he felt only fear. One amongst the coven of scryer surgeons had had to convey news of the battle upon the planet below. That unpleasant duty had fallen to him.

'The auguries in flesh were clear, my lord. We saw through the lens of the screaming veil all that transpired below. They are all dead.'

The master of auguries was a hunched creature, swathed in perfumed robes, bent double beneath the weight of the metal fetishes that pierced his flesh. Before the unwavering gaze of his masked and armoured lord, the lumpen creature cowered lower still.

When he spoke, Lord Excrucias the Flawless' voice slithered from the lips of his gilded mask in a silken whisper. Still it carried to the furthest corners of the cavernous bridge.

'If our enemies are slain, then why do you grovel so? Was it an… untidy… victory?' Excrucias' thoughts turned to his golden flensing knives with a tingle of anticipation. They would have delightful work to do, if his servants had made a hash of his elegant battle plans.

'No, my lord.'

'Then what?' hissed Excrucias. 'Reticence is a flaw.'

The master of auguries flinched. He gathered himself before replying.

'My lord. Some of our enemies were slain. Not all. It is our warriors who lie dead.'

Silence fell across the bridge of the *Herald of Pain*. Gold-armoured Chaos Space Marines stood statue-still, watching with avid excitement. Cultist crew and slave-mutants halted mid-sentence, leaving astrogation readings unfinished and vox exchanges hanging. Even the captives locked within dangling excruciation-cages turned their screams to whimpers. Only the distant rumble of the ship's drives and the mindless binharic babble of servitors disturbed the quiet.

'All of them…?' asked Excrucias.

'Yes, lord,' replied the master of auguries. The creature abased itself before Excrucias' living throne, veiled face pressed to the decking.

'How?'

'The enemy, lord. They had traps. Defences. They fought like daemons.'

'Truly,' whispered Excrucias. 'You assured me that your scryer surgeons detected but thirty-one souls on that world. I despatched two hundred warriors to effect their sacrifice. There were Terminators amongst our ranks. The battle was to last seventeen minutes and thirty-two seconds, no longer. Instead, it has been more than an hour since I gave the order to attack. And you say that these thirty-one enemies... slew them all?'

'Yes, lord,' whimpered the mutant.

'How many of these mysterious foes did we kill in return?' asked Excrucias.

'We believe... perhaps half...' The master of auguries' voice was little more than a croak.

'Fascinating...' said Excrucias, running his tongue delicately along the serrated edge of his mask's lips. His armour hummed as he rose from his squirming throne.

Excrucias' sorcerer, Phelkorian Twyst, detached himself from the shadow of the throne and lumbered in his wake. Phelkorian's body was encased in a gem-encrusted suit of power armour, but the cowl of his rubberised cloak did little to hide the bloated mass of tentacles and fangs that was his face. Gasping wet, eager breaths, the sorcerer joined his master at the marble railing of Excrucias' command dais. Before them, looming large in the bridge's primary vid-screen, was the planet of Bloodforge.

'It looks like a blinded eye,' panted Phelkorian from his lamprey-like mouth. 'As though our divine mistress slipped a needle into one of the Blood God's vacant orbs.'

Excrucias let slip a murmur of agreement, staring intently at the planet below. Two hundred, slain by just thirty-one. He should feel anger, he supposed. Instead, he was fascinated. Oh, his knives would taste blood, of course, pleasurable offerings cut from his living flesh and given to Slaanesh to atone for this failure. But still, an opportunity presented itself.

'Prepare the teleportarium,' ordered Excrucias.

One of his attendant champions slammed a fist to his breastplate in salute.

'I shall bear your orders, my lord,' he barked eagerly. 'I beg the honour of leading the next attack for myself and my Kakophanarii.'

Excrucias gave a slight shake of his head.

'No, Gaiuss. I go alone.'

'My lord?' said Phelkorian, tentacles squirming in agitation. 'Is that advisable? Whoever they are, they cut down Lukian and his Writhe-kin like dogs. Not to mention that we are deep within the Eye. Teleportation has its risks. Prideful victory is an act of worship, but arrogance...'

'...is a flaw,' finished Excrucias. 'I know. Prepare the teleportarium.'

The slighted champion saluted once more and strode away. Excrucias placed one fleshmetal palm upon the pommel of his sword. He caressed the weapon's hilt, and the entity within it crooned softly.

'Ensure that the magi are ready to extract me at a moment's notice, Phelkorian,' he said.

'Of course, my lord,' replied the sorcerer. 'And I shall gather my magicks, in case they are required,' he added with relish.

'As you will,' murmured Excrucias, before gesturing to the master of auguries who still grovelled before his throne. 'As for that, it is flawed. I've no further use for it.'

The master of auguries let out a piteous wail and scrambled to his feet, but with a sorcerous gesture, Phelkorian froze him in place.

Excrucias strode from the bridge, leaving his sorcerer leering delightedly over the weeping mutant.

Excrucias' senses sang as an empyric tempest raged around him. His consciousness expanded while reality wheeled dizzyingly. For a split second he felt the feather-light touch of questing tendrils and raking claws upon his flesh, his mind, his soul. Then, with an ear-splitting crack, he rematerialised upon the surface of Bloodforge. Kaleidoscopic lightning danced around the Chaos lord before flickering away into nothingness.

Excrucias stood in a place of deep and profound silence, amidst the tumbledown ruins of what looked to have once been a mighty fortress. The sky above was the colour of cataracts, streaked by wisps of blood-hued cloud. A sallow breeze hissed fitfully through hollow archways and over crumbled ramparts, rattling grit against his armour plates. The quiet was sepulchral.

Slowly and deliberately Excrucias took in his surroundings, leaving his weapons sheathed. He had teleported down close to his warriors' initial drop coordinates, and had a clear view of the devastation they had triggered. Rubble and corpses were scattered on every side, littering an area cratered and blackened by the aftermath of multiple detonations. The bodies wore the purple and gold power armour of Emperor's Children, or else the tattered remains of Slaaneshi cult robes and masks. Dozens had died here. Excrucias tasted traces of fisilite and magnitorian det-chems upon the air, along with burned blood and the dust of shrapnel-torn stone. His unnaturally sharp senses suggested that his warriors had teleported directly into the midst of a minefield constructed from short-fused demolisher shells. The size of the craters and the condition of the corpses reinforced his supposition.

Through magic, or technology, or some other means, his enemies had known precisely where his warriors would deploy, and had managed to salvage the ordnance for their trap, in such a bleak and desolate place.

Intriguing.

Excrucias set off through the bolt-cratered ruins, following a trail of his warriors' sprawled bodies. Some, he noted, had been riddled with shells or had their armour rent open by detonations. Others lay with neat holes punched through the eye-pieces of their helms where sniper rounds had found their mark. He tasted a hotchpotch of propellants and alchemical traces upon the air, some so strange that even he couldn't place their origin.

Cultists sprawled in bloody heaps, blade-slain or torn open like fleshy flowers. Sections of stonework and pillars were deformed and blown apart by sonic bombardment where his followers appeared to have fired wide of their marks.

Whoever the enemy were, they had channelled his forces into killing zones in courtyards and alleyways. Booby traps had brought down high stone ramparts, crushing the faithful of Slaanesh. In one broad and lonely square, Excrucias found a deep pit, which had evidently been concealed in some fashion until the Terminators of the Writhe-kin strode across it.

Their corpses lay at the bottom, half-dissolved by acidic ooze that still bubbled and popped as it ate away at ceramite and flesh.

Excrucias moved cautiously, straining his keen senses for threats, but at the same time he felt his fascination and excitement grow. This enemy had picked apart his warriors with efficiency and invention. Yet still he didn't see a single slain foe. Perhaps half, the master of auguries had claimed. Where, then, were the bodies? Here and there, Excrucias noted scuff marks and blood trails, tell-tale suggestions that power-armoured corpses had been hastily removed.

'Your very secrecy gives you away,' he murmured.

'Not entirely,' came a voice to Excrucias' left.

'No,' came another from his right. 'I'd say it kept us hidden just long enough. Wouldn't you, brothers?'

'Yes,' came a third, rumbling voice to Excrucias' rear. The Slaaneshi lord stopped dead, giving a slight sigh as multiple lock warnings chimed in his ear. Carefully he looked left and right, seeing bulky, armoured figures slipping from the shadows with their guns pointed at him. As they advanced, they swept aside the cameleoline cloaks that had concealed them, and Excrucias saw metallic blue armour that confirmed his suspicions.

Alpha Legion.

The warriors now flanking Excrucias were unhelmed, and their facial features were remarkably alike. Both possessed high, noble brows, strong jaws, shaved scalps and quick, sharp eyes. One had slit-like pupils of deep jade green, while the other's armour was festooned with what appeared to be the salvaged tools from a Techmarine's servo harness.

The wargear of both warriors was worn and battered, their armour a patchwork of scavenged and repainted plates. Excrucias' own armour shone by comparison. He was a god against these ragged ghosts. And yet they had confounded even his exceptional senses and surrounded him. It was an impressive display.

He hissed as he felt the muzzle of some large firearm thump him none too gently in the back.

'Don't try anything clever,' came that third voice from behind. 'These aren't the only guns trained on you.'

'It'd be a shame to spoil all that pretty gold armour,' said the one with the tools, disdainfully. 'Except that ugly damn mask. You can keep that.'

'Kassar wants to talk to you,' said the Alpha Legionnaire with the snake's eyes.

'And who is… Kassar?' asked Excrucias, earning himself another shove from the gun muzzle at his back.

'He's someone who wants to talk to you,' said its owner. 'As we said. So, move. Forward up that alley, and keep your hands where we can see them. You don't want to try for your weapons. Really.'

Despite his predicament, Excrucias was calm. He felt no indignation at being spoken to in such a fashion, regardless that no living thing had dared to do so in many long centuries. He felt only a growing certainty that his suspicions were correct.

Excrucias was marched at gunpoint through the ruins to a partially collapsed mausoleum, and ushered through its tumbled entrance into a chamber lit by flickering lamps. Kassar awaited him, leant casually against an ancient tomb fashioned from some squamous black substance. His facial features echoed those of his brothers, save for a long, tight scar that ran up one cheek and over his right eye. A short-shaved mohawk clung to his scalp, but he bore no other distinguishing features of rank or seniority. Despite this, Excrucias sensed Kassar's quiet authority at once. Here, without a doubt, was the leader of this strange warband.

Excrucias' guards motioned him to stand before their leader. The three of them, including the big brute whose heavy bolter had nudged Excrucias in the back, spread out and kept their weapons trained on him.

Kassar was running a cloth along the black blade of an ornate sword, and as he set the weapon aside Excrucias' eyes widened in recognition. The reaction was not lost on Kassar, who observed his guest with hooded eyes.

'You know this sword?' he asked.

'It… belonged to one of my most… accomplished champions,' hissed Excrucias. 'Sethriel. Several centuries ago.'

Kassar gave a grunt of acknowledgement.

'I remember him,' he said. 'I remember all the warriors I've killed, but he stands out. Good fighter, swift as air, gave me this scar. Possessed?'

'Not Sethriel,' said Excrucias softly. His eyes drifted to the blade.

'You're wondering why it hasn't taken me the way it did him,' said Kassar. 'The thing bound into this blade.'

'The Hexling,' nodded Excrucias. 'It is a… persuasive… entity.'

'It tried,' said Kassar. 'It failed. Is that why you're here? Sethriel and his sword?'

'Sethriel and his warriors are the original reason I came to this place,' replied Excrucias. He wondered how much he should divulge; how much they might already know. The Alpha Legion, it was said, had their ways.

'Do you know the legend of Bloodforge?' he asked instead.

The Alpha Legionnaire with the tools snorted a laugh.

'Know it, your golden grace? We've been living it for more than three hundred years.'

Kassar glanced at his warrior, who shrugged.

'We know it,' said Kassar. 'Two daemon princes, the Butcher and the Blade. One a World Eater, one a Night Lord. Their rivalry led them to create a world of eternal war, this world, upon which they could finally settle their score. Only their war ran out of control, fed upon itself. It drew the champions of the gods like flies to offal. The Butcher and the Blade drowned in the bloody flood they had created, and still the war raged on. An endless contest where the greatest servants of Chaos could prove their might, hone their skills. The Bloodforge.'

'Just so,' said Excrucias. 'Such was the legend that reached me, many years ago. When I discovered that Bloodforge was real, I sent my Eternals to find it. Led by Sethriel, they were to battle here, to earn glory and reward from Slaanesh so that, when I returned, those that lived would be flawless, living weapons.'

'Except when you arrived, all you found was us.'

Excrucias nodded slowly.

'Only you, from a world of champions, of perpetual war. What happened here?'

'We won,' said Kassar simply.

'Evidently,' said Excrucias. 'And who are you, you victors of the Bloodforge?'

'We are the Unsung, and we prevailed, as we always prevail. Killed your men. Killed all the others. Not without cost, but…' Kassar spread his hands. 'Here we are.'

'Here you are…' echoed Excrucias. 'Victorious but… still here, amidst the rubble. I wonder why…'

Kassar smiled without humour.

'Never ask the Alpha Legion a question, lest they tell you seven truthful lies,' he said. 'Besides, except for coming down here alone, I'm sure you're not stupid. You know why.'

'You lack a ship,' said Excrucias. 'You sit trapped amidst the ruin of your conquest, waiting to suffer the finishing blow by the hand of the next powerful enemy that comes along. An enemy like me.'

'There's more to you than there seems,' said Kassar. 'Elaborate armour, gold daemon mask, impressive blade, sense of power coming off you in waves. But you came here alone. An error. You could hurt us, but I've enough brothers left that we'd kill you before you finished the job.'

'How quickly do you think you could land the blow?' asked Excrucias. 'I have an entire fleet in orbit. A word, and they teleport me out… then fire on my last location. This entire region would be nothing but rad-fire within moments.'

'Hm,' grunted Kassar, seeming to ponder the point. 'I thought you might say something like that. It's why I had Haltheus here put together a teleport jammer before you arrived.'

The tool-festooned Alpha Legionnaire brandished a crude-looking device, all exposed wires and runic circuitry.

'Haven't activated it yet,' he said cheerfully. 'It might not even work. Or it might just scramble your teleport signal enough to deliver you to your destination inside out. I've told them more than once that I'm no Techmarine, but...' He shrugged.

'An... impasse, then,' said Excrucias, his outward poise showing nothing of the excitement he felt within. He hadn't foreseen the teleport jammer, and the sense that he had placed himself in real, mortal danger was exhilarating.

'Perhaps,' said Kassar. 'Perhaps not. You said that your warriors were the *original* reason that you came to Bloodforge. Implying that something has changed. You know what we want, to get off this gods-blighted rock while some of us still draw breath. What about you?'

'I came here in search of living weapons,' said Excrucias. 'Flaw-less killers. I am engaged in... an ongoing conflict. My... rivals have proven more problematic than I had hoped. I sought to bolster my ranks with warriors who could... conclude matters on my behalf.'

'But we killed them,' said Kassar.

'But you killed them,' echoed Excrucias. 'And for that insult I should flay you all alive. But instead, I wish to offer you a bargain.'

'Go on,' said Kassar. Around the chamber's edge, his warriors had become very still, watching the exchange with intense interest.

'You have butchered a world of warriors,' said Excrucias. 'What more perfect living weapons could I hope to find than you? Perhaps you do not have the magnificence, the sheer might that my Eternals possessed, but what I have seen here suggests that you make up for this lack in... murderous guile. Fight for me. You have won one war already. Now help me to win another.'

Kassar's face was an unreadable mask. 'And in return?' he asked.

'In return... a ship, a frigate from my fleet with a full and loyal crew, warp capabilities, firepower. Freedom, to do with as you will.'

Kassar nodded slowly, then motioned for Haltheus to lower his teleport jammer.

'Let me speak to my brothers,' he said. 'You'll remain here as insurance, just long enough for the Harrow to assemble and to vote. Then you'll have your answer.'

Excrucias made a show of considering Kassar's demands, then graciously acquiesced. Inside he already knew. He had been right. He had come to Bloodforge in search of flawless, living weapons. And, by the grace of Slaanesh, he had found them.

Soon enough, the Beacon of Tsadrekha would be his...

PART I

CHAPTER ONE

The waves of the Risen Sea crashed on the flanks of Hive Endurance, beating endlessly against the immense structure's metallic hide. Endurance shrugged them off as it had for thousands of years, looming over the ocean like a man-made mountain whose minareted peaks pierced the clouds.

Partway up the southern face, several hundred feet above the choppy waters, Captain Dysorian wrapped his bear-like arms around another marble block. Bracing his legs, he rose, armour servos whining as they lent their prodigious strength to his own. With a grunt, Dysorian swung the block into place atop the barricade, then stepped back. He cast a critical eye over the growing barrier, heavy grey brows beetled.

'Sergeant Loriyan,' said Dysorian, addressing one of the Primaris battle-brothers labouring at the barricade. 'What is our Chapter famed for?'

'Grit,' replied the looming Intercessor, hefting another block flush into place next to Dysorian's. 'Determination. Loyalty. Siege-craft. The Imperial Fists are the Emperor's praetorians, my captain, and deservedly so.'

'Indeed,' said Dysorian. 'None amongst all the Emperor's servants know better than we how to fortify a position, and how to hold it for as long as it must be held.'

'Yes, my captain,' said Sergeant Loriyan, stooping to heft another block into place. His brothers worked alongside him, bolt rifles slung as they raised a defensive wall across the mouth of the access-arch. It was but one of many such entrances set into the lower flanks of Hive Endurance, archways linked to cargo-conveyors that brought fuel and materiel up from the sprawling piers far below. As they laboured, the Intercessors showed no outward reaction to the rhetorical nature of their captain's questions. Never mind that their simplicity would have insulted a yearling novitiate.

'This is a reputation that we sons of Dorn have upheld for many thousands of years,' said Dysorian. 'It is integral to who we are, and we all must earn it anew with every day that dawns, whether long-serving veteran or newly ascended battle-brother.'

'I understand, my captain,' said Sergeant Loriyan, placing another block with a hard clunk of marble on marble. 'My brothers and I will not disappoint you in this.'

'I do not doubt it, sergeant,' said Dysorian, though even he could hear that his tone of voice did not quite match his words. 'Raise this barrier another five feet before the servitors monobond these blocks, then begin the second layer in a staggered grid behind it.'

'Yes, my captain, and then the fire step behind that, with raised platforms for unaugmented human weapons teams. It shall be done to a standard that would make the primarch proud.'

Dysorian nodded.

'Good. Proceed, sergeant.'

He turned away, back into the dingy electro-candle illumination of Main Hive. A chevron-lined cargo corridor took him through Endurance's skin, his metal-on-metal footfalls ringing away down service pipes and grilled vents. Dysorian's practised eye noted rust and spot-welds where the salt air of the ocean had taken its toll. He allowed himself a sour grunt.

Dysorian reached the end of the corridor, where Tsadrekhan defence troopers were erecting an emplacement of prefab barricades and sandbags. The men ceased their work as he strode through their midst, each making the sign of the aquila and averting their eyes.

'Enough of that,' said Dysorian irritably. 'Be about your labours. You can genuflect later.'

Looking mortified, the men resumed their work with fresh urgency. The Imperial Fists captain strode on down the transitway. Looming manufactory units rose on either side, turning the street into a metal canyon filled with jaundiced light. This hive-level's ceiling loomed high above, half lost amidst criss-cross girders and hazy smoke. Dysorian caught movement amongst the fumes, gargoyle-like cherubim of the Ministorum winging their way through the gloom, and his scowl deepened.

The captain's vox-bead chimed once.

'Pavras,' said Dysorian. 'You are contacting me to report that the south pier redoubt is complete, no doubt?'

'Within the hour,' replied the Techmarine. 'As I'm sure you know, my captain.'

Dysorian heard the wry smile in Pavras' voice.

'Something about this situation amuses you, Techmarine?'

'No, my captain,' said Pavras. 'I am merely comforted by the dour cynicism I hear in your voice. The stars may have turned to madness, the Emperor's light may be hidden from us, but it is good to know that some things remain the same.'

'How is your inspection proceeding?' asked Dysorian by way of response, ignoring his old comrade's jibe.

'As well as can be expected,' said Pavras. 'Where our battle-brothers apply themselves to shoring the defences, they rise as Dorn would have wished. Where the Tsadrekhan defence troopers and hive labour gangs are working...? Well, the defences appear adequate.'

'What of the Adepta Sororitas?' asked Dysorian.

'They still concentrate their efforts and those of their frateris on further fortifying the spire,' said Pavras. 'I believe Canoness Levinia feels that their efforts are best focused upon defending the levels around the beacon itself.'

'Understandable,' said Dysorian. 'Though she must know that if Main Hive or the Underbilge falls, her convent prioris will be next, no matter how well defended it is.'

'When we spoke earlier, my captain, I did mention that line of reasoning,' said Pavras. 'The canoness told me that I must have faith…'

'We place our faith in adamantium and bolt shells,' said Dysorian. 'Now, what of the Primaris battle-brothers? You have overseen their labours also?'

'I have, my captain,' replied Pavras, his tone dry. 'Just as you instructed. The barricades they raise are every bit as solid and redoubtable as those built by the other battle-brothers of the Fourth Company. Indeed, I would say they work somewhat more quickly than the rest of us with those augmented physiques of theirs.'

Dysorian grunted. He turned left at a junction and climbed a set of metal steps onto a suspended walkway bustling with robed menials and hive militia. Skull braziers burned along the walkway's edges, and candle-lit grav placards drifted in the air, inscribed with exhortations to faith and labour. Below, a six-lane transitway thundered with groundcars and transporters, while overhead a mag-train hove through the smoke upon its electrified lines.

'Captain,' voxed Pavras. 'Paetrov. The Primaris are sound. More than sound, they carry something of the primarch within them. Most of our warriors venerate them. They are valuable assets, and they are our battle-brothers. But you still don't trust them, do you?'

'We have fought the long war against Chaos without them for ten thousand years,' replied Dysorian, subvocalising so as not to be overheard. 'New genetics? New weapons? Spawned from the work of a tech-magos trying to imitate – no, worse – to improve upon the Emperor's own labours? Battle-brothers who do not even serve time in the Scout companies or the Devastators before taking their place in the line? I neither trust nor need such warriors amongst my ranks, Pavras. Dorn's fist, they're not even proven in battle!'

'Only because they have not had the chance,' replied Pavras. 'My captain, the living primarch himself ordered their creation and vouches for their excellence.'

'Not our primarch,' said Dysorian, marching onwards as the crowds melted away before him.

'My captain…' began Pavras, but Dysorian cut him off.

'Cease your fretting, Pavras. I've my orders from the Chapter Master and I shall not be derelict in fulfilling them. The Ultima Founding occurred whether I like it or not. I'll use the Primaris battle-brothers just as I would proper, proven Imperial Fists. But I will keep a weather eye upon them, and no amount of hectoring from you will change my mind on the subject. Do I make myself clear?'

'Yes, my captain,' replied Pavras, recognising that the subject was closed.

'Now, where are you?' asked Dysorian.

'Level six-twenty-four,' replied Pavras. 'Main Hive. I have just finished inspecting the defences around generatorum block Kilphor.'

'Good,' said Dysorian. 'Sweep through to the Hive Spine and take a grav-lift to level eight-one-seven. Vox Lieutenant Lydanis, have him meet us at south teleportarium hub beta. I remain unconvinced of the efficacy of the tech-priests' failsafe rituals.'

'Yes, my captain,' said Pavras, then cut the link.

Dysorian reached the teleportarium hub to find his subordinates already waiting for him. The Techmarine and the Primaris lieutenant stood near to a set of heavy bulkheads stamped with the cog mechanicus. They were illuminated by flickering electro-sconces and deep in earnest conversation. Pavras was stocky and square-jawed, and half of his skull and his right eye boasted finely worked augmetics. By comparison, Lieutenant Lydanis was tall and broad, his eyes ice blue and his hair shaved close to his scalp. Two sallow-skinned servitors lingered near the conversing warriors, and their eyes and weapon systems lit with warning runes as Dysorian approached. Pavras' servants scanned the captain with ocular auspex before emitting binharic blurts and subsiding.

'Brothers,' said Dysorian, returning their aquila salutes. 'Lydanis, report on your sweep.'

'I have completed my inspection of the Underbilge defences,' said

Lieutenant Lydanis. 'All pressure-locks and sub-aquatic bulkheads are confirmed sanctified and secure. Heavy defensive positions have been established in concentric rings around the oceanic-mag-rail transit station. As per your orders, mixed Primaris and Mk VIII squads have established patrol routes and guard posts throughout primary oceanic-mag-rail support tunnels three through nineteen, with emphasis placed on securing those routes that connect to the outer fortress islands, drilling rigs and with Hives Dryspire and Immersia. All is in readiness.'

'What of the Tsadrekhans?' asked Dysorian.

'Our patrols and positions have been reinforced with significant deployment of Tsadrekhan Defence Platoons,' reported Lydanis. 'And Canoness Levinia has released squads of Retributors and Battle Sisters to further reinforce the checkpoints leading up through the primary Underbilge–Main Hive transit portals.'

Dysorian nodded.

'Then let us attend to this next matter. I thank the Emperor and the primarch for this period of grace, but our enemies will not wait forever to launch their assault. We will not allow Hive Endurance to meet the fate of Hive Eternum. Clear?'

Lydanis and Pavras chorused the affirmative, though both knew that the captain's words were aimed mostly at his Primaris lieutenant. If that fact troubled Lydanis, he did not allow it to show.

Dysorian stood directly before the bulkhead, and announced in a clear voice:

'Captain Paetrov Dysorian, Imperial Fists Fourth Company. I demand audience with Magos-ethericus Corphyx.'

From above the doorway, gargoyle-faced scanner servitors swept the Imperial Fists with crimson auspex beams. If they found anything amiss, punisher turrets would deploy from the walls to either side of the bulkhead and fill the corridor with a hail of high-calibre rounds.

A sonorous chime echoed along the corridor, and with a hiss of escaping gas the cog mechanicum revolved, then slid apart. Amidst crackling electrolight, the bulkhead doors rumbled open, and Dysorian led the way into the teleportarium beyond.

Each of the hive's three teleportaria clung to Endurance's outer skin like huge mechanical tumours. They dotted the south flank from down near the waterline to the highest gothic spires of the convent of the Order of the Crimson Tear. Two were lesser substations, automated servo-shrines. South hub beta was a far more substantial bastion, festooned with empyric antennae, crackling energy coils and a plethora of strange mechanical protrusions that only an adept of the Machine-God could hope to comprehend.

They were also afforded a degree of natural daylight within their chambers and corridors, a rare and considerable honour below the spire itself.

Dysorian and his brothers strode through wisping clouds of steam and crackling arcs of energy, through high-ceilinged chambers and along cable-thick corridors. Light fell in kaleidoscopic patterns through stained armourglass domes that depicted the great works of the Omnissiah. Servitors lumbered, hobbled, slithered or rumbled in the fumes, dead sensor eyes fixed forwards on whatever labours were theirs to perform. Tech-priests, too, swept through the murk, hunched figures in rubberised red robes who clutched data-slates in metal claws. They peered from their cowls with glowing red eyes. None approached the Space Marines, instead remaining aloof and mysterious as they went about their business.

'Quite a place,' murmured Pavras as they strode across a walkway above vast, thrumming capacitor arrays. 'The very air sings with the power of the Omnissiah.'

'I care only that, if these places must continue to operate, they do so without presenting chinks in our armour,' replied Dysorian. 'What they sing with is of no interest, Pavras.'

'No, my captain,' said the Techmarine.

'Could we not simply order that the teleportation shrines be rendered quiescent until the threat has passed?' asked Lieutenant Lydanis. 'Surely the hive has stockpiles of fuel and ordnance sufficient to see out a substantial siege?'

'Clearly,' said Pavras with a grim smile, 'you have never dealt with the adepts of the Machine-God. This transfer of fuel from the rigs is more than logistics to them, lieutenant. It is a holy act of tribute and communion with the Machine-God, the pumping of the Omnissiah's promethium blood. It is for the same reason that they will not cease the movement of the maglev trains through the undersea tunnels. The tech-priests would no sooner stop these things than they would allow their own hearts – or whatever passes for them – to stop beating.'

Dysorian and his companions entered a huge chamber. Brass steps a quarter of a mile wide led up from its entrance arch, into an artful spill of crimson and gold light falling through stained-glass windows high above. Every hundred feet, the steps were flanked on either side by baroque teleportation platforms, broad, sigil-inscribed discs surrounded by incomprehensible banks of machinery. The air stank of ozone and crackled with esoteric energies as consignments of promethium barrels flashed into being. Each fresh manifestation sent thunderclaps rolling through the cavernous shrine. Gangling cargo-servitors descended on hydraulic booms to gather up the holy cargo and spirit it away to destinations throughout the hive.

The Imperial Fists climbed the steps quickly, ascending hundreds of feet beneath the cold stares of tech-magi, servitors and weird cyber-cherubim. At the top, they found their way barred by a conclave of electro-priests, behind whom rose banks of ancient machinery. The priests parted at an unspoken signal, making a corridor through which a bulky figure lumbered. Wheezing and gurgling, tattered robes doing little to conceal that he was more grotesque machine than living flesh, Magos-ethericus Corphyx came to greet them. Tentacular mechadendrites snaked from within his robes, and three piston-driven legs carried him forwards with a thudding gait.

'Imperial Fists,' his voice buzzed from a vocal emitter set somewhere within his central mass. 'Omnissiah's blessings upon you. Your presence is an honour both unexpected and unlooked for.'

'Magos-ethericus Corphyx,' said Dysorian, inclining his head in what could generously have been called a gesture of respect. 'Myself and my brothers are engaged in the task of inspecting and assessing the defences of Hive Endurance, on behalf of Canoness Levinia.

Several more of my senior battle-brothers are still sweeping the upper and lower levels. Meanwhile, we are here to inspect the security of your teleportarium, and by extension that of all the teleportaria in this hive.'

'Commendable,' buzzed Corphyx. 'But eminently unnecessary. My apologies that you have wasted your time, captain.'

Dysorian bristled. 'Magos-ethericus,' he began, 'the nature of the technologies you are using here presents a clear potential risk of infiltration. Should enemy forces gain possession of another of this planet's teleportarium facilities, they could storm this site from within and secure a foothold that could see the whole Hive conquered. Tsadrekha has faced two Chaos invasions within the last month alone. We are cut off from the outer systems of the Unity now, and the beacon does not just light the way for the servants of the Emperor to find this world. You know as well as I that Tsadrekha is the prize over which our enemies fight, and that when their killing blow lands, it will land here, where the beacon is kept alight.'

'These are empirical facts,' said Corphyx. 'Their pertinence to this situation is nil, however.'

'What my captain is saying, honoured magos,' said Pavras, 'is that our system monitors claim the enemy are coming soon, likely in very great numbers. It is still unclear whether it was a teleportarium breach that allowed the sack of Hive Eternum, but my captain wishes me to inspect your facilities for any potential defensive weaknesses that our enemies might exploit. We are of the Imperial Fists. I am sure you are aware of our expertise in such matters.'

'I am aware of your Chapter's experiential familiarity with matters of conventional siege warfare,' said Corphyx. 'It is, again, irrelevant to this scenario. The capacity to build or demolish ferrocrete walls efficiently is in no way synonymous with an understanding of the deeper mysteries of the Omnissiah. Your assistance is not required at this time, and your continued presence is becoming a sub-optimal variable.'

'Unacceptable,' said Dysorian, his voice loud enough that the Fulgurites to either side stiffened their stances. Electricity buzzed through their staves. 'I have been charged with the defence of this entire hive, and I do not intend to fail in my duty because some obstreperous–'

The captain's words were drowned out amidst the sudden wailing of alarm hymnals. The shrine's electro-sconces strobed a deep, blood red, and spools of rune-covered parchment began to spill from the chattering data-banks behind Corphyx.

Dysorian and his brothers reached for their weapons, while the Fulgurite priests hefted their staves, looking for enemies.

'Magos,' shouted Dysorian over the booming alarms. 'Are we under attack?'

'Insufficient data,' replied Corphyx, his emitter's volume increased to painful levels. 'I will consult with the motive force and interpret the inload-revelations of the Omnissiah. Remain if you wish.'

The magos turned away, and the ranks of Fulgurites closed behind him. Dysorian fought down the urge to shove his way through them, instead turning to his battle-brothers.

'Pavras, I want you to commune with whatever sensor inputs and vox-channels you can. Gather information and compile. Lydanis, ensure that all battle-brothers are in a state of full combat readiness and patched in to channel seven-aleph.'

'This much arcane technology may interfere, my captain,' said Pavras. 'It may take time.'

'Be as swift as you can, Pavras,' replied Dysorian. 'We need information. Now.'

As his battle-brothers followed his orders, Dysorian sent a priority vox-hail to Canoness Levinia via the hive's hardened supreme command channel. This was her city, her Order's world; if anyone had a clear view of what was occurring, it would be her.

Dysorian did not have to wait long for a response. The canoness' voice filled his ear, stern and sharp as cut glass.

'Captain Dysorian.'

'Honoured canoness, I assume that alarms are also sounding in the spire. Are we under attack?'

'We seek revelation on that matter even now, brother-captain. There appears to be but a single visible contact, high up on the very edge of the auspex net, beyond the tempestosphere.'

'Ordnance?' asked Dysorian. 'Some form of cyclonic warhead or viral payload?'

'Unlikely, brother-captain. The scryers inform me that it is moving too slowly, and appears too small, to be a warhead.'

'I've little patience for mysteries,' growled Dysorian, turning away from the muttering priests and hastening back down the steps of the shrine.

Minutes later, he led his brothers out onto an external rampart several levels above the shrine's armoured dome. Dysorian hurried into the watery daylight of the Tsadrekhan dawn. The hive wall stretched vertiginously above and below. Waves boomed distantly against the city's lower slopes, while salt-wet winds howled around the rampart, causing its supports to creak and groan. There were skitarii arrayed neatly along the rampart's fire step, the teleportarium well below and the armoured battlement to their fore.

The Mechanicus soldiery were staring up into the churning clouds, fusils and rad carbines at the ready. Dysorian ignored them and gripped the rungs of a ladder set into the hive's metal hide. He climbed quickly, skirting a huge stained-glass window until, several hundred feet up, he reached a sloping roof.

Showing none of his three centuries, Dysorian clambered up onto a roof between crackling antenna and thrumming sensor dishes, ignoring the sickening drop and the screaming winds that plucked at him. Still the hive loomed up and up above them. Pavras and Lydanis followed, as fearless and tireless as their captain. The lieutenant had unslung his bolt rifle, while Pavras was checking the charge of his plasma pistol.

'If something is coming, better to see it for ourselves,' said Dysorian over the wailing wind.

So saying, he clamped his helm in place and magnified its optics to maximum. Running through visual filters, the captain scanned the clouds until, at last, he caught sight of a golden glow swelling into being.

'Not a warhead,' voxed Pavras. 'It almost looks like–'

'It's a person,' said Lydanis. 'Armoured. Female. She… are those wings?'

'It looks like an angel of the Emperor…' breathed Dysorian. 'No such thing. What trickery is this?'

At last, his hail to Canoness Levinia was answered, a choral chime giving way to a clear channel.

'Brother-captain, we are blessed,' she said, and in her voice Dysorian heard a note of rapture that made him wary. 'Vid-capture and archival interrogation confirm it. Her aspect, the blade she wields, the way in which she descends from the clouds on high in the hour of our greatest need. Captain Dysorian, this is Celestine, the Emperor's Living Saint!'

'How do you know this, Levinia?' asked Dysorian. 'It could be some ruse of the enemy's, some malefic manifestation of the Great Rift.'

'No, captain,' said Levinia firmly. 'My heart tells me it is so in a voice that can only be the Emperor's own. I have faith, captain. It is she, and she will deliver us.'

Amidst the alarms rose a tumult of tolling bells and amplified plainsong. The angel descended into its midst, clearly visible now to all three Space Marines as she swept gracefully down through the tattered clouds. Celestine's face was a mask of cold beauty, distant and ethereal as her hair danced about it like a halo. The metallic wings of her jump pack flexed dextrously, holy light and spectral flame wreathing them as the Living Saint descended upon Hive Endurance. In one hand, Celestine bore a blade of sublime craftsmanship. The other was empty, held outwards as though in benediction.

'The Living Saint,' breathed Pavras with something resembling awe. 'Remarkable.'

'They say she was instrumental in bringing back Primarch Guilliman,' said Lydanis. 'That she fought alongside him all the way to Terra. They say she even stood and fought on the killing fields of Cadia, before the end.'

'And look how that turned out,' said Dysorian gruffly. 'If it's even really her.'

The angelic figure had passed from their sight now, sweeping down upon the spire.

'The saint comes to us, captain,' said Levinia. 'I must greet her in person. The scriptures say that she shall choose two of our sisterhood to attend her and walk in her blessings as her Geminae Superia. It is my duty to preside over the choosing. Go with the Emperor's grace, Captain Dysorian, and be glad, for today is a rapturous one.'

With that, Levinia cut the link.

From the hive spire high above, proud hymns carried upon the storm winds, echoing out across the slate-grey immensity of the ocean until they were swallowed by its endless indifference.

'All right,' grunted Dysorian. 'Not an attack, then. Not yet. But whatever the provenance of this miracle, we still have a task to perform. And I fully intend to investigate the safety measures in this shrine, even if I have to take that magos by the mechadendrites and–'

The renewed blare of alarms drowned Dysorian's voice out again, silencing the captain for the second time in a matter of minutes.

'Dorn's fist, what now?' he snarled.

'Perhaps the Emperor's seen fit to send us some more saints?' suggested Pavras, but his words died away as the clouds lit with angry trails of flame. As they watched, streaking beams of light stabbed down across the horizon, artificial lightning strikes that raised distant plumes of fire at the furthest reaches of the Space Marines' vision.

'That was Fort Gloriana,' said Dysorian grimly.

'Orbital bombardment,' said Pavras, checking his auspex readings. 'More signatures incoming. And massive energy readings from the outer orbital envelope.'

'They're here at last,' said Dysorian.

'That is the other thing they say of the Living Saint,' said Lieutenant Lydanis. 'That she is the herald of woe. The harbinger of disaster. She appears in the darkest hour, when her aid is most needed, but never without a price.'

'Sounds suspiciously like superstitious nonsense to me, lieutenant,' said Dysorian over the howl of the wind. Above, the first black specks could be seen, plunging down through the cloud cover as the skies blazed ever brighter with fire.

The waves reflected the crimson glow, and for a moment they seemed to stand above an ocean not of water, but of blood.

'Whatever the case, my captain, we should get back inside the hive,' said Pavras. 'We've sighted the foe, and we know what's coming. They'll be raising the void shields. We'll be needed for the defence.'

'Well said, Pavras,' said Dysorian with a stern nod. 'Speculation won't get us anywhere. Now is the time for steel and fire, boltguns and blades and sheer damned grit. Now begins the battle for Tsadrekha, and it is a battle we *will* win.'

Dysorian clambered back down the ladder and headed into the teleportarium shrine with his battle-brothers close upon his heels. High above, the Living Saint was being welcomed with a mixture of delight and religious terror by the Adepta Sororitas while, higher still, the servants of Chaos blazed down through the Tsadrekhan skies.

The invasion had begun.

CHAPTER TWO

Tsadrekha was a mote amidst the darkness. The planet wore an artificial halo of wreckage, a sprawling veil of blasted warships and ravaged defence platforms that extended for many miles. Some of the butchered hulks still crawled with voidfire, or trailed fat sparks as they drifted.

Out beyond the fringes of the stellar abattoir, reality flickered. Oily streamers of light flowed into screaming faces and monstrous shapes that were gone as swiftly as they appeared. The disturbance grew, clawing and ripping at the fabric of real space until it tore like flesh. Hellish light spilled from many wounds. The ships of Excrucias' fleet surged with their drives lit and their gun decks unshrouded. Dozens of craft thundered from the warp, trailing ectoplasmic streamers of anger and sorrow, regret and lust that burned away in the harsh light of the real. Captained by supremely skilled warriors, the warships fell swiftly into formations as elegant as they were deadly.

They arced away towards the distant planet, leaving behind them a ragged swathe of torn reality and writhing warpstuff that would not heal as it should.

* * *

Kassar sat upon a grotesque chaise longue fashioned from gold, glass and living flesh. He and the warriors of his Harrow were surrounded by deranged opulence, from marble flooring and mats of human skin, to garish works of art framed in gold and painted with noisome substances Kassar didn't care to identify.

Electro-candle chandeliers dangled from a vaulted ceiling busy with obscene frescoes. Weird furnishings and objets d'art made from precious metals, sinew and bone thronged the room.

When they had first been led to their quarters, Haltheus had looked at his comrades' dusty, battered armour and laughed dryly at the contrast. Yet for all its grandeur, as the door slid closed and locked firmly behind them, the Alpha Legionnaires had recognised their prison cell for what it was.

The opulence, though distasteful, hadn't troubled Kassar overly. After having his warriors subtly rearrange the room's furnishings for optimum cover in the event that their hosts turned on them, he had simply ignored it.

By Kassar's count, the door had closed seventeen days, six hours and twenty-three minutes ago. It had opened since only to admit robed menials who brought excessive feasts, and bore away the mostly untouched and rotting foodstuffs from the day before.

Beyond sparring and tending to their wargear, there had been little to occupy the Unsung during their enforced captivity. Yet they had not been idle.

'Did you feel that?' asked D'sakh, the Harrow's vexillor, idly spinning one of his foot-long knives between his fingers.

'Pressure change,' nodded Kassar. 'Empyric shift.'

'Warp translation,' said Makhor, seated nearby at a table of jade and gold. He slotted the magazine back into his bolt pistol and sighted down its barrel before giving a grunt of satisfaction.

The thump and whine of heavy footfalls announced Ges'khir, the Harrow's last surviving Terminator. Ges'khir had not removed any section of his spiked armour for many years now. Kassar doubted he still could.

'Our wait is over,' said the Terminator, his voice rumbling from his helm's vox emitter.

'Or this is simply a brief halt to regather the fleet, and account for empyric drift,' said Makhor. 'We do not know that we have reached our destination.'

'Ever the voice of optimism,' said D'sakh sourly.

'I would be a poor naysmith, were that the case,' said Makhor without rancour.

'True enough,' said Kassar. 'But...' With a thought, he sent a complex string of clicks through the Harrow's encoded vox-channel. A signal in their own private battle cant, serpenta.

'Continue with your tasks. Converse in fourth cypher. Information exchange.'

Clicks of acknowledgement came back from the Harrow, who continued to spar, check weapons or give the appearance of meditation.

Just sixteen of them now. Kassar could remember when the Harrow had stood at a full century, proud and determined to do the primarch's bidding. Hundreds of years had passed, but still he saw them clearly in his mind's eye. Kassar never forgot anything. He had not decided whether that was a blessing or a curse.

Kassar mentally assessed them, gauged their readiness. His brothers, still alive. To the untrained eye, most of them were indistinguishable. They bore the same markings and insignia, eschewing almost all personal honours, while unhelmed their features were – for the most part – eerily alike.

Kassar knew them all, though, down to the last nuance and detail.

Haltheus and A'khassor, the Harrow's Techmarine and Apothecary, both brothers serving in roles that necessity had forced upon them.

The twins, Phaek'or and Phalk'ir, one brooding over his disassembled heavy bolter, the other squatting on his haunches with a slight smirk as he whetted his blade.

Skaryth, the Scout, in his tally-scored armour, and Sha'dor, the sword fighter.

Skarle, broken in mind, cradling his flamer and chuckling at some incomprehensible jest.

Thelgh, the silent sniper, seated cross-legged in his meditation pentagram.

Ulkhur and Reskh, adepts in demolition and linguistics respectively.

Kyphas, the black-eyed spymaster.

D'sakh, the bladed vexillor.

Makhor, the naysmith.

Finally, looming at the edges of the gathering, Ges'khir and Krowl, the Harrow's blunt instruments of destruction.

Kassar nodded slowly to them all. Their captors, no doubt watching and listening, would see only a nod. Yet the Harrow had already begun their conversation. Serpenta was a private language not only of vox clicks and hisses, but also of coded words, gestures and nuanced posture, whose meanings were in turn determined by the numbered cypher chosen for the conversation. Developed over long centuries, Kassar prided himself that it was every bit as versatile a communication tool as unfettered speech, and utterly beyond even the most devious mind to decipher.

When the Harrow spoke in serpenta, their words were for them alone.

'This captivity chafes,' said Kassar. 'I long for battle.' His brothers saw and heard a different utterance entirely.

'*We've broken warp. What do we know?*'

Kyphas indicated that he would answer first, and Kassar acknowledged with a meaningless verbal platitude about attending to the spirits of their wargear.

'*When last the servants came,*' began Kyphas, '*I expanded my influence upon them. Hypnotic suggestion and subvocalised interrogation.*'

'*You were careful, yes?*' asked A'khassor. The Apothecary appeared, to outside observers, to be talking about the sanctity of the gene-seed canisters he bore upon his belt.

'*I know my work, as you know yours,*' replied Kyphas stiffly. '*The slaves have no notion that they answered my interrogations, and will have given no outward indication of doing so.*'

'*What did you learn?*' asked Kassar.

'*They indicated a belief that we were nearing our destination,*' said Kyphas. '*And intimated that their master was greatly agitated by the prospect. It seems that Excrucias is not the only warlord of the gods who seeks to claim this world of Tsadrekha.*'

'*Why have you waited until now to tell us this?*' asked D'sakh.

Kyphas made a dismissive gesture.

'*Secrets are as precious as bolt shells, knife-bearer. They should be stock-piled carefully.*'

D'sakh bristled, but Kassar shifted to a posture that forestalled further antagonism.

'*Anything else, Kyphas?*' he asked. '*A dead man with a full clip is still dead.*'

'*They speak of a time of glory,*' replied the former spymaster. '*They claim that Abaddon has broken Cadia. That the warp is spilling through the skin of reality like a flood tide, and that the victory of the Chaos Gods draws nigh. They talk of a great rift, and a pall of darkness.*'

'*Broken Cadia?*' exclaimed Makhor. '*You are sure of this? The pretender has been beating upon that door for millennia!*'

'*It is what they said,*' confirmed Kyphas.

'*The rift again,*' said Kassar thoughtfully. '*Excrucias spoke briefly of it before we departed Bloodforge. What has happened to the galaxy in our absence?*'

'*A great deal, clearly,*' replied smirking Phalk'ir. '*You stranded us on that rock for too long, Kassar.*'

'*Know your place,*' gestured D'sakh, his finely inscribed blade spinning to a sudden stop in his fist. Phalk'ir inclined his head in a gesture of deference, but his smirk remained.

'*Skarle feels a shifting,*' said Skarle suddenly, making no effort to converse in serpenta. '*Skarle feels a slowing. This ship decelerates. We have got where we are going.*'

His piece said, Skarle stifled a snort of laughter. Kassar saw the looks that passed between the Harrow and understood them. Yet Skarle could still fight, still followed orders. He was still useful, and he was one of so very few brothers left.

'*Haltheus,*' said Kassar. '*Skarle is right, we're slowing down. While there's time, what can your data daemons tell us?*'

'*I've recalled them,*' said Haltheus. '*But don't expect miracles. This ship is hideously corrupt. Its machine-spirit is ancient and evil, Heresy era and absolutely seething with Slaaneshi taint.*'

'*We don't need data daemons to tell us that much,*' said Skaryth, garnering a snort of amusement from Ges'khir.

'*Context, brother,*' said Haltheus. '*I'm explaining why barely half my familiars have made it back intact. Hostile environment.*'

'*The ship detected the others?*' asked Kassar in alarm, but Haltheus made a gesture of reassurance.

'*I'm not some fumbling Imperial tech-babbler,*' he said. '*Any of my helpers that got entangled or cornered, they self-immolated. No trace, no indication of foul play.*'

'*Good,*' said D'sakh. '*So what did the survivors find?*'

'*Fragments were the best they could garner,*' said Haltheus. '*But I believe from astrogation data that we're somewhere in the galactic north east. This craft obviously doesn't utilise the Astronomican to navigate but...*' Haltheus paused as if working out how to express a particularly alien concept.

'*But it seems impossible to detect,*' he said.

Kassar stiffened with shock.

'*Is it gone, or are we just cut off from it? In either case, how can that be? Does that mean that Terra is gone as well, that the long war is at an end? Has the throneworld fallen?*'

'*Unclear,*' replied Haltheus. '*But seems unlikely. Our new 'allies' surely would have been crowing such vast news from their highest towers, and it would be all over their dataspools and auto-chantries. No, I believe something else has occurred. Perhaps something is blocking its light, warp storms and the like, or else the Emperor has withdrawn his guidance from his unworthy servants? Or maybe Abaddon has achieved more than merely breaking down the Cadian Gate, and has worked some artifice to blind our foes. Whatever the case, this region of the galaxy is shrouded in darkness. Nothing to indicate the direction of Terra whatsoever. Nothing for Imperial ships to steer by. Except it seems that there is.*'

Kassar made another questioning gesture, demanding elaboration.

'*One of my daemons scavenged fragmentary mentions of Tsadrekha. Somehow this planet is holding a spread of Imperial systems together using some form of psychic beacon.*'

'*Impossible,*' said Makhor. '*If the Imperials had that sort of technology they wouldn't need the Astronomican.*'

Haltheus' stance approximated a shrug.

'It's what my data daemons picked up. Make of it what you will.'

Kassar's next question was interrupted by the sharp hiss of the chamber's door sliding open. Through it marched a squad of Emperor's Children clad in riotously coloured armour and dripping with furs and finery. The warriors wore helms whose vox grilles were hugely enlarged and ringed with fangs, the mouths of hideous daemonic lampreys. They bore sonic weaponry, and Kassar felt a tinnitus ache build behind his eyes at the mere presence of the deadly guns. At the head of the procession strode a haughty warrior with a high-crested helm and a flowing cloak of white fur. He looked straight at Kassar, even though his helm was eyeless, and made an imperious gesture. His voice sounded like a disharmonic choir fighting to be heard over one another's wailing.

'You are to follow me. Lord Excrucias the Flawless demands your presence.'

Wincing, Kassar rose to his feet. The Harrow gathered around him, and at a gesture from their leader all fixed their helms in place. Kassar did the same, embracing anonymity. It was an old tenet of the Alpha Legion, and a good one.

Knowledge is power. Gather all that you can, and give none to your enemies.

Kassar and his men strode onto the bridge of Excrucias' flagship. Their escorts led them across the teeming lower decks and up an elegant stairway of blood-slicked crystal towards the strategium. Though they remained outwardly unmoved, across their encrypted vox-channel Kassar heard his brothers exclaim in revulsion at the excess and insanity displayed around them.

They moved through clouds of shimmering incense, between bio-organic instrument stations where hideously bloated cultists worked their controls. Bodies hung suspended upon hooks and chains, many writhing and keening with pain. Shadowy figures moved through the murk, and nameless fluids made the decking sticky and foul.

'Grotesque,' commented A'khassor to Kassar over coded vox. *'And*

how do they work in this infernal din? The screaming alone is enough to drown out orders, surely.'

'It stinks,' replied Kassar. *'It's not often I regret the sharpness of my senses.'*

'Depravity of the worst kind,' said A'khassor. *'Utter indiscipline. We've nothing to be wary of in this place, Kassar. Creatures this debased are not the ones fated to end our punishment.'*

Kassar kept his reply to himself. He typically avoided engaging with his Apothecary's strange superstitions, and had long since stopped trying to dispel them.

They reached the head of the stairs and found themselves upon a huge, gilded platform. Broad enough to marshal a full company of Space Marines upon, the wide open space was dominated by twisted statues of massive stature, and a revolting throne fashioned from the stitched and slowly writhing bodies of dozens of living beings. Fat tubes gurgled as they pumped fluids into the bloated abomination, while from braziers to either side of the throne billowed pungent clouds of incense in which Kassar detected potent hallucinogens. Excrucias himself sat on the throne, surrounded by freakish champions that Kassar took to be his war leaders. The rest of the dais was crowded with knots of robed and masked figures engaged in acts of drugged debauchery.

'This is how they offer devotion to their god,' voxed Kyphas. *'Such wanton hedonism is intended to garner the blessings of Slaanesh.'*

Kassar's lip longed to curl in revulsion, but neither he nor any of his warriors betrayed any outward sign of their disgust as they were led through the spectacle of foul excess to stand before Excrucias' throne. As one, the Slaaneshi champions turned to stare at them. An array of compound eyes, glowing lenses, black sensory pits and bulging ocular orbs regarded the Alpha Legionnaires. Kassar read undisguised hatred and contempt in those stares, and satisfied himself with the thought that the feeling was mutual.

'Ah...' sighed Excrucias with an expansive gesture. 'The Unsung. My... secret weapon. Perhaps you can rescue me from this daemon's bacchanal of flaws and failure.'

Kassar waited in silence, unwilling to be drawn in by such false bonhomie. His brothers followed his lead, standing silent and still as statues.

'Insolence!' squealed one of the Slaaneshi champions, a massively obese thing with a yawning jaw. 'Answer when the Lord Excrucias addresses you, heathens.'

'Lord,' panted another champion eagerly, this one a scarecrow of flayed skin and barbed armour. 'Allow me the pleasure of punishing them for their insolence.'

'No, me!' trilled another champion, whose plethora of eyes were held open with cruel metal sutures.

Kassar slowly moved his hands towards his weapons, and sent a swift burst of serpenta through the vox.

Be ready. Pattern Scylla if forced.

'Presumptuous wretches,' came a phlegm-thick voice. 'You know well your lord's perfect wisdom. Stay your writhing tongues. The flawless one shall do as he deems fit.' From the shadow of Excrucias' throne shambled a huge figure in baroque power armour and a rubberised, many-coloured robe. In the shadow of the figure's cowl, Kassar saw constant, writhing movement.

Slowly, deliberately, Excrucias rose from his throne. He made a show of caressing the pommel of his blade, eliciting a crooning sigh from the weapon.

'None shall punish them,' he said softly. 'For though they might seem... plain, and barbaric... these warriors are as close to flawless as any I have seen.'

The Slaaneshi champions subsided, though the resentment in their stares deepened.

'Noble Kassar,' said Excrucias. 'Which are you? Will you not speak to me in this most sacred of places? Does the power of Slaanesh awe you so?'

Kassar's vox clicked, D'sakh questioning whether he should play the role of his captain. Kassar clicked back. *Not today.*

'I can speak,' said Kassar, taking a step forward. 'I simply await pertinent information. I assumed this would be a mission briefing?'

Several of the Slaaneshi champions hissed with outrage. Others burst into wild shrieks of overly affected mirth.

'Of a sort,' replied Excrucias. 'We have arrived, and I shall now tell you of the task that you are going to perform for me.'

'We have reached Tsadrekha, then?' asked Kassar. 'This will have something to do with the beacon, yes?'

Excrucias hid his surprise well, but Kassar saw the tell-tale cues. It was a tactic he favoured: a calculated reveal of intelligence, meant to leave your enemies guessing as to how much you knew. At worst, it threw others off balance. At best, it could shake loose far more information than it surrendered.

'That… is correct,' said Excrucias, rallying smoothly. 'I would ask how you knew of this but… what is it they say? The Alpha Legion have their ways…'

Kassar remained silent.

'Yes,' said Excrucias after a moment. 'We have reached Tsadrekha. It is a world I mean to see conquered, and you shall be my instruments of conquest. My champions are displeased with this notion. They believe they should have the pleasure.'

'Why don't they?' asked Kassar.

'They have tried,' breathed Excrucias, venomously. 'They have proven flawed.'

'What's the mission?' asked Kassar. 'Who are we facing? What strengths? What's our edge?'

From behind Excrucias' mask came a skin-crawling hissing that Kassar realised was laughter.

'You will forgive me, Kassar,' said Excrucias. 'I am not accustomed to dealing with… such unadorned bluntness. We Emperor's Children have a more… elegant manner than the lesser Legions, but it is perhaps not as swift. Sometimes, perfection is a curse.'

Again, Kassar remained silent. For long moments, the screams of agonised slaves and the moans of writhing cultists were the only sounds.

'Phelkorian,' said Excrucias eventually. 'Enlighten our allies as to their duties upon this world.'

'You are going to corrupt the Beacon of Tsadrekha,' panted the cowled figure with the writhing face. 'That is your mission, Kassar of the Unsung. You will defile it in the name of great Slaanesh, and in so doing prove our infinite superiority over the crude hordes of Lord Khordas the Slaughterer, and Ganshorr of the Iron Fist.'

'We will be facing rival Chaos warbands, then?' asked Kassar.

'Potentially,' said Phelkorian, a fanged leer splitting the squirming darkness beneath his hood. 'Primarily, however, your enemies shall be corpse worshippers. They defend their beacon with all the fervour of the desperate faithful. It is their only light, now, amidst a terrible darkness, and it is your task to extinguish it.'

'What exactly does the beacon do, that the Astronomican cannot?' asked Kassar. 'Why is it so important to them?'

A ripple of contemptuous laughter passed through the Slaaneshi champions.

'There *is* no Astronomican,' shrieked the flayed champion gleefully. 'Not this far out. Not since the rift opened, and the time of glory came. The Dark Prince has blinded the eyes of our foes and given us the run of the galaxy, that we might revel in the corpse worshippers' exquisite torments.'

Behind his faceplate, Kassar quirked an eyebrow. So Haltheus had been correct. Whatever this rift was that the Emperor's Children kept talking of, it must have brought the darkness with it. How far did that extend? he wondered. How much new-found freedom had the Traitor Legions been afforded? Now wasn't the time to reveal his ignorance with further questions, however.

'As Shemlok says,' gasped Phelkorian. 'The Astronomican cannot reach beyond the rift, but the Beacon of Tsadrekha has afforded the Imperials a light in the darkness. Its reach is comparatively short, a few neighbouring systems, but it is enough to give them hope and coherency. The Tsadrekhan Unity, they call it. But it cannot last.'

'No?' asked Kassar, though he could guess why.

'Too rich a prize,' said D'sakh in his ear. *'Too obvious. Silkwings to a brazier.'*

'The beacon is a light in the darkness... its glare is visible to all,' said Excrucias. 'He who extinguishes this flame of defiance shall know the beneficence of the gods in great measure. And to allow any other to steal this prize from us… that would be a flaw of the gravest magnitude.'

Kassar noticed Excrucias' tongue flicker along the lips of his mask, drawing a runnel of blood. In some strange way, the Slaaneshi lord relished the thought of failure, he realised. Or perhaps just its consequences. Kassar filed the information away for later consideration.

'So the Imperials have a psychic beacon, and you are in competition with other warlords to smother it,' he said. 'Their defences must be formidable, to hold you all off.'

'You will see for yourself, soon enough,' panted Phelkorian. 'We have more information for you, topographical charts, enemy strengths, an exfiltration plan, logistical tedium of that sort. All shall be made available to you before you begin your mission. But for now, I wish you to meet Syxx.'

Phelkorian unslung a staff from his back, a thing of bone and sinew scrimshawed into obscene shapes and daubed in unnameable fluids. Kassar felt raw psychic power build in the air, a potent charge rising fast around Phelkorian's staff. A sorcerer, then, he thought.

'Arrogant, to use his powers in such a place despite the risks,' said A'khassor.

'He is Emperor's Children,' replied Kassar. *'He's likely addicted to the danger.'*

Throwing back his hood to reveal a disgusting mass of fleshy tentacles and bulging eyes, Phelkorian opened several, fanged maws and gave vent to an obscene string of jarring syllables. The air shuddered with overpressure. With a fizzing crack and a blaze of dirty light, a figure appeared, knelt before Phelkorian. Human in stature, though built strong and tall like a fighter, the figure was clad head to foot in a dark, rubberised bodyglove. Its head was hooded, its pale face half concealed by a bronze grotesque mask, and bulky, overly elaborate armour encased much of its body.

The figure stayed kneeling, head bowed.

'Lord Phelkorian,' it said. 'How may this servant do your bidding?'

Despite the servile words, Kassar detected vocal tells suggestive of burning resentment and hatred. Interesting.

'Syxx,' said Phelkorian with a wet leer. 'Stand, and meet your deliverers.'

The masked human rose and turned towards the Alpha Legionnaires. If their presence surprised him, he hid it well, instead bowing deeply.

'My lords,' he said. 'The blessings of Slaanesh upon you.'

'Syxx is one of my most accomplished mortal acolytes,' explained Phelkorian. 'He has endured that which would have killed lesser men thrice over, and earned our Dark Mistress' blessings with his devotion.'

'He sounds as though he were talking about a favoured hound,' voxed Sha'dor.

'Of course,' replied Phalk'ir. *'It's only a mortal.'*

Kassar clicked for silence.

'What is this slave to us?' he asked aloud. 'How does he bear upon our mission?'

'He is to be greatly honoured,' said Phelkorian, clamping one huge hand upon Syxx's shoulder. To the mortal's credit, Kassar noted he didn't flinch. Much.

'Syxx has been ritually marked with the sigils of Slaanesh, his flesh branded and scarified to render him a conduit for the Dark Prince's favour. You need only bring him safe to the Beacon of Tsadrekha, Kassar of the Unsung. His presence, and the words of power that he has learned, will do the rest.'

'And if he does not make it to the beacon alive?' asked Kassar, though he knew the answer already.

'Then our… compact shall be declared flawed,' said Excrucias. 'And you will know my sternest displeasure.'

'Alive doesn't necessarily mean fully intact,' voxed Haltheus. *'Just a thought.'*

'This changes things,' said Kassar to Excrucias. 'It is one thing to take my Harrow down onto the planet's surface to effect sabotage, but quite another to keep a fragile mortal alive throughout a drop-insertion into an active warzone. I will need time to factor this into our plans.'

'Unfortunate,' said Excrucias. 'As time is a pleasure that you cannot afford.'

The Slaaneshi lord gestured to the strategium's primary vid-screen, which shimmered obediently to life. On it, Tsadrekha was depicted as a flickering beacon of white light, wreathed by runes denoting orbital defences, wreckage belts and previous stellar engagements. Kassar picked out the livid pink runes of Excrucias' fleet, hanging in a defensive formation above Tsadrekha. Flooding towards the world from its opposite side was a far larger concentration of runes picked out in a rusty crimson hue.

'The rune of Khorne,' said Kassar. 'One of your rivals moves against Tsadrekha?'

'Even as we speak,' hissed Excrucias. 'Khordas the Slaughterer is a dull oaf, but he has vast numbers on his side, and he attacks with a single-minded lack of restraint.'

'You're sending us in straight away, aren't you?' said Kassar.

'This just keeps getting better,' voxed A'khassor in his ear.

'You have an hour to prepare yourselves, Kassar,' said Phelkorian with obvious relish. 'Any longer and you risk Khordas beating you to the prize.'

'Very well,' said Kassar. 'We will require unlimited access to your armouries, a suitable transport vehicle to effect insertion, and all the information that you can provide upon the beacon's location, its defences, local meteorological and atmospheric conditions…'

Excrucias cut Kassar off with a dismissive gesture.

'Whatever you need will be yours,' he said airily. 'I give you leave to depart my presence. Your escorts will lead you to the primary embarkation deck. From there we shall interfere no further lest our… differing methods of war introduce needless flaws.'

Kassar nodded and turned to go. As he and his warriors marched away from the writhing throne, Excrucias called out to them.

'There is one other thing you should be aware of, my perfect warriors. Something to lend a little speed to your step, perhaps. Our long-range vox thieves intercepted a fragment of this transmission, broadcast on all frequencies from several of Khordas' drop-ships. If it is… legitimate, then I fear that even my magnificent Unsung will have their work cut out for them, no?'

The strategium vid-screen switched, the image filling with hundreds of crimson-hulled attack craft framed against the void. Though Kassar kept walking and showed no outward reaction, his blood ran cold at the bestial chant that boomed through the strategium.

'*Kill! Maim! Burn! Kill! Maim! Burn! Kill! Maim! Burn!*'

Amidst the opulence and frenetic bustle of the *Herald of Pain*'s embarkation deck, the Unsung prepared. They worked with calm efficiency. Haltheus moved from brother to brother, testing armour components and muttering benedictions to machine-spirits.

All the Alpha Legionnaires carried favoured weapons that they had personalised and bonded with over centuries of war, but that didn't preclude them from girding themselves with additional equipment. Bolt pistols, hand flamers, dozens of grenades, power swords and more were selected from the weapons racks that Excrucias had provided. Magazines, fuel cells, sniper rounds, all were stocked up on until the Alpha Legionnaires could carry no more.

As they armed up, the Legionnaires assessed the reams of data that Excrucias had exloaded directly into their helm cogitators and auspexes.

'*Massive defences around the primary hives,*' observed D'sakh in second cipher serpenta. '*And Hive Endurance looks to be the most well defended of them all.*'

'*Unsurprising,*' said A'khassor as he fastidiously cleaned his reductor's blades. '*They know that if they lose the beacon, they lose the war.*'

'*Adepta Sororitas,*' said Phaek'or. '*Do you remember Cordam City?*'

'*Of course,*' replied Makhor. '*Only two hundred of them trapped on Bloodforge, no hope of rescue, but they fought like daemons.*'

'*Until Thelgh took the head off their canoness from a thousand paces,*' chuckled Phalk'ir, mag-locking frag grenades to his belt. '*That took the fight out of them somewhat.*'

They glanced at the silent sniper, who paused in his scope-calibrations long enough to tip Phalk'ir a slight nod.

'*Lots of secondary structures dotted across the oceanic surface,*' said D'sakh. '*Check through this ill-disciplined mess of data for methods of transportation between them. Could be useful.*'

'*Could be,*' agreed Ulkhur. '*But is no one else going to speak of what we heard as we left the strategium? That war chant. You know what that means, yes?*'

'*We know what it might mean,*' said Makhor. '*Khorne worshippers are forever shouting about murder and maiming. Let us not jump to the assumption that he is here. I'd prefer to know what a Primaris Space Marine is. There are several mentions of them amongst this garbled mess, but I can't find any details.*'

'*Could be a Chapter we've not heard of?*' suggested Haltheus. '*Just another watered-down echo of the Legions' glory?*'

'*It's just another name for soon-to-be-dead corpse worshippers,*' said Phalk'ir, raising chuckles from several of his brothers.

Kassar let his warriors debate freely, knowing that, between them, they would pick apart the information they had been given and formulate the best plan of attack. Despite the pitifully short planning window for this operation, he already had a notion of how they would reach the surface of Tsadrekha alive, but he wanted all the input his Harrow could provide to hone the plan to a sharp point.

Kassar glanced at Syxx, leaning against a munitions crate a little way from the Alpha Legionnaires, his shoulders hunched. Thus far, the Harrow had ignored their human cargo completely, though much had been said in code about how their living burden could be kept alive until mission's end. Now Kassar strode over to the acolyte, looking him up and down in frank appraisal.

'I won't slow you down, lord,' said Syxx. 'I can fight. I am fast and strong.'

'You would have to be, to live long in this place,' said Kassar. 'What are you to these degenerates?' Syxx flinched, shooting a quick glance around to see if any Emperor's Children had overheard.

'I am a higher cultist, lord,' he said. 'The property of Phelkorian Twyst. His sixth high acolyte.'

'An auspicious number for your masters, I would imagine,' said Kassar.

'Yes, lord, and for me. The blessings of Slaanesh are many and bounteous.'

'So I've seen,' replied Kassar. 'But you despise your masters, don't you, Syxx?'

'I...' the cultist paused, and lowered his voice to a bare murmur. 'I despise Phelkorian, lord, yes, more than any of them. To be in his service is...'

'Unpleasant,' finished Kassar, and Syxx nodded.

'Horrific, my lord, in ways of which I shall not speak. He is truly an instrument of the Dark Prince.'

'You can fight?' asked Kassar.

'I can,' said Syxx, gesturing to the autopistols holstered at both hips.

'But you won't,' said Kassar. 'Not unless you are left with no choice, and none of my brothers can aid you. Without you, we don't complete our mission, we don't get a ship. We don't get our purpose back. You will stay safe, and keep up, and do nothing else unless you must. Do you understand?'

'Whatever you require of me, lord,' replied Syxx.

Kassar nodded and walked back towards his Harrow, preparing themselves in the looming shadow of their waiting gunship. Kassar narrowed his eyes as he looked over the armoured craft. They would start with that, he thought, and began issuing his orders.

CHAPTER THREE

The leading waves of Khordas the Slaughterer's invasion thundered down upon Tsadrekha. Dreadclaw drop pods and Heldrakes jostled furiously with hundreds upon hundreds of drop-ships and landing craft. Stormbird and Thunderhawk gunships, bullish daemon-engine transporters, captured Astra Militarum mass conveyors packed with frothing cultists, all burned down through the planet's atmosphere. Flames danced across hulls daubed bloody red and encrusted with spikes, battle-scars and Khornate runes. Aboard each craft, Heretic Astartes bellowed praise to the Blood God and swore mighty oaths to claim more skulls than their rivals. Meanwhile, a monstrous voice bellowed through the vox, Khordas exhorting his warriors to strike hard and fast, to smash the enemy's hives open with brute force as Khorne would expect, and to shed their blood for the Blood God.

Amidst the descending waves flew a battered old Thunderhawk, smoke billowing from rusted exhausts, tangles of razorwire trailing from its blocky hull. Aboard, seated in the co-pilot's throne, Haltheus felt the drop-ship's controls shudder as it punched down through the planet's atmospheric envelope. Fire washed across the cockpit armourglass in waves, before parting like a curtain to reveal an incredible vista below.

'Through atmosphere,' reported Haltheus as the Thunderhawk's shuddering subsided. 'Endurance Hive sighted, spire-top five miles and closing fast.'

'Find me a weak spot, Haltheus,' said Kassar through the helm-vox.

'Auspex is sweeping,' said Haltheus, speaking fast as the controls bucked in his grip. 'According to Excrucias' data, the entire hive spire is a convent prioris for the Order of the Crimson Tear. Occupies the top fifteen per cent of Hive Endurance entirely. It's an impressive fortress. Void shield cover is one hundred per cent. Every structure massively armoured. Dark Gods, the flak fire in this quadrant is immense!'

Seen from above, the hive filled the windscreen, a titanic metal mountain whose flanks were wreathed in smoke and fire, and whose feet were lost amidst choppy ocean waves. Hundreds of drop-craft arced down upon it, but sawing streams of fire from Imperial flak batteries blew them apart. Dreadclaws became plummeting fireballs that glanced off the hive's flanks and tumbled away. Khornate fighter craft jinked madly, weapons spitting death, before exploding. Larger craft wallowed painfully off course, trailing fat columns of smoke and flame as they executed graceless death-dives into the waves below.

Haltheus cursed as a bright fireball erupted to his left, Imperial missiles hitting the prow of a heavy lander and blowing it to bits. Shrapnel clattered against the Thunderhawk's hull, and damage runes lit up across its instrument panel.

'Kassar, this is hellish,' said Haltheus as he helped to haul the gunship into a spiralling evasive manoeuvre. 'There's no vertical access. Nothing. The hive spire isn't viable.'

'Damn,' said Kassar as more craft exploded around the Thunderhawk. They were almost on top of the highest spires now, gothic turrets and weaponised gargoyles looming up to fill the armourglass. Over the howl of its engines and the constant roar of gunfire came the bellowed chant, ringing across every vox-channel.

'Blood for the Blood God! Skulls for the Skull Throne! Kill! Maim! Burn! Kill! Maim! Burn!'

Haltheus hauled at the controls again, swerving the Thunderhawk to one side at the last moment and skimming down the flank of a fortified cathedrum. Void-shield energies arced and crackled around the gunship's hull, and fire spat from every window and battlement.

'We'll be dead in seconds at this rate,' said Haltheus tightly. 'Suggestions, Kassar?'

'None,' Kassar replied. 'This attack is doomed to fail.'

Uncoiling across the sky like the tines of a whip, three streams of flak fire converged on the Thunderhawk and ripped through its armoured hull. The warriors crammed into its hold died without even seeing their enemies, burned to ashes or sent tumbling out through wounds in the aircraft's hull, to fall to their deaths thousands of feet below. Haltheus hissed as his instruments exploded, and the controls bucked in his hands hard enough to break bone. He heard the pilot beside him snarl a last prayer to the Blood God, then everything was fire and crushing impact.

Haltheus wrenched the wires out of his helm-augmetic and let them drop. He sat back in his pilot's throne and muttered a string of creative profanity.

'That's three runs,' said Kassar, stood in the gloom behind Haltheus' throne. 'No sign of an infiltration point.'

'Do you need me to begin another possession ritual?' asked Haltheus, sitting forward and making minor adjustments to the Stormbird's controls. Attitudinal thrusters fired a silent burst to maintain its drift. 'There's bound to be plenty more ships with servitors on board...'

'No,' said Kassar. 'I need you fresh and capable of piloting when we make our actual approach. We've gathered enough data on their defences and fire patterns.'

Haltheus nodded gratefully.

'That's for the best, anyway,' he said. 'I'm no warpsmith, Kassar. It felt like the daemon might fight free on that last one.'

Beside the pilot's throne sat a black iron box from which extended several fleshy-looking sets of wires. Three of these were spliced crudely into the rune-daubed auspex and vox systems of the borrowed

Stormbird. The others, Haltheus had just uncoupled from his helm. The box was giving off a strong stench of brimstone, and the runes on its flanks were glowing an infernal red.

'That would be unfortunate,' said Kassar. 'We may have more need of the Coffer before this is over.'

'It would be more than unfortunate,' replied Haltheus with a grim laugh. 'You know what lurks in this box, Kassar. If it got loose, I doubt any of us would survive.'

'Uncouple it and perform your rites of appeasement,' said Kassar. 'But do it quickly. Khordas' attack is in full flow, and we can't risk him beating us to the punch.'

Leaving Haltheus to gingerly neutralise the Coffer, Kassar moved back through the Stormbird towards its transport compartment. His boots clanged with every step, mag-locks sticking and releasing as he walked through the low gravity. The Stormbird was running on minimal power as it drifted through Tsadrekha's debris field, just another ravaged derelict whose course happened to be taking it towards the planet. Still, the gloomy half-light was enough to show Kassar the garish Slaaneshi sigils and biomechanical corruption that riddled the ship's interior. It was not somewhere he wanted to remain for any longer than he absolutely had to.

Stepping through a doorway, Kassar entered the drop-ship's troop bay. Here, the rest of the Unsung sat, fully armoured and strapped into grav harnesses ready for the drop. Syxx sat amongst them, between Thelgh and Kyphas. The cultist wore a rebreather mask to compensate for the minimal life support, and shuddered with cold despite the thermocowl he had wrapped around himself.

'So?' asked Phalk'ir. 'Do we have an insertion vector yet?'

'Nothing primary,' replied Kassar, ignoring the impatient edge to Phalk'ir's tone. 'The spire isn't viable, and from what Haltheus has picked up, Khordas is deliberately withholding direct bombardment to bring the shields down. Some impractical zealotry about blood and honour and the warrior's way.'

'Inconvenient, but unsurprising,' said Ges'khir. 'What is our plan, then?'

'Fall upon them from on high,' said Skarle in a whispered sing-song. 'Loose the fire, watch them die.'

'Nobody asked you, lunatic,' said Reskh.

'Skarle is our brother,' said Kassar sharply. 'You will remember that.'

Reskh offered his captain a warrior's salute and subsided.

'My guess would be insertion scenario quadra,' said D'sakh. 'If the hive is that heavily defended.'

'Correct,' said Kassar. 'I intend to utilise our fourth iteration attack plan. It avoids extreme risk, without compromising speed. Comments?'

'Must we absolutely abandon the notion of gaining access to the spire directly?' asked Makhor. 'It is a large area of complex, armoured structures. Can we be sure that three runs is enough to rule it out altogether?'

'The Coffer is becoming irate,' said Kassar. 'Haltheus has done everything he can on that front. Survivability of Khornate drop-ships within the spire's flak umbrella is vanishingly small. There is no chance of success by that route.'

'This plan will take us outside of the main invasion vectors being followed by Khordas' forces,' said A'khassor. 'I would challenge the assumption that hull camouflage alone is enough to deflect attention from one craft moving so radically off course.'

'They're Khorne worshippers,' said Skaryth scornfully. 'They'll be breaking off from their flight patterns all over, wherever their blood thirst takes them. It's doubtful that anyone else will even notice us stray off course.'

'The Imperial gunners might,' said Makhor. 'All it takes is one servitor crew or sharp-eyed helot to spot an easy target, out in the open, and we're mission fail.'

'The risk is negligible,' said Haltheus, swinging himself through the hatchway to join the discussion. 'The Imperial gunners are keeping the Khornate hordes at bay for now, but Khordas has a *lot* of ships. One craft, high up, veering well off course? We should encounter no difficulties. Probably.'

'Probably?' echoed Phaek'or.

'Have a little faith,' said Haltheus. 'I have an additional innovation ready, in case anyone picks us out.'

'What about personal camouflage?' asked Skaryth. 'And mask protocols?'

'No armour swaps unless a specific opportunity presents itself,' said Kassar. 'We've insufficient intelligence on their protocols and rites. We would blend poorly.'

'Some of us more than others,' said Phalk'ir, looking pointedly at Skarle and Krowl. The former stifled a snigger, while the latter sat still, silent, golem-like, as he always did when not specifically ordered otherwise.

'Mask protocols are seventh pattern, if invoked,' continued Kassar. 'D'sakh will play the role of leader, should the need to obfuscate seniority arise.'

He noticed that Syxx was watching proceedings intently, his body language conveying bewilderment as well as borderline hypothermia.

'You have a question, cultist?'

The Harrow turned their collective gaze upon the human in their midst.

'My lord,' he began, teeth chattering. 'With respect, this is unfamiliar. Lord Excrucias instructs that to question the orders of your superiors is a flaw.'

D'sakh snorted. Makhor and A'khassor looked away, immediately disinterested.

'That's not our way,' said Kassar. 'The Alpha Legion prize initiative at every level. As a collective, we formulate our attack plans, utilising all available information to ensure that we have a counter to every eventuality. Once an attack strategy is chosen, it is questioned and tested before being put into action.'

'You wouldn't wield an untempered blade,' said Haltheus. 'Plans are no different, but sorry, Kassar, why are we explaining this to the baggage?'

'Because if he understands a little of our ways, we stand a better chance of keeping him alive,' replied Kassar. 'And because information is fair exchange, and he can tell us things that Excrucias hasn't.'

'Anything, lord,' said Syxx.

'Let us begin with Ganshorr of the Iron Fist,' said Kassar. 'His name was mentioned by Excrucias, only once, as being the third warlord in contention for Tsadrekha. Yet we've heard nothing more of him, except that he is of the Iron Warriors. Why?'

'It is a matter of wounded pride, my lord,' said Syxx, trying to control the chattering of his teeth. 'Ganshorr assumed an approach of steady, methodical conquest where my master and the butcher Khordas both struck straight at Tsadrekha. They have both been defeated by this world, but Ganshorr has so far overrun three of the Unity's outer planets.'

'Choking off the supply lines, no doubt,' said D'sakh. 'Typical Iron Warriors.'

'He's probably waiting for his rivals to dash themselves to pieces upon Tsadrekha's defences before moving in to finish the job himself,' said Haltheus, nodding.

'There's more to it, though,' said Kassar. 'Isn't there?'

Syxx paused, as though Excrucias might hear him.

'Yes, lord.'

Kassar waited.

'Ganshorr defeated Excrucias, lord,' continued Syxx.

'Where?' asked Kassar. 'When? How?'

'I don't know all of the details, lord,' said Syxx. 'It was death to even speak of it. But Phelkorian implied that Excrucias led an attack to remove Ganshorr from the campaign altogether, believing that one so dull and unimaginative would prove easy prey.'

'Arrogance cost him,' said Kassar. 'And in its aftermath, he found himself in need of elite warriors to replenish his ranks. The sort he abandoned on Bloodforge.'

Syxx nodded.

Before Kassar could ask his next question, the electro-sconces gave a single crimson pulse.

'Ah…' said Haltheus, disappearing back through the hatch.

Wordlessly, Kyphas unharnessed himself, and he and Kassar followed.

* * *

The Stormbird had three thrones in its cockpit, two forward-facing and side-by-side for the pilot and co-pilot, and a third on a recessed level above them, facing back towards the craft's tail. Kassar had never seen a variant of this sort before, but it hadn't taken him long to determine that the third throne was for a dedicated gunner. While Haltheus and Kyphas strapped in to the pilot's and co-pilot's thrones respectively, Kassar propelled himself up to the gunner's throne.

'Haltheus?' asked Kassar. 'Are we detected?'

'No,' answered Haltheus as he worked his instruments. 'Servitor-guided mines, by the looks of it. Probably been out here a while. Just our bad luck they've picked up life signs aboard.'

'Three thousand yards and closing,' said Kyphas, one eye on the auspex as he engaged his motive controls. 'Their thrusters are firing sporadically. They look ill-maintained.'

'Can we light our void shields, drift through them and endure?' asked Kassar.

'Stormbirds are tough, but not that tough, and if this old war-horse still has void shield generators I don't know where Excrucias' warpsmiths have hidden them,' said Haltheus. 'I'm reading plasmic signatures. Even if the mines didn't blow us to pieces, there's no way we'd be in fit shape for orbital insertion.'

Kassar thought quickly. To engage the Stormbird's primary drives and weapon systems would allow them to deal with the incoming ordnance, but it would also betray their position as if they had run up a flag.

'Distance to the edge of the debris field?' he asked.

'Two point three miles,' replied Haltheus. 'Then another twenty to bring us onto our approach vector.'

'Two thousand five hundred yards, still closing,' said Kyphas. 'I read a dozen mines, Kassar.'

Their craft had already drifted through over thirty miles of orbital debris. Excrucias' ships had been left far behind, lurking beyond the engagement zone. The Unsung were alone, unsupported, and very much in harm's way.

Precisely where they did their best work.

'Haltheus,' said Kassar, 'the Coffer?'

'Slumbering,' said Haltheus. 'We couldn't wake it now even if we dared.'

Kassar nodded.

'All right then,' he said over the squad's vox-channel. 'Stealth's no use to us if we die here. Haltheus, keep to manoeuvring thrusters but take what evasive action you can, and we'll hope that there's still enough debris between us and the enemy to hide it. Kyphas, patch squad vox through the ship's emitters, highest sensitivity, and direct it towards the nearest wrecks. Focus the auspex beams on the same locations and see if you can't generate some heat.'

'False life signs,' said Kyphas, already working his controls. 'Heat. Breathing. Heartbeats. Clever.'

Kassar didn't reply, instead focusing on his targeters, and the weapons slaved to his command. Along with several racks of missiles, Stormbirds boasted four heavy bolter turrets, two set fore and aft along each flank, and normally crewed by dedicated gunners. This Emperor's Children gunship instead gave full control of all weapons to one individual; if Kassar had to guess, some element of obsessive or excessive psychology was the root of such a decision, but now was hardly the time to ponder it. Instead, he watched intently as runic designators flashed up to indicate the plasma-warhead orbital interdiction mines closing to within eighteen hundred yards.

The gunship lurched, and Kassar felt sudden pressure as Haltheus swung them around a drifting hunk of metal that had once been a warship's prow. The mines changed heading to follow them, and two silent flashes lit the cockpit in quick succession. On Kassar's targeter, ten runes remained, closing quickly.

'Kyphas,' said Kassar.

'Focusing resonance now,' said the former spymaster.

Kassar heard the weird feedback loop of his and his brothers' breathing and heartbeats magnified through their vox-channel, before Kyphas sent their signal out through the void. On Kassar's screen, another rune winked out as it chased their false life signs into an ancient enginarium, followed by three more that ploughed in quick succession into the gutted hulk of a Sword-class frigate.

'Six left,' said Haltheus, triggering the Stormbird's thrusters again. The gunship tumbled onto its side, sliding neatly between the skeletal spars of a drifting leviathan. Fingers of wreckage scraped their hull, causing screeches and groans to echo around them. Drifting globules of promethium spattered the armourglass of the windshield then wobbled away.

'Five,' said Kassar as another of the runes winked out. The rest filtered through the wreck behind them, red eye-lights pulsing in skull sockets as they tracked their prey.

The gunship emerged from the huge wreck, and Haltheus gave its thrusters a sudden punch, spinning them vertical and propelling them away towards the edge of the debris field. Kassar watched as the mines jetted after them, accelerating.

'Kyphas?' he asked.

'Still transmitting, no response,' replied Kyphas.

'We won't outrun them on manoeuvring thrusters, Kassar,' said Haltheus. 'It's engines or gunfire.'

'Guns then,' said Kassar. 'Lesser of two evils. Give me a clear shot.'

'Nine hundred yards,' said Kyphas.

Haltheus worked his controls and, with another surge of thrust, the Stormbird rolled to present its belly to the oncoming mines. Hanging sideways in his restraints, Kassar swivelled all four twin-linked heavy bolters so they were pointing at the onrushing ordnance. Four weapons' worth of targeting data flooded in, taxing even his superior cerebral capacity, yet his breathing remained steady, his actions calm and measured.

'Eight hundred yards,' said Kyphas.

'Kassar...' said Haltheus.

Kassar drank in data, mentally processing trajectories, velocity, energy output signatures. One by one, lock signatures appeared above the target runes.

'Six hundred yards,' said Kyphas.

'Captain!' urged Haltheus.

Breathing slowly out, Kassar depressed his runic triggers. Eight heavy bolter muzzles flared silently in the void, a single shell bursting from each gun on a jet of fire. The heavy calibre shells sped through the darkness in tight pairs, converging on their targets with lethal speed. Fierce detonations followed. The Stormbird bucked as though kicked by a giant, Haltheus and Kyphas wrestling with the controls as they rode out the shockwave from multiple plasma flares. Kassar hung on grimly, eyes still fixed on the static-washed screen of his targeter.

The gunship's tumble righted itself and the instruments cleared. Kassar sat back from his screen as the targeter showed empty.

'All hostile contacts eliminated,' he reported. 'Kyphas, can you get us visual confirmation?'

'One moment,' said Kyphas, working his instruments.

'Cutting things fine, Kassar?' asked Haltheus.

'Minimising shots fired,' replied Kassar. 'There's a dozen reasons why old ordnance might detonate within this debris field, but sustained streams of heavy bolter fire don't just happen without someone directing them.'

'Agreed,' said Haltheus. 'I almost hope the skull-lovers *are* looking this way. At least then all this effort and danger would be justif–'

'Single contact remains,' said Kyphas. 'Damaged but mobile, must have been pushed clear of your fire by its comrades' detonation, Kassar. Two hundred yards, eighty-two degrees starboard.'

Reacting instantly, Haltheus triggered the Stormbird's port thrusters, kicking the gunship into a sharp turn. At the same time, Kassar swung the starboard guns to bear, sighted on his target and depressed his triggers. Again the Stormbird's guns spat shells. Four bolts slammed into the target, and a raging storm of plasma erupted into space.

Haltheus cursed as damage runes lit amber on the Stormbird's panel, and Kassar clung grimly to his restraints as he was shaken like a rag doll. Then they were drifting again, clear of the blast and nearing the edge of the debris field.

'Damage?' asked Kassar. For a moment, the only answer was the click and hum of his brothers working their controls, stabilising the craft, performing diagnostic genuflections to its machine-spirit.

'Tolerable,' said Haltheus eventually. 'Outer plating on the starboard wing is partially melted, and there's a coolant leak somewhere in there. I wouldn't chance firing those missiles unless I had a clear shot at the Golden Throne, and we're going to have to watch the wing during re-entry. But we're still mission capable.'

'Good,' said Kassar. 'Give us enough thrust to take us onto our approach vector, then let the machine-spirit compose itself for a few moments. We want it calm and willing before we commence our approach.'

Haltheus muttered something about his own calm and willingness, but followed his orders. Kassar switched back to the squad vox-channel, which Kyphas had now returned to its normal configuration and re-encrypted.

'Unsung, report,' he voxed.

'The Harrow is mission capable,' replied D'sakh. 'No damage sustained, though the package was rendered unconscious during that second blast.'

'He was harmed?' asked Kassar.

'Nothing serious,' replied A'khassor. 'I have checked him over, as best I can without exposing him to lethal levels of cold. No compromising damage. As an observation, though, what flesh I saw – scalp and neck mostly – is absolutely crawling with branded sigils. You'd need a psyker to confirm it, Kassar, but I'd wager there's empyric power bound into the mortal's body somehow.'

'Noted,' said Kassar. 'Phelkorian spoke of markings that would taint the beacon, but he was vague as to their exact purpose. We'll be doubly cautious until we can determine what power our guest brings with him.'

'A shame that you were forced to put an end to Nehkt'sha,' said Kyphas, joining the vox exchange. 'A skilled sorcerer might have been able to decipher the purpose of those runes.'

'A shame indeed,' added Phalk'ir bitterly. 'And what was his sin but embracing the gifts that we have all earned thrice-over by now?'

'Nehkt'sha was possessed,' said Kassar. 'And this is an old, tired argument, Phalk'ir. The gifts of the gods are nothing of the sort. They are corruption and death.'

'Or they are power,' replied Phalk'ir. 'Fairly earned and richly deserved.'

'I won't have this argument with you again, brother,' said Kassar. 'We are no longer trapped on Bloodforge, and once we complete this mission we will have our freedom. If you wish to part ways with the Harrow on that day, to pursue the cursed boons of the Chaos Gods, I won't try to stop you. That goes for any of you who still hunger for their gifts despite all we have seen. But for now, we have a mission, one that we must complete. Focus on that.'

'Yes, Kassar,' said D'sakh. 'How long?'

'We will be out of the debris belt in under a minute,' said Kassar, grateful for his vexillor's loyalty. 'We'll drift for another three minutes and then enter an approach vector. Providing the enemy do not see through our ruse, we'll begin our drop six minutes and ten seconds after that. Final preparations.'

Assenting vox pips came back to him, the Harrow beginning ammunition checks and pre-battle rituals, and their final benedictions to their machine-spirits.

'No prayer,' he added in a tone of voice that brooked no debate. 'We are our own masters.'

Kassar cut the vox-link and began a thorough check of his own wargear, taking slow, meditative breaths as he did so.

'Phalk'ir is a preening cretin,' said Haltheus quietly. 'But he does make you think. We don't owe the gods anything, but do we owe Excrucias any more? We're already free, Kassar. I'm just saying, we could shoot the cultist, turn our prow and disappear.'

'No, brother,' said Kassar. 'I hear you, but where would we go? This is not a warp-capable ship, and we haven't the numbers to board one that is.'

'Just "questioning and testing",' replied Haltheus, a smile in his voice. 'I assumed you'd say something of that sort.'

'Besides,' said Kassar. 'If we broke our word so easily, we'd prove ourselves no better than the rest of these degenerates. We're better than that. We're Alpha Legion.'

Kassar continued with his checks, quietly reflecting upon the other, deeper reason for his determination to see this mission through. On the planet below, redemption waited, a chance for him to atone for the lives lost on Bloodforge. A chance for the Unsung to be their own masters once again. Kassar vowed to himself, there and then, that he would do whatever it took to win them that chance.

Whatever came after, could wait.

CHAPTER FOUR

Engines fired in the darkness, spitting tongues of blue-tinged flame. Adamantium and ceramite accelerated, driven on by the mounting force from behind. Sluggish at first, but swiftly gaining momentum, the Stormbird swept down towards Tsadrekha.

Ahead lay swarming masses of drop-craft, red-hulled murder ships filling the orbital approaches to the planet like wind-blown spores. They flooded from the launch bays of lumbering battleships and cruisers, which even now were hauling themselves closer to the planet, desperate to join the frenzied attack.

'Warp, will you look at all this?' said Haltheus as he guided the gunship towards the massed craft. 'Kassar, if they've been losing ships at the rate we saw…'

'Millions dead already,' agreed Kassar from the gunner's throne. 'And doubtless millions more before they secure any meaningful beachhead.'

'Khorne cares not…' said Kyphas, leaving the old invocation hanging.

'Evidently not,' said Haltheus, fingers dancing over the controls. 'Kyphas, choristry please.'

'At once,' said Kyphas, attending to his own instruments. Deftly, the spymaster isolated the voxponder signatures of a random string of Khornate gunships from the masses ahead. Working fast, Haltheus marked the signal's key binharic beats and replicated them within the gunship's onboard cogitator, before setting the data-hymnal to repeat. The Stormbird's voxponder output was now masked by an agglomerate approximation of their enemies', sufficient to fool all but the most determined auspex.

'Unsung,' voxed Haltheus. 'A moment's frenzied idiocy, if you please. Belligerence is key, try to make yourselves heard over Krowl.'

In answer, the vox filled with the Harrow's dutiful bellows.

'Kill! Maim! Burn! Kill! Maim! Burn!'

'Sufficient,' said Kyphas, manipulating the gunship's vox to broadcast the shout as a repeating mantra across every open vox-channel.

Haltheus flared their gunship's engines, coaxing more speed and dirty smoke from them even as he subtly adjusted his piloting to match the more aggressive, heavy-handed approach typified by the Khornate craft. Coupled with the crimson paintwork and Khornate runes applied by deck-servitors before the Unsung departed, it was everything they could do to camouflage their craft.

The seconds ticked by. The Khornate armada swelled in the windscreens. Auspex chimes rang out as passive scans swept them. Cogitator guidance subroutines awoke. Haltheus found himself holding his breath as they swept over the gun-studded spine of a Carnage-class cruiser. They passed over the ship's name, *Murderer's Fist* picked out in scorched black letters larger than their Stormbird.

'Kassar,' said Haltheus, 'are those turrets tracking us?'

'Hard to tell,' said Kassar, noting the spiked emplacements Haltheus had spotted. 'Just stay on course.'

Brutish cannons and lascannon arrays swung their way. Haltheus' hands hovered over his instruments, ready to begin evasive manoeuvres, for what good they would do.

Then they were past, the rumbling cruiser a looming cliff face at their backs, and a hurricane of attack craft ripping past on every side.

Haltheus breathed out slowly.

'First test passed,' he muttered. 'Now things get really challenging.'

'Entering flight pattern, such as it is,' voxed Haltheus, switching seamlessly to sixth cypher serpenta, the variant the Harrow used whenever staging a vehicular infiltration. *'Infiltration successful. Welcome to the Blood God's service, brothers.'*

'Do not even joke of it,' growled Skaryth.

'Good work Haltheus, Kyphas,' said Kassar. *'Stay alert, all of you. Prepare for drop. Krowl?'*

A low grunt came back across the vox.

'The cultist is your responsibility. Keep him safe at any cost, understood?'

Another grunt, indistinguishable from the last, but Kassar knew that Krowl would protect Syxx with his life.

'The enemy have attack corridors flowing down on all five Tsadrekhan hives,' reported Kyphas as stolen data streams filtered across his vid-screen. *'They're scattering secondary offensive waves to strike at island fortifications and orbital batteries, while roving hunt groups prowl in search of the hives' promethium rigs, macrofactory fleets and air interdiction assets.'*

'We're nestled in the trailing edge of the Hive Endurance attack corridor,' informed Haltheus. *'Ready for the descent.'*

A monstrous flash of light filled the cockpit. As the glare died away, Kassar checked the external feed and saw the *Murderer's Fist* breaking gradually into two halves. Secondary explosions rippled through the cruiser's superstructure, while around it dozens of craft drifted as blackened wreckage.

'Defence lasers,' said Kassar, squinting as the vid image washed out once again. A volley of mile-long energy bolts seared up through the planet's atmosphere and struck a battleship to the Stormbird's rear. The huge craft's void shields held, and it began to pivot into bombardment position, lining its lance batteries up to return fire. Drop-ships still poured from its launch bays, adding to the endless locust swarm of attack craft.

'Kassar,' said Kyphas urgently. *'Reports suggest Khordas is leading the attack on Endurance in person.'*

'*Unfortunate, but not unexpected,*' said Kassar. '*We'll stay out of his path. Anything further?*'

'*No,*' said Kyphas. '*Nothing pertinent.*'

'*Fifteen seconds to atmosphere,*' said Haltheus. '*Brace, brace, brace.*'

Kassar tested his throne's restraints one last time, checked his armour's seals, and prepared himself for the violence of atmospheric re-entry. He reflected, not for the first time, that a doctrine of self-reliant godlessness was all well and good, until you found yourself powerless to affect your situation. As he always did at such moments, Kassar chose to believe in his brothers instead of distant, disinterested gods, and to draw strength from them.

Then the Stormbird hit the upper atmosphere of Tsadrekha with an almighty jolt, and gravity took them in its merciless claws.

Kyphas felt the force of their descent push him back into his throne, armour servos whining as they compensated. The armourglass of the windscreen filled with flame, and proximity warnings chimed as Khornate attack craft nosedived all around them. He held his controls steady, helping Haltheus to keep the craft within the approach vector shown on their cogitator screens.

Kyphas' mind whirled with possibilities. He should tell Kassar the rest of what he had seen in that data-transcript. Why had he not? This had a serious bearing upon their mission. It could cost his brothers their lives. Yet Kyphas felt his avarice for secrets strongly. Information. It was the lifeblood of the Alpha Legion and, until the last of his cultist spy networks had died out upon that cursed daemon world, it had been Kyphas' greatest gift. The steady flow of secrets through his fingers had ensured his status in the Harrow.

They had defined him, given him purpose.

That loss had been a bitter blow. But the Unsung were no longer trapped on Bloodforge, and once again the information had begun to flow. It was his to give or to keep as he saw fit, his to hoard until the opportune moment.

And really, wasn't he doing his duty by sparing his brothers from distracting information until it became truly relevant? Wasn't he obeying his Legion's old tenet? *Gather as much as you can. Give none away.*

Yes, he thought as the fires flickered from the heat-shielded prow of their gunship, and the endless oceans of Tsadrekha spread out far below. These secrets were his, his power, and he would deign to part with them only when he was ready.

With a gesture, Kyphas wiped his vid-screen, diverting the flow of information directly to his retinal display and hoarding it away detail by detail, word by word.

Name by name.

Strapped in the gunner's throne, Kassar felt the descent as a constant, savage pressure from behind. Mag-locks held his shoulders and helm in place, preventing him from smashing forwards into his targeters, but still he was thankful when the Stormbird punched through into open sky and the pressure eased.

'Kyphas, *route external vidcams to all retinal displays,*' he ordered. '*Brothers, surveillance and threat recognition.*'

The view outside their gunship was anarchic madness. Haltheus had guided them in on the far eastern edge of the Hive Endurance attack corridor, but still there were craft plunging down all around them. Troop transports, war engine landers and attack craft fell like bloody rain.

Away to the west rose Hive Endurance, its towering enormity crowned by the gothic macrostructures of the convent prioris. A corona of fire surrounded the hive, millions of defensive guns roaring their defiance at the swarms of attack craft that hurtled towards them.

Most of the Khornate craft were angling towards the hive, or turning their noses towards outer fortresses that clung to rocky islands and artificial rafts in the open ocean. The structures formed a loose ring around the hive, adding their substantial firepower to the defence. Lasers, missiles and shells filled the air. Wreckage fell, and the ocean waves teemed with floundering bodies and burning promethium slicks.

'*I can see why they've had no luck invading this place,*' said Haltheus through gritted teeth. '*How do you even establish a toehold?*'

'*Brute force,*' replied D'sakh over the vox. '*Look.*'

An optic feed flashed in Kassar's peripheral vision and he brought it forward with a thought. He saw a magnified view of an ocean fort, one flank of which had been smashed open by a drop-ship's prow. The craft had broken in half with the force of the impact, and smoke billowed up from fort and drop-ship alike. Tiny figures moved amidst the wreckage. Daemon engines, Kassar realised, iron beasts hauling themselves from the devastation to fall upon the fort's defenders.

'*Impressive,*' said Phaek'or, his voice lurching as Haltheus rolled to avoid incoming fire.

'*If they can succeed there, then given enough time and lives they can break into the hive as well,*' said Kassar. '*Haltheus, it's time we diverted.*'

'*Understood,*' said Haltheus. '*Deploying smoker.*'

Haltheus unclamped a handheld detonator from his belt and, piloting one-handed with Kyphas' aid, he pumped the device's pressure-plunger. On the third click, there was a muffled bang from the second port-side engine. In the external vidstreams, thick black smoke began to billow from it, accompanied by flickering flames.

'*Effective,*' said A'khassor. '*We look winged.*'

'*Switching to true attack heading,*' voxed Haltheus. '*Expect a little chop, brothers. The smoker may have worked a touch too well.*'

Their craft lurched sideways, narrowly missing a hurtling squadron of Helblades as it arced away from the attack column. Their new heading took them out over open ocean, through a gap between two of the defensive fortresses and away west above the turbulent chop of the waves.

Kassar could see flames still spilling from the engine cowling, while the Stormbird had developed a definite shudder.

'*I asked for the semblance of a direct hit, Haltheus,*' he said. '*Not the real thing.*'

'*Firstly,*' replied Haltheus. '*I'm a little busy piloting us through an active war-zone. Secondly, still not actually a Techmarine. You all ask an awful lot of me, Kassar, considering my expertise is in blowing things up, not repairing them.*'

'Agreed,' said Kassar, switching back from serpenta as the ocean forts receded behind them. No enemy forces were nearby, and the effort of conversing in serpenta became wearing over time. 'But I ask a lot of us all, myself included. There's not enough of us left to do anything but our best.'

'Understood,' said Haltheus, his voice stiff.

'Can we still reach our destination with the engine compromised?' asked Kassar.

'Easily,' said Kyphas. 'This craft is resilient and powerful. Besides, its machine-spirit carries the taint of Slaaneshi corruption. It likely revels in the experience of battle damage.'

'Speaking of which,' said Kassar, 'how is the cultist?'

'Conscious,' replied D'sakh. 'Mission capable.'

Behind them, the warzone around Hive Endurance shrank until all that could be seen was the hive's dark silhouette, wreathed in an ever-shifting veil of drop-craft and smoke.

'So many ships,' said Makhor. 'This Khordas must be a warlord of incredible power to muster so many. I've not seen numbers like that since the ancient days.'

'If this great rift is all that the Slaanesh worshippers claim, that may account for it,' said Kassar. 'Imagine, our forces able to move at will through the galaxy, while the corpse worshippers take their turn to be trammelled like dogs.'

'The irony is not unappealing,' said Makhor. 'And you may well be right. Our numbers are likely greater within the darkened regions of the Imperium, than in those where the Astronomican shines.'

'Destination coming up,' said Kyphas. 'Five minutes.'

'Ready yourselves, brothers,' said Kassar, double-checking his bolter's magazine. An old pre-battle ritual, though needless. Mortis was an exceptional weapon, and had never failed him.

'What should I do, my lord?' Syxx's voice sounded firm on the vox, no hint of the nausea or shock that Kassar had expected.

'What I told you,' he answered. 'Stay close to Krowl. Keep him between you and any gunfire.'

'And what if he is killed, lord?' asked Syxx.

'If they've got anything that can kill Krowl,' said Sha'dor, 'then we'll probably all be dead anyway. But in extremis, get behind Ges'khir.'

'I am not a barricade,' rumbled the Terminator. 'Hide behind me at your peril.'

'Three minutes out,' said Haltheus. 'Prepare yourselves for a rough landing, brothers. Auspex is reading a lot of firepower and... damn it, a combat air patrol.'

Promethium extraction rig *Bountificus Omnissium* towered a thousand feet above the ocean waves. In the gunship's forward feed it looked like an armoured behemoth, an ogre of plasteel and ferrocrete built to shrug off the most violent excesses of a Tsadrekhan hurricane. The Stormbird's long-range auspex picked out the distinctive barrels of hydra batteries scanning the aerial approaches, while life signs were densely clustered throughout the rig's chevron-painted industrial battlements.

As he guided the Stormbird in towards its destination, however, Haltheus' first concern was the pair of runic contacts showing in the rig's local airspace.

'Stormhawk interceptors,' he said. 'Our long-lost brothers in the Imperial Fists, extending the hand of welcome.'

'*They'll assume we're Khorne worshippers,*' said Kassar in sixth cypher. '*My guess is they'll swing out on our flanks, try to herd us into the teeth of the rig's flak.*'

'*It will be my pleasure to surprise them,*' said Haltheus.

'*Stormhawks moving away from the rig,*' reported Kyphas. '*You were right, Kassar, auspex shows them breaking right and left. They're accelerating to combat speed.*'

'*Perfect,*' said Haltheus. '*Engaging right. Kassar, be ready with the guns and remember those starboard missiles.*'

'*Last resort only, brother, understood,*' said Kassar, fingers dancing across the arming runes as enemy contacts flashed on his targeters. The Stormbird tilted around him as Haltheus took them into a tight turn, lining up on his target. On the vid-screens, a compact yellow and red interceptor swung into view, streaking low over the waves.

The Stormhawk was far smaller than their Stormbird, but Kassar guessed that its firepower was wildly disproportionate to its size, and its armoured hull a great deal more resilient than it looked.

'*Engaging,*' said Haltheus, and the Stormbird leapt forward on full thrust. The enemy pilot, clearly surprised at having to face the larger craft alone, wavered for a moment, banking aside.

Kassar depressed his firing runes, chasing his target with streams of bolts and sending a missile streaking away for good measure. A crackling halo of frag charges burst from the back of the Stormhawk, detonating in mid-air and triggering Kassar's missile. The bolters did better, clipping the interceptor's tail assembly. Smoke burst from the wounds, but the Imperial Fists craft stayed airborne, hauling itself out of the Stormbird's attack path and fleeing back towards the rig.

Kassar could already see the Stormhawk's wingman sweeping around on their flank, gaining on them fast.

'*Can we drive them off long enough to land?*' he asked, sending thumping bursts of fire towards the enemy craft.

'*There's a lot of flak down there, Kassar,*' replied Haltheus. '*I'd risk it, maybe, if we didn't have the baggage, but he'd never survive that sort of combat drop. Besides, that would leave the Stormhawks free to hit us from above.*'

'*Agreed,*' said Kassar, working his fire controls as fast as he could, striving to trap the Stormhawk in a web of flak. It was still coming, though, straight at their damaged starboard side, spiralling around his shots.

'*Warp damn it,*' cursed Kassar. '*This one's a born dogfighter.*'

The interceptor's guns roared, lascannon blasts and cannon shells ripping into the Stormbird's wing and flank as it streaked overhead. The gunship shook furiously, and sparks showered from overloaded systems.

'*Damage report,*' demanded Kassar.

'*We've lost an engine,*' said Haltheus. '*Luckily the one the smoker damaged already. We're also shedding fuel.*'

'*Kassar,*' voxed D'sakh. '*Ges'khir's dead. Lascannon rounds punched through the hold and nearly tore him in half.*'

Fifteen, said a cold voice in Kassar's head. Fifteen left, and their last Terminator-armoured brother fallen.

'*Understood,*' he said, his voice cold. '*He'll be avenged.*'

'*If so, we need to do it quickly,*' said Haltheus. '*We've maybe ten minutes in the air before we're running on fumes. And that bastard has linked up with his wingman.*'

On Kassar's targeter, the two designator runes for the Stormhawks had converged out beyond the rig. They were coming in for another run, the damaged interceptor flying top cover for his comrade. Lumbering on three engines, the Stormbird was swinging around to meet them, but not fast enough. Kassar sent a broadside of bolt rounds whipping towards the incoming craft.

'*Haltheus,*' he said. '*Bank away from them. Lower the rear ramp.*'

'*She'll handle like orks built her, and it'll take us in towards the rig's flak umbrella, but all right,*' replied the pilot. '*We're already outmanoeuvred, what's a little more handicap?*'

Kassar continued to spray fire, and grinned savagely as he managed to clip the wing of the already damaged interceptor. It wobbled, and tried to climb away. Kassar hammered its underbelly with bolts, ripping the Stormhawk open and scattering its wreckage across the waves.

'*Harrow, out of your restraints and find cover,*' he barked. '*Ramp opening. Thelgh, you know what to do.*'

A single vox pip was Thelgh's acknowledgement.

Kassar switched his vid feed to show the interior of the hold, and the Unsung scattering to take cover behind bulkheads, stanchions, anything that would shield them. Power armour provided magnificent protection, but it wouldn't stop a lascannon blast. Krowl stood firm behind a plasteel support, Syxx crouched at his back.

Only Thelgh remained in the open, walking calmly towards the lowering ramp with his sniper rifle Somnolence in hand. He had taken that weapon from one of the Raven Guard's elite Mor Deythan during the madness of the Scouring, and had slain hundreds of enemies with it since. Perhaps thousands.

Ignoring the blasts and shells spitting from the closing Stormhawk, Thelgh mag-locked his boots to the decking, swept his cameleoline cloak back, and took careful aim. A lascannon blast spat directly over his shoulder, searing a line across Thelgh's armour and causing a violent explosion to blossom beyond the vidcam's view. Kassar was thrown sideways in his seat by the force of the impact, but Thelgh swayed with it, utterly focused.

Kassar switched his view to the pursuing craft in time to see a small, crimson dot slide up its nose, across its canopy, and settle on the thin, armoured vision slit of the Stormhawk.

More shots hammered the Stormbird as the rig's flak batteries awoke. Haltheus cursed as he fought to break right.

Kassar's hearts skipped a beat as Thelgh's aim swayed with the sudden manoeuvre, and the Stormhawk's lascannon barrels seemed to yawn like caverns.

Then Thelgh fired.

A slight, almost silent thump as the round left the barrel.

A muted flash from the suppressed muzzle.

The Stormhawk wobbled, and Kassar's superhuman vision picked out a spatter of blood painting the inner surface of its vision slit. Then the Imperial Fists interceptor listed off course and fell away. Its nose guns clipped the waves, and the aircraft flipped head over heels before becoming a tumbling, cartwheeling fireball.

Kassar slammed one fist against his throne's armrest in triumph, hearing the shouts of his more bellicose warriors ringing across the vox. Thelgh calmly chambered another round, shrouded his weapon, and returned to his seat.

'Bring the ramp up, and prepare for a combat landing,' ordered Kassar. 'And Thelgh, that was masterful.'

On Kassar's retinal display, Thelgh gave a slight nod.

'Don't celebrate yet, brothers,' said Haltheus as he closed the Stormbird's ramp. 'That last hit displeased the machine-spirit mightily. I'll do what I can, but we're going down.'

Kassar's jubilation evaporated, replaced by steely focus. Calmly he checked the Stormbird's ammunition counters, recalibrated its targeters, and readied himself as Haltheus hauled the shuddering gunship's nose around.

'We have one chance at this,' he voxed. 'For the sake of all those we've lost, for our chance at a future, make it count.'

Haltheus climbed as much as he dared, getting breathing space between his stricken craft and the merciless ocean. He checked his instruments, silently cursing the powerful westerly wind that had risen during the dogfight. Black clouds were rolling in from the deep ocean, lit by forked tines of lightning. The waves were rising, white froth cresting them. Unless Haltheus missed his guess, the storm would be on them in minutes, but that didn't trouble him too much.

By that time, they would be on the rig, or they would all be dead.

'I'm going to bring us in on the rig's left flank,' he voxed. 'I'll try to keep our most intact armour turned towards their guns. We're going to take fire, its unavoidable, but I'll do what I can to minimise it. Stay in your restraints, but keep your weapons to hand, brothers. I'll swing us around the back of that guard tower at the rig's far corner and ditch in the storage hangar at its feet. That should give us a few moments to take position before they can mass on us.'

Privately, Haltheus had his doubts, and a quick glance at Kyphas' hunched posture told him his brother felt the same. But Haltheus' natural pragmatism was shot through with a strong vein of optimism, and a fierce determination that he was the master of his own destiny. He wouldn't give in without a fight.

'Rally point is here,' said Kassar, blink-clicking a designator onto the Harrow's retinal displays on the edge of the storage hangar. 'Fall-back position is here.' Another click, another rune lit on their auspex maps at the foot of the guard tower. 'Look to your wargear, and your brothers.'

'Not for gods. Not for warlords,' said his warriors as one.

'For the primarchs, and the Harrow,' Kassar replied. It was an old battle mantra, adopted on Bloodforge, and it had served them well.

The shuddering of the Stormbird had become a violent shaking. Runes flickered from amber to red across its cockpit instruments, and warning chimes sounded through the craft. Its electro-sconces flickered to deep crimson, and the smell of smoke filled the air.

Hydra barrels swivelled and began to thump, streams of shells converging on the gunship as it thundered in over the waves. Kassar heard Haltheus curse, and gripped the arms of his throne as the Stormbird executed a wallowing series of evasive manoeuvres. The clang of impacts suggested they weren't entirely successful.

'*Coming up on the rig,*' said Haltheus. '*Give me what cover you can, Kassar.*'

Kassar was already sweeping for targets, the auspex flickering across armoured turrets, humming vox-nests and rearing battlements that thronged with warriors. Selecting his victims with veteran skill, he sent multiple warheads streaking away from the port wing.

The first missile punched through a plascrete redoubt and into the magazine behind, detonating a flak battery and a score of Imperial Guardsmen. The second was clipped by flak, tumbling off course into the rig's towering industrial superstructure. It exploded amidst a cluster of fuel tanks, and flames lit Kassar's screens as an almighty fireball bloomed skywards. The last shot struck the supports of an armoured vox-tower. It fell, wreathed in electricity, to crush another Hydra battery and scatter the Adepta Sororitas hunkered in its shadow.

Then the missiles were gone, and Kassar was down to heavy bolters. He played his targeters across the enemy positions, raking them with explosive rounds, but the rig was huge and their enemies many. Bodies tumbled in bursts of blood. A third flak battery burst into flames.

Engines howling, hull aflame, the Stormbird floundered around the flank of the rig, taking more hits as it went. A section of the cockpit cowling tore away, and suddenly the wind was screaming around Kassar, the sky yawning overhead.

The rig's superstructure hurtled past, their dropsite approaching fast. The guard tower loomed up before them, its guns spitting fire.

'*Kassar!*' D'sakh's voice, barely audible above the scream of the wind and the roar of engines and gunfire. Whatever the vexillor's message, Kassar didn't have to hear it. At precisely that moment another stream of flak raked them, and he was slammed into his seat by an almighty explosion.

On his instruments, everything pulsed angry red, then cut in a shower of sparks.

'*Starboard fuel tanks,*' shouted Haltheus. '*Forget what I said, Kassar, get those war-damned missiles away!*'

'*My controls are dead,*' Kassar shouted back, amplifying his voice over the cacophony of battle. '*I can't.*'

Kassar's world filled with light and fire as the fuel tanks touched off the gunship's trapped missiles. The Stormbird jolted sideways with bone-breaking force. Kassar felt a terrible wrench as the deck buckled and tore. Then everything turned upside down, the rig raced up to meet them, and the sound of impacts and explosions melded into a deafening bellow cut off by sudden, silent darkness.

CHAPTER FIVE

Consciousness returned, a sharp transition from nothingness to mayhem. Kassar's eyes opened, and his mind engaged.

He was upside down, hanging from his throne's restraints. The roar of flames filled his ears. Amber alert runes flashed in his peripheral vision, his armour warning of damage and minor injuries. A quick check confirmed that Mortis was still mag-locked to his thigh, and Hexling remained in its sheath at his hip.

Kassar uncoupled his restraints and dropped from his throne, landing in a fighting crouch on what remained of the cockpit roof. A quick glance showed that the gunship had slammed into a building, probably the guard tower, punching through into the structure's interior. The explosion had torn open the Stormbird's hull, and the subsequent crash had ripped the craft apart, segments of it smashing through chambers and corridors. Kassar stood, fires burning all around, choking smoke obscuring wreckage and rubble on every side. There was no sign of anyone else.

'Unsung,' he voxed. 'Report.'

Rubble shifted to his right, lumps of ferrocrete tumbling down to clang on the metal decking. Kyphas hauled himself free, jade eye-lenses burning amidst the dust. Wordlessly, the spymaster unholstered his bolt pistols.

'Kassar,' came a shout from amidst the smoke. Haltheus' voice, no cypher.

Kassar and Kyphas hurried through the wreckage towards the source of the shout. On their way, they all but tripped over the sprawled body of Reskh, his armour scorched and his head nowhere to be seen.

Fourteen left, thought Kassar grimly.

They found Haltheus pinned under the wreck of the gunship's nose. Together, Kassar and Kyphas hauled the mangled metal aside, and Haltheus clambered to his feet. Blood leaked from a rent in his side, but otherwise he looked uninjured.

Kassar's vox pinged now with a steady stream of clicks and hisses, the Unsung confirming that they still lived. Quickly, efficiently, they rallied on their leader.

'The baggage lives,' said D'sakh as he limped from the smoke. 'Krowl took a stanchion through the chest, still hasn't managed to rip it out, but the cultist? Barely a scratch. Something's watching over him.'

Kassar felt a tightness unlock in his chest as he saw Syxx stumble into the firelight, rebreather clamped to his face. Krowl loomed alongside him, both gauntlets wrapped around a jagged spear of metal driven into his breastplate. With a grunt, he wrenched the offending spar from his flesh and threw it aside. Brackish blood spattered after it, but through the crack in Krowl's armour his flesh could be seen reknitting.

'Several minor injuries and flesh wounds,' reported A'khassor as he moved from brother to brother, his narthecium flashing. 'Makhor has a broken arm. Skarle's secondary heart is punctured.'

'Sha'dor? Ulkhur?' asked Kassar, seeing that both were missing. D'sakh shook his head.

'They were closest to the starboard ordnance when it blew,' he said. 'I saw them both die.'

Twelve left; the voice sounded again in Kassar's mind like a death-knell. Angrily, he drove it away.

'We could have suffered far worse,' he said. 'And we are still mission capable. But the enemy will be on their way.'

'The crash will have weakened the tower, also,' said Haltheus. 'We don't want to be in this structure any longer than we have to.'

'Skarle, Thelgh, spread out and stand guard,' said Kassar. 'I'll join you. Krowl, watch over the cultist, stay near me. Skaryth, scout our location and find me a route out of this place before it burns to the ground. The rest of you, strip the wreck and the dead. Follow Haltheus' lead. Two minutes.'

Flames roared. Waves of heat rolled over Kassar. The structure of the tower groaned and settled around him, rivulets of ferrocrete dust trickling from the ceiling. Somewhere above, a string of secondary explosions rattled like gunfire, causing him to snap his bolter up in search of targets. As his brothers laboured to gather ammunition, armour segments, serviceable weapons and supplies, he felt the tower shudder.

The building was mortally wounded. It wouldn't live long.

Haltheus came to his side. The Coffer was mag-locked to the underside of his armour's power pack, and belts of tools, explosives and miscellaneous devices festooned his armour. The rest of the Unsung had spread out into a guard formation, crouched amidst fire-lit rubble and wreckage, awaiting orders.

'We've got everything we need, Kassar. The rest we can leave.'

'Good–' began Kassar, only to be interrupted as bolt-rounds whistled past him to detonate amidst the wreck. At the same moment, strong, clear voices were raised in hymn, the Emperor's Battle Sisters voicing the words of their faith.

'Enemy contact,' he voxed. 'Switch to second cypher. *Formation gorgon.*'

At once, his warriors readied their weapons and pushed outwards, hunting for targets of opportunity amidst the smoke and flame. Knowing that thermal vision would be useless, Kassar instead called up a wireframe motion-filter. Several targets lit up with designator runes, the outlines of Battle Sisters suddenly visible, crouched behind a half-collapsed wall.

Using serpenta, Kassar issued his orders.

'Krowl, get the cultist into cover then draw their fire. Haltheus, flank right. I'll go left.'

Even as his warriors acknowledged, and Krowl's bolter barked, Kassar was moving. He bent low, loping through rubble and ruin. Off to his right, more self-propelled bolts cut through the smoke to burst against Krowl's armour.

Kassar spun around a demolished column and raised Mortis, sighting on the nearest Battle Sister. The woman's hair was bleached white and cut in a severe bob. Her bolter was flaring as it spat shells at Krowl. Her armour was half onyx black and half bone white, and her cheeks boasted jewelled ruby tears.

The beautiful adornments vanished in an eruption of blood as Kassar placed a bolt neatly through the woman's cheek and blew her head apart. Shouting, her two Sisters spun towards him, only for the furthest to stagger as a foot-long silver blade burst, point first, from her jugular. Blood jetted, and the Battle Sister pawed weakly at the blade, then crashed forward onto her face.

The last Sister spun again, spraying shots at D'sakh where he crouched, ready to hurl his second knife. Kassar charged in from behind and hacked the Battle Sister's head from her shoulders.

Tasting blood, Hexling squealed with delight and writhed in his grip. Teeth gritted, Kassar rode out the blade's demands for more, crushed down its sibilant hissing in his mind, mastering it with his will as he always did.

Bolter-fire sounded throughout the crash site, muzzle flare marking where the Unsung were engaging. Plainsong echoed across the battlefield. Nearby, Kassar caught the tell-tale *phut, phut, phut* of Thelgh's sniper rifle, a moment before Phaek'or's heavy bolter kicked in with a bombastic roar.

'Kassar,' voxed Skaryth. *'Exit secured. Transmitting.'*

A rune flashed up on Kassar's retinal display, four hundred yards to his right.

'D'sakh, Phaek'or, Phalk'ir, Thelgh, covering fire. Everyone else, gather on Skaryth then cover their retreat. Haltheus…'

'*I'll leave them a gift,*' said Haltheus, unclamping several explosive charges.

Kassar spotted another group of enemies moving in through the smoke. He lobbed a frag grenade into their midst before falling back with his bolter roaring.

Forging through the smoke, ignoring the bolt-rounds bursting around him, Kassar found the rest of the Unsung – minus their rear guard – gathered around the entrance to a pneumo-lift shaft. Its doors had been forced open, mechanisms still drizzling sparks.

'*Lift's inoperable, and I wouldn't trust it anyway,*' said Skaryth. '*But there's a service ladder. Looks to lead right down into the inner structure of the rig.*'

'*Good work,*' said Kassar. '*We won't follow it that far though, too obvious. Skaryth, take point. Krowl, carry the cultist and keep him safe. Get down as far as ground level then make us an exit onto the outer decking.*'

Around him, his brothers' guns roared. Kassar's rear guard backed away through the smoke, firing as they went. With less than ten yards to go, D'sakh was punched off his feet by a direct hit to the helm. The vexillor shook his head and hauled himself upright, blasting his assailant and blowing her apart.

One by one, Kassar's brothers followed Skaryth into the lift shaft. Syxx yelped as Krowl clamped one arm around his midriff and disappeared into the shaft, but he had the sense not to struggle. The rear guard knelt in cover, snapping off shots at each clear target. They conserved ammo where possible, and maximised the protection offered by their surroundings. Not for the Alpha Legion the bravado that saw Space Marines eschew cover. They trusted in their armour, but also adhered to the doctrines that every advantage should be seized, and that martial pride was a fair sacrifice for victory.

'*Their numbers are increasing,*' said D'sakh.

'*What a shameful end it would be, to be overrun by mere mortals,*' commented Phalk'ir.

'*Then you should talk less, and shoot more,*' said Kassar.

Now only Kassar, Phalk'ir, Haltheus and D'sakh remained. Bolter-fire was pouring in on their position, and Kassar could see several dozen enemy pushing closer through the devastation.

'Haltheus?' he asked.

'On your command,' replied Haltheus. *'We'll need to move with a purpose, though.'*

'Unsung,' voxed Kassar, ducking an explosion of masonry. *'Drop if you can. Clear the shaft. We're coming down hard.'*

Vox pips of acknowledgement sounded in his helm.

'Phalk'ir, D'sakh, go.' The two Alpha Legionnaires turned and dived into the shaft, not even bothering with the ladder.

'Do it,' said Kassar.

Haltheus pumped the detonator he held in his gauntlet, then they both turned and ran.

Kassar felt the decking buck under his feet and heard the deep boom of detonations. Charges, affixed to columns and walls by Haltheus as he retreated, blew in sequence. The smoke billowed outwards as shockwaves roared through the ruined floor. Shrapnel whizzed and rattled. Battle Sisters were immolated or hurled through the air like rag dolls. As Kassar ran for the elevator shaft, the entire floor began to collapse behind him, the last structural supports giving way.

Then he leapt into the darkness.

The walls of the shaft rushed past, Kassar watching his auspex read-out intently as he dropped like a stone. Emergency lumen whipped by. Above, the lift shaft filled with fire as the fury of the explosion spilled into it.

Now, he thought as he saw sparks below him. Kassar grabbed the edges of the ladder, creating sparks of his own as the metal supports passed through his gauntlets at speed, slowing his momentum. Below Kassar, a rectangle of light flashed up towards him. Haltheus launched himself from the ladder and vanished through it. Kassar followed suit, pushing off with arms and legs as hard as he could. He propelled himself through the open hatchway bare seconds before a mass of flame and rubble thundered down the shaft.

Kassar rolled to a stop, flames licking over him from the elevator hatch. He registered dark clouds overhead, sluicing rain hissing against his armour, and ugly, walkway-hung towers looming all around. Then he was hauled to his feet.

'Move,' said A'khassor. *'The whole tower is coming down.'*

Kassar ran, following his warriors, footsteps clanging on rain-slick metal. At his back, flames spat from the guard tower as it shuddered then buckled, collapsing in on itself. Rubble crashed down. Smoke billowed. The decking shook while, overhead, lightning split the clouds.

Clear of the building's collapse, Kassar joined his brothers in the cover of a servitor processing-unit. Thelgh and Phaek'or were standing guard while the rest of the Harrow rapidly reloaded and counted clips. Syxx was crouched in the Alpha Legionnaires' midst, sheltered by their armoured bodies.

'Reading enemy movement all around,' said Kyphas. *'They'll be on us in moments. Substantial numbers.'*

'We keep moving,' said Kassar. *'Two of you on the cultist at all times, shield and preserve. According to Excrucias' intelligence, our primary objective is located on underdeck four, directly above the drill chambers.'*

'Fastest route is through the promethium processor block ahead,' said Kyphas, cycling swiftly through map schematics of the rig. *'There's a main rampway they use to haul crude promethium up from the drill chambers to processing. Open, but we can follow it all the way down.'*

Kassar vox-pipped acknowledgement, then broke from cover, running for a heavy iron hatchway that led into the processing block. Las-fire slashed around him, falling amidst the rain from walkways above. Tsadrekhan defence troopers were dashing into position, their flak armour and grey-blue uniforms partially hidden under bulky foul-weather cloaks.

Kassar spun, slamming his back up against the wall next to the hatch and returning fire as his brothers followed. The Harrow shrugged off the las-fire, their weapons spitting death back at their attackers. Sniper rounds found grenade packs and power cells, blasting men apart in savage explosions. Bolts ripped through armour and flesh. Skarle's flamer spat tongues of emerald fire, melting support stanchions and sending men screaming to their deaths as their vantage points collapsed. One unfortunate hit the ground nearby, his bulky vox-caster cushioned from the impact by his broken body.

'Grab that,' said Haltheus. 'I need it.'

Skaryth obeyed, lunging out through the las-fire and dragging the corpse into shelter.

'Krowl. The door,' ordered Kassar.

Krowl gave a grunt then accelerated into a run, dropping his shoulder. The hatch was six-inch-thick plasteel, secured with adamantium locking bolts and designed to keep out the fury of a deep-ocean hurricane. Krowl hit it at speed, smashing it inwards with its locking bolts sheared.

The Harrow filed swiftly through the open hatch, ducking in with guns raised. Inside, a well-lit security corridor led to a second, larger hatch that was slowly rumbling shut. Beyond could be seen the industrial hurly-burly of the processing manufactorum still in full operation. Kassar had a fleeting glimpse of dozens of Tsadrekhan troopers and Battle Sisters dashing into position behind barricades and barrels.

Several Tsadrekhan soldiers stood between the Unsung and the closing hatch. To their credit, they raised their lasguns rather than retreat. They were shot down all the same, Kassar leading his Harrow along the corridor at a run. Krowl lunged between the closing doors and braced them with arms outstretched.

Servo-motors whined and gears ground. Sparks showered from motivator units set into the hatch frame, and then with a stink of smoke, the door stopped closing. Krowl grunted in satisfaction, then a missile hit him square in the chest. The blast hurled him backwards and left him sprawled and scorched near the entrance hatch. Krowl's armour was torn open, his chest a hideous red ruin. Syxx cried out in horror.

'Cultist,' barked Kassar. 'You stay on me now. No more than five paces away, understand? And unholster those guns, you'll need them.' Syxx nodded.

'Phalk'ir, A'khassor, get Krowl,' ordered Kassar, ignoring Phalk'ir's hiss of irritation. 'Vox access?'

Haltheus had wrenched the vox-pack off the fallen Guardsman, but only after cracking the man's skull open and taking several bites of the grey matter within. The Unsung had been a long time away from the Emperor's light, but they retained many of the gifts he had given them. Consuming a man's memories along with his flesh was but one.

'*Getting the vox-channels now,*' reported Haltheus. '*Give me a moment.*'

Several krak grenades flew through the exterior hatch. They bounced along the corridor, only to be kicked back out by the Unsung. At the same time, another missile streaked through the jammed interior hatch, forcing the Alpha Legionnaires to throw themselves up against the walls to avoid its blast. A'khassor thrust Syxx none too gently behind him, shielding the cultist with his body.

'*Haltheus…*' said Kassar.

'*Got them,*' said Haltheus, re-affixing his helm and running a wire from its side to the pilfered vox-pack. The jack at the end of the wire was a squirming biomechanical leech that dug hungry fangs into the device. Haltheus' helm emitted a series of static blurts as he adjusted its vox-modulator, another improvisation of his that had served the Harrow well during their campaign against the Whispersmiths of the Black Valley.

'*Lieutenant DeLares,*' he voxed, his voice sounding like an unaugmented human's.

'*DeLares,*' came the response. '*Who is this?*'

'*Lieutenant,*' voxed Haltheus urgently. '*You're being outflanked! The heretics in the corridor are just a distraction, sir. There's a much larger force moving up from the drill chambers.*'

'*Emperor's teeth!*' exclaimed the lieutenant. '*Hobbs, Decker, keep your squads covering those bastards beyond the bulkhead. Everyone else, redeploy to cover the primary rampway. Plasma guns front and centre. Soldier, who is this, are you able to reinforce?*'

'*Fourth platoon, sir,*' said Haltheus, glancing at the insignia on the corpse at his feet. '*We'll move in on your left flank.*'

'*Good man,*' said the lieutenant. '*When you reach us, take position between Sister Grace's Retributors and Sergeant Morlin's squad.*'

'Yes, sir,' said Haltheus. 'Let's show these heretics that the Emperor's servants aren't so easily fooled!'

'That's the spirit, lad, we'll beat them yet,' replied DeLares, before breaking the link.

Haltheus chuckled as he slung the bulky vox-pack casually over one shoulder.

'Skarle,' said Kassar. *'You're rear guard. If anything comes down this corridor, burn it.'*

Skarle nodded, shaking with silent mirth.

'The rest of you,' said Kassar, *'ready to advance up the left flank. Skaryth, lead us in.'*

Skaryth began by lobbing a bulky alchemical bomb through the jammed doors. The device coughed sparks and jetted clouds of greasy smoke as it bounced across the decking. Skaryth threw two more smoke bombs, veiling the entrance in obscuring fumes, before ducking through. He went unhelmed, his warp-touched sight unhindered by the smoke. Ahead, spread out between a ground-level barricade and a raised walkway, he saw the souls of twenty men, shivering blue with fear.

Speculative fire slashed around him, but Skaryth evaded it with ease. He went left, sliding into cover behind a heavy barrel conveyor, then pipped his vox to signal his comrades. As they moved up to his position, Skaryth hefted another alchemical smoke bomb and hurled it as far as he could towards the right flank.

'Predictable fools,' he muttered to himself as the Imperial soldiers swung their aim towards his false trail. Another missile lashed down from the gantry, well aimed but striking nothing living.

Skaryth heard Skarle crooning over the vox, and more distantly the roar of his flamer discharging. Their pursuers had caught up.

'D'sakh, Thelgh, Kyphas,' ordered Kassar. *'You take the squad on the gantry. The rest of you, the squad on the ground.'*

The three warriors slung their weapons and began to climb, swarming silently up through the rumbling industrial machinery. Meanwhile, Skaryth and his remaining brothers worked quickly around their enemies' flank, staying low and unseen. Fuel barrels rumbled along conveyor belts. Processing units and consecration vats steamed and hissed.

'*They should have deactivated their machines,*' Skaryth voxed Kassar.

'*Perhaps they thought all the movement and fumes would confuse our assault,*' replied Kassar. '*Or maybe their war effort is so thinly stretched that they need every barrel of promethium they can produce, even during battle?*'

'*Either way, it is their mistake,*' said Skaryth with a cruel grin. '*It makes this all the easier.*'

The Alpha Legionnaires halted scant yards from their victims, crouched in cover. Skaryth felt his flesh tingle beneath his armour. Not now, he thought, closing his eyes and taking slow, deep breaths. They were finally off Bloodforge. They were finally out of the warp. He could recover now, he knew it, but only if he remained the master of his own flesh. Somewhere between his shoulder blades, Skaryth felt a sensation both alien and familiar. An eyelid, blinking. He grimaced in revulsion.

Skaryth's reverie broke as a body fell from the gantry above. The Tsadrekhan troopers yelled in shock, seeing one of their comrades with his throat slit ear to ear, his blood fountaining across them. The troopers turned their guns upwards, spraying panicked fire at half-seen, armoured monsters.

As they did so, Skaryth, Kassar and the others struck. Skaryth vaulted a chugging generator and fired his bolter, bursting the nearest trooper like a sack of meat. Two more Tsadrekhans fell in quick succession as Kassar and Haltheus gunned them down. Then Phaek'or's heavy bolter roared to life, carving a bloody line through the panicked soldiers. Men detonated and severed limbs flew. Blood painted every surface. Skaryth wove through the carnage, slashing with his combat knife and blasting with his bolter, ignoring the nausea churning in his guts and resolutely not thinking about the brothers they had lost to spawndom along their road. This was his purpose, slaughtering the lapdogs of the Imperium, and he neither wanted nor needed the gifts of the gods to fulfil it.

The sergeant of the Tsadrekhan squad ran at him, screaming in anger and fear, a running chainsword in his hand. Skaryth evaded the man's wild swing, snatching him up by the face and plucking the chainsword from his grip as though taking a toy from a child. Almost casually, he reversed the man's roaring blade and eviscerated him with it, relishing every moment of suffering as its teeth howled through armour, flesh and bone.

'That's all of them,' said Kassar. 'Skarle, what's your status?'

'Many burned, many dead,' came the singsong response across the vox. 'Some are ash, the rest are fled.'

Skaryth growled in distaste at the warp-touched madness in his brother's voice.

'Good,' said Kassar. 'Rejoin us. The rest of you, advance, formation Furia. Those up high, shadow us.'

Skaryth felt the squirming in his flesh subside, as it always did after sufficient bloody murder, as though the taint was sated.

Switching a new clip into his bolter, he moved out, senses sharper than ever, across the processing-plant floor.

They came upon the Imperial forces from behind, exploiting the gap their enemies had left for reinforcements that would never arrive. Bolters roared. Grenades thumped. Tongues of green flame turned Imperial servants into living torches. Kassar had his warriors attack from several angles and multiple heights, sowing further confusion with well-placed smoke bombs. Though the Unsung were outnumbered at least five to one, they carved through their panicked enemies.

Kassar drove Hexling through a Battle Sister's breastplate, kicking her convulsing corpse off the blade just as flames engulfed him. Ignoring the fire dancing across his armour, he turned and shot his attacker in the face. The Retributor's helm caved in and she toppled backwards down the primary rampway, her heavy flamer spilling from her hands.

'Kassar,' came Kyphas' voice on the vox. 'I'm reading substantial energy build-up below.'

'The teleportarium?' asked Kassar, beating out the stubborn flames that clung to his right arm.

'I believe so,' said Kyphas. 'Energy readings are empyric in nature, so unless someone is summoning entities…'

'Finish this fight, brothers,' voxed Kassar to the Harrow. 'We must make haste.'

A pair of Tsadrekhan troopers dashed from behind a barricade, pouring fire at him. Kassar hissed as a lucky shot struck the seal of his gorget and drew a scorched line across his neck. D'sakh dropped from above, landing on the two troopers and bearing them to the ground. His knives flashed, silver inscribed with the Harrow's numerals and honour-markings.

The only banner the Unsung had ever required.

'How fare the colours, D'sakh?' called Kassar.

'Blood red,' snarled D'sakh, completing the old refrain as he ripped his knives from his two lifeless victims.

Overhead, Thelgh's rifle coughed and another Battle Sister plummeted, crashing to the decking with a neat hole punched through her forehead.

Kassar heard Syxx cry out. He spun, bolter raised, in time to see the cultist gun down a Tsadrekhan. The soldier had been mere paces from Kassar, a belt of krak grenades in hand. Syxx lowered his smoking autopistols, and Kassar favoured him with a slight nod.

One by one, the Unsung gathered on their leader at the head of the rampway. Lined with black and yellow chevrons, wide enough to drive a Baneblade down, it disappeared into the steam-shrouded depths.

'We've broken their strength,' reported Haltheus, still plugged into the Tsadrekhan vox-channels. 'But they're rallying what they have left to the teleportarium. It's a fair guess they know where we're headed.'

'Skaryth, Kyphas, take point,' ordered Kassar. 'Double-time. How's Krowl?'

The blasted crater of Krowl's chest had all but repaired itself, flesh, muscle and armour reknitting with grotesque slurping sounds. The big warrior was groaning and twitching.

'He can walk,' said Phalk'ir, letting go of Krowl's right arm and letting him drop to one knee. A'khassor shot an annoyed glance at Phalk'ir, but released Krowl's left arm and let him stagger, groggily, to his feet.

'Just,' added the Apothecary. *'He should stay to the rear, and I with him.'*

'Agreed,' said Kassar.

They set off down the ramp, footsteps clanging, senses alive for any hint of danger. Guide-lumen flashed in the steamy murk. Every hundred yards, the ramp switched back on itself, wending steadily down into the deep, metal-walled pit. They passed first one sub-deck, then another, masses of platforms and girders and thumping machinery. Labour gangs and crew helots fled in terror from them and were ignored, as were the muscular, promethium-spattered servitors that continued at their mindless labours.

'Any indication what they're doing down there?' Kassar asked Kyphas and Haltheus.

'Readings still building,' reported Kyphas. *'They could be trying to bring in reinforcements?'*

'Some officer-level vox chatter about Dysorian Protocols,' said Haltheus. *'But my knowledge donor didn't know anything about that.'*

'Whatever it is, we don't want it to happen,' said Kassar. *'Pick up the pace.'*

A hail of firepower greeted them as they reached sub-deck four. Bolt shells and las-fire spat from industrial loading hatches, over which empyric warning sigils and cogs mechanicus were stencilled.

'No time for subtlety,' said Kassar. *'Grenades, then storm the breaches.'*

His warriors complied, a hail of frag charges sailing down the ramp to bounce through the fortified entrances. Even as dull explosions rippled within, they were already charging.

Kassar burst through the smoke into a red-lit chamber. The frag-torn corpses of several Tsadrekhans sprawled on the floor. More were falling back, ducking behind circuit-pillars and runic consoles, firing as they went. Las-fire splashed from his scorched armour.

'Keep at them,' he bellowed. *'Break their line.'*

To his right, Phalk'ir lunged through a hail of shots to impale a screaming Tsadrekhan. Phaek'or followed his twin at a steady stride, his heavy bolter deafening in the low-ceilinged space.

'*Careful of the damned consoles,*' snapped Haltheus as he locked blades with a Battle Sister. '*Don't damage anything that looks important.*'

The Sister stepped back and swung her chainsword, chewing through Haltheus' shoulder guard in a spray of blood. Haltheus hacked his opponent's legs out from under her, catching her by the throat as she fell and hoisting her to eye level.

'That hurt, mortal,' he snarled. The Battle Sister spat in his face. In return, Haltheus head-butted her, caving her skull in and discarding her twitching corpse.

Kassar pushed deeper into the teleportarium, aiming his shots with pinpoint care, trying to avoid severing bundled cables or damaging thrumming consoles. Huge armourglass tubes rose floor to ceiling, caged lightning dancing within. Kassar strode between them, down a set of ironwork steps, gunning down charging Tsadrekhans as he went.

Beyond their tumbling corpses, Kassar saw that the steps descended into a lightning-wreathed metal pit surrounded by arcane machineries. Huge cargo-conveyors fed in through the pit walls, leading to a teleportarium dais of enormous size. Figures swarmed around it, armoured Tsadrekhans and hunched tech-priests, but Kassar caught no more than a fleeting glimpse before a hail of plasma fire drove him back into cover.

'The last of them are making a stand around the dais,' he voxed. 'Surround them and–'

'*Kassar,*' said Haltheus urgently. '*There's no time. The energy readings don't match any teleport signature I've seen. They're far too high. They're going to overload the teleportarium.*'

'Blast radius?' asked Kassar.

'*Conservative estimate, the entire rig,*' said Haltheus. '*That's if it's even a conventional blast. They could tear a warp rift…*'

Kassar felt real fury rise inside him, and the familiar old hatred of the Imperium. How long he had laboured to keep his warriors alive, never despairing, always resisting the sick temptation to some vainglorious last stand and the relief that would bring. Yet one battle turning against them, and these nihilistic zealots were willing to kill themselves to the last man. It was so wasteful, so narrow-minded.

'*How do we stop them?*' he asked.

'*My best guess,*' said Haltheus, '*is we kill the priests performing the ritual.*'

'*Without them, we won't be able to use the teleportarium,*' said Phalk'ir. '*We'll be stranded, mission fail.*'

'*We'll fail either way,*' said Kassar. '*Better alive than dead. Unsung, kill the tech-priests.*'

Kassar and his warriors burst from cover, sending a hail of fire whipping down into the pit. A red-robed priest sprawled onto his face, blood and oil leaking from gaping bolter wounds. A round from Thelgh's rifle threw another against the pit wall in a spray of gore. A'khassor let fly with his plasma pistol, burning a third tech-priest to ash.

The surviving Tsadrekhans, perhaps a dozen or so troopers and officers, fired back. Kyphas was clipped by multiple las-bolts and driven back into cover. A krak grenade detonated at Kassar's feet, throwing him onto his back as a fresh spread of warning runes lit up in his peripheral vision. Phalk'ir sidestepped a plasma blast, only for another searing bolt to graze his helm. Armour melted and Phalk'ir dropped with a howl of pain.

The last tech-priest ignored the blizzard of fire whipping around him, and his fallen comrades littering the teleportarium dais. He proceeded solemnly from one console to the next, working his ministrations, sending arcs of unnatural lightning leaping between the empyric vanes of the machinery. Consoles began to rupture and burn, and a terrible whine filled the air.

Kassar pulled himself into a sitting position, struggling to aim a shot at the priest. His first round flew wide. His second blew out the chest of a selflessly heroic Tsadrekhan who threw himself into its path.

'*Someone…*' he barked into the vox.

There was a flash of silver in Kassar's peripheral vision, a streak of light on metal, and a foot-long silver blade sprouted at the base of the tech-priest's skull. The Martian staggered, reached out for the nearest console with shuddering mechadendrites, then collapsed in a robed heap, unmoving.

* * *

The last few Tsadrekhans turned their guns on the teleportarium in desperation. The only practical effect of this defiant gesture was to speed their own extermination as the Unsung shot them down in short order.

Limping, Kassar made his way down into the pit, examining the machineries as they flickered and sparked. The caged lightning was dying away, the whine fading.

'It's dead,' he said.

'It is,' agreed Haltheus, surveying the devastation. 'Far beyond anything I could repair, before you ask.'

'How, then, do we proceed?' asked Makhor, joining them. 'This plan called for the speed of the teleportarium. Without our gunship, we may well be stranded here altogether, and even if we could get airborne, we would once again face the problem of overcoming Endurance's flak cover.'

'My lords,' said Syxx. 'We cannot fail in this. We must reach the beacon. I *must* get there.'

'You don't make demands of us, mortal,' growled D'sakh. 'If there's another way to reach our objective then we'll find it. Otherwise, you stay very silent and hope we don't discard you.'

'How *do* we proceed now?' asked Kassar. 'Thoughts?'

'I don't know, myself,' said Kyphas with relish. 'But I've found someone to ask…'

Stooping, he grabbed one of the fallen Tsadrekhan officers by the arm and hoisted him off the floor. The man made a lunge for his pistol, but Kyphas slapped the weapon away.

The Unsung gathered around Kyphas and his prize, menacing figures looming in the gloom.

'Ah,' said Haltheus to the sweating, wounded officer. 'Lieutenant DeLares, I presume…'

Flames roared. Metal shuddered. Harsh voices bellowed oaths to the Blood God. Lit red, the interior of the Dreadclaw stank of dried blood and chemical sweat.

Strapped into his restraints, Khârn ignored it all. In his mind's eye, the Betrayer saw a singular figure, limned in blinding light. A winged angel, blade in hand, ancient eyes in an ageless face. A divine champion of the Emperor, who had walked a road of faith to return the Primarch Guilliman to life.

Khârn cared nothing for Khordas, for Tsadrekha, or for this war. He had come as the instrument of Khorne's punishment, the headsman's axe that would lop this angel's skull from her neck so that it might be set at the Blood God's throne.

Sudden impacts rang the Dreadclaw like a struck bell. Holes spackled its flank. Blood sprayed as high-velocity rounds punched through the drop pod, shredding the Berzerkers within and sending it looping off course. Khârn snarled, gripping his restraints as punishing g-forces pressed him back against the hull.

Spinning. Shuddering. Jolting. The Dreadclaw's interior went dark as its power failed, the only illumination the harsh bars of daylight stabbing through the bullet holes. The pod was spinning madly, turning on its side.

Muscles straining, Khârn hefted Gorechild and triggered the axe's motors. It revved in his grip, a monster awoken and glad to serve its master.

Khârn swung Gorechild once, twice, carving through the rusted metal of the Dreadclaw's hull. The third blow saw a slab of metal tear loose and spin away. Wind whistled through the gap, and for a moment Khârn saw the ocean revolve below, swelling rapidly closer.

A corpse fell against Khârn, a fellow Berzerker, and he kicked it away with a growl. Then, breaking his restraints, the Betrayer grabbed the edge of the ragged hole he had carved and launched himself into the open sky.

Khârn fell, the wind whipping around him, Gorechild clutched firmly in one fist. His stricken Dreadclaw tumbled away, falling faster, trailing smoke. It hit the waves and detonated.

The Betrayer steered himself as best he could, bringing his arms and legs in as the waters rushed up to meet him. The impact was like being run over by a battle-tank. It hammered the breath from his body, and knocked him momentarily unconscious. Only his power armour and his unnatural fortitude prevented it from shattering every bone in his body.

Khârn plunged deep, the waters closing over his head. Fire lit the waves above. Below him was only darkness.

With powerful kicks, he drove himself back towards the surface, the image of the angel still burning in his mind. Nothing would keep him from his quarry. He was the Blood God's weapon, and he would strike.

Khârn broke the surface. Overhead, the stormy sky was filled with fire, plummeting drop-craft and streams of flak. Wreckage and corpses bobbed and sank all around. In the distance rose Hive Endurance, where his Dreadclaw was supposed to have landed. Closer, less than a mile distant, Khârn saw an armoured fortress. It clung to a jutting island of stone, its defence cannons spitting fire into the skies.

Feeling rage building within, Khârn struck out for the fortress.

'You have not saved yourselves, lapdogs,' he snarled. 'You have only prolonged your suffering…'

* * *

Khârn hauled himself up the rocks hand over hand, his eyes fixed on the fortress rising above him. Algae and squirming, tentacled things squelched under his gauntlets. The rhythmic pounding of the fort's guns filled his ears, warring with the jackhammer beating of his hearts. Khârn saw the aquila emblazoned across its flank, and felt a swelling surge of hate.

It seemed that no one on the walls had spotted him yet. Their eyes were turned skywards. Khârn would punish them for that.

Unholstering his plasma pistol, Khârn revved Gorechild and strode to the foot of the fortress wall. Several swift blows and a section of verdigrised metal crashed inwards. Khârn stepped through, into a pipe-lined corridor. He took a deep breath, scenting flesh and blood nearby.

'**Kill!**' he bellowed, his vox-grille amplifying his words into a stentorian boom. '**Maim! Burn!**'

Picking his direction at random, Khârn set off down the corridor. He loped up a set of metal steps and burst through a bulkhead door into a brightly lit chamber. Human soldiers were scrambling for their guns, overturning tables for cover. He saw, within the space of a heartbeat, how each one would act. How each one would die. He saw every axe-stroke and pistol shot, as he had seen billions before.

Then the violence began. Las-bolts slashed around him, some splashing from his armour. Khârn ignored them and charged headlong, swinging Gorechild in an almighty arc. The axe's teeth whirled through flesh and bone, blood exploding from the sundered bodies of three Tsadrekhan troopers. Khârn gunned down another two, his plasma pistol howling, then kicked an overturned table across the room, smashing another Tsadrekhan into the wall in a burst of gore.

More shots hit home, but his enemies might as well have been throwing stones for all the good they did. To one side, a trooper was frantically fumbling with the charge-modulator of his plasma gun, jabbering prayers as he did. Khârn lopped his head from his shoulders then shot down another Tsadrekhan who ran at him with bayonet levelled.

The last troopers were falling back, fleeing for the chamber's other exit. Khârn accelerated into a charge and ploughed through their midst, every blow felling another victim. Heads bounced across the floor, expressions *locked in terrified grimaces. Blood jetted from the stumps of necks. Not a single Tsadrekhan escaped the chamber alive.*

Khârn moved on, the butcher's nails pounding in his skull, a furnace of hate and fury roaring within him.

*'**Blood for the Blood God!**' he roared as he crashed into another chamber, this one some kind of magazine. Huge shells and crates of rounds filled metal racks on every side, and Tsadrekhans hunkered behind makeshift barricades between them. They died, just as their comrades had died.*

Just as everyone who faced Khârn died.

The Betrayer's rampage continued, the body count climbing by the minute. Panic spread quickly, the Tsadrekhans yelling orders and desperate pleas through their vox-casters. They came at Khârn whole squads at a time, and he butchered them like livestock. Where they tried to hem him in, trap him and pound him with firepower, the Betrayer smashed his way free. Where they tried to block his path, or overwhelm him with numbers, Khârn hacked them apart with contemptuous ease. Where brave heroes duelled him, he reduced them to bloodied meat in moments.

At last, Khârn found himself near the fortress' peak, in amongst the gun decks and flak turrets. Here the pounding roar of gunfire was constant, red armoured drop-ships exploding and falling from the sky above. One by one, Khârn silenced the guns, cutting down their crews and firing plasma bolts into their mechanisms and power supplies until an inferno raged all around.

A commissar and his squad of ogryns delayed Khârn, buying time for the final turret to hammer off a few thousand more rounds into the skies. Then the last of the abhumans crashed, headless, to the decking, and the commissar's chest was reduced to cinders by Khârn's pistol. The Betrayer hacked open the armoured hatch of the final turret and butchered the crew, painting its interior dripping red.

The fortress had fallen in less than an hour. Khârn's armour was scorched, his flesh nicked and burned, but he didn't notice. The tally of skulls had been started on this world, and he would build a mountain of them before he finally slew the angel for Khorne.

As Khornate drop-craft lumbered in overhead and Dreadclaws slashed down to land upon the fortress' battlements, Khârn turned and plunged back into the depths. Down there he had seen signage for an undersea maglev. A route into the hive. His path to the angel.

'**Kill**! **Maim**! **Burn**!' roared Khârn, and at his back, the massing warriors of the Blood God took up the cry...

PART II

CHAPTER SIX

They descended on an industrial lift, a broad platform that rumbled ponderously into the depths. Hazard lumen strobed around them as steam jetted and pipes gurgled.

The Unsung were all there, those that still lived. Thelgh, Skaryth and Krowl remained apart from their brothers; the sniper meditated, his rifle across his knees; the lunatic muttered benedictions over his flamer, his hand flamers, his incendiary bombs; the golem, healed now, loomed still and silent. The rest of the Harrow cradled their weapons, speaking quietly together in small groups.

A'khassor crouched by Makhor, tending to the naysmith's broken arm.

'I've done what I can,' he said. 'The bone is setting, the muscle mending. A few hours, perhaps a day, and the limb will be fully serviceable again.'

'A day is a long time, Apothecary,' replied Makhor, running one-handed checks on his weapons.

'Which is why,' said A'khassor, in a tone unique to piqued physicians the galaxy over, 'I'm going to give you a shot of combat stimms.'

'Is that wise?' asked Makhor. 'We have few enough doses left. Assuming you didn't risk appropriating anything from Excrucias' stocks.'

A'khassor barked a laugh.

'I wouldn't inject that filth even if we were all down and dying,' he said. 'Who knows how the degenerates have tainted it?'

'You'd have me seeing three-breasted daemonettes dancing around the enemy,' said Makhor with a painful chuckle.

'If you were lucky,' said A'khassor. 'More likely you'd just haemorrhage and die. No, this is Legion issue. And as the Harrow's last living Apothecary, Makhor, yes, I deem it necessary.'

A'khassor's time-worn narthecium hissed as it dispensed the chemicals through a valve in Makhor's armour.

'Our brothers?' asked Makhor, wincing as the stimms hit his system. 'The fallen ones. They are with you?'

'Of course,' replied A'khassor, tapping the small, armoured canisters locked to his belt. 'Their gene-seed lives on, if only for posterity. Their punishment is over. I envy them.'

Makhor sighed, clenching and unclenching his fist, working feeling into his damaged limb.

'Your superstitions are unbecoming for one in your position, A'khassor. We aren't being punished.'

'Of course we are,' the Apothecary's words bore no rancour, just acceptance. 'For the twofold betrayals of our Legion. For our refusal to select a faith, in a galaxy of manifest gods. For the brothers we've slain. How could this slow winnowing *not* be a punishment?'

Makhor shook his head.

'We've been around this loop before, A'khassor. I should know better. You are just so level-headed about everything else.'

'I only hope that our living brothers can be as peaceful as our fallen,' said A'khassor, brusquely deflecting the conversation. 'The operation has gone somewhat awry, has it not?'

'Kassar has never failed us,' said Makhor. 'And we have a route onwards again. These undersea maglev tunnels. We will complete our objective yet.'

'Will we?' asked A'khassor, busying himself with cleaning his narthecium's blades. The device no longer auto-sanctified as it should. 'Haltheus lost more of his precious gadgets in that crash than he's letting on. We're lucky he still has the Coffer.'

Makhor glanced at their ad-hoc Techmarine, hunched over Phalk'ir's partially melted helm, muttering to himself as he worked at its plating with a stolen las-torch.

'And Phalk'ir,' said A'khassor, subvocalising beneath the rumble of the platform. 'I've treated his wounds, but his plasma burns are extensive. He'll bear those scars for the rest of his days.'

'And you know who he'll blame for that,' replied Makhor.

The swordsman crouched in Phaek'or's shadow, making no effort to hide the hideous, red-raw wounds that marred one side of his face. He stared fixedly at Kassar, where he stood speaking with Kyphas, Skaryth and D'sakh. Phaek'or's helm was in place, leaving his expression unreadable, and he seemed wholly occupied with keeping watch.

'What of his twin?' murmured A'khassor. 'Which way does Phaek'or lean, do you think?'

'Blood is loyalty,' mused Makhor. 'But Phaek'or has been loyal to Kassar a long time, also. His character hasn't... eroded... like his brother's.'

'Then there's our erstwhile spymaster,' said A'khassor. 'And you know how I feel about him.'

'His methods have certainly become less restrained,' said Makhor.

'His gauntlets are still red to the elbow!' hissed A'khassor. 'I care nothing for the suffering of mortals, don't mistake me. But he enjoyed that whole interrogation far too much, and took far too long. I could have extracted the information we required in half the time, and with a lot less theatre.'

Makhor nodded slowly.

'And then there is his reticence to impart the information he gathers,' said A'khassor, warming to his subject. 'I can't be the only one to have noticed it. I don't believe for a moment that he has told us everything he knows about this operation. The warp knows why, but he's keeping secrets.'

'This wouldn't have anything to do with that business on the Bone Ridge, would it, brother?' asked Makhor.

'No!' said A'khassor. 'Yes. Somewhat. But that doesn't change the fact that he has become untrustworthy.'

'Perhaps,' allowed Makhor. 'But still useful, and very capable. Either way, we are loyal to Kassar, this much we know.'

'We are,' said A'khassor firmly. 'D'sakh and Skaryth too, I'm sure. But is that enough to see this thing to its end?'

'Our pact?' said Makhor warily.

'The canisters I carry are the only memorial our brothers will ever have,' said A'khassor.

'And they are the only hope of our Harrow's future,' replied Makhor. 'I know, brother. And what I said before, it stands. If Kassar falls then I will ensure that you make it out alive. The Unsung must have a worst-case contingency, and we are it.'

A'khassor nodded, clapping a palm against his brother's shoulder guard.

'There's someone else here who I don't believe has told us all that he knows,' said Makhor. 'Perhaps we should let Kyphas have a conversation with the baggage…?'

Syxx had stayed close to Kassar ever since the battle in the processing plant, lurking behind him even now. The cultist's body language radiated a desire to be ignored.

'He certainly looks nervous, especially for one who professes to worship the Dark Prince,' said A'khassor. 'But then, wouldn't you be, were your situations reversed?'

Makhor grunted noncommittally.

'Be that as it may,' he said. 'If Kassar doesn't wring some answers from him soon, I may take it upon myself.'

'I hope you won't need to,' said A'khassor.

'We'll know soon enough,' said Makhor, clambering to his feet and rolling his shoulder experimentally. 'Feel that juddering? Braking. We're nearing the bottom.'

The platform shuddered beneath Kassar's feet, arrestor plates clamping to slow its descent. He had been discussing exit strategies and logistics with Skaryth, Kyphas and D'sakh. Now he broke off, and drew his bolter and blade.

'Third cypher,' he said. *'Helms on.'*

'You'll have to give me a moment with–' Haltheus' words were interrupted as Phalk'ir snatched the battered helm from his hands and clamped it in place. Kassar winced at the thought of the still-hot metal pressed against the swordsman's wounds.

'It's fine,' voxed Phalk'ir bitterly. *'Pain reminds us we're still alive, does it not? Unlike our brothers.'*

Kassar sighed, refusing to rise to the bait.

'Formation Arakhna,' he ordered, dispersing the Unsung around the platform's edge in firing crouches. Until it cleared the ferrocrete shaft, there was no telling on which side the platform's exit lay.

'Reading background life signs,' said Kyphas, studying his auspex. *'Energy signatures indicative of dormant machineries. Nothing that looks like warriors, or weapons.'*

'Vigilance,' voxed A'khassor. *'We're not the only ones capable of duplicity.'*

Amid strobing lights and grating hymns, the platform juddered to the base of the shaft. Massive ironclad doors were revealed, thick with warning sigils and runic lumen, currently all showing crimson. The Harrow snapped their weapons up as gears ground in the shaft walls, and another set of heavy doors rumbled out to lock together with a resounding clang above their heads. The shaft was sealed above them, leaving the Harrow inside a sizeable cell.

'Perfect,' spat Phalk'ir.

'A trap?' asked Kyphas.

'Haltheus?' said Kassar.

'There are no access panels in the walls, Kassar,' said Haltheus. *'Nothing I can hook into to reverse those doors.'*

'Wait,' said Skaryth. *'Feel that? Pressure change.'*

'Yes,' said Kassar. At his back, Syxx grunted in discomfort, working his jaw. *'We're a long way down now, deep enough for atmospheric change. This is an airlock.'*

One by one, the runic designators flicked from red to green and then, with a rush of stale air, the automated doors before them cracked open. They slid slowly apart, grinding on rusted runners.

'*Nobody has come this way in some time,*' said Haltheus.

'*Move up,*' ordered Kassar. The Unsung advanced, filtering through the opening bulkhead and into the maglev terminal beyond.

They entered a broad, low-ceilinged chamber a good few hundred yards across. Aquilas and cogs mechanicus stood out in bas-relief on the walls, alongside peeling, faded bill-posts exhorting hard labour, faith, tireless vigilance and the like. Algae grew in patches on the walls, and water dripped slowly through the ceiling to pool on the ferrocrete floor. Two rows of thick columns ran down the chamber's middle, girdled with heavy iron panels from which nests of wiring emerged. Gathered around these were servitors, their biological components wasted and their metalwork tinged with rust. Their foreheads rested against the pillars, whose wires flowed into their bodies.

'*One exit,*' said Kassar, gesturing with his bolter. At the chamber's far end was another heavy bulkhead. Stencilled above it was MAG-LEV TUNNEL XXI along with pictographs indicating that outgoing barrels should stay right, incoming left.

'*No hostile readings,*' said Kyphas.

'*Three groups, move up, one down the middle, two flank the columns,*' ordered Kassar. The Unsung responded smoothly, flowing apart and advancing on the far doors. The servitors twitched and murmured. Water dripped.

When they reached the chamber's far end, most of the Harrow dropped into guard stances. Haltheus moved up to the doors, which had remained obstinately shut.

'*They won't open?*' asked Kassar.

'*Give me a moment,*' said Haltheus, running instruments across the bulkhead and tapping at its runic panels. '*Could be they've locked down because the tunnel beyond is flooded? Hopefully not...*'

Kassar watched as Haltheus ran wires into sockets, levered off an inspection panel, muttered ritual benedictions and applied unguents.

'*Ah...*' he said at last, stepping back.

'Ah?' prompted Kassar.

'Code-locked,' said Haltheus. 'When they decommissioned this facility in favour of their teleportarium, they locked it all down for security. Without the binharic pass phrase, these doors are staying shut.'

'Can we acquire the pass phrase?' asked Kassar. 'Kyphas, did the lieutenant tell you anything about this?'

Kyphas shook his head.

'He insisted the route would be clear. My guess is that, even broken, he did his best to lead us into a dead end.'

'And leave us entombed below the waves,' said Phalk'ir. 'What chance that we'll find the elevator platform now locked down also?'

'Impressive...' said Kyphas. 'For one so fragile.'

'No,' said Kassar. 'Unacceptable. Haltheus, can we cut through?'

Haltheus blew out his breath.

'We've no equipment fit for the job. Krowl could go at it with his power fist, but we'll be here a while.'

'Could the Coffer help us?' asked D'sakh. 'All those servitors?'

'They'd be no use,' said Haltheus. 'Look at them, wasted and rusting. Besides which, they're loader units. Strong, but only good for picking things up and putting them down. And I could only possess them one at a time anyway.'

'Another route?' asked Makhor, but Kyphas shook his head.

'This is the only way,' he said.

'We don't have time for this,' said Kassar. 'Everyone back. Haltheus, blow it open.'

'Kassar,' said Makhor. 'We don't know how stable this structure is, how much separates us from the ocean. If we should punch a hole through and flood this place we might survive, but the baggage...?'

'It won't be quiet, either,' said Haltheus, though Kassar could hear the eagerness in his voice. 'If anyone else is down here with us, they'll definitely know we're coming.'

'Regardless,' said Kassar.

Breaking ranks, Phalk'ir came to stand before him.

'Not enough that you've killed four of us on this planet already?' he snarled. 'Now you aim to drown the rest? If this is all some elaborate *adventure in self-termination to atone for your failings, I can just shoot you right now and–'*

'*Phalk'ir,*' interrupted Kassar, voice steady. '*Stop talking. Move back. Do it now.*'

The two Alpha Legionnaires stood, still as statues, the jade lenses of their helms locked.

Nobody moved.

Water dripped.

Phalk'ir shrugged, turning and walking back down the chamber.

'*Very well, drown us then,*' he said. '*Saves me a bolt.*'

The rest of the Harrow followed, leaving Kassar and Haltheus before the doors. Syxx still hovered close by, clearly unsure what was happening or where he should go.

'Cultist,' said Kassar. 'Stay close. Haltheus, do it, but do it safely.'

Kassar retreated, Syxx hurrying at his side. Haltheus folded his arms, staring up at the tightly sealed bulkhead and its thick, armoured panels.

'All right then,' he said with relish. 'Machine-spirits, I'll ask your pardon in advance…' Haltheus began unhooking explosives from his equipment belts, and set to work.

The detonation was controlled, considering. Its roar faded quickly to echoes, as metal shrapnel pinged and clattered off the Alpha Legionnaires' armour. Kassar held his breath at the distressed groan of metal and stonework, waiting for the black flood of seawater to pour in.

When no inundation was forthcoming, he rose from his crouch and led the way towards the smoke-shrouded bulkhead.

'*Unsung,*' he voxed. '*On me. We have a long distance to cover, and a scarcity of time.*'

He stepped through the ragged hole that Haltheus had blasted in the bulkhead, quietly admiring his brother's work. Haltheus made a poor Techmarine, much of the time, for he had never known schooling in the deeper mysteries of the Mechanicus. But in the field of demolitions, he was an artist.

Beyond the doorway lay a gloomy terminus, an echoing space so huge that it vanished back into shadow, with a high ceiling of rein-forced armourglass. Up there, the black waters of the deep ocean could be seen pressing to get in. No daylight reached this far down, and Kassar thought that – but for the strange, luminescent arthropods flut-tering through the water – it could almost have been the void of space.

The rest of the hangar had clearly served as the loading and unload-ing terminus for maglev trains. Several raised rails ran in from cavernous entrance tunnels in one wall, dividing and flowing into sidings between raised metal walkways of considerable width. Chev-ron patterns marked loading corridors, and the chamber's back wall was stacked high with industrial trolley units that would have borne the barrels to the trains.

The chamber was dimly lit by hanging lumen globes through which power still flickered, and dominated by two structures. The first was a blocky tower that rose at its centre, ringed with viewing bays and busy with aerials, auspex pickups, power cabling and machineries whose functions were a mystery to Kassar. The other was a huge maglev train, listing off its rails in the furthest bay like a slain beast.

'That's impressive,' commented D'sakh. 'I hadn't realised the convey-ances would be so imposing.'

'I don't know how far back it stretches,' said Kassar, 'but it must meas-ure in miles.'

The train rose several storeys high, its carriages slab-sided and com-posed of pipework tangles, heavy fuel bowsers, walkways, ladders and transit compartments. The engine at its prow was monstrous and muscular, an ironclad beast of fusion drivers and crew decks emblazoned with an aquila thirty feet high. It was a monster, even canted at an angle and going to rust.

'It's more like a mobile refinery,' said D'sakh. 'A shame it is so clearly no longer mobile.'

'Imperials,' said Haltheus, moving to join them. 'So bloody wasteful. They've just left it there to rust. No doubt they've trains to spare, and tele-portation is so much quicker…'

'Yes,' said Kassar. 'It would have been. Meaning we've no time for rumi-nation. Haltheus, could you make it work?'

'Highly doubtful,' he replied. 'I'll need to look it over. Search that tower, which I'd guess is the control hub for maglevs coming from this terminal. It could take hours.'

'Did you expect there would just be a ready train, idling here for us to take?' asked Makhor.

'I hoped for a stroke of fortune,' said Kassar. 'Something with crew, that we could take at gunpoint. I didn't expect anything.'

'Give me twenty minutes to run a quick sweep of the tower,' said Haltheus. 'I'll exload the tunnel maps from their systems, scavenge anything usable in there…'

'You have ten,' said Kassar. 'Tunnel maps are priority. Find us a working terminus, a running maglev, something to speed us along.'

Haltheus pipped acknowledgement and set off, gesturing Skaryth and Krowl to accompany him.

The Harrow deployed into a guard pattern. A recycled breeze sighed through the dark tunnel entrances, making them moan. Small, many-legged things scuttled and crawled in distant corners, fighting over vermin even smaller than themselves. Kassar, meanwhile, beckoned Syxx. Trailed by the Slaaneshi cultist, he strode away from his brothers, far enough to be out of earshot.

Stopping on a walkway that soared high above an empty siding, Kassar removed his helm and leant against the railing.

'What am I missing?' he asked.

'Lord?' asked Syxx.

'About you,' said Kassar. 'About all this? I'm Alpha Legion, cultist. We know things. It is what we do. But I am left with a lingering sense that, with regards this operation, there are things I do not know. Important things.'

'Lord,' said Syxx. 'I will tell you whatever I can, of course. But what I could tell one so mighty as yourself–'

'Alpha Legion also disparage blandishments,' said Kassar. 'Your masters revel in egotism. They expect worship. I value plain speaking. Such false idolatry irks me. I don't want compliments from you, cultist, I want intelligence.'

'Lord,' said Syxx, wary. 'Please. Ask me what you will.'

'What do you know of the beacon?' asked Kassar, watching glowing jellyfish the size of Rhinos quiver overhead.

'It is the light that unites the Tsadrekhan Unity, lord,' replied Syxx. 'It is the prize that Excrucias and his rivals seek above all else.'

'Yes,' said Kassar. 'But what *is* it? Do you know? Do they? Technology? A choir of psykers? Or has the Imperium become so desperate in this strange age that they have truck with other, darker entities?'

'I do not know, lord,' said Syxx. 'I am sorry. Phelkorian said only that the beacon first shone after the great blackness came, and the rift split the heavens. He said that the corpse worshippers claimed that it was deliverance, sent by their Emperor.'

Kassar grunted.

'And you,' he said, dropping his gaze to pin Syxx in place. 'Why, of all Excrucias' many servants, has he sent a mere mortal to corrupt this thing? What is so special about you?'

'I am one of Phelkorian's longest serving acolytes,' said Syxx. 'He took me from amongst the bilge-tribes of the flagship when I was still young, and he was not kind. Has never been kind. But he taught me much. Rituals. Words of power.'

'And you are going to, what, speak these words of power when we reach the beacon?' asked Kassar. 'Is that how you will corrupt this ineffable source of the Emperor's light?'

'The runes upon my flesh,' said Syxx. 'Lord Phelkorian… branded them there himself. I need speak no words of power, my lord, only a triggering chant for these runes. I wear them across my body, and when I stand in the light of the beacon, they will do what must be done.'

'The gifts of the Dark Gods are never free,' said Kassar. 'What do you gain by doing this? And what will it cost?'

Syxx hesitated.

'You seek it yourself, lord,' he said. 'Escape.'

'Your masters do not expect you back? They will just let you go free?'

'No, lord,' said Syxx. 'Never that. But… I did not choose the circumstances of my existence. I didn't choose my tribemother's death, my enslavement to Lord Phelkorian, the worship of the Dark Prince. The things that I have done, and that have been done to me…'

'And yet you remain master of your own mind,' said Kassar thoughtfully. 'Rare, especially in mortals. The worship of the Dark Gods is destructive and all-consuming, the temptations they offer fit to overwhelm even the strongest-willed. We ourselves have fought those temptations for years. Many have failed the test. Am I to believe that you have endured where my brothers did not?'

'Hate, lord,' said Syxx. 'From the first, I hated our masters. I hated their god. I saw their gifts for the abominations they are, and I wanted none for myself. I have endured, but never embraced such worship. But you are right. Nineteen years, I have fought this corruption, but I know that I am losing. The temptation grows greater with every day. Lord Phelkorian sees this, and delights in it. But he has told me that if I do this thing, it will all end. The ritual, the words… they will kill me, lord. And then I will be free.'

Kassar nodded to himself, running his hand over the pommel of his blade. The Hexling murmured.

'I know a little of that fight,' he said eventually. 'And I commend you for your strength, even as I spit upon your cowardice in seeking your own destruction.'

'Lord–' began Syxx, but Kassar cut him off.

'I have fought for centuries to resist the temptations of the Dark Gods,' he said. 'On Bloodforge, even before. If the date-stamps I have seen since departing that world are correct, then time passed very differently in real space than it did for us, but still. My war of self-belief has lasted for dozens of times your pitiful span. And I haven't just fought for me. I have fought for them.' Kassar gestured to the warriors of the Harrow. 'My Unsung. My brothers. Keeping them out of the clutches of the gods, true to the old Legion, the old ways.'

'We cannot all be our own gods, lord,' said Syxx bitterly.

'That's not my point,' said Kassar calmly. 'What I am saying, mortal, is that I have done many terrible things in the service of my brothers. And if you are omitting information that will jeopardise them, or lying to me, then I will hurt you for it in ways that will make the torments of Phelkorian Twyst look like the inept fumbling of a broken servitor.'

Syxx swallowed with a dry click.

'I swear to you, lord, I have told you all that I know. There is no sense in punishing me, or threatening me. I do not willingly embrace Slaanesh, but that does not mean that I don't benefit from some of his gifts. You would struggle to inflict sensations that would discomfit me.'

'Long centuries have made me inventive,' said Kassar. 'And there is always Kyphas. But, you see? Plain speaking. Despite our reputation, it is something my Legion excels in, when required. We understand each other now.'

Syxx nodded, clearly shaken by the tone the conversation had taken.

'Thank you for your honesty,' said Kassar after the silence had stretched a while. 'You have nothing to add, clearly, so let us rejoin the others, and hope that you have chosen wisely.'

Syxx nodded again and followed Kassar back to the Harrow, hanging a little further back than before.

Haltheus returned with a full schematic of the maglev system, loaded onto a pilfered data-slate that he had coaxed to life.

'*Here,*' he said, stabbing a finger at a rune-marked intersection. '*It's twelve point two miles on foot, but this transit hub should allow me to hook up the Coffer and redirect one of the operational trains from tunnel seventeen to our location.*'

'*Then we just hijack it, ride it into the base of Endurance Hive, and find a way to the beacon at its peak,*' said Kassar. '*It will serve.*'

'*We had best make haste, then,*' said D'sakh. '*And the baggage will have to keep up.*'

'*Krowl can carry it, if it falls behind,*' said Haltheus dismissively.

'*We move,*' said Kassar.

As one, the Harrow moved out. Weapon sights swept the gloom of the nearest tunnel mouth. Vision filters were set to low light, thermic augurs activated to overlay the Alpha Legionnaires' sight. Climbing down a maintenance ladder to ground level, the Unsung spread out into a loose formation and advanced into the gloom of the unused maglev tunnel.

They kept the powered-down rail to their right and moved at speed, adopting a steady lope that they would be able to maintain for hours, even days if required. Syxx was forced to run to keep up, staying ahead of Krowl and Thelgh, who thumped along as rear guard. The cultist could barely see in the low light, and Kassar had ordered that they stay at his back to ensure he did not stumble and fall behind.

The tunnel bored on in a dead straight line, the black waters of the ocean occasionally visible outside through armourglass inspection ports. Twice the rail reached a junction, a right then a left fork curving away into the gloom. Both times, Haltheus consulted his leprously glowing data-slate and motioned them to keep on, straight down the primary tunnel.

Kassar saw maintenance hatches set into the tunnel walls, high up near the curved ceiling, accessed by ladders and gantries.

'The maintenance tunnels run across the ocean floor,' said Haltheus, noting his interest. 'They connect these tunnels by foot so the servitors can move from one to the next without getting run over. They wouldn't help us though, I checked. They go the wrong way.'

The Harrow ran on, the minutes ticking past, Syxx's ragged breathing loud in their ears. Suddenly Skaryth, ranging ahead, came to a halt with one fist raised. Immediately the Unsung dropped into fighting crouches, sighting for any potential threat. Krowl forced Syxx down, the cultist gulping great lungfuls of air.

'What is it?' voxed Kassar.

'Hostile contact ahead,' voxed Skaryth. 'I scent Adeptus Astartes, Kassar. But... there's something wrong with them.'

'Elaborate,' said Kassar. 'Theorise.'

'Blood chemical makeup tastes wrong,' said Skaryth. 'Something in their chem-sweat. It's potent.'

'Haltheus, Kyphas, what can you add?' asked Kassar.

'The tunnel carries straight on,' said Haltheus, checking his data-slate. 'We're still four miles shy of the transit hub, in out-of-service tunnels. No junctions ahead. Nothing to remark on.'

'*Auspex is picking up multiple energy signatures and life signs,*' said Kyphas. '*Just on the edge of range, still nearly a mile ahead. How can he smell them that far out?*'

'*Skaryth's senses are sharp, you know this,*' replied Kassar. '*Focus. Cloaks over, move up, stealth approach. Keep your eyes open, I want us to see them before they see us. Kyphas, tell me the moment you know more.*'

Pips of acknowledgement came back and the Harrow advanced. Slowly now, cautiously, swathed in their camo cloaks, quieting the machine-spirits of their armour to two-thirds power output. They moved near-silently for such huge, armoured figures, and peered ahead through targeters set to maximum magnification.

Skaryth spotted the enemy first, motioning for a halt and easing himself down into a crouch. Kassar moved up alongside him, staring at the distant figures moving behind a barricade stretched across the tunnel ahead. The maglev rail ran through the barricade's centre, breaking its line.

'*Space Marines,*' he said. '*Imperial Fists from the yellow, but I've never seen anything like that mark of armour.*'

'*Do they look… bigger… to anyone else?*' asked Haltheus. '*It could be me, but…*'

'*Their guns are different too,*' said Makhor. '*Some sort of elongated bolt-gun. I've never known the Imperium to innovate, but this is something new, surely.*'

'*Primaris Space Marines,*' said Kassar. '*That was what they called them. I don't know precisely what they are, brothers, but we must have made the Imperium desperate indeed if they're resorting to tinkering with the Emperor's own work.*'

'*They're dug in behind prefab barricades,*' said Phaek'or. '*But nothing big enough to upset our aim. We could harass them from here. Kill a couple, draw them out, take the rest in the open.*'

'*There's only five of them,*' said Kassar. '*And I don't see any special or heavy weaponry. But they're Imperial Fists. I'd expect them to have fortified their position more, especially if they heard Haltheus' bomb go off. We're at quite a remove, but they might have caught the echoes.*'

'*And what are they doing out here?*' asked D'sakh.

'I think our enemy is clever,' said Kassar. 'I'd be willing to bet that the same Dysorian who ordered the teleporter destroyed has laced these tunnels with watch posts and patrols.'

'I found a little information on these Primaris Marines,' said Kyphas. 'During the drop insertion.'

'And you hoarded it,' said A'khassor. 'Again.' His brothers looked angrily at Kyphas.

'I am telling you now,' said Kyphas. 'They are something new, the work of the Adeptus Mechanicus if that is to be believed. Allegedly stronger, faster and tougher than normal Space Marines. Shock troops. These are Intercessors, and they carry something called a bolt rifle. Superior range and stopping power over the standard bolter. Impressive.'

'But few in number, here,' said D'sakh. 'And a perversion of the Emperor's work. He may be a rotting corpse, but he created perfection in the Legiones Astartes. I cannot imagine for a moment that some arrogant magos biologis will have done anything but flaw that work beyond redemption.'

'Agreed,' said Phalk'ir. 'If we try to draw them out, we give them the chance to vox a warning of our approach. We should hit them now, fast and hard. We'll overcome them in moments.'

'That seems viable,' said Kyphas.

'And if these assumptions prove mistaken?' asked Kassar. 'If they are stronger, more resilient? We cannot afford more losses.'

'Nor can we afford the delay,' said Phalk'ir. 'You said so yourself. You are the greatest of us, Kassar. With you leading the charge, they will not long resist us.'

Kassar ignored the spiteful attempt at manipulation. Phalk'ir would take any chance to place him in harm's way, but he was right about the time pressures. Even now, Lord Khordas' Berzerkers could be smashing their way into the spire and taking the beacon for themselves.

Every second mattered.

'They may be few, but we cannot risk them getting a vox message away. We must retain the element of secrecy if we can. Haltheus, what can you do about blocking their vox-channels?'

'Nothing,' said Haltheus. 'I lost my last handful of chaff bombs in the crash. The cacodaemonicum, too.'

'Then we'll have to silence them fast,' said Kassar. 'D'sakh, take Skar-yth and Kyphas. Slip over the rail and move up the right flank. Hold to the shadows until you're over the barricade, then encircle. The rest of us will advance as close as we can, then rush them,' he said, easing Hexling from its sheath. 'Skarle and Krowl at the fore with me. Thelgh, Phaek'or, covering fire. The cultist stays with you. The rest of you move up on my heels. When I give the signal, we strike.'

CHAPTER SEVEN

The advance began slowly, the Unsung staying low and gliding along the tunnel like shadows. Kassar felt their movement around him, their presence at his back. Thelgh and Phaek'or would be setting themselves up, taking prime firing positions, the cultist shielded behind them.

Gradually, Kassar, Krowl and Skarle pulled ahead of their brothers, bunching up into a spear tip and moving fast to gain ground. Their task would be to focus attention, to distract the enemy with their sudden assault. The second wave would then unleash a point-blank firestorm even as D'sakh's group struck from the flank, ending the fight before it had truly begun. Anything that endured would face Kassar's charge and the winnowing fire of the back rankers. It was a tactic that had served them well on Bloodforge.

Gradually the gap closed, the barricade drawing closer. Kassar strained his auto-senses for any sign of buried munitions or ambushing enemies. He could detect nothing.

The Primaris Marines seemed unaware of their approach, a couple patrolling back and forth, the others standing guard, unaware that death slid closer with every heartbeat. Any second their auspex must pick up movement, they must catch a sound or a glint of metal approaching.

A string of vox pips indicated that his shooters had selected targets, and that D'sakh and his brothers had slipped around the edge of the barricade unseen.

'Now,' voxed Kassar, surging from his crouch and straight into a headlong charge. Krowl and Skarle followed, the latter letting go a shrieking laugh that echoed along the tunnel.

Kassar opened fire. Even as his weapon spat shells, the Intercessors were already firing back. They moved with impressive speed, and showed no signs of panic or confusion. Bolt shells flew back and forth as Krowl added his fire to Kassar's. More shots whipped in from the right as D'sakh and his warriors swept back their cloaks and ran to cut off the Primaris' retreat.

A shot burned over Kassar's shoulder. Another glanced off his greave, staggering him. Krowl took a direct hit to the chest, the shell bursting with a sharp crack and blasting a crater in his armour.

Kassar's own rounds hit the nearest Primaris Marine, but ricocheted off his shoulder guard. A shot from Thelgh's rifle followed, punching through the Intercessor's face plate and knocking him off his feet. Kassar cursed as the felled warrior pushed himself back up and kept firing.

Skarle hurled an incendiary bomb that burst against the barricade and wreathed it in flame.

Kassar closed the gap, firing as he went.

A roar filled the tunnel as Phaek'or's heavy bolter stitched a line of shells up their left flank. He blew out a section of the barricade before slamming several shots into an Intercessor's chestplate. The Primaris Marine went down on one knee, only to rise again with a vox-amplified roar.

'Stubborn corpse worshippers,' voxed Haltheus.

D'sakh and his brothers were now behind the Primaris, dropping into firing crouches and pinning them in a crossfire. Rounds sparked from the Imperial Fists' armour, but to Kassar's surprise they weathered the storm and kept firing.

He was ten yards from the barricade when a tight group of shells hit Skarle in the chest and blew him onto his back. Blood sprayed.

'A'khassor,' voxed Kassar, and kept running.

Sweeping through the flames, Kassar vaulted the barricade with blade in hand. Three shells hit him point blank in the chest as he landed. The impacts drove the air from his lungs and threw him back against the barricade.

An Intercessor came at him with a roar, swinging the butt of his bolt rifle.

'Die, filthy traitor!'

Kassar took the blow on his shoulder guard, hard enough to dent its plating. In return he brought Hexling's point up, ramming it through the Space Marine's guts.

Blood welled around the blade, and his enemy grunted in pain, but even transfixed the Intercessor swung another clubbing blow that rang Kassar's helm like a bell.

Dazed, hemmed in, Kassar had little room for skill or subtlety. Instead he dropped Mortis and wrapped both hands around the hilt of Hexling before ripping the blade upwards with all his strength. Unnatural energies arced as the weapon tore through the Intercessor's chest, bursting organs and sending blood sluicing across the ground.

The Imperial Fist gurgled in agony, convulsing. He tried to bring the muzzle of his bolt rifle around but Kassar pushed off the barricade and drove his enemy back. Carved open from stomach to throat, the Intercessor stumbled and the weapon dropped from his hands.

Kassar ripped Hexling free, the blade steaming with blood, runes glowing eldritch along its length, and let his opponent fall. He glanced about, taking in the scene.

The fight was progressing far slower than he would have liked. D'sakh and his brothers had shot down one of the Intercessors, concentrating their fire on him until his armour was a crater-blasted ruin. Another looked to have been blown apart by Phaek'or's heavy bolter.

Somehow, though, the last two Intercessors were still fighting, back to back in a closing ring of blue-green armour.

'Kill them,' ordered Kassar. 'Now!'

With a bellow, Krowl charged in and tackled one of the Intercessors off his feet. Krowl wrestled with his pinned victim, and Kassar's eyes widened as the Primaris Marine began to pry the golem-like Alpha Legionnaire off him. Krowl was as strong as several orks. Kassar had never seen him outmatched in such a fashion.

Evidently the same realisation had pierced the fug around Krowl's mind. He gave an angry grunt, firing a volley of bolt shells point blank into his enemy's face. The Intercessor fell back and Krowl raised his power fist, delivering a clubbing blow. Blood sprayed, but Krowl struck again, and again. By the fourth swing, nothing remained of the Intercessor above the neck.

The last enemy was struck by bolt shells from several different angles. He staggered, but didn't fall. He fired back, spinning D'sakh off his feet.

Seizing his chance, Phalk'ir lunged in from behind.

The Intercessor spun, fast as lightning, and blocked Phalk'ir's descending blade with his bolt rifle. The humming sword hacked the gun in half. The Intercessor clubbed Phalk'ir with the ruined halves, before delivering a furious head-butt to his faceplate. Phalk'ir staggered, but as he did Kyphas drove one of his envenomed knives through a blasted rent in the Imperial Fist's armour.

The Intercessor arched his back and stumbled. Phalk'ir, rallying, spun on his heel, blade whipping around in a glowing arc, and lopped the loyalist's head from his shoulders.

Kassar let out a breath, and leant back against the barricade.

'That,' he said, *'was harder than it should have been.'*

The Unsung gathered on their leader. Several of them nursed fresh wounds from the fight.

'Skarle will live,' said A'khassor. *'His back carapace is cracked, and there's organ damage, but nothing he can't recover from. It'll just hurt, and slow him down for a while.'*

'Pain is how we know we live,' sang Skarle.

'Are you mocking me?' hissed Phalk'ir, but Skarle wasn't done.

'Pain is how we know we live, what they inflict I'll thrice-back-give.'

'*Simpleton,*' said Phalk'ir.

'*We have to assume they got a message away,*' said D'sakh, blood still drying in a rent in his side. '*They had the time.*'

'*Direct hits didn't drop the bastards,*' said Haltheus. '*I mean, nothing gets up again when Thelgh shoots it.*'

'*Apparently, Primaris Space Marines do,*' said Kassar. '*There will be more of them ahead, no doubt. If nothing else, we'll better understand their capabilities now. But we must assume that we're compromised. We make straight for the maglev hub, and get clear of this area before Imperial reinforcements reach us.*'

'*We should check over the corpses first,*' said Kyphas. '*Gather more intelligence on these warriors. Scavenge what we can.*'

'*Thirty seconds,*' said Kassar.

The Unsung fell upon the bodies like vultures. Grenades were seized. Haltheus tore off two helms and clamped them, one after the other, to his belt. Thelgh hefted a bolt rifle experimentally, testing its weight. He nodded to himself, mag-locking the weapon across the base of his backpack and gathering up clips.

Phaek'or stood guard as they worked, still and silent as a statue. Syxx hovered near him, pistols in hand.

'*Kassar,*' said Haltheus. '*You need to see this.*'

Kassar joined Haltheus where he knelt beside one of the fallen Intercessors, inspecting a small, flashing device at the warrior's belt.

'*What is it?*' asked Kassar.

'*Some kind of short-range choral transponder, with a servitor-brain component,*' said Haltheus, turning the runic box over in his hands. '*It's emitting a signal of some sort. Not a message, though. And not a homing beacon. The signal is… intermittent… like it's hailing something else and getting no response.*'

He ran an auspex wand over the device, Kassar watching intently.

'*A bomb?*' he asked. '*Do we need to get clear?*'

'*No, it's not attached to any sort of explosive,*' said Haltheus, the frown audible in his voice. '*Unless… Oh, warp curse it! Yes, we need to get clear. Back down the tunnel to the last fork, now!*'

'*Unsung–*'

Kassar got no further. The device flashed again, then went dark. Above, dug into the tunnel's ceiling, its twins followed suit. Each was attached to a heavy demolition charge and, having ascertained beyond reasonable doubt that the Intercessors' life signs had all dropped to zero, the device in Haltheus' hand sent them a command.

Detonate.

A triple roar shook the tunnel. Searing firelight hurled back the shadows, extinguished the next moment by thundering darkness. Ferrocrete rained down, and a flood of icy water came with it.

Syxx cried out, cowering beneath the fury of the blasts. A chunk of masonry slammed down beside him, peppering him with stone shrapnel.

Water jetted from above, pressurised by the immense depth. Kassar and Haltheus were knocked from their feet by one gushing spume. Thelgh dived clear of another. The water flooded across the tunnel floor with shocking speed, white froth boiling on its surface.

'Shutters!' yelled D'sakh.

Alarms were howling along the tunnel. Warning lumen were pulsing. And in both directions, adamantium shutters were lumbering down from the tunnel ceiling to seal off the compromised section.

Kassar gauged the distance in a heartbeat.

'Onward,' he barked. 'Thelgh, grab Syxx. Get past that shutter!'

They ran, as water sluiced around their greaves in buffeting waves. It was pouring in at a furious rate, a triple waterfall whose sheer pressure was cracking the tunnel roof.

'That whole section is going to rupture,' said Haltheus as they ran. 'I give it less than a minute.'

Kassar powered through the rising waters, riding out each wave that slammed into his back. Water was pouring around them, spilling past and under the lowering shutter. The roar was constant, deafening.

The distance readout in Kassar's retinal display dropped by the second.

Three hundred yards.

Two fifty.

The shutter rumbled lower. It was maybe fifteen feet from the floor of the tunnel now.

A chunk of masonry buffeted Kassar from behind, nearly throwing him forward into what was now waist-high water. He regained his footing and pressed on.

One hundred and fifty yards.

The shutter was barely ten feet from the ground, the water rising swiftly to meet it.

A glance showed his brothers also forging towards the exit. There was Thelgh, Syxx thrown over one shoulder. Kassar noted that Skarle and D'sakh were both falling behind, their wounds slowing them.

'Move with a purpose, brothers,' he voxed. 'I haven't kept you alive this long just to see you drown.'

'Trying,' gasped D'sakh.

The shutter was forty yards away now. Thirty. Twenty. It was below the surface, though, still shuddering downwards.

'Krowl, brace it!' shouted Kassar. Krowl splashed forward through the chest-high water, disappearing under the surface as he grappled to find the shutter's underside. Kassar dived, immersing himself in time to see Krowl get a grip on the shutter's underside barely a foot from the ground.

Kassar kicked forward, intending to help his brother, but it was no use. Krowl might as well have tried to pick up a Land Raider. The shutter ground down and Krowl, doggedly following orders, let it crush both hands into the floor as he strove to fight its motion.

'Krowl,' voxed Kassar, righting himself. His helm barely broke the surface now, and the water was swirling furiously around him as it crashed against the shutter. 'Get clear of there.'

Obediently, his brother surfaced, dark gore drizzling from the mangled stumps where his hands should have been.

'What now?' asked Phalk'ir. 'The shutters are down. This place will soon flood. The baggage will drown and at this depth even our multi-lungs won't keep us alive forever.'

'Blast our way through?' suggested D'sakh, treading water.

'No time,' said Haltheus. 'Besides, I've got nothing strong enough.'

The water pounded into the tunnel, more of the roof giving way by the second. A great tumble of masonry pummelled down and the ocean followed with redoubled force. Cold, dark water rose around them at alarming speed.

'Maintenance tunnels,' said Kassar. 'Is there one in this section?'

Kicking to stay afloat, Thelgh raised his rifle out of the water and sighted along its scope. After a moment, he pipped his vox once in the affirmative.

'Back,' said Kassar. 'Everyone back, make for the maintenance hatch.'

They turned and swam through the rising water. Power armour was heavy, and far from buoyant, but Legiones Astartes strength was enough to drive them along regardless.

A many-legged sea-creature tumbled past Kassar, its fragile body split open by the sudden pressure change. Rubble drifted and thudded below him. The barricade passed underneath, the corpses of the Intercessors jerking in the savage current as though back from the dead.

Overhead, the water neared the ceiling. Thelgh stayed on the surface, keeping Syxx from submerging. The rest of them powered on quicker, kicking for the maintenance hatch. Power armour had its own oxygen supply that could last for days, but most of the Unsung had taken battle damage during the fights on the rig and now here, in this tunnel. Air leaked in bubbling streams from cracks and rents.

Kassar knew that he and his brothers could breathe and filter oxygen from water for a time, but Syxx had no such luxury. Besides, at this depth the pressure was likely to crush even their power-armoured forms within a matter of minutes.

And then the tunnel was flooded entirely. As of now, Kassar knew, Syxx would either drown or be crushed to death.

Ahead, the maintenance hatch swam into view through the murk. Set into the tunnel's ceiling. A now-redundant ladder led up to it, and a small platform allowed access. Ignoring the warning runes on his armour, and the feeling of water sluicing cold against his skin, Kassar mag-locked his boots to the platform. The Unsung slammed down around him, Thelgh still trailing Syxx's body.

'Haltheus, get it open,' voxed Kassar.

Haltheus took slow-motion steps to stand below the runic control panel, each footfall locking to the platform with a muffled clang. He reached up and stabbed at the controls, then again more insistently. Red lights flashed, and he swore vociferously.

'Locked out,' he said. 'Must be a failsafe if the tunnel floods.'

'Krowl?' asked D'sakh, but even submerged in the dark, they could see that their brother's hands were still nothing but bloody stumps.

Kassar could feel the pressure increasing on his armour, hear little groans from its stressed plating. Within his helm, the water was up to his chin.

'We can't open the hatch with the controls, and we can't tear it from its hinges. And even if we could, that would risk flooding the maintenance tunnel,' he said. 'Ideas?'

'Profane the controls?' asked Kyphas.

'The tools I'd need to achieve that aren't waterproof,' said Haltheus. 'All I'd do is wreck the panel.'

'Is there another route?' asked Makhor. No one answered him. Air drizzled from their groaning armour.

'How does it know?' asked D'sakh. 'How does the door's machine-spirit know that the tunnel is flooded?'

'If we're unlucky, it's all in chorus with the shutter controls,' said Haltheus. 'But if not then some kind of augur, probably external... senses the breach... the pressure change. There!'

Above the hatch and to one side, they saw an aquila-stamped panel with several augury-blisters standing proud of its surface.

'If you can get us out of this,' said Kassar, 'do it quickly. The cultist has been submerged for too long already.'

'I know,' said Haltheus angrily. 'But I need some way to... ah! I really hope they didn't innovate too much with these things.'

He unlocked one of the Primaris helms from his belt and, barging past his brothers, clamped it over the sensor. Haltheus grasped one of the rebreather feeds in the grille of his faceplate and tore it loose. Oxygen bubbled from its end. Water surged into his helm.

Moving fast, he peeled away a section of armour on the Primaris helm and revealed its own rebreather feed. Deftly, one-handed,

Haltheus worked the component out and then leaned in and held his oxygen feed firmly against the other helm's hollow socket.

Kassar watched as water currents moved around the Primaris helm. He saw what his brother was doing, and urged it to work. He was breathing ice-cold water now, his armour compromised, his body feeling the groaning stress of the deep ocean pressing down on it.

With a mute click, the control panel's runes turned green as sufficient oxygen passed over the augurs to fool them. Kassar lunged, punching the rune to open the hatch. Locking bolts disengaged, the hatch slid back, and the tunnel above was revealed.

Kneeling beside the dark pool of the open hatch, Skaryth and Skarle gripped Krowl's shoulder guards and hauled him up into the tunnel. He was the last.

Kassar slumped against the wall, water drizzling from his armour. He wrenched off his helm and let out a long, slow breath. A wave of dizziness struck him as oxygen bubbles formed in his blood from the sudden pressure change, but it passed as his Adeptus Astartes physiology asserted itself.

Electro-sconces flickered to life with stuttering pings, their light marching away down a metal corridor that stretched into the distance. Pipes ran along its walls, interspersed with occasional clusters of machinery.

'Report,' he gasped, receiving confirmations from all his brothers. Everyone present, and alive.

'Except the baggage,' said A'khassor grimly, crouching over Syxx's bedraggled body. 'He's gone.'

'Curses,' spat Kassar. 'We should have got air into him the same way Haltheus did with that lock.'

'It wouldn't have helped,' said A'khassor. 'We couldn't have made a seal for him to breathe inside the helm, and forcing air down his throat would just have ruptured his lungs. Besides, none of it would have helped the pressure. His bones, his organs, they're surely all crushed.'

'Then all this was a waste of time and lives,' said Makhor, glancing at the Apothecary. 'We're mission fail, and we haven't even reached the hive.'

'Warp damn it,' said Haltheus. 'Damned fragile mortal. It's my fault, Kassar, I missed that bomb.'

'What now?' asked D'sakh, looking to Kassar.

'We do what we ought to have done to begin with,' said Phalk'ir. 'We fight our way to a transport. We get off this drowned rock and leave these fools to fight amongst themselves. Let them waste their lives, not ours.'

'And then what, Phalk'ir?' asked Makhor. 'Assuming we manage to acquire a transport capable of breaking atmosphere. And assuming we get clear without being shot down. Where then do we go, without warp capabilities, in a galaxy we no longer understand?'

'Anywhere,' spat Phalk'ir. 'Stow away on a warship. Steal something at gunpoint.'

'There's twelve of us,' said Kassar. 'We wouldn't have the strength to capture a warship. Not even close.'

'But we could,' said Phalk'ir. 'If you would stop forcing this curse upon us. If we claimed what was rightfully ours!'

'No,' said Kassar. 'Not this, again. We do not enslave ourselves to the Dark Gods, Phalk'ir.'

'What slavery?' cried Phalk'ir, slamming his fist against the wall in frustration. 'I look at the chosen of the gods and I see power! Power we have earned a thousand times over, if we would just open ourselves to their worship. You all know I'm right.'

Uncomfortable silence reigned.

It was broken by a sudden, whooping gasp.

Syxx rolled onto his side and retched a great spume of water and bile. He coughed desperately, more water bubbling between his lips, then slumped, gasping, in his own fluids.

'No...' said Haltheus in amazement. A'khassor crouched by Syxx, hastily running the instruments of his narthecium over the cultist's head and chest.

'He lives,' he said simply. 'Some pressure trauma, but...' A'khassor shrugged and stood, letting Syxx slump back into a heap. The cultist dragged in great draughts of air, spitting and gagging to clear the last of the water from his lungs.

'You see, Phalk'ir,' said Kassar. 'We don't need the gifts of the gods to succeed here. If this mere mortal can endure that which Tsadrekha throws at him, how can we not?'

'For all we know, Kassar, that *was* the aid of the gods,' said Phalk'ir, but his heart wasn't in it. He could clearly sense the Harrow's mood turning against him again.

Kassar crouched by Syxx. He gripped the cultist's dripping chin in his gauntlet and raised his face. Syxx stared up at him with blood-shot eyes, the skin that Kassar could see spider-webbed with burst blood vessels.

'Can you walk?' Kassar asked. Syxx blinked and nodded. Kassar noted blood trickling from the cultist's nose.

'I... think so, lord...'

'Good,' said Kassar. 'Then we move.'

'Where?' asked Kyphas.

'The only way we can, for now,' said Kassar, gesturing down the passage. 'Until we can find something that will bring us back towards our original objective. Skaryth and Haltheus take point, eyes peeled for anything that will help us get back on mission. The rest of you, two by two, fifth cypher. *With luck, any Imperial reinforcements will believe we drowned back there, but in case they think to sweep this passage, be ready for a firefight. Krowl, guard the cultist. Keep him in the middle of the Harrow with you.*'

So ordered, the Unsung moved off, water still dripping from armour and weapons.

They moved at a brisk march, fast enough to eat up the distance but slow enough to be wary of sudden threats. Krowl carried Syxx, cradled like a newborn in limbs that were still regenerating.

Haltheus kept a weather eye on the instrument panels they passed. His broken helm was clamped to his belt, along with the two Intercessor helmets. Until he had time to repair it, the Techmarine would go bare-headed.

Near the column's rear, A'khassor fell in with Kassar, speaking to him on a private vox-channel.

'You know what I'm going to say, Kassar,' he said.

'I do,' said Kassar. *'There's no way he could have survived that.'*

'None,' said A'khassor. *'The mortal drowned. And he was ruptured. Inside. Eardrums burst. Eyes full of blood. Tissues ruined. That much pressure, we might as well have cycled him through an airlock.'*

'Then how?' asked Kassar.

'I have absolutely no idea,' said A'khassor. *'Except to say that our baggage has a great deal more about him than meets the eye.'*

'I miss Nehkt'sha more than ever, at times like these,' said Kassar, sombrely. *'A psyker could pry into the cultist's mind, discover what he's hiding. Perhaps even make sense of the brands on his flesh.'*

A'khassor murmured agreement.

'There's Kyphas?' said Kassar.

'Only if you want the baggage broken beyond repair,' said A'khassor scornfully. *'That one hasn't the restraint left to know when to stop.'*

'Cogitator panel here,' called Haltheus. *'Let's see what we can see.'*

'Just bear it in mind, Kassar,' said A'khassor as the Unsung drew to a halt. *'And watch him carefully.'*

Several minutes and several unrepentant offences to the Omnissiah later, Haltheus barked in triumph.

'What do you have?' asked Kassar. *'A route back to the hub?'*

'What? No,' said Haltheus. *'No, that'd take us hours to circumnavigate back to. I have us a much quicker way onwards.'*

'Elaborate,' said Kassar.

'This tunnel goes on for another two miles,' said Haltheus. *'Then it splits. One fork would take us on towards the hub on foot, but as I said, hours. The other leads directly to tunnel thirteen. An active route direct to the hive.'*

'What use is that?' asked Makhor. *'We'd still be on foot... unless... Haltheus, what are you planning?'*

Haltheus grinned at them all.

'Well, brothers,' he said, *'if we move quickly, there's a train coming...'*

CHAPTER EIGHT

The Khornate horde battered at Hive Endurance. Up and down the city's metallic flanks, Imperial defenders rained fire upon those heretics that had gained a toehold. Directly below the shuttered mechanical cavern of the Divinitus Aerodocks, halfway up the hive's north flank, a thin line of Tsadrekhan militia and Adepta Sororitas held the barricaded entry-ports to the lower docks. They were led by a dozen Imperial Fists, and Captain Dysorian himself.

Dysorian snapped off a shot from his bolt pistol, blasting out a Khorne Berzerker's throat. The warrior's lifeless body tumbled back down the armoured mountainside of the hive's outer shell, falling towards the waves below.

'Reloading,' said Dysorian, calmly ejecting his clip and slamming a new one into place as shots ripped the air around him. Bolt shells struck the barricade he stood behind, exploding against monobonded marble and leaving black scorch-marks. A storm of small-arms fire whipped up and down the hive's flank, fired by Tsadrekhan defence troopers and clambering cultists.

'Two more drop-craft coming in at seventeen one-one,' voxed Sergeant Valynas. 'They're making the most of that hole in our flak cover.'

'Brother Yoldas,' said Dysorian. 'Did you receive that?'

'Yes, my captain,' came Yoldas' voice, crackling with atmospheric interference. Yoldas had authority over a pair of Hunter anti-aircraft tanks, locked down on a commercia access ramp two levels up. As Dysorian kept firing, the Hunters let fly. Guided by mummified servitor-savants, their skyspear missiles arced away on trails of smoke and flame.

One struck a renegade Stormraven head on, sending its flaming wreckage plummeting away. The other clipped a crimson-hulled bulk hauler.

'Direct hit, starboard nacelle,' reported Yoldas. 'Target listing… Dorn's fist, the pilot's aiming straight for us. Brother Lumas, get us cl–'

The hauler, belching smoke from its blasted engine, lurched drunkenly over Dysorian's head and slammed into the hive. The captain ducked as a titanic explosion lit the evening gloom, raining flaming wreckage around him.

Dysorian magnified his auto-senses and surveyed the blazing ruin of the drop-ship, and the two Imperial Fist tanks that had been crushed by it.

'Curses,' he muttered sourly, then continued shooting. The captain was flanked by Sergeant Valynas' Primaris Hellblasters, their plasma incinerators howling with every shot. Khorne Berzerkers clambered towards them hand over hand, gripping antennas, pipes and cables, brandishing chainaxes and firing bolt pistols.

One by one, the Hellblasters shot them back down.

The last of the Khorne Berzerkers somehow evaded the hail of shots, putting on a burst of speed and hauling himself up onto the barricade. Dysorian stepped up and drove his power sword through the Berzerker's neck. The corpse toppled backwards, crashing into a nest of antenna and dangling there like macabre fruit.

'Attack wave neutralised, my captain,' said the Hellblaster sergeant. He motioned for his brothers to begin appeasement rituals on their plasma incinerators, which were glowing and venting wisps of steam.

'Vigilance, Sergeant Valynas,' said Dysorian, sheathing his blade. 'No doubt the foe shall be upon us again soon enough.'

'Yes, my captain,' said Valynas.

Dysorian took a moment to survey the strange battlefield. The clouds had thickened above Endurance, lightning crackling through them to strike at the distant towers of the convent prioris. Enemy drop-ships still fell like rain, many flaring out in fireballs as streams of gunfire found them. The waves below were frothing, smashing against the hive's flanks hard enough to send spume several hundred feet into the air. Wreckage and bodies churned amongst them.

Out on the horizon, plumes of smoke rose, tell-tale signs of other battles being waged on rigs and ocean forts. With atmospherics so poor, little word had come from the planet's other hives, but what fragments had reached Dysorian's ear sounded less than encouraging.

Closer to home, the hive's skin crawled with invaders like mites on a grox. Not every drop-ship could be shot down, and of those that were, some still managed crash landings that their passengers could survive.

Gradually, by dint of sheer numbers and aggression, Lord Khordas' forces were gaining footholds.

'*They're still coming, my captain,*' voxed Techmarine Pavras. '*Their numbers are more akin to orks.*'

'A lot of cultists here, Pavras,' replied Dysorian. 'A lot of renegades and mongrels bulking out the elite. Still, their numbers cannot be inexhaustible. We need only endure.'

'*And we shall,*' said Pavras. '*We shall make the primarch proud.*'

'We shall,' agreed Dysorian gruffly. 'How fares the battle in the Waterline districts?'

'*The line is holding down here,*' said Pavras. '*We've been coordinating with the Sororitas and the Tsadrekhan officers to keep reinforcements flowing. Docking piers four and six are overrun, but we're keeping the enemy pinned with Thunderfire batteries. One breach in Waterline sector tertius nine minutes ago, driven back by overwhelming deployment of Tsadrekhan militia reserves.*'

'Good work, Pavras,' said Dysorian. 'The Primaris?'

'*Fighting like born heroes, my captain,*' said Pavras. '*As you have no doubt witnessed for yourself.*'

'They fight with courage, determination and skill,' replied Dysorian. 'Which is the bare minimum I would expect from an Imperial Fist. But I grant, their presence is not an active disadvantage.'

Dysorian switched channels from his old friend's wry chuckle.

'Canoness Levinia,' he said. 'What news of the battle on high?'

'*The hive spire remains unbreached, captain,*' came Levinia's reply, warped by ether-static. '*The Saint leads us, and the heretics fall like chaff. The Tsadrekhan vox-men report that your warriors are leading the defence below in a similarly successful fashion, yes?*'

'Thus far, that is so,' replied Dysorian. 'The hive's strategic command decks are faring admirably in keeping us informed of enemy threats as they develop. My commendations to their officers.'

'*I shall see that your message is passed on, captain,*' said Levinia. '*It will boost morale considerably. Your praise is known to be hard to win.*'

'Let me know if anything changes, canoness,' said Dysorian. 'And we will hurl these scum into the ocean together.'

Dysorian switched through further channels, absorbing strategic exloads and listening in on officer vox exchanges before cycling on again. He maintained a strategic picture of the hive in his head, far more complex than anything a mere mortal could have envisioned.

'Lieutenant Lydanis,' he said, switching channels again. 'How fare the defences in the Underbilge?'

'*Minimal enemy contact thus far, my captain,*' replied Lydanis, his voice fading in and out as the channel strove to cut through miles of hive structure and electrical systems. '*The defences around the maglev hub remain untested. Levels zero-zero-five through one-zero-six are likewise patrolled, but unassailed, probably due to depth and difficulty of enemy access. The levels directly below the Waterline districts have seen isolated break-ins and two flood warnings. Berzerkers have sawed their way through several airlocks. All enemy ingressions have been swiftly eliminated.*'

'See that it remains thus,' said Dysorian.

'*Yes, my captain,*' replied the lieutenant.

'And what of the tunnels?' asked Dysorian, raising his voice as a squadron of Land Speeders roared overhead, then dived away on a strafing run.

'Several reports of contact from patrol groups and guard posts, my captain. Isolated bands of enemies gaining access via outliers, all neutralised. Two flood events, one of which appears to have cost us Intercessor Squad Ledarno.'

'Enemy involvement?' asked Dysorian.

'Unclear,' replied Lydanis. *'One instance appears to have been caused by macro-lander wreckage impacting the tunnel roof. In the other case, Sergeant Ledarno attempted a vox transmission prior to the collapse, but under-ocean atmospherics are extremely poor. We received only fragments, which Techmarine Savandys is attempting to decipher. I have despatched response forces to both locations, but the distance is considerable and the maglev network is still running, which presents a substantial hazard that must be circumnavigated. Even in armoured transports, it will take them time to reach their destinations, my captain.'*

Dysorian grunted. 'Keep me appraised, lieutenant,' he said.

'In Dorn's name,' replied Lydanis.

Dysorian continued his vox sweep, speaking to his commanding officers and sergeants, appraising himself of the strategic situation. Overall, he found himself cautiously optimistic. The enemy had made a number of localised gains, but their casualty rates had been phenomenal, enough to turn the waters around the hive red, and as he had said to Pavras, they could not be infinite. Afternoon was dimming towards evening, but thanks to the cloud cover they would not have to endure the ugly, glowing scar of the Great Rift splitting the stars above. Dysorian didn't hold with omens, but had he, that would surely have been a good one.

Canoness Levinia's rune flashed in Dysorian's peripheral, a priority hail. He blink clicked acknowledgement, returning to their open channel.

'Canoness Levinia,' said Dysorian.

'Captain Dysorian,' said Levinia urgently. *'The Saint has given us a warning. The foe are about to force a breach on the southern face of floor five-two-two. We must relocate our forces appropriately, for they will do this within minutes, captain.'*

'How does she know this?' asked Dysorian, heavy brows beetling.

'Because she is a Living Saint of the Emperor, Captain Dysorian,' snapped Levinia. *'She is party to holy revelation. Do you lack faith in her word?'*

'I have faith in intelligence reports, auspex scans, auto-seances,' replied Dysorian, ignoring the resumed howl of gunfire from the Hellblasters. 'None of which have reported any enemy threat to that sector. Canoness, with respect–'

'Captain,' interrupted Levinia, steel in her voice. *'If you do not trust the revelations of the Saint, then trust me. We have fought to defend this world for long months now. You know I am not some habit-wringing novitiate.'*

Dysorian hesitated for a moment, then growled in annoyance.

'Very well,' he said. 'I am relocating now.'

Dysorian switched channels, swiftly ordering those reserves he could spare towards southern face five-two-two and hoping to Dorn that he was doing the right thing.

Stepping back to the barricade, Dysorian emptied his bolt pistol's clip into the blood-cultists scrambling frantically up towards it. Clad in mangy robes and skull masks, many badly burned from the crash of their transport, the men burst like blood blisters as his shells hit them.

'Sergeant Valynas,' he said. 'Not a single foe crosses this barricade.'

'Understood, my captain,' said Valynas. 'It shall be as though Dorn himself stood watch.'

'Good enough,' nodded Dysorian as the howl of powerful engines approached.

Swinging in low around the hive's flank came a yellow-hulled Stormraven. Its guns cut a swathe through the clambering cultists, then the pilot brought his craft around, its nose lowering as though bowing to Dysorian. Hydraulics whined, and the gunship's assault ramp lowered.

Offering a quick salute to the Hellblasters, the captain vaulted atop the barricade then leapt onto the ramp, cloak streaming behind him. He locked gauntlets with one of the Tactical Squad already riding in the gunship's hold, and was pulled in. As the ramp closed behind him, the Stormraven was already swinging away, bullets pinging from its armoured hull as it fired its thrusters and set off for level five-two-two.

'Oh, Throne,' breathed Dysorian in horror.

Overhead, a leviathan blazed down through the clouds.

Standing behind the pilot's throne in the Stormraven's cockpit, Dysorian stared up at the vast metal shape, still wreathed in flames, that was plunging towards the hive's southern flank.

'Augurs suggest a Hellbringer Mk II light cruiser, my captain,' said the gunship's pilot. 'Approximately one mile long. No battle-damage showing. Collision course with Endurance south flank, floors five-one-nine to five-two-four. Two minutes to impact.'

'A cruiser,' said Dysorian. 'Those lunatics are going to ram the hive!'

Recovering himself, Dysorian began issuing orders over the vox.

'Imperial Fists forces within three-level proximity to south face five-two-two, withdraw to higher or lower levels, effective immediate. Brace for macro-ordnance impact. Any Tsadrekhan Militia reserves or Adepta Sororitas in vicinity of level five-two-two, this is Captain Paetrov Dysorian of the Imperial Fists ordering an immediate withdrawal from south face combat zone. In the Emperor's name, if you wish to live, move now.'

Responses came back, some brisk and efficient, others panicked militia requests for confirmation or additional detail. These latter he ignored. He had more important matters to attend to than the coddling of fools.

Overhead, the blazing spear of the Hellbringer was arcing towards the hive, flames still dancing around its prow. Flak fire reached out to hammer the craft, but splashed harmlessly from flickering void shields.

'Canoness Levinia,' voxed Dysorian. 'Do you see it?'

'I have the abomination in my sights, captain,' replied the canoness.

'Do we have anything that can shoot it down?' asked Dysorian.

'We are trying. All southern batteries have retasked. But it's below the arc of our orbital lasers.'

Missiles streaked away from the convent prioris, slamming into the ship's void shields until they collapsed in a polychromatic spray. Las blasts and explosive warheads pummelled the Hellbringer's prow. Still it roared closer.

'There's no time,' said Dysorian. 'It's going to hit.'

'*My captain,*' came Pavras' voice over the vox. '*Vox-intercept from the cruiser. You need to hear this.*'

Dysorian's ear filled with the sound of a bestial voice.

'...and now, as we plunge down upon the weakling city like a blade cast from the hand of mighty Khorne, know that I lead you to glory in person. The eye of the Blood God is upon me, as it shall be now upon all of you, and in his sight, we shall reap such glory from the field of battle...'

'Primarch's fist,' said Dysorian. 'Khordas. He's on that cruiser, isn't he?'

'*I think so, my captain,*' said Pavras. '*The Arch Heretic has tired of waiting. He comes.*'

The impact was phenomenal. Triple-layer, reinforced plasteel built to withstand the most furious bombardment crumpled like paper under the cruiser's prow. Like a javelin hurled into the flank of some towering behemoth, the Hellbringer plunged deep into Hive Endurance. Explosions blossomed around the impact point. Choked screams and thunderous rumbling filled the vox-net, cutting off as the ship tore through decking, hab-units, bulkheads, manufactorums, exchanger pipes, generatorums and shrines.

The cruiser suffered for its insane aggression. Its superstructure warped and crumpled as the titanic force of the impact radiated along its length. Fireballs erupted from collapsing gundecks and munitions stores. Stained glass fell in blizzards. Spiked gargoyles and gun towers tore away, smashing into the flanks of the hive and trailing secondary detonations all the way to the ocean.

'It's going to tear the hive in two,' said Dysorian.

'*If its warp drives don't go critical first,*' voxed Pavras, voice shuddering.

Groaning like a dying god, the Hellbringer ground to a stop, over two-thirds of its length driven into the meat of the hive. Frantic reports claimed that its mangled prow had missed the hive spine by less than a thousand yards. Fires blazed furiously all around the breach, which had ripped through the superstructure of five-two-two and several floors above and below.

Wreckage rained down.

The cruiser's hindquarters settled, threatening to tear away under their own weight.

'Movement,' reported Dysorian's pilot, magnifying the cockpit vid-feed and panning it across the breach. 'Multiple hostiles emerging from the wreck and entering the hive.'

'Canoness,' voxed Dysorian. 'It looks as though your Saint spoke the truth. Whatever you have available, deploy it. We need to push them back, now.'

'The Saint herself is on her way, captain. She will lead the counter-attack, and I would ask that you support her with everything you can.'

'In Dorn's name,' said Dysorian. He issued a quick string of orders, stripping away all but the most essential forces from the surrounding combat zones and requesting initial casualty reports. They were not encouraging.

'Brother Haldyne,' said Dysorian to his pilot. 'Get us down there.'

'At once, my captain,' said Haldyne. 'Brace for flak.'

Dysorian swung himself back through the hatch into the Stormraven's troop bay, gripping a restraint as the Tactical Marines around him did likewise.

'Brothers,' said Dysorian as he felt the craft accelerate into a dive. 'For the Emperor and the primarch.'

The Stormraven swept in low along the spine of the crashed cruiser, making for the ragged breach it had torn in the flesh of the hive. It streaked through a fire-lit hell, weaving left and right as shots stabbed up at it.

'I can't land,' voxed Haldyne through gritted teeth. 'It's taking all I've got to evade the fire from the cruiser's functional turrets. Prepare for a combat drop.'

Haldyne brought the Stormraven low and decelerated as much as he dared before lowering the rear ramp. As flames and mangled metal flashed by below, Dysorian and his brothers leapt.

Dysorian's boots hit decking and he dropped into a roll, softening the impact and coming up with blade in hand. He found himself in the ragged stub of a corridor, one end part-sealed by a seized bulk-head, the other a torn wound open to the darkening skies. Checking his auspex feed, Dysorian dropped from the corridor's end, landing on the exposed hull plating of the Chaos cruiser. Flames danced around him, and the monstrous superstructure of the warship loomed, spiked towers still menacing despite being shattered and canted.

'Dorn preserve us from their taint,' he muttered.

Smoke billowed. Gunfire and the roar of chainaxes sounded from nearby and Dysorian, still alone, followed it.

Running down the Hellbringer's hull, the captain ducked under a splayed web of melted girders and found himself amidst the charnel ruin of a hab block. A honeycomb of sundered floors and chambers surrounded him, punched through by the cruiser's passage. Bodies, or what remained of them, lay under heaps of rubble or sprawled in burning profusion. The wreckage of ruined lives was everywhere.

'Captain,' came a shout from ahead. Two of the Tactical Marines, Sergeant Vynus and one of his brothers, were battling several Khorne Berzerkers amidst the ruins. Dysorian broke into a run, firing his bolt pistol.

He managed to knock one of the traitors off their feet with a shot to the chest, but another carved his chainaxe through Vynus' neck, sending the sergeant's head tumbling away. Dysorian roared in anger, crashing headlong into the bellowing Berzerker and running him through. Ripping his power sword free, Dysorian swung it in a crack-ling arc that lopped an arm from the third heretic. Blood sprayed, but the Khorne worshipper kept howling even as his axe arm clanged to the floor.

He fired his pistol into Dysorian's chest, staggering the captain. In return, the surviving Tactical brother swept the Berzerker's legs from under him, then emptied a clip of bolt shells into his helm.

Gulping a lungful of air, Dysorian nodded.

'My thanks, Brother Lytor. Let us find our comrades.'

The two of them set off, clambering down through a mangled mishmash of warship and hab block. Dysorian picked up four more of squad Vynus as he went, still making for the clangour of combat.

They dropped through a torn patch of decking, landing in a fire-blackened chamber. A mangled heap of machinery dominated half the space, and beyond it could be seen the flash and flare of gunfire.

'Brothers,' said Dysorian. 'With me.'

As one, the Imperial Fists gripped the blackened tangle of machine-parts and heaved them aside. As they did, a desperate battle was revealed.

Beyond the chamber's end lay a broad communal plaza. Half of it was buried beneath the titanic bulk of the cruiser, which rose as a ruptured wall of crimson armour and profane sigils from floor to ceiling. In the shadow of the ship's carcass lay a toppled statue of the Emperor and beyond it, a wide rampway leading through a hundred-foot-high arch into the commercia district beyond.

On that ramp, hunkered behind scattered lumps of rubble and wreckage, a thin line of Tsadrekhans and Imperial Fists was making a desperate stand. Teeming masses of dagger-wielding blood cult-ists surged into the loyalists' gunfire, exhorted by bellowing Heretic Astartes in the colours of some Khorne-sworn renegade warband. At their head stamped a blood-spattered Helbrute, heavy bolters chat-tering as they raked fire across the defenders.

'For Dorn and the Emperor!' cried Dysorian. 'Enfilading fire!'

The brothers of Squad Vynus let fly into the traitors' flank. Bolters roared. Frag grenades exploded amidst the cultist mass with thump-ing booms. Brother Volnys hefted his squad's missile launcher and sent a krak missile arcing over the fight to explode between the Hel-brute's hulking shoulders. The hellish machine staggered and ichor sprayed, but it stayed on its feet.

From the ramp, Intercessor Sergeant Loriyan voxed Dysorian.

'It is good to see you, my captain.'

'Report status,' replied Dysorian, firing his bolt pistol.

'Two brothers down from my squad,' said Loriyan. 'Devastator Squad Lynarus have lost three more. The Tsadrekhans have suffered approximately seventy per cent casualties and rising.'

'Hold, brother,' said Dysorian. 'More aid is on its way.'

Loriyan pipped acknowledgement, firing his bolt rifle into the onrushing masses. Meanwhile, a portion of the horde spilling from the cruiser had now redirected their charge towards Dysorian and his brothers. Shrieking praise to Khorne, hundreds of cultists flowed towards them over the bodies of the dead.

'This is Captain Paetrov Dysorian, Imperial Fists,' voxed the captain across all channels. 'Priority alert to all Imperial forces in the region of south face five-two-two. Overwhelming enemy forces disembarking from the cruiser. Multiple breaches. We hold one, but there are others, and we shall soon be overrun. All available forces, converge and repel invaders before we lose the hive!'

Then the cultists' charge slammed home, and Dysorian focused his mind upon the fight. Individually, these malnourished lunatics were no match for the Imperial Fists. Yet there were hundreds of them, a screaming, frothing mass, and they fought with lunatic fury.

Bullets ricocheted off Dysorian's armour. Blades clanged against it. The captain gunned down a swathe of enemies, and hacked his blade through two more.

Hands clawed at his limbs. His cloak tore from his shoulders. A jagged blade found a join in his armour, snaking through and drawing blood. Point-blank gunfire sprayed into his face, cracking one eye-lens.

With no time to reload, Dysorian clamped his pistol to his thigh and gripped his blade's hilt with both hands. Swinging the weapon in wide arcs, he carved away the mass of foes pressing in around him, buying himself room to breathe.

'Fight, brothers,' he shouted, vox-amplifying his voice so it boomed across the chamber. 'Fight for Dorn, for the Emperor, for Tsadrekha!'

To his right, Brother Lytor crashed to his knees, a crude bayonet jutting from one eye-lens. Nearby he heard Brother Volnys cursing in pain and anger.

A masked fanatic lunged at Dysorian, only to have his head swept from his shoulders. Another came from the side, firing his pistol point blank. Dysorian lopped him in two. Another cultist came at him, and another, stabbing and firing frantically. One clamped both arms around one of Dysorian's and refused to let go, weighing down the captain's blade. To Dysorian's disgust, yet another cultist tried to bite into his power-armoured gorget, shattering his teeth to bloodied stumps.

Dysorian felt the sting of a wound behind his knee, another where a shot had cracked his breastplate. He couldn't see Squad Vynus any more, just a sea of chanting cultists on every side.

'Captain,' voxed Sergeant Loriyan. 'We can't hold them! The Helbrute–'

Dimly, Dysorian heard the war machine roaring, its guns hammering.

'To the last man,' he bellowed. 'No weakness! No surrender!'

Another blade found his elbow joint, drawing a line of fire across his flesh. Finally dislodging the lunatic on his arm, Dysorian stamped on the man's skull then whirled his sword in a glowing arc, driving the enemy back. The move earned him seconds, long enough to see Chaos Space Marines closing on him with evil leers.

'I'll make you suffer for it,' snarled Dysorian, bracing himself for their attack. 'Come on, you traitorous filth.'

It was then that blinding light suffused the chamber, and Dysorian heard a pure, crystalline note singing in the air. The Khorne worshippers faltered at that sound, many clutching their heads and snarling in pain. As they reeled, so came the Saint.

She descended from on high, the metallic wings of her magnificent jump pack spread wide. A halo flickered about her head, and beneath its radiance, Dysorian felt the pain of his wounds lessen. Celestine swept down upon the Chaos horde with the Ardent Blade held high, the pair of jump-pack-wearing champions known as the Geminae Superia dropping on pillars of flame at her side.

Celestine hung above the fight for a moment, a star radiating the pure light of divine judgement. Imperial soldiers cried out in rapturous voices at the sight of her, and even Dysorian was surprised to feel fervent emotions swelling in his chest. By comparison, the heretic cultists quailed in terror, while their renegade masters shielded their eyes from the Saint's luminescence and spat vile curses through their vox grilles.

Then she fell upon her foes, slamming down into their midst like a comet while her Sisters rained bolt shells upon their heads. Dysorian lost sight of the Saint as she plunged into the enemy, but the glowing luminescence and sprays of heretic blood told him precisely where she was.

At the same moment, fresh gunfire sounded from the head of the ramp. Dysorian caught a fleeting glimpse of Battle Sisters in black-and-bone armour, pouring into the chamber with their guns thundering. They cried out praise to the Saint, and their eyes seemed to flash with a holy light.

As the enemy around him wavered, Dysorian felt his fatigue lift, replaced by surging new strength. His first swing cut down three cultists, his next another two. Shouldering between the reeling fanatics, Dysorian managed to reach the lead Chaos Marine and hack him down in turn with a savage lateral cut. Gaining momentum, leaping the traitor's corpse, Dysorian carved a path through his foes. The cultists milled in panic, the fervour driven out of them by Celestine's divine aura. Cursing, clubbing, their Heretic Astartes masters tried to force them back into the fight.

Another of the traitors fell to Dysorian's blade, then another. The fourth managed to carve a bloody wound into the captain's side with his chainsword, but then bolt-rounds blew out the traitor's helm and threw his body into the cultists behind. Blood leaking from the blade still jammed into his eye socket, Brother Lytor bulled his way through the panicking cultists to stand alongside his captain. With him came another Tactical Marine, Brother Tylorn, clutching a pair of combat knives that were red to the hilt.

'Brothers,' said Dysorian. 'Together.'

'Yes, my captain,' said Lytor and Tylorn, and together the three of them hacked their way towards the Saint.

* * *

As the final rank of cultists fell before them, Dysorian bore witness to the Saint's true glory for the first time. He felt her presence like a physical blow. She was glorious, stern, merciless. She was death incarnate.

Celestine fought with perfect form, duelling five Chaos Space Marines at once as though she fought in a practice cage. She leapt and spun, using bursts of propulsion from her ornate jump pack to carry her high above her enemies' heads, and to evade their wild swings. The Ardent Blade sang as it cut through the air, lopping the arm from one traitor then the head from the next. Celestine sprang backwards from a furious lunge, kicked the blade elegantly from her attacker's hand, then landed in a crouch and eviscerated him.

'She is magnificent,' breathed brother Lytor.

At her back, one of the Geminae Superia lay in a pool of blood. The other stood over her body, raining merciless fire into the cultist masses and driving them back.

Recognising that the Saint needed no aid, Dysorian and his brothers sprang to help her living Sister, hurling back those few cultists with fight left in them. At the same time, Dysorian heard Sergeant Loriyan's voice in his ear again.

'*Captain, we have them! Permission to pursue.*'

'Granted, Loriyan. Drive them back and we will crush them as they come to us. We stand in the Emperor's light. These traitors can know no victory!'

Dysorian's words were proven true in a matter of minutes. There came a hissing roar from the head of the ramp, a Battle Sister's multi-melta carving through the hull of the Khornate Helbrute and blowing it apart in a shower of molten wreckage. Shorn of the Heretic Astartes who had driven them into battle and the beast that had led them to war, the cultists collapsed. They became a surging, panicked crowd. Some screamed in fear, or fell to be trampled. Others, the truly devoted amongst them, attacked their comrades, hacking and stabbing to spill as much blood as they could before the end. Some fought, frantic as cornered rats, but against the resurgent Imperial warriors they stood little chance.

The last of their number fled back into the cruiser, or else scrambled away into bolt-holes amidst the wreckage.

'Brothers,' ordered Dysorian. 'Charges into the cruiser hatches. Blow them. Entomb the foe.'

Dull booms shook the chamber as the captain's orders were followed. Gunfire stuttered here and there as the Imperial forces put down the enemy stragglers. Meanwhile, Captain Dysorian knelt before the Saint.

She looked upon him, her visage ageless, peaceful, infinitely wise. Though she had fought outnumbered against the murderous warriors of the Heretic Astartes, there was not a mark on Celestine's armour, not a scratch on her alabaster skin. Bathed in her light, Dysorian felt disbelief and wonder warring within him.

'My lady,' he said. 'Saint Celestine. My thanks for your timely aid.'

Celestine smiled at Dysorian, motioning for him to stand.

'You remind me of another,' she said. 'A brother from amongst your Chapter's successors, who fought valiantly at my side when our need was most desperate.'

Dysorian rose, with the sense that he had just been paid a significant compliment.

'Saint Celestine, I believe that our need is desperate on this day, also. And I thank you again for your intercession. But the enemy will have forced many breaches here. And I did not see Lord Khordas amongst the fallen. I have more warriors on their way, but we must press on lest we lose the hive.'

'I admire your ardour, Captain Dysorian,' said Celestine. 'And so we shall. But first I must attend my fallen Sister, for the Emperor's work is not done.'

Dysorian went to utter words of condolence for the Saint's loss, but something stopped him. Instead he watched as Celestine paced across to the fallen Seraphim and knelt in her blood. The Saint cradled her Sister's head, brushing the hair back from her pale forehead. A single tear welled from Celestine's eye. It glittered as it fell, splashing upon the Seraphim's cheek, and Dysorian's eyes widened in amazement as the fallen Battle Sister gave a sudden gasp. Her eyes snapped open, and for a moment she fought frantically in Celestine's embrace. Then her eyes focused, and as she looked upon the face of the Saint she too wept, this time in love and gratitude.

A murmur of hushed awe flowed through the crowd of onlookers, for surely they had witnessed a miracle. Dysorian shook his head slowly, at a loss to explain the incredible phenomenon that had just occurred.

Celestine rose, her armour stained with the blood of her resurrected Sister, and turned to Captain Dysorian.

'In three centuries of courageous service, you have never seen anything to prove the literal truth of the Emperor's divinity, have you, Paetrov?' she asked gently.

Dysorian shook his head. 'Some psychic ability?' he asked. 'Medicae tech? None can bring the dead back to life... Not even the primarch had such a power.'

Celestine smiled. 'Tell yourself whatever you wish, Captain Dysorian,' she said. 'But know that the Emperor's light shines upon you, and what is ordained to befall in this place shall do so in his name. Take heart in that.'

'As you say, my lady,' said Dysorian.

'And now, captain,' said Celestine as the Battle Sisters, Imperial Fists and Tsadrekhans gathered around them, 'you are correct. The battle lies before us, and the fate of the beacon hangs in the balance. In the Emperor's name, lead us on, Brother-Captain Dysorian. To battle.'

CHAPTER NINE

Deep beneath the ocean, some miles distant from where the dark waters had almost ended their mission in disaster, the Unsung crouched on a long metal gantry in the gloom of tunnel thirteen.

'This is insane,' said Makhor. 'I've mentioned that, haven't I?'

'Several times, brother,' said D'sakh.

'And yet…' said Makhor.

'You worry too much,' said Haltheus. 'This is by far the fastest and most efficient way of reaching the hive city.'

'Only if we survive it,' said Makhor.

'Haltheus' plan isn't without its risks,' said Kassar. 'But he's right, it's the quickest way at this stage, and we cannot afford to lose any more time. Your concerns are noted, Makhor.'

'Well, that's a relief,' muttered Makhor. 'I don't see why we have a naysmith if no one ever listens to my objections…'

Ignoring Makhor's dark mutterings, Kassar surveyed his warriors, assessing their readiness. The Unsung had a scattering of injuries between them, from Phalk'ir's hidden facial burns and D'sakh's cracked shin to the ugly wound that marred Skarle's chest. Their armour, repainted for this mission, already looked every bit as grimy, dented, blood-spattered and scorched as it had upon their departure from Bloodforge, and several of their camo cloaks had been reduced to tatters. They clutched an assortment of weapons, some their own, some scavenged from the dead, many low on ammunition or suffering damage in their own right.

None of that mattered. They were his Harrow, his Unsung, and they would win through as they always had, without the aid of the Dark Gods. For all their flaws, corruptions and failings, they were the only ones he trusted in the entire galaxy. And that was enough.

'Are we all clear on the plan?' asked Kassar.

'It's hardly complex,' said Haltheus. 'Wait until the train is passing below us, then we jump, grab hold, rally to you, and ride it all the way to our destination.'

'The vehicle is likely to be travelling in excess of one hundred miles per hour,' cautioned Kyphas. 'It will be no easy matter to time our drop correctly, or to land safely atop it.'

'Are we sure that the baggage will survive this?' asked Makhor. He gestured to where Syxx clung to Krowl's backpack. The cultist had been firmly lashed in place with plasteel rappelling lines, and was now doing his best to avoid the biomechanical vents that drizzled hot, wet steam from Krowl's power pack.

'He'll be fine,' said Haltheus dismissively. 'So long as he keeps his limbs tucked in and hangs on, those lines will hold him in place. And you know Krowl would go under the maglev before he let the baggage get injured when he's been ordered not to.'

'Besides,' said Phalk'ir, darkly, 'it survived drowning, and crushing. I'm sure it can survive this, too…'

'Has anyone considered that we might not be the only ones trying this?' asked A'khassor. 'Stealing a ride on the maglev into the city, I mean. We may be about to leap onto a train crawling with Khorne worshippers just as eager to reach the city as us.'

'Or Imperials,' said Makhor. 'If they've kept the trains running while there's an invasion under way, you can believe they've garrisoned them.'

'If we run into resistance,' said Haltheus, 'I have a backup plan. Trust me, brothers.'

'Trust in all of us,' said Kassar. 'In each other.'

Murmurs of appreciation greeted his words, drowned out by a rising wind that moaned along the tunnel. Overhead, strip-lumen pinged and ticked as they burst to life, a bow wave of light and air rushing before the approaching leviathan. The thunder of the train's approach built for longer than Kassar expected. The gantry to which they clung began to quiver, its railing humming with vibration, its mesh decking emitting a tinny rattle.

When it came, it did so with breathtaking suddenness. One moment the tunnel was empty. The next, Kassar had a fleeting impression of the engine hurtling beneath them, furiously alive and spewing smoke and steam. Then the carriages were whipping past just feet below, fast and lethal.

'We'd as well jump into a rock grinder,' breathed Makhor, aghast.

'Now or never,' said Haltheus.

'Then it's now,' said Kassar, and sent his signal, three vox pips in quick succession.

As one, the Unsung jumped. They slid off the gantry with eerie synchronicity, and fell.

Kassar dropped, and the hurtling train hit him like a battering ram. He flipped helplessly over, backwards, tumbling like a leaf in a gale, then managed to clamp one hand around a railing. The metal bent under his sudden weight, but held, and Kassar slammed down onto a walkway with a grunt.

'Kassar, back here,' voxed D'sakh. Kassar glanced back to see the vexillor hunkered down between a pair of heavy fuel bowsers. 'Join me,' said D'sakh. 'Better place to rally the troops than out there in the open.'

'Agreed,' said Kassar. Still clinging firmly to the railing, he lurched back to join his brother.

Thelgh was first to arrive, sliding wordlessly down into cover with his rifle ready. Makhor and Krowl came next, Syxx lolling unconscious but alive on Krowl's back. Their other brothers followed, Haltheus the last of them. Blood clotted a gash in his temple, and more of it spattered his armour.

'It's not all mine,' he said. 'I clipped a pipe, got knocked up into the air and came down two carriages back. Slid head first into the side of a crew compartment. It stopped me from being thrown right off the back of the train, but it did this.' He gestured to his head.

'Were you detected?' asked Kassar. 'Does anyone know we're here?'

'I was, but no, they do not,' said Haltheus while A'khassor inspected his wound. 'My impact brought a handful of cultists out to investigate. None of them survived their curiosity long enough to call for help.'

'Good,' said Kassar. 'But we know the enemy are here, now. Can we determine in what numbers?'

Kyphas was already hunched over his auspex, deftly working its controls.

'I'm reading a lot of power signatures and Khornate helm-vox exchange, all unshrouded,' he said. 'It appears Khordas' followers are here in substantial numbers. No suggestion of weapons discharge though, so we must assume that any Imperial forces originally present have already been neutralised.'

'We know we can't stay out here,' said Makhor. 'The corpse worshippers will have fortified the hub beneath Hive Endurance. If we're exposed like this when the train arrives, there's a good chance we won't all survive. I'd rate the baggage's chances even lower.'

'Moving inside risks triggering a fight we can't win,' said D'sakh. 'One message gets through on the vox, one auspex sweep runs over whichever carriage we're in, and we'll have a train full of enemies coming down upon our heads.'

'That is already a danger, even out here,' said Phalk'ir. 'You all know this. If any of the Khorne worshippers has the wherewithal to be scanning the train for threats, there's nothing we can do to mask our power packs' signatures.'

'How far to the hive?' asked Kassar.

'According to the cogitator information I accessed,' said Haltheus, 'from our drop point, one hour. So approximately forty-five minutes from here.'

'Too long to be trapped on a train full of hostiles,' said Kassar. 'All right, Haltheus, we go to your backup plan.'

'We move back along the train,' said Haltheus. 'All the way to the back, noting and rune-marking alternative routes as we go. Once back there, we ensure weapons fire and a voxed warning or two.'

'You want us to intentionally reveal our presence?' asked Makhor.

'Correct. We get their attention. We've all fought Khorne worshippers before, so we know they'll come running at the chance to claim our skulls.'

'I fail to see how this would be advantageous,' rumbled Phaek'or.

'By the time the enemy reach the rear carriage, we will have split into Formation Scylla to evade them,' said Haltheus. 'In small groups we move around the Khornate charge, and rendezvous here.'

A rune flashed up in Kassar's helm display.

'The carriage behind the engine,' he said.

'We're owed a little good fortune,' said Haltheus. 'If the enemy take the bait the way I expect they will, this carriage and the engine itself will be all but deserted. We storm the engine, take control, then I use my last demolition charges to blow the coupling between us and the rest of the train.'

'And when we reach the hub?' asked Makhor. 'And face the guns of the Imperial defenders alone?'

'We conceal ourselves before we get there,' said Haltheus. 'Let the servitor guidance take us in. The Khornate forces will be in full pursuit on foot, an obvious heretic threat pouring along tunnel thirteen. Our enemies turn their attention to Khordas' warriors, and when they do we cut down through the underside of the engine chassis, and slip away.'

'That will have to be enough,' said Kassar. 'Ready your weapons. Skaryth has point, Thelgh is rear guard. Single file, and stay high to reduce chances of premature contact. Let us begin.'

They moved swiftly along the roof of the speeding train, bracing themselves against the screaming wind using grab rails and pipes. Partway down the third carriage they came across the crew compartment that Haltheus had struck. Behind this carriage was another, and then another. They leapt, landed, swept and cleared, keeping moving at a steady pace. Kassar watched the chron on his retinal display.

Thirty-seven minutes until they reached the hub, if Haltheus' cogitations were correct.

'I think it is safe to assume that the greatest strength of our enemies must be in the front carriages,' said Kassar as they pressed on. 'Khorne worshippers. They will be eager to fight, keen to be at the forefront the moment the enemy is in sight.'

'If there's no enemy to fight back here,' said Makhor, 'we may simply have to discharge weapons and hope that it is enough to attract their attention.'

One more leap, and they were atop the final carriage. A heavy bolter turret surmounting it pointed back down the tunnel, and bunker-like hatches and viewing slits dotted its armoured structure.

'Troop transport,' said Kassar. 'Garrison carriage.'

'Auspex definitely has energy signatures,' said Kyphas. 'Could be a concentration of warriors, but it reads wrong for that. Maybe a stowed tank or two, or part of the train's machinery?'

'Let us find out,' said Kassar. 'Time is pressing.'

Moving up, they kept watch while Skaryth clamped a melta bomb onto the nearest roof hatch. A hissing detonation later, and the Unsung dropped, one by one, through the glowing rent.

Kassar landed in gloom, his auto-senses instantly adjusting. He had a moment to register heat, fiery light, something big moving fast, and then a titanic impact lifted him off his feet and hurled him through the air. Kassar struck a bulkhead wall with a clang, then crashed to the floor. Pain blossomed in his chest. He felt blood running freely from ragged wounds, and his thoughts seemed to have come loose in his head, rattling and jumbling together. Something big, hurtling closer. An impact that had thrown him here...

'Kassar, move!' D'sakh, bellowing at him. Kassar's mind snapped into focus, triggering his instincts. He threw himself sideways just as huge brass claws tore into the wall where he had been slumped.

Kassar rolled to his feet, shunting aside the blizzard of warning runes flashing in his vision. He ripped Hexling from its sheath, then threw himself into another dive as monstrous claws split the air where his head had been.

'Daemon engine!' shouted Haltheus.

Kassar had a fleeting impression of a large space, a shattered holo-lith table, gantries and ladders torn down and mangled, equipment racks smashed to wreckage. Huge claw gouges marred the floor and walls, and the bloodied remnants of servitors and cultists sprawled like rag dolls. Then it was coming at him again, a roaring mass of animate metal and flame. It was tank-sized, a nightmarish amalgam of hunting cat, feral hound and enraged bull, eyes glowing, fangs gnashing, thick steel tendrils lashing around it.

Desperately, Kassar threw himself backwards as the daemon engine pounced, then rolled aside as its spike-tipped tendrils stabbed into the decking where he had landed.

'Kill it!' he roared.

The Maulerfiend reared up on its hind legs, tore at the air with its claws, then lunged straight for Krowl. Protecting Syxx, Krowl had backed into a corner. With nowhere to go, he met the Maulerfiend head on with a thunderous uppercut from his power fist. The beast managed to rake its claws across his chest, spraying brackish gore, but in return his punch smashed its head upwards and it staggered back.

Darting in from the side, D'sakh slashed his blades through the metal tendons of one of the Maulerfiend's back legs. Lubricant sprayed and the daemon engine roared again. Its tendrils lashed out like whips, cracking across D'sakh's faceplate and chest. He was thrown from his feet, fetching up amidst a heap of bloody corpses.

'Keep at it,' shouted Kassar. 'Keep it off balance.'

The Unsung lunged in and darted back, like hunters baiting some ursine monster. Yet the Maulerfiend struck blows as well. A mighty claw-swipe caught Phaek'or under the chin, ripping his helm off and hurling him into a pile of wreckage in a shower of blood.

'Kassar,' shouted Kyphas. 'We need to finish this. Auspex has massive movement flowing down the train, carriage to carriage. The enemy has taken our bait.'

Kassar spared a split-second glance at his chron. Less than thirty minutes to the hub.

The momentary distraction was all that the beast needed. Knocking

Makhor and Phalk'ir from their feet, it hurled itself at Kassar. Its claws swung down, then stopped, inches from Kassar's helm.

'Move,' shouted a pained voice, thin with strain. Kassar glanced to his left and saw Syxx, leaning from Krowl's back, one hand outstretched.

'I can't hold it,' shrieked the cultist, and Kassar flung himself aside. The Maulerfiend's claws finished their swing, sinking deep into the carriage wall. Snatching up Hexling, Kassar angrily pushed down the blade's hissed mental challenge, and raised it high. He swung his sword down double-handed, and scythed its blade through the Maulerfiend's neck. Metal shrieked. Hellish energies crackled, and the blazing fire in the monster's eyes went out as its ironclad skull crashed to the deck. Kassar staggered back as the thing slumped, now no more than a heap of debris.

'First cypher,' panted Kassar. '*A'khassor, get down here, now. See to the wounded, get everyone up and ready to move. We don't have time for recuperation.*' As the Apothecary dropped down with a clang, Kassar jogged to D'sakh's side and rolled the vexillor over. D'sakh pushed Kassar's hands away and sat up, shaking his head.

'*Can you move?*' asked Kassar.

'*Of course,*' said D'sakh, staggering to his feet and shaking his head again. '*I'm fine.*'

'*Good,*' said Kassar, before turning to Skaryth. '*I need at least four egress routes from this carriage, now. The enemy are almost upon us, and we need to slip around them like ghosts. Otherwise, we'll be trapped in here and slaughtered.*'

Skaryth nodded and moved off. Kassar turned to Syxx.

'You, cultist, stay where you are. Krowl will continue to carry you, so that you don't slow us down.'

Syxx nodded weakly, swiping away the blood trickling from his nose.

'*Kassar!*' said Makhor, gripping his arm. '*Are we not going to speak of what just happened? The baggage… that was psyker manifestation! He has powers!*'

'I know,' said Kassar. 'And yes, our guest here is going to tell us everything about himself that we don't already know, or I shall give him to Kyphas, and damn the mission. But not now.'

'I... lord, I don't know how I did that,' said Syxx. 'I swear to you, I have some slight ability, it's why Phelkorian picked me, but so minor a talent that–'

'I said not now,' said Kassar. 'There's no time. The enemy are upon us. But understand this, cultist. If you use those powers again before we have had our conversation, I'll kill you myself.'

'*Everyone's on their feet, Kassar,*' said A'khassor. '*More injuries, and that's the last vials of stimms gone. If anyone goes down from now on, they stay down until their body heals.*'

'*Egress routes assigned,*' reported Skaryth, and fresh runes lit in Kassar's retinal display, plotting his projected path along the train.

'*How close?*' asked Kassar. Timing would be everything with this manoeuvre. Kyphas was watching his auspex intently. '*Front runners just reached the next carriage along,*' he said. '*It's time. We... stop, wait.*'

'*What?*' asked Kassar, eyeing the time. '*Kyphas, what is it?*'

The former spymaster struggled for a moment, as though he couldn't force the words out. When he finally spoke, his voice strained with effort.

'*He should be at the hive, not here.*'

'Kyphas!' barked Kassar. '*Who? What are you saying?*'

'*The Betrayer,*' said Kyphas. '*Khârn is here. He's leading the charge. Kassar, he's almost upon us!*'

CHAPTER TEN

'We should meet him head on,' said Phalk'ir. 'All of us, the champions of Bloodforge, ambush Khârn the Betrayer and finally lay him low.'

'And earn the rewards of the gods,' said D'sakh angrily. 'That's what you really want, isn't it, Phalk'ir? To force us into this fight in the hopes you'll finally get your divine reward?'

'We would win such incredible boons!' hissed Phalk'ir, squaring up to D'sakh, helms almost touching. 'Are you so dull and blind that you cannot see that?'

'We cannot and will not fight the Betrayer,' said Kassar. 'Especially not with an army at his back. Formation Scylla. And leave a spread of long-fuse krak grenades in our wake – we might not be able to defeat the Betrayer, but let's see if we can't slow him down the Alpha Legion way.'

Kassar unclamped two krak grenades from his belt and thumbed their primers, allowing the detonation count to spiral upwards before letting them go to clatter across the floor. According to the runes that Skaryth had exloaded, Kassar's egress was a nearby side hatch. He slid through into the service corridor beyond, a low-ceilinged space filled with the roar of the maglev and the flicker of tunnel-lumen whipping by. Makhor followed him, also assigned to this route.

As Kassar jogged along the corridor he watched the runes on his auto-senses disperse, his Harrow splitting up while Khârn and his warriors surged closer. Skaryth went with Krowl and Syxx, Phaek'or with Haltheus, Thelgh and A'khassor with Phalk'ir, D'sakh with Skarle and Kyphas.

'We'll make it, Kassar,' said Makhor. 'It's a solid plan, if a risky one. Skaryth and Krowl have the safest route.'

'I know,' said Kassar. 'It's us I'm worried for. This route is slow, we'll be close for time.'

Makhor laughed mirthlessly.

'Better this than stay and meet the blood worshippers.'

The two Unsung had now reached the end of the corridor. The Khornate forces could be heard getting closer, axes revving, boots pounding the decking. Kassar and Makhor took hold of the floor hatch at the corridor's end and, muscles straining, wrenched it open. The hatch swung wide, Makhor catching it before it could slam against the deck. Below, a dark, echoing pipeline could be seen stretching away along the underside of the train.

Kassar dropped down through the hatch. As he did so, a series of blasts shook the carriage, causing the pipe to creak and shudder alarmingly. Travelling at such speeds, with the mag-repulsor field of the train pounding the ground below, if their weight proved too much and tore the pipe loose it could prove fatal.

'Hurry, Kassar,' urged Makhor, lowering himself in behind Kassar, then pulling the hatch shut with a clang. 'They're in the carriage.'

'Then let us waste no time,' said Kassar, beginning to crawl, arm over arm, into the darkness.

'At least it isn't swimming,' said Makhor. 'And if it gets us clear then I may revise my decision to kill Skaryth when I next see him. Freedom had better be worth all this.'

'It's the only thing that is,' said Kassar.

* * *

Kassar's chron read eleven minutes to the hub when he and Makhor cut their way out of the empty fuel bowser. Slipping from concealment, they narrowly avoided a band of Khorne Berzerkers who pounded past on a lower walkway, bellowing war cries.

Following their runes, Kassar and Makhor clambered out through a webwork of pipes and onto an outer gantry that ran along the side of several carriages in a row. Free of entanglement they ran, heads down into the howling wind, conscious of the seconds ticking away. As they crossed a transit bridge, they heard shouts below them.

Glancing down, Kassar saw a mob of cultists pointing frantically in their direction, waving blades. Bullets started to whine around him, ricocheting off the gantry.

'No time for subtlety now,' said Makhor. 'We just have to stay ahead of them.'

'Agreed,' said Kassar, legs and arms pumping as he sprinted along the gantry. Ahead, a ladder led up to the higher walkways. He clambered up it several rungs at a time, Makhor on his heels.

'Unsung,' he voxed. 'We're detected. Coming to you at speed, enemies close behind. Report.'

'In position,' said Skaryth. 'Haltheus was right, the foremost carriage was mostly empty. Nothing living in here now but us.'

'We're with them,' said A'khassor.

'At the couplings and setting up,' said Haltheus. 'Phaek'or's standing guard. There's a lot of machinery here, Kassar. I'll do what I can, but I can't promise a neat separation.'

'Any sort of separation is acceptable at this point,' said Kassar, vaulting a tangle of pipes and charging along a walkway. The shouts of cultists and the vox-amplified roars of Berzerkers could be heard close behind.

'We're almost at the rendezvous,' voxed D'sakh. 'Do you need us to turn back and provide support, Kassar?'

'Negative, stick to the plan,' said Kassar. 'We'll make it.'

Kassar kicked through a doorway into a crew compartment, and crashed straight into a Berzerker coming the other way. The Khorne worshipper bellowed a battle cry, that turned into a bloody gurgle as Hexling slid point-first through his throat. Sheathing his knife, Makhor snatched up the warrior's fallen chainaxe and revved it experimentally.

'Cumbersome,' he said. 'But more use than a knife against power armour.'

They ran on, bursting from the crew compartment onto another walkway, then another ladder, another tangle of pipes. From behind them came an echoing roar, as of some rampaging daemon on the warpath. Kassar looked back, and his blood ran cold as he saw the distant but unmistakable figure of Khârn pursuing them. The Betrayer reached the end of a carriage and leapt, straight through the screaming headwind and onto the one beyond. He kept running, closing the gap by the moment.

Kassar kept running.

At last they burst through a hatch and saw Haltheus and Phaek'or waiting for them at the rear of the next carriage. A single transit bridge remained to cross the gap. Any others had been reduced to smouldering stumps. Kassar and Makhor dashed across the bridge, over the yawning gulf and the crackling lightnings of the grav tethers. As they did, Phaek'or's heavy bolter thumped to life, spitting shells back the way they had come. Cultists burst in bloody sprays as fist-sized shells blew them apart. The rest dived back into the cover of the carriage.

'Sever that last walkway, will you?' asked Haltheus, hunched over the explosives that he was rigging to the grav tethers. Kassar swung Hexling and, in a single powerful blow, scythed through the end of the transit bridge. It sagged under its own weight, clipped the energies of the grav tethers, and was ripped away and pummelled beneath the train.

'That will slow them down,' said Haltheus.

'Not all of them,' said Kassar. 'The Betrayer was not far behind us. Work quickly.'

'I'm doing what I can,' said Haltheus. 'I'm not a Techmarine, Kassar.'

'But you are an expert in blowing things up, and you're the only hope we have,' said Kassar. 'So get it done.'

Leaving Phaek'or and Makhor to cover Haltheus, Kassar ducked through another hatch into the last carriage. As at the rear of the train, this was a garrison car, though thankfully this one had not been used to house a daemonic monstrosity. Kassar's brothers waited at its far end, guns pointed at the bulkhead door that led through to the engine. He noted that Thelgh's armour had a ragged new rent on one side of the torso, clotted blood still drying around it. Otherwise the Harrow looked intact.

'D'sakh, A'khassor, get back there and help Phaek'or and Makhor cover Haltheus. Keep the enemy off him until the bomb is ready.'

Vox pips answered, the two warriors checking their weapons and hastening away. Kassar felt the maglev shift beneath him, its floor angling slowly upwards. They were climbing the slope of the ocean floor, approaching the submerged foot of Hive Endurance.

Not long now.

'The rest of you on me,' he said. *'Krowl, the door.'*

Krowl swung a thunderous punch into the engine bulkhead, denting the doors. Lubricant sprayed. Sparks drizzled. Krowl rumbled deep in his chest and swung again, smashing the doors inwards with a loud crash.

Kassar swept past him, bolter up, the Unsung on his heels.

He advanced between thundering pistons and roaring boilers, crackling electrodes and chuntering parchment-feeds. Running up a ramp onto the control deck, he was caught amidst a sudden hail of autogun fire. Snarling, Kassar weathered the storm and launched himself into the knot of cultists who had been left to guard the engine. His sword swung in slicing arcs. His warriors piled into the fight alongside him, using blades and fists to avoid damaging anything crucial. Blood splattered the servitor train crew, wired obliviously into their podiums and working their controls.

In seconds, the cultists were dead and the control deck was theirs. The chron read three minutes and nine seconds.

'Haltheus,' barked Kassar. *'We have the engine. Tell me you're ready.'*

'Almost,' said Haltheus through gritted teeth. *'I just need to–'*

'Khârn!' yelled D'sakh. *'Atop that carriage! Phaek'or!'*

Over the vox, a heavy bolter roared.

'*Haltheus, if Khârn gets onto this carriage we're all dead,*' shouted Kyphas. '*Just blow it now!*'

'*Detonating,*' said Haltheus.

For several, torturous seconds they heard nothing. Around them, the engine's thunder changed pitch as its crew began their breaking rituals.

'*Detonation fail,*' voxed Haltheus angrily. '*I didn't have time... To the warp with it, it's failed. Kassar, we're still attached.*'

'*He's jumping the gap!*' shouted D'sakh. '*Kassar, Khârn just leapt right over us. He's on the carriage roof.*'

'*We need to get back to them,*' urged Phalk'ir. '*They can't face that monster alone.*'

'*We're still attached, and we're two and a half minutes out,*' said Kyphas. '*If we don't do something to break free, we're all dead. We'll be caught between the defenders and the Khorne worshippers.*'

They heard a throaty sawing sound, furious and ominous, echoing from beyond the ruptured bulkhead.

'*He's cutting his way into the carriage,*' said Skaryth. '*He's between us and the others.*'

Kassar's mind spun furiously. Khârn was mere moments from cornering them in the engine. For a moment he was tempted to believe his more superstitious brothers, that the Dark Gods were punishing them for refusing to kneel. The plan was in tatters, and Kassar was running out of time to formulate a new one. His eyes roved the engine intently, absorbing every iota of detail, looking for an edge, a trick to get them out alive.

'*Berzerkers,*' barked Phaek'or over the thump of his heavy bolter. '*They're trying to jump the – A'khassor, there. He's used the end of the transit bridge.*'

'*I see him,*' said A'khassor, and a bolter roared.

'*Another one above,*' called Makhor, no cypher. '*And another. Come on, you mindless fanatics.*' Behind his words came the throaty rev of a chainaxe.

From the garrison car came a loud clang, followed by the heavy impact of boots meeting decking.

'**Blood for the Blood God!**' roared Khârn. '**Your skulls belong to Khorne!**' Syxx quailed at the monstrous voice, and even the Unsung recoiled instinctively.

In that instant, Kassar finally spotted their edge. It was desperate, costly, but it was all they had.

'*Cover the bulkhead,*' he barked, his warriors immediately obeying. '*Drive him back if he comes through. Haltheus, can you reach us?*'

'*They're jumping across the broken bridges,*' said Haltheus, his voice punctuated by grunts of exertion as he fought. '*They're all over us, Kassar. And Khârn is between us and you. No, we can't reach you.*'

'*Acknowledged,*' voxed Kassar, voice cold and steady as he directed his channel to Haltheus, D'sakh, Makhor, Phaek'or and A'khassor. '*I'm sorry for this, brothers. If you survive, make for rendezvous point beta. We'll wait if we can.*'

D'sakh paused for a split second before responding.

'*Understood. Good fortune, Kassar.*'

'*We make our own fortune, brother,*' Kassar replied. '*For the primarchs and the Harrow. We'll see you at point beta.*'

The roar of gunfire filled the control deck as the Betrayer charged. Bolts, sniper rounds and krak grenades hammered him in a storm, driving him back but doing little to injure him.

Kassar spun, raised his bolter, and blew out the skulls of the crew servitors in quick succession. He lacked Haltheus' knowledge of mechanisms, but the controls of the maglev were insultingly simple. Identifying the heavy brass levers that governed the engine's speed, he ripped away dead servitor hands and thrust the levers forward as far as they would go. Numerals spiralled upwards and warning chimes sounded. Around them, the engine's generators roared like enraged daemons.

The deck lurched beneath Kassar's feet, staggering him as the train, which had been slowing for arrival, put on a sudden surge of speed.

'Kassar,' shouted Phalk'ir. 'What are you doing? We can't hold him back.'

'He's going to crash the train into the hub!' said Kyphas. 'It'll hit like a missile.'

Khârn was coming at them again, shrugging off direct hits, his flesh bloody and his armour scorched. His plasma pistol spat incandescent bolts, and Kyphas threw himself sideways to avoid them. A shot blew out a section of the train's armourglass windscreen, and a shard-filled gale screamed around them.

'Up!' shouted Kassar. 'Up to the top deck. Look at the signs, there's a saviour chamber up there!'

Firing off a last volley, the rest of the Harrow made for the upper deck, leaving Kassar at the head of the ramp. Phalk'ir stayed by him, the two of them firing their bolters at Khârn.

'What about the others?' said Phal'kir. 'You can't just leave them to die.'

'They know the crash is coming. They have the rendezvous coordinates. Phalk'ir, *move!*'

Khârn came at them with a furious roar. The Unsung had battered him with their firepower, but had achieved little more than to enrage him.

The Betrayer swung Gorechild in a mighty arc, and Kassar threw himself backwards. Phalk'ir was slower, diving aside at the last moment. Khârn's axe hewed through his shoulder guard in a spray of blood, and hacked one of the exchanger vents from his backpack.

Kassar hit the decking and kicked out, trying to swipe Khârn's legs from beneath him. He might as well have kicked a Dreadnought. Pain exploded up his leg as it met the Betrayer's armoured shin. Khârn ignored him, following Phalk'ir, swinging Gorechild up for a killing blow.

Warning lumen flashed red and emergency klaxons howled as the maglev crested the rise in the tunnel and hurtled towards the hub. It gave a titanic lurch, almost slewing off its rail, and Khârn staggered.

Seizing his chance, Phalk'ir scrambled to his feet and fled, dashing up the ramp towards the upper deck. At the same time, Kassar launched himself back to his feet and drove his blade at Khârn's back with all his might.

The Betrayer spun on his heel, faster than thought, parrying the blow with his vambrace. Hexling's point scythed through Khârn's side in a shower of gore then tore free again, leaving a smouldering gash below his ribs.

'Kassar,' shouted Skaryth from above. 'Twenty seconds! Hurry!'

'Just seal the chamber,' yelled Kassar, backpedalling furiously as Gorechild swung at him. Churning teeth cut the air an inch before his faceplate. 'Save the cultist. Get that ship and make this worth it!'

Gorechild came at him again, a buzzing terror that promised instant death. He threw himself aside, the axe chewing into a console in an explosion of sparks.

From above came the sound of the saviour chamber's bulkhead slamming shut.

Kassar blocked another swing from Khârn's axe, Hexling shrieking with pain in his mind. Khârn swung again, again, again. The blows came at a blistering pace, jarring the muscles in his arms. Kassar couldn't think about offence, couldn't consider finding somewhere to survive the crash, couldn't even worry about the sickening view through the broken windscreen as the end of the rail raced up to meet them.

He caught a fleeting impression of dashing figures, strobing lights, gunfire flaying the engine with desperate intensity, but Gorechild was all he could think about.

Shots struck the engine, blowing out its remaining armourglass, tearing through its hull and ripping open generators. Flames billowed around them. Still Khârn pressed his attack, hideously single-minded.

'**Your skull will make a worthy offering,**' he snarled.

Kassar cried out in agony as Gorechild swept around again and carved through his chest in a shocking explosion of blood. Even as he staggered backwards, the axe reversed its swing and scythed through his arm at the elbow. Mortis clanged to the deck, still clutched in Kassar's hand.

Kassar crashed down on his back, blood gushing from the killing wound in his chest, the severed stump of his arm. Weakly, he tried to raise Hexling, but the blade weighed a hundred pounds. It wavered above his chest, then clanged down on him, useless.

'**Now you die for the glory of Khorne!**' bellowed Khârn.

Behind him, the pandemonium of the hub raced up to meet them.

'You… first,' coughed Kassar, then the train slammed into the Hive Endurance rail hub at one hundred and fifty miles per hour, and fire swallowed Kassar's world.

Her blade sang through the air, holy light dancing in its wake. It cut through tainted armour and poisoned flesh. It tore the rotted soul from her enemy, and cast it into the warp. There would be no reward for these sinners beyond the veil. Only damnation, and the dismal wages their treachery had earned them.

Another one came at her, roaring with fury. Serene, she disarmed him with a flick of her wrist, then spun and struck off his head. With a thought, the Saint triggered her ornate jump pack and soared aloft, alighting upon a jutting gargoyle.

She surveyed the battle, and found it good.

They fought at the mouth of the Triumphus Processional, quarter of a mile back from the breach torn by the traitor spacecraft. Red-armoured heretics and clattering daemon engines hurled themselves against several breaches in the barricades, but the weight of Imperial fire was holding them at bay.

She, Captain Dysorian and a Tsadrekhan militia colonel named Hespus were coordinating the ongoing defence, and they were meeting with success. The tolling bell of battle had swung away from the Emperor's servants, yet now it was swinging back with every Chaos worshipper that fell.

The Saint knew fighting raged on other levels, above and below this one, and that the renegades were forcing their way deeper into the city. She knew, also, that their efforts would not suffice. They would cause suffering, misery and death in great measure. They would send many a martyr to sit at the Emperor's table.

But even with their butcher lord leading them, their attack would fail.

Celestine knew this as surely as though she had seen it happen already. She knew it because she had faith in the revelations that the Emperor sent to her. They had never proved untrue.

Below, Captain Dysorian led a courageous charge against a Khornate daemon engine trampling its way over the barricade. The Imperial Fist charged through fleeing Tsadrekhans, a small band of his brothers at his side. As one, they hurled krak grenades into the abomination's workings, driving it back in a flurry of blasts. A missile streaked in and struck it in the chest, finishing the daemon engine off. Its legs crumpled beneath it and it slumped over the barricade like some grotesque, dying spider.

Such were the works of heretics, reflected Celestine. Fearsome, repugnant, but ultimately flawed.

The captain, though. There was a true hero of the Imperium. Like so many of the Adeptus Astartes, he did not believe in the Emperor's divinity, but that was of no matter to Celestine. Dysorian believed in the Imperium. He would fight and die for it no matter the odds, and that was all that she required of him. A time of sore testing loomed for the veteran captain, and Celestine pitied him the triumphs and tragedies he would soon know. But such was Dysorian's place in the Emperor's plan, and he was privileged to fulfil it with blade in hand, master of his own will.

Few were afforded such an opportunity in these dark times, she thought sorrowfully.

Always, now, Saint Celestine perceived the hideous rents that yawned across the galaxy. She sensed the massing of vast armies, the swelling of traitor warbands into conquering hordes like the one they faced in this place. She felt the tainted winds of Chaos as they spilled from the mouth of the warp to pollute the Emperor's realm.

Ever since she had journeyed at the primarch's side she had seen a dark fate approaching, borne towards her on those same tainted zephyrs. It drew close now. She felt it looming.

Yet she had work still, on this world, and she would not allow the darkness to take her before her duty was done.

The revelations that Celestine received were not visions like those experienced by astropaths or seers, not clearly perceived paths to be walked into the future. Her road was an invisible bridge, spanning an endless gulf, lit by candles that only shivered to life at her passing. The Saint had to trust to her faith in the Emperor that, with each footfall, the bridge would be there. She proved her devotion to Him every day by continuing that walk of faith.

Celestine prepared to launch herself from her vantage point and rejoin the fight. Her Seraphim Sisters were hard-pressed below, and needed her aid.

Something stopped her, a presentiment of sudden knowledge. Foreboding rose within her mind as a new revelation came to her. The next steps of her path were illuminated, and they shook her to the core.

Though she was too far away to feel its shockwaves, Celestine knew that a ferocious string of explosions was ripping through the Underbilge maglev hub. She knew that a train had emerged from tunnel thirteen travelling at breakneck pace, that it had smashed into the grav-baffles at the end of its line and blown them out like a battering ram shattering a castle gate. She knew, as certainly as she knew her own name, that the blazing juggernaut had flipped and tumbled through the defences of the hub, fuel tanks and generators exploding, hurtling wreckage killing hundreds of good, loyal soldiers.

She knew, also, as it skidded to a halt, as its wreckage settled and the fires spread, that the train had brought agents of fate to this city. Murderers? Despoilers? Or saviours? Or simply lost souls whose actions bore greater weight than they could know? To such insight, Celestine was not yet party.

But she knew, now, what must happen next, and the weight of it settled upon her shoulders as so many terrible burdens had before.

Stepping from her perch, Celestine dropped into the melee. She scythed through the heretics attacking her Seraphim Sisters, her expression grim. Every blow was swift, economical, flowing into the next, and the next. In moments, the Saint had reduced her immediate enemies to bloodied corpses, while her Geminae Superia kept firing.

With a gesture, Celestine called them to her. She would need their aid in the hours to come. Dysorian and Colonel Hespus would have to continue this fight without her, for as long as they could. Canoness Levinia would have to spare more of her precious Sisters for a foray into the depths, for there, too, the enemy must be held back for as long as possible. Opening a channel in the ornate gorget-vox of her armour, Celestine began issuing her commands, even as she led her Sisters upwards, back towards the convent prioris. Back towards the Tsadrekhan beacon.

She did so with a heavy heart for, in the moment of the train's impact with the hub far below, this battle had changed. It was no longer a question of whether Hive Endurance would fall, but when.

She knew it, as surely as all her other revelations. Sometimes, Celestine thought sadly, she would give almost anything to simply not know.

PART III

CHAPTER ELEVEN

Let me help you…

No…

You die…

Yes…

You need not…

I did this for them…

A sacrifice…

Yes…

Do you know what I am… Who I am…

I do…

You have wielded me for many years, and resisted me for all that time…

We do not kneel, to gods or to daemons…

You are strong…

My brothers are strong…

But without you, they will falter…

No…

They will fail…

No...
They will die...
No!
Let me show you...

You lie...
You know that I do not...
You know that I can help you...
You know that I can save you...
And your price...?
There is no time...
Tell me!
Yes... or no... Let me in, or let them perish...
For them, then...
For them...you must say it...
Yes!

Kassar opened his eyes to smoke, flame and twisted metal. He was gripping Hexling firmly, its blade laid flat across his chest and giving off a weird, tingling heat. Mortis was clutched in his other hand. A quick check of his armour's systems revealed that it was in good condition. No major damage sustained.

Somehow.

'Alive,' he breathed, incredulous.

Metal groaned nearby. Something heavy fell, causing sparks to billow. Accepting, for the moment, his mysterious survival, Kassar took stock of his surroundings.

He was still in the engine of the maglev train, or what was left of it. The wreckage around him was barely recognisable. Decking was torn and buckled into strange shapes. Consoles were ruptured, nests of cables spilling from them like intestines. Boilers and generators were little more than ruined shells. The entire engine was laid on its side, and Kassar was buried in loose detritus. Everything was lit by dancing flame, whose roar and crackle oppressed all other sound. Smoke coiled thick and oily through the crumpled control deck.

truly will be l
teachings of the
and give none t
what strength of
'I will begin
said Kyphas. 'I
'Good,' said k
Kyphas take po
before we burn

Skaryth led th
his heels. Fire
glass crunchec
helm, feeling i
had to keep i
brothers, to n
tempers runni
Skaryth had
sively, but betv
to retain contr
showed disres
free. Privately,
alive within th
that had retur
Under his ar
and Skaryth re
his armour an
not the time c
'Anything yet
Ahead, the
black smoke
advanced care
Knight's shin
'The garrison
there now. And

'Khârn!' gasped Kassar, leaping to his feet and sending wreckage bouncing and clattering. He brandished Hexling and sought his enemy, but of the Betrayer there was no sign. A sensation struck him, then, a phantom agony in his chest and the fleeting vision of his own severed arm striking the floor. He stumbled, shook his head, brushed it off.

'Later,' he promised himself. 'We will get to the bottom of this later.' For now, he had more pressing concerns.

'Unsung,' he voxed. 'A'khassor, Haltheus, D'sakh… Anyone?'

'Kassar,' came a shout.

'Skaryth?' called Kassar. 'Is that you, brother?'

'Kassar, thank the primarchs that you live!' came Skaryth's voice through the smoke.

Following his armour's localised auspex, Kassar picked his way through the roiling smoke. He clambered over tumbled heaps of wreckage, nerves alive for any hint of foes. Even if Khârn was nowhere to be seen, some of his followers would surely have survived the crash. And then there were the Imperial defenders to consider.

Kassar hauled himself up over a twisted railing and reached the saviour chamber. The kinetic damper cradle around the armoured box had crumpled during the crash, and the chamber listed drunkenly on its side. Its door was buckled in its frame, a little crimson light spilling through the gaps.

Kassar tried to haul it open. Just then, the digits of Krowl's power fist drove through a gap and got a firm grip, crumpling metal like cloth. Kassar stood back as Krowl tore the door away from inside.

Krowl ducked through the hatch. Syxx followed him, staggering drunkenly, one hand pressed to a bloody gash on his temple. The cultist's mask was broken, and Kassar felt a moment's surprise at how young Syxx looked, but it was swallowed by relief that he still lived.

The others followed, emerging from the chamber one by one. Skaryth, Thelgh, Kyphas, Skarle and finally, Phalk'ir.

'Unsung,' said Kassar. 'I am glad that you live.'

'What of the others?' asked Skaryth.

'Nothing on the vox,' said Kassar. 'Not yet, anyway.'

'They ma
immediatel'
'Or they n
like he has
'Phalk'ir–'
'I don't wa
be sacrificed
Phalk'ir. 'Bu
we even thir
us into. Anc
'You ungr:
sar's quick tl
'Yet he dic
perate pass i
'It wasn't
they were fu
and jabbing
withheld the
engagement
tempted to v
'Prod me v
will sever it
'Restrain y
ing, and if o
He turned
'You are er
I will serve ɑ
you that has
A'khassor wɑ
Haltheus wa
maintain ou
rifice such as
'Regardless
'You will tr
ing this incre

'Advance with caution,' said Kassar. 'We'll sweep for our brothers and scout out the lie of the land, but beware enemies. If it isn't already, this area will surely be crawling with Imperials soon.'

'Not to mention that Khârn is still out there somewhere,' muttered Skaryth to himself. 'No maglev crash is putting an end to the Betrayer…'

With hand gestures, he indicated for Kyphas to flank right while he went left. Kyphas pipped acknowledgement, and the two Alpha Legionnaires stalked out through the smoke with their bolters raised.

'I don't know what this place looked like before the crash,' voxed Skaryth. 'But it's a real mess now, Kassar. Chunks of train wreckage, burning debris, toppled columns, wrecked barricades… I can't even work out where we are, and the smoke's too dense to see far even with auto-senses.'

'We're at the bulkhead now,' replied Kassar. 'Can you locate a cogitator station, something we could access to exload maps of this area?'

'I'll do what I can,' said Skaryth, doubtfully. 'Meantime, I'll see if I can locate a higher vantage.'

'Kyphas,' said Kassar. 'Any response from our brothers? Any indication of their whereabouts?'

'Nothing,' said Kyphas. 'But Kassar, it looks as though the train broke up and scattered through the hub. The speed we were travelling, and the weight of the carriages… I don't know how big this place is, but they could have been carried a long way from us.'

'Not to mention they may well not all be together, even if they have survived somehow,' said Skaryth as he clambered up the underside of the engine, and onto its raised flank. 'If we want to try to find their bodies, though, we may be looking for a while.'

Smoke drifted in thick banks, but from atop the wreck Skaryth had a better view of the hub. It looked apocalyptic.

The space itself was huge and open, a curving metal undersea cavern a hundred feet high that arced away around the feet of the hive. It surrounded an armoured central pillar like a metallic mountainside, into which countless doorways, tunnels and hatches led, and from which walkways and gantries extended like the strands of a spider's web.

Skaryth could see the mouth of tunnel thirteen, yawning in the wall hundreds of yards away through the smoke with its designator numerals stencilled in stark black above it. Other numbered tunnel mouths were visible, marching away into dim distance around the curvature of the hub. Closer, the maglev lines terminated in grav-baffles and transit platforms, which in turn were flanked by masses of concourse buildings whose purposes Skaryth could only guess at. Administratum, warehouses, shrines, commercia, guard posts and the like, no doubt.

All of it appeared to have been heavily fortified to resist assault from the tunnels, but it hadn't proved nearly enough to stop a speeding maglev. All that remained of tunnel thirteen's defences was wreckage and blazing ruin, ammunition crates crackling and popping as they cooked off amidst the flames. Corpses lay everywhere, crushed, incinerated or simply burst by the explosive shockwaves of the carriages' detonations. He saw a handful of larger, yellow-armoured corpses scattered amongst the fallen Tsadrekhans, and felt a sting of spiteful satisfaction.

More bodies were scattered further out, sprawled bloodily on gantries, platforms and stairways. Many were headless.

Checking that his brothers weren't watching, Skaryth unclasped his helm and removed it, allowing all the scents and sounds of the ruined hub to wash over him. There, he thought, distantly echoing down passageways from afar. Gunfire. Revving chain weapons. War cries. Skaryth replaced his helm, and reopened his vox-channel.

'I would wager my bolter that Khârn survived the crash, and that many of his Berzerkers did the same,' said Skaryth. 'There's plentiful evidence of them ripping through the Imperial defences in the aftermath. My guess is they've driven deeper, pushed up into the surrounding zones.'

'That would explain why we've not been swamped by foes,' said Kassar. 'Any sign of our brothers from up there?'

'None,' said Skaryth. 'But that doesn't mean anything amidst all this.'

'We should spread out and search,' said Phalk'ir. 'If the corpse worshippers are busy fighting the blood-mongrels then that leaves us free to find our brothers.'

'Agreed,' said Kassar. 'But Phalk'ir, I'm allowing us ten minutes, no longer.'

'*Ten minutes?*' snarled Phalk'ir. '*Why not just dismiss them as dead now?*'

'*Any longer and we risk giving Khârn an unassailable lead. That's if Khordas' forces haven't already broken into the hive somehow and stolen the prize. We need to gather intel, learn the shape of the battle and the quickest route to our goal. Besides which, for all we know our brothers may be waiting at rally point beta even now.*'

'*Vox range amidst all this interference is extremely poor,*' said Kyphas. '*A few hundred yards at best. Lots of angry data spirits loose in the air. If they have progressed to beta then we would not be able to contact them, or vice versa.*'

'*Very well,*' said Phalk'ir, stalking out beneath Skaryth's perch with his blade drawn. '*Then let us stop wasting time and search…*'

They spread out, combing through the devastation with their weapons drawn. Kassar rooted through heaps of rubble, kicking over smouldering slabs of metal and hefting aside the heat-fused remains of luckless Tsadrekhan troopers. He scanned the ground for any hint of shimmering green-blue armour, tatters of camo cloak or strewn wargear that belonged to his missing brothers.

All the time he watched his helm chron, and kept his eyes on the gantries above, the firelit approaches to the concourse and the plethora of entrances to the hive pillar. Danger could emerge from anywhere, at any time, and with his few remaining warriors so spread out, the Harrow would be hard-pressed to defend themselves.

As he searched, Kassar also wrestled with the fact of his own survival. His thoughts felt fractured, his memories somehow incomplete. Again he saw an axe ripping across his chest, a killing blow tearing him open. Yet it was a faded image, the phantom pain nothing but an echo that grew dimmer the harder he tried to recall it. Had such a thing happened at all? Or had he suffered a strange premonition, a death omen that had not come to pass? If the opening of the Great Rift had tainted reality as fundamentally as he had been led to believe, Kassar supposed that such a thing was possible.

His ruminations were cut short by a shout from Kyphas.

'Is it them?' asked Kassar as he hurried towards Kyphas' position. 'Vox contact?'

'No,' said Kyphas. 'I've found... Kassar, it's an arm.'

Kassar felt a moment of dislocation and horror, flexing his bolter hand as though to check it was still there. He shook his head, frowning in confusion at the sensation, then hurried to join his brothers.

Kassar found Phalk'ir, Skarle and Kyphas already there when he arrived, stood in the shadow of a partly demolished shrine. Phalk'ir was holding a severed arm up by the wrist. An arm clad in Alpha Legion plate.

'This is all that's left of him,' said Phalk'ir, turning and thrusting the severed limb at Kassar. 'See it? This is what you left of him.'

'You can't know that that is Phaek'or's limb, Phalk'ir,' said Kassar. 'It could have belonged to any of them.'

'That hardly makes this better,' said Kyphas, earning himself a glare.

'I know that, Kyphas,' he said. 'Whatever this betides is grievous news, but we don't know which of our brothers has suffered this hurt, or whether they lived or died.'

'It's Phaek'or's,' said Phalk'ir angrily. 'You think I don't know my own flesh and blood?' The swordsman still held his blade in one hand, and now he brandished it angrily.

Skaryth, Thelgh and Krowl had arrived while they spoke. Syxx looked on uneasily from Krowl's shadow.

'I think,' said Skaryth, 'that you *want* it to be Phaek'or's.'

Phalk'ir rounded on him.

'You think I'd wish death on my twin?'

'I think you want a pretext,' pressed Skaryth. 'You want an excuse for your vendetta against Kassar. I don't think you care whether Phaek'or lives or dies, so long as it gives you just cause to stick a knife in the captain's back.'

'You've let him lead you for too long, if you think I would throw away Alpha Legion lives so cheaply,' said Phalk'ir scornfully. 'His contempt for us has poisoned your thinking.'

'The only poison here,' said Skaryth, 'is what drips from your tongue every time you speak. This isn't about Phaek'or, is it? This is about you wanting to take charge, and steer us into the arms of the gods. Again. You're obsessed.'

'Obsessed?' spat Phalk'ir. 'If anything I'm simply not as blind as the rest of you. This futile quest to stay untouched by the powers of the warp, the influence of the Dark Gods. To stay untainted. We're already tainted, all of us!'

Phalk'ir stared around at each of them, knuckles clenching and unclenching on the hilt of his blade.

'Look at Skarle, driven mad by the warp. Kyphas, becoming as closed off and poisonous as the secrets he keeps. Krowl... the Dark Gods only know what Krowl is turning into, but even a legionnaire shouldn't be able to heal the wounds that he can. For all we know, Thelgh already prays to the pantheon. How would we tell?'

The sniper maintained his silence, his stance betraying not even the slightest hint of a reaction to Phalk'ir's allegations.

'And you?' said Phalk'ir to Skaryth. 'Oh, I can practically *smell* the corruption coming off you in waves. You think you hide it, but it's there for all to see. Kassar just turns a blind eye because–'

Phalk'ir got no further. Skaryth launched himself at his brother, locking his hands around Phalk'ir's throat and slamming him back into the shrine's outer wall. Kassar lunged, grabbing Skaryth and hauling him away. The scout resisted, until Krowl joined Kassar and hefted Skaryth easily backwards.

Phalk'ir pushed himself off the wall with a cruel chuckle.

'Touchy, brother,' he said.

'Phalk'ir,' said Kassar angrily. 'We have no time for these theatrics. I've told you before, if you want to leave and pursue the path to glory then I won't stop you.'

Phalk'ir turned upon Kassar, and flung the severed arm at his feet.

'No,' he said. 'You won't stop me, because I don't take your orders any more, you murdering hypocrite. I saw Khârn engage you in combat. You were outside the chamber when we crashed. If this is all that remains of Phaek'or, then how did *you* emerge so completely unscathed?'

A phantom pain. A roaring blade. A severed arm hitting the decking.

'I was lucky, Phalk'ir. Abominably so, yes, but we were due some fortune at last.'

'You're a liar,' said Phalk'ir. 'A fraud. I don't know what you did, but you broke your own damn rules to survive that crash, the rules you've held us back with for so long. And I won't stay and tolerate it any longer. Any of the rest of you who want to join me, feel free. We'll seek our glories together.'

'Phalk'ir, I can't let you just break away mid-mission,' said Kassar warningly. 'You know that. You could compromise us.'

'I do know,' said Phalk'ir. 'Which is why, when I pulled the vox-bead out of an Imperial Fist's helm a few minutes ago, I kept the find to myself, then kept you idiots talking until they reached our position.'

Even as Phalk'ir spoke, a hail of bolt shells and las blasts rained down upon the Unsung. Kassar spun to see Battle Sisters and Tsadrekhans running along the gantries above them. Several squads had drawn up in firing lines, while the rest made for ground level. Seraphim dropped on trails of flame, and a Primaris Marine in a crested helm led them with sword drawn.

'And unlike you,' spat Phalk'ir from behind him, 'when I say I'll do something, I keep my warp-cursed word.'

Kassar wheeled back towards Phalk'ir. He saw the swordsman's blade thrusting towards him, aimed straight for his throat. There was a loud crack and the blade was driven aside, shattering down its length.

Phalk'ir fell back with a cry, clutching the haft of his broken blade. Smoke still wisped from the barrel of Thelgh's rifle where he had shot Phalk'ir's weapon in half.

Kassar levelled his bolter to blast Phalk'ir, but was hit in the back by several shells. He was thrown onto his face, Mortis skittering from his grasp as more shots whistled and exploded all around him.

'*Get to cover,*' gasped Kassar. '*Return fire.*'

He regained his feet, snatching up his bolter in time to see Phalk'ir running full tilt for the mouth of tunnel thirteen. Kassar fired a string of shots after him, but Phalk'ir vanished behind a blazing mound of wreckage and Kassar's shells flew wide.

'*I lost him,*' said Kassar wearily, swinging himself into cover.

'*He was lost a long time ago,*' replied Skaryth as he dived into the lee of a ruptured fuel tank. '*But we will be too if we don't fight.*'

'*There's a lot of them, Kassar,*' said Kyphas, hurling a frag grenade from behind the wreckage of a barricade. It detonated amongst a charging knot of Tsadrekhans. '*Do we fall back?*'

'*No,*' snarled Kassar, feeling a tingle run up his arm from Hexling's hilt. '*We've run enough. Formation Baphamet.·We break their will to fight, then mop up the survivors. And leave a couple alive for Kyphas to interrogate.*'

More Tsadrekhans were charging towards the Harrow through the wreckage. Skarle flung incendiary bombs at them, shrieking with laughter as the luckless men staggered and burned. Thelgh snapped off shots at the Battle Sisters on the gantries above, killing several before one of his rounds struck a heavy flamer's fuel tank. A ferocious explosion flared above the battlefield, and burning, armoured corpses rained down.

Amidst the firestorm, Kassar rose from cover, Mortis held out steadily before him. Ignoring the bolts and blasts of the foe, he strode towards them, and the Harrow provided cover. Formation Baphamet was a demonstration of contempt, a shock tactic intended to crush the enemy's morale by proving the Harrow's apparent invincibility.

Kassar strode at a steady pace into the teeth of the fight, aiming and snapping off single bolt shells at key targets. His brothers levelled a storm of fire to eliminate each enemy that turned their gun Kassar's way. Thelgh's rifle spat again and again, the sniper picking off special weapon troopers, Battle Sisters and sharpshooters with mechanical efficiency. Ragged streams of shells from Krowl's bolter-fist ripped through the Tsadrekhans. Kyphas and Skaryth played their bolters along the enemy lines. Skarle advanced in Kassar's wake, sending tongues of flame licking out to incinerate encircling enemies as they dashed through the smoke.

Kassar's first shot struck a Tsadrekhan sergeant in the face, exploding his head as though he'd swallowed a grenade. His second round caught a Battle Sister square in the chest, pulping her insides and spilling her meltagun to the floor. His third and fourth shots brought down the leader of the Seraphim squad, then ruptured a heavy bolter before its Tsadrekhan crew had even had time to finish setting it up.

All the while, beneath the expert covering fire of his brothers, not a single shot struck Kassar. He strode through the eye of the storm, smoke billowing around him, gun flaring and kicking. He saw the zeal burn out in his enemies' eyes, replaced by panic as he moved closer.

A Tsadrekhan raised his lasgun to shoot Kassar, and a bolt from Kyphas plucked him off his feet. A Sister Superior ran at Kassar with a roaring chainsword, only for Thelgh to shoot her in the throat. She crumpled to her knees, and Kassar shot her in the face then stepped over her corpse. Three more Tsadrekhans dropped into firing crouches, lining up their lasguns, only for Krowl to riddle them with shots.

None but the most exceptionally skilled, veteran, unified warriors could even have attempted such a manoeuvre, yet the Unsung made it look contemptuously simple.

Untouched, untouchable, Kassar walked into the heart of the foe and raised his blade, pointing it straight at the Imperial Fist. The warrior was clearly some sort of leader, and at Kassar's challenge he mag-locked his bolt rifle to his thigh and raised his power sword.

'Come and meet your end, heretic!' he roared. 'I am Lieutenant Lydanis of the Imperial Fists, and I shall strike you down in the Emperor's name!'

'I am Alpharius,' spat Kassar, 'and I am death.'

The Imperial Fist charged at him, swinging his power sword in a high arc.

Kassar shot him three times in the face, deforming his helm and smashing him onto his back.

Yelling in outrage, the last of the Seraphim Sisters launched themselves at Kassar. Shots struck him at last as their bolt pistols thundered, and he hissed as their volley smashed him off his feet.

Emerald fire engulfed the Seraphim, Skarle playing his flamer across them with glee. Two of the jump troops crashed to the ground, writhing and burning, while another was hurled spinning into the sky as her jump pack's fuel reserve ignited. She managed a last scream before the device exploded like a cannon shell.

Kassar scrambled up and turned to finish the Imperial Fist, only to find that the warrior had regained his feet. His buckled helm lay discarded, and his skull was clearly cracked. Blood ran from a deep gash in his forehead, and wept from around one eye. Still he fixed Kassar with the other, and lunged.

Kassar turned the blade aside with a deft parry then tried to shoot his opponent in the face again. The lieutenant was ready this time, backhanding the gun from Kassar's grip. In return, Kassar drove Hexling's point straight up, trying to ram it through his opponent's jaw.

Lieutenant Lydanis pulled his head to the side, evading the killing thrust, and drove his knee into Kassar's midriff. Armour cracked and the breath whooshed from Kassar's lungs, doubling him over. Lydanis smashed the pommel of his sword into the back of Kassar's helm, driving him onto his hands and knees, then swung his blade down in a beheading strike.

Kassar rolled aside from the blow, which sliced a line through his shoulder guard instead. Coming back to his feet, he circled the lieutenant, tossing Hexling from hand to hand as gunfire roared around them. Blood dripped from the lieutenant's chin to patter to the floor.

'What are you?' asked Kassar. 'What is Primaris? Some Mechanicus perversion? Another failed experiment of the Emperor's?'

'We are vengeance given form,' spat Lydanis. He turned with Kassar, keeping his guard up and his good eye locked on him.

'Yes, but what *are* you?' pressed Kassar, feinting then dropping back, circling further. 'You're damnably hard to kill.'

'We were made to defeat heretics like you,' said Lydanis, launching a sudden flurry of blows at Kassar. Hexling parried them all, except for a swift cut across the ribs that shed Kassar's blood. Kassar slammed his shoulder into his opponent's chest, a desperate move to gain breathing space.

'We are your bane,' Lydanis spat. 'For we are the perfect weapons to fight the servants of Chaos.'

'I see that,' said Kassar. 'And you have fought well. But, lieutenant, this is a fight that you will never win.'

With that he dropped his guard, and then his weapon, ignoring Hexling's surge of anger as it clattered to the floor.

Lydanis readied his blade, good eye darting around in search of some ruse, all his attention focused upon his defenceless opponent. A single vox pip sounded in Kassar's ear and, as the lieutenant drew back his sword for the killing blow, Kassar dropped to the floor.

Lydanis' face exploded as Thelgh's sniper round burst from the bridge of his nose. Gore spattered Kassar, and his opponent's twitching corpse crashed down next to him.

Rolling, Kassar swept up his blade, then went to retrieve his bolter. Around him the fight was concluding, the last reserves of courage driven from the Tsadrekhans by their leader's death. Here and there, knots of Battle Sisters still fought, but they did not last long.

Calmly, Kassar wiped his blade clean on Lydanis' corpse, then sheathed it. He checked the clip in his boltgun, switching it out for a new one.

His Harrow gathered upon him, those that were left. Kyphas hauled a terrified-looking Tsadrekhan sergeant with him by the scruff of the neck.

Six, whispered the voice in his mind, but Kassar spat upon it.

'Our brothers may yet live,' he said. 'And though we have been betrayed by one of our own, we will not let his cowardice undermine us. He called us tainted, yet he was more twisted by desire for the gods' regard than any of us. Our objective lies above. Our enemies battle one another, or flee from us in tatters.'

'Let's finish this,' said Skaryth. 'For the primarchs.'

'And for the Harrow,' nodded Kassar. 'Unsung, move out.'

CHAPTER TWELVE

They set off in tight formation, Skaryth scouting ahead and Thelgh acting as rear guard. Kyphas maintained his vox sweep for their lost brothers.

Clattering up a corpse-strewn stairway, they filtered through an open hatch into the central pillar, and into the enormity of the hive proper.

The runic marker for rally point beta flashed on their auspex maps, deeper into the region known as the Underbilge. They had designated it based upon partial maps that Haltheus had inloaded while raiding the cogitators of the abandoned transit hub. However, it soon became apparent that those maps were woefully out of date.

'Another dead end,' spat Skaryth. 'There used to be a hatch here, I think, but it's been replaced with a pipe conduit.'

'Does your captive know anything, Kyphas?' asked Kassar.

Kyphas hefted the bleeding sergeant, pinning him back against the wall of the corridor they were in.

'What is your knowledge of this area?' Kyphas snarled through his vox-grille. The sergeant squirmed and shook.

'I… I won't tell you anything… heretic…'

'Brave,' said Kyphas. 'But pathetic.' With his free hand, Kyphas unlocked his helm and pulled it off, clamping it to his belt. The sergeant stared into his hard, yet weirdly anonymous face. Kyphas leant in close, holding the man's head so that he couldn't recoil. He whispered something in the sergeant's ear, a subvocalisation that Kassar didn't catch.

The man's body went slack in Kyphas' grip. His eyes glazed.

'Now,' said Kyphas, setting the Tsadrekhan on his feet. 'What is your knowledge of this area?'

'This is Underbilge level zero-zero-five, west sector,' said the sergeant, his voice dull as though he fought sleep. 'Its productivity output is thirty-two per cent, population–'

Kyphas whipped one of his daggers from its sheath, snake-fast, and sliced a neat line up the man's cheek.

'Strategically relevant information only,' he said. 'Do you know this region well enough to expedite our swift navigation through it?'

Blood welled from the cut on the Tsadrekhan's face. Black lines of corruption were spreading from the wound, Kyphas' poisons going to work.

'I am from the level one-zero-eight garrison,' he said, wincing unconsciously at the poison seeping through his flesh. 'Our patrol routes are confined to twenty-floor radiuses. This is the first time I have ever been to this level.'

Kyphas slashed the man's other cheek. Kassar felt disquiet as he watched the relish on his brother's face at this act of casual violence. Power over others had become a drug for Kyphas, he realised. Perhaps even more than that.

'Do you know of any location wherein we can gain a clear and concise knowledge of our surroundings, of the layout of the Underbilge, and of the strategic situation within the hive?' Kyphas demanded. The Tsadrekhan, who was twitching now as the poisons built up in his system, struggled to answer.

'Yes,' he started, before coughing a mouthful of bloody vomit and starting again. 'Yes. The Adeptus Arbites precinct on level zero… zero… eight… has access… to…'

The Tsadrekhan dropped to his knees. Black blood was weeping from his eyes and nostrils, and his flesh was purpling. Kyphas gripped him by the chin, crushing his swollen face, and hoisted him back into the air.

'Access to what?' he asked.

'...hngh... vid... feeds... gggnnnnh... vox... thieves... gh... gh...'

The sergeant's jaw worked.

'Mark it,' said Kyphas, thrusting his auspex at the man. 'Mark it on here. Now.'

The Tsadrekhan tried to comply, raising one twitching, darkening hand and stabbing his finger at the auspex map. It took him three attempts.

'You're sure?' asked Kyphas.

The sergeant tried to speak, but more gory bile spilled from his lips, drowning his words. Foam followed, as his flesh darkened from purple to black. Kyphas spun his dagger up and punched it through the man's eye, piercing his brain. He ripped the blade free and savagely cut the man's throat, before slamming him backwards against the wall hard enough to dent the metal. Kyphas dropped the bloodied corpse, then closed his eyes and steadied his breathing. He wiped his blade, spinning it back into its sheath.

'What was that?' demanded Kassar.

'Arbites precinct, level zero-zero-eight,' said Kyphas. 'We have what we need.'

'Not that,' began Kassar, but Thelgh placed a hand on his shoulder and shook his head.

Not the time.

Kassar nodded. Another problem, he thought, that had to be set aside until this mission was done. Another brother at breaking point. That was the burden of leadership, though. And at least there were some conversations that he would not have to delay any longer.

'It will take us too long to progress to point beta at this pace. Knowledge is power. We reroute to the Arbites precinct and hope that Kyphas' victim provided us with an accurate location for it.'

'There will be signage, as we get closer,' said Skaryth. 'The corpse worshippers revel in their petty authorities and oppressions.'

'True,' said Kassar. 'Then let us move with a purpose. Cultist. You will walk with me.'

They moved quickly, Syxx forced into a half-jog-half-walk to keep up. He came to Kassar's side reluctantly, his posture hunched and defensive. The bleeding from his head had stopped, leaving barely a mark to show where he had been hurt. Syxx saw Kassar notice, and tried to shift his broken mask to conceal it.

'What are you?' asked Kassar, keeping his voice low while unable to speak in serpenta.

'Lord, it's as I've told you. I am an acolyte of Phelkorian,' said Syxx. 'And the bearer of the incantation that will desecrate the beacon in the name of Slaanesh.'

'I am not one to gamble, when I can help it,' said Kassar. 'I do not take unnecessary risks unless I must. I weigh the cost of every decision, using what information I possess to make informed judgements. Do you understand this?'

'I do, lord, but why are you telling me this?'

'Because,' said Kassar as they crossed an intersection and started up a spiralling ramp lined with abandoned hovels, 'I am performing that calculation while we speak. I am weighing what I believe I know about you, against the condition you must be in to remain mission viable.'

Understanding dawned across Syxx's features. He paled.

'My lord,' he said. 'Please. You must believe that I have told you everything I know.'

'No. I do not have to believe that,' said Kassar, voice still quiet and calm. They reached the top of the ramp, picking their way through a breached barricade littered with headless corpses.

'I don't know precisely what the incantation will do,' said Syxx urgently. 'Phelkorian didn't tell me, but I know him and I do not believe it will be a pleasant way to die. But whatever it does, it is still worth it to escape him.'

They were moving now through a wide-open space, with a low, pipe-thick ceiling pressing down from above. Some kind of shanty-market, Kassar thought, looking at the demolished remains of tarpaulins and stalls, scattered gewgaws and blood-spattered promethium lanterns.

'I believe everything that you have just told me,' said Kassar. 'But you know that is not what I am asking about. If you evade the question, I will hurt you before asking again.'

'I should have died,' said Syxx. 'In the tunnel. When it flooded.'

'You *did* die,' said Kassar. 'We could survive those conditions for some time. You could not. And yet...'

Syxx picked his way through a litter of broken bodies and torn cloth. When he looked back at Kassar, his expression was equal parts fear and confusion.

'I don't understand it, lord. Honestly I don't. Perhaps Phelkorian... did something to me? Perhaps it's the effect of the incantation worked into my flesh?'

If the man was lying, then Kassar had rarely met a mortal who could do so as convincingly as this.

'What about in the garrison car?' he asked. 'With the daemon engine? Why did you not tell me that you were a psyker?'

'I should have said something,' said Syxx. 'I am sorry that I didn't, but I didn't realise that you would care. My masters dealt with such potent entities and exhibited such outlandish gifts, they have never taken any interest in my pitiful powers.'

'We are not the Emperor's Children,' said Kassar. 'We are Alpha Legion, and unless a great deal has changed since we were marooned upon Bloodforge, our Legion does not embrace the corruption of the Dark Gods in the same way that our erstwhile brothers do. But that is beside the point. I wouldn't call holding back a daemon engine pitiful.'

'I can sometimes sense if someone is speaking falsehoods,' said Syxx. 'On a few occasions I have conjured pyrokinetic manifestations. And countless times I have served as one of a coven of acolytes when Lord Phelkorian summons daemons. But lord, please believe me that I have never managed anything even remotely resembling what I did today.'

They left the market by way of an arched transit tunnel, finding more devastated barricades stretched across its width. Strip lumen flickered fitfully overhead, illuminating an abattoir scene.

'Ominous,' said Skaryth. 'I have seen no fallen Berzerkers, and surely the Tsadrekhans would have managed to kill at least some of their attackers.'

'Unless their attacker was just one warrior,' said Kyphas. 'One they couldn't lay low.'

'Be cautious,' ordered Kassar. 'But stay on this route. With luck, we will follow in his slipstream right through the defenders' lines.'

He returned his attention to Syxx as they pressed on through the flickering gloom of the tunnel.

'Assuming for the moment that I believe you,' said Kassar, 'this does not make my calculation any easier.'

'But I haven't deceived you!' said Syxx, frustrated and fearful.

'Maybe not,' said Kassar. 'But now we have a psyker in our midst, whose powers appear to be growing, perhaps beyond his comprehension or control. I've been in this situation before, cultist.'

'What happened?' Syxx asked quietly.

'It ended badly,' said Kassar. 'I don't mean to see this mission go the same way.'

'What are you going to do with me?' asked Syxx, and again Kassar found himself impressed.

'You don't plead, or beg, as most mortals would,' he said.

'When you have lived as the plaything of the Emperor's Children, you soon learn that begging and pleading will do you no good,' Syxx replied.

'They're degenerates,' said Kassar. 'We are not. But I need to know that you won't endanger my warriors. You must stay alive and, I presume, whole for your incantation to work and our mission to be successful. Besides, the powers of survival you have displayed have been significant. I've no guarantee that if we tried to kill or dismember you for our own safety, we wouldn't simply rouse whatever power it is that seems to be protecting you.'

'Will you bind me, then? Gag me? Beat me unconscious?' Syxx sounded resigned, conditioned to violent solutions.

'No,' said Kassar. 'That would require Krowl to carry you again, and with so few warriors left I cannot spare him. No, cultist. I'm going to trust you.'

Syxx blinked.

From ahead, Kyphas sent a string of vox pips to halt their progress. He checked his auspex, then indicated a ladder that led up to a hatch in the tunnel's ceiling. Skaryth nodded and started climbing. The rest of them followed.

'My lord,' said Syxx. 'I will be worthy of your trust, I swear to you.'

'Don't mistake me,' said Kassar. 'This implies no fondness on my part. If I could see another, safer path I would take it. But you have not knowingly betrayed us yet, and weighing all the information I possess, the scales tip this way.'

'Yes, lord,' said Syxx.

And, thought Kassar, if you break my trust I will turn the entire Harrow upon you and between us we shall put the lie to your apparent invincibility.

Gripping the rusted rungs of the ladder, he began to climb.

Their route took them up a narrow shaft, then through a snarl of maintenance crawlways and pipeline gantries. As they traversed them, they passed close to the ironclad skin of the hive, and heard the groan of the ocean waters pressing outside. They passed through an abandoned skavvy encampment, where water dripped from the ceiling into salty pools, then they emerged through another hatch into an alleyway between two hab blocks.

A dead Tsadrekhan lay on his face nearby, sprawled amidst a toppled stack of aquila-stamped crates. Close by, Kassar heard gunfire, and bellowed battle cries. He and his surviving warriors swathed themselves in the remains of their cameleoline cloaks, and crept to the end of the alleyway.

Kassar looked out along a wide processional. Hab blocks towered to either side of the ferrocrete roadway, rising into a sky lost amidst glowing vapours, winking lights and precarious-looking gantries. Groundcars and Tsadrekhan troop transports were strewn around, many rolled onto their roofs or piled in heaps where they had collided at speed. Fires burned. Bodies lay where they had fallen.

'There,' said Skaryth, pointing through the smoke. 'Combat.'

Magnifying his auto-senses, Kassar saw a pair of armoured transports parked nose to tail across the transitway. Rhinos, their hulls black and bone. Around and atop the tanks stood grim-faced Sisters of Battle, their guns blazing as they held off an onrushing mass of Khornate cultists.

'The corpse worshippers are winning,' noted Kyphas. 'But they are also occupied. We need to go that way, but we should be able to skirt around them.'

'Quick and quiet,' said Kassar, gesturing for the Unsung to move out.

They ghosted through the smoke, sliding around wrecked vehicles and staying low. Just because they hadn't seen any other enemies, didn't mean there weren't any. Bolter fire echoed between the hab stacks, mingled with the roar of engines and the screams of the dying. In such a tangled warzone, death could come from any angle.

'That alleyway,' said Kyphas, studying his auspex. 'We follow it around the rear of this block, then climb the stack ladder at its rear. From there we should be able to follow the rooftops and stay above any fighting all the way to the Arbites precinct.'

An overturned Chimera currently blocked the mouth of the alleyway. They could climb over it, but doing so would expose their silhouettes to any who might be looking.

Better to go beneath.

'Krowl,' said Kassar, gesturing to the wrecked tank.

With his customary grunt, Krowl crouched beside the wreck, braced himself, and hefted one end upwards a few feet. Immediately, Skaryth dropped to his belly and crawled under the wreck to the far side, rising in a firing crouch. Kyphas followed, then Syxx, then Skarle. Kassar came after them, crawling beneath the crushing weight of metal as Krowl dutifully held it up.

Thelgh came last, leaving just Krowl on the wrong side of the tank.

While Thelgh and Kassar kept watch, Kyphas, Skaryth and Skarle braced the tank between them. Answering Kassar's vox-pip summons,

Krowl scrambled through and joined them, helping his brothers to lower the wreck back down. Between their strength and care, it barely creaked as it settled on its roof.

'*Alleyway looks clear,*' said Skaryth.

'*Then let's move,*' said Kassar.

They climbed the stack ladder, swarming up its switchback rungs and platforms to the roof of the hab. It was a gruelling climb, especially for Syxx. By the time they passed through the hazy clouds of the cavern's microclimate and reached the rooftops above, the cultist was gasping and shaking. No one aided him, but Kassar was ready to catch him if he fell.

They found the hab-zone rooftops to be a different world. Above the clouds and smoke, everything was starkly lit by the huge arc-lumen that dangled from the ceiling high above. They looked like captive stars, thought Kassar, albeit sad, crude, anaemic ones.

The hab-tops marched away from them in a grid, with yawning gaps between them where the transitways ran. Flocks of scruffy avians fluttered and swirled in the distance, disturbed by the violence of battle far below. Huge ventilator units and generatorums hunched atop the roofs, studded with baroque gargoyles and old, corroded servitors. The salt tang of the ocean was strong here, though Kassar couldn't have said why.

They set off quickly, following Kyphas' directions. Gasping to regain his breath, Syxx kept up.

Kassar had feared they might have to jump between rooftops, but narrow metal bridges spanned the gaps between the habs. Recycled wind wailed around them, shaking the thin metal of their construction and singing through the guide-wires that formed their flimsy railings.

'*Do not fall,*' he said to Syxx, who had shrunk into himself at the sight of the perilous crossings. The cultist looked at him and nodded.

They made the best time they could, edging carefully across the juddering bridges, bracing themselves against the puckish winds that threatened to pitch them off and into the clouds below.

Down there, Kassar could still hear the distant thump and roar of battle. Occasionally a large explosion would underlight the cloud cover. But nothing came their way. They skirted the warzone, staying focused on the mission.

After a perilous and exhausting hour, Kyphas at last called a halt. They crouched in the lee of a chugging generatorum, Thelgh keeping watch through his scope. Kassar noticed that Syxx was visibly shaking, though whether with fear, exhaustion or cold he didn't care.

'The Arbites precinct fortress is directly north of here,' said Kyphas. 'But it is not part of this rooftop network. The building looks to stand alone in a wide plaza, presumably to provide it with protection and good sightlines from all sides.'

'Back to ground level, then?' asked Skaryth.

'Many guns I hear them fire, I'll throw their wielders on the pyre,' sang Skarle.

'You will not,' said Kassar. 'There is a great amount of gunfire down there. Sounds like a pitched battle in full swing. Is there no other route to reach the precinct fortress?'

'Yes,' said Kyphas, though Kassar heard again a note of struggle in his voice as he revealed the information. 'The electro-conduit wires that stretch from atop this generatorum look to span the gap and connect to capacitors on the fortress' side.'

'Hardly perfect security,' said Skaryth contemptuously. 'Why have a fortress whose power can be cut so easily?'

'They'll have backup generatorums,' said Kassar. 'Oceanic world means scarce resources. This sort of practice is likely an efficiency measure. Kyphas, are you suggesting that we climb across on the wires? Will they take our weight? Are they live?'

'The generatorum is running, so yes, I would say there is a good chance that the wires are live, but so long as we do not break their sheaths then we should remain insulated from the motive force. As to them taking our weight, let's inspect them.'

Clambering atop the generatorum left them exposed to the full force of the ventilator winds that howled across the cavern. Krowl kept a firm grip on Syxx, preventing the terrified cultist from being plucked off the rattling mass of pipes and scaffold.

At the generatorum's highest point, a bulky metal tower jutted up, the wind singing through it. A thick braid of taut electro-conduit wires stretched away from it, vanishing at a steep angle into the clouds below.

Hanging on to precarious handholds, Skaryth climbed up and grabbed hold of the wires. He tugged on them, carefully at first and then with increasing aggression. At last, he turned his back to the drop and signalled that the wires would hold them.

'It would be a long and arduous climb,' said Kassar. 'We'd risk losing the cultist, even if we tied him to Krowl again. Besides, it would take too long.'

'The ground, then?' asked Kyphas.

'No,' said Kassar. 'Remember the Tetanyphic Fortress on Bloodforge?'

'Hah!' barked Skaryth. 'Perfect. Krowl, the guide-wires from that last bridge we crossed should be thick and long enough. Fetch them.'

Krowl lumbered off through the glare, returning minutes later with two thick coils of metal wire. Clasps still dangled from them where he had ripped them away from the bridge. He clambered back up onto the generatorum, and laid the coils at his brothers' feet.

Kassar cut the wires into sections, Hexling slicing through them as though they were binding twine. He lifted a length, wrapped it several times about each of his gauntlets, then pulled on it as hard as he could. He nodded with satisfaction. Straining with his full strength, Kassar couldn't snap the cable.

'This will work,' he said. 'Weapons mag-locked. Bind the cultist to Krowl again.'

The Unsung prepared themselves. Syxx panicked when he realised what his guardians intended, but didn't fight them as he was hoisted up and bound securely to Krowl's backpack. Kassar could hear the cultist's heart racing, though, and smell his fear sweat.

'My idea,' said Kassar, clambering up to the precarious spot below the wires. 'So I'll go first. Krowl is to follow me, then Skarle. The rest of you, bring up the rear in whatever order you choose. Give it a firm ten count between each of us. I'd rather be outnumbered on the other side than have the wire snap under too much weight.'

Kassar received vox pips of acknowledgement.

'*Good luck, captain,*' said Skaryth.

'*See you on the precinct roof,*' said Kassar. Then, before he could think too hard about what he was going to do, he looped his length of wire over the electro-conduits, made sure its ends were bound around his gauntlets and gripped securely, then leapt out into space.

The wind howled around him, and he plunged through it. His length of guide-wire skimmed over the electro-conduits from the generatorum, forming an improvised zip-line. Weighed down with armour and wargear, Kassar hurtled down it at a ferocious speed.

Murky clouds veiled his destination, ripping apart as he plunged through them. His twin hearts thumped as the yawning drop sped beneath him, undoubtedly lethal even for one such as he. Gunfire and tank engines raised a muffled cacophony from below.

Runes flashed in his auto-senses, urgent proximity warnings. Something huge and dark loomed up through the murk. Kassar brought his knees up to his waist, bracing for an uncertain landing.

He whipped in over a parapet of black metal, seeing fleeting impressions of armoured men pass on either side. Then he struck the side of another generatorum block, this one encased in black armour and stamped with grim gold aquilas.

Kassar dropped, falling fifteen feet and slamming down on metal decking. His auto-senses were alive with target locks and threat warnings. Mortis was already in his hand.

The top of the building formed a metal crater fifty feet across and fifteen deep, with the generatorum jutting from its centre. It was ringed on all sides with armoured battlements, and on the fire steps behind them stood Adeptus Arbites in bulky spotter-helms, sniper rifles clutched in their hands.

The men were turning in shock, to stare at the Heretic Astartes who had just hurtled out of the clouds to land in their midst. The huge optic lenses of their helms made them look like insects.

Kassar shot one man before his enemies had even reacted, throwing his body back against the battlements. His second bolt hit another

Adeptus Arbite in the face, exploding his helm. Kassar saw some of the men trying to wrench their helms off, while the optics of others were hissing and clicking as their wearers frantically refocused. They must have been firing down into the battle below, he realised, using the optics to compensate for the cloud cover and extreme range.

'They won't help you now,' he said, and gunned down another two of the Adeptus Arbites before ripping his sword from his scabbard and charging.

Sniper rounds whipped around him, a couple of lucky shots ringing from his armour, but his enemies were at a horrible disadvantage.

Kassar slid in low, running one man through, then spun, sliding his blade free and slashing it across another of the Adeptus Arbites' throats.

Krowl rushed in overhead, Syxx clinging to his back like grim death. Krowl's boots hit the decking, and his bolter gauntlet roared to life.

Another sniper shot hit Kassar, this one punching through his power pack and lodging in the meat of his back. He cursed, feeling his armour's power dip as its systems struggled to compensate. Spinning, Kassar shot his attacker through the chest, killing him.

Skarle flew overhead, landed, and unleashed the fury of *Gift*.

Shots rang out again, and Kassar saw sparks rain from the side of the generatorum.

'*They're trying to shoot out the wire,*' he voxed. '*Stop them!*'

He, Krowl and Skarle launched themselves into the Adeptus Arbites. Men were hacked and bludgeoned, rent and blasted. Blood sprayed.

Thelgh arrived, unlocking his stolen bolt rifle and adding its point-blank salvoes to the fight. Kyphas followed, dropping into what was rapidly becoming a massacre.

Kassar gutted another enemy and turned in time to see the last of the Adeptus Arbites running for the generatorum. The man had torn his helm free, and unholstered a bolt pistol from his hip.

'No!' roared Kassar, firing his bolter.

Too slow.

Even as he was punched from his feet, the Adeptus Arbite managed to loose off a bolt that struck the electro-conduit cables where they met the generatorum. There was an explosion of sparks, a whipping report, and the cables snapped backwards like a released slingshot.

Over the vox, Kassar heard Skaryth utter a frantic curse.

'Skaryth,' voxed Kassar. 'Skaryth!'

For a beat, none of the Unsung moved, appalled at the sudden loss of another of their brothers. He would be falling. Plunging to a crushing, ignominious death.

Then they heard Skaryth's voice, tight with effort.

'I'm here,' he said. 'Just. Get up here and pull me in before I lose my grip!'

Kassar leapt up onto the fire step, letting out a shout of triumph as he saw Skaryth's fingers clinging to the lip of the parapet. One hand. He had just made it.

Leaning over the sickening drop, Kassar grabbed Skaryth's wrist. The scout was dangling over the dirty clouds, boots kicking against the smooth metal of the fortress' flank. The electro-conduit had fallen away into the chasm below.

Skaryth swung his other arm up, Kassar gripping that too.

'Up you come, brother,' said Kassar.

'Gladly,' gasped Skaryth as he was hauled over the rampart. The two Alpha Legionnaires crashed to the fire step in a heap, then clambered to their feet.

'Too close,' said Skaryth.

'Fifth cypher,' said Kassar. *'Glad to have you with us, Skaryth.'*

'Thanks for pulling me up,' said Skaryth. *'Now, let's get what we came for.'*

'Agreed,' said Kassar. *'Lead the way.'*

It took them twelve minutes to reach the command sanctum of the precinct fortress. The Adeptus Arbites were occupied with the besieging forces outside their walls, fighting a furious battle to repel the Khorne worshippers that bayed all about. The din from outside was phenomenal, the barely controlled panic within the fortress palpable. The Adeptus Arbites did not realise that the subtle venom of the Alpha Legion had been injected into their stronghold until it was too late.

The Unsung cleared one chamber after another. They kept to their knives and blades, approaching their victims from the shadows and silencing them before any alarm could be raised. Finally, they swept into the command sanctum, blade work and sniper fire eliminating the senior enforcer and his command staff before they even realised they were under attack.

Kassar saw one man, wounded but still breathing, reaching for a vox headset. He crushed headset and hand alike beneath his boot, before hoisting the Adeptus Arbite to his feet.

'Cogitator access,' Kassar said as Thelgh sealed the sanctum door. 'Vid feeds. Vox access. Everything you have. Do not make my brother ask you a second time.'

Kassar glanced at Kyphas, who had unsheathed a pair of knives, and who growled menacingly through his vox grille.

Shaking, the Arbite nodded.

'Please,' he said. 'I have a family.'

'Then obey, if you wish to see them again,' said Kassar.

The Arbite nodded and hurried to a console, stumbling in his fear. Sweating, hands shaking, he punched runic keys.

'Don't try to deceive us, corpse worshipper,' rumbled Kassar. 'Your death need not be quick. Nor those of your loved ones.'

The man shot a fearful glance at him. With a final clatter of keys, he unlocked the warding of the console and brought up the primary information feeds for the hive.

'Under... Underbilge and Main Hive,' he stammered. 'We don't have clearance to observe the spire. The Battle Sisters rule there. Our laws don't apply.'

'This is everything?' asked Kassar. The man nodded eagerly.

'Yes, everything you asked for,' he said. 'Now, please, I won't tell anyone that you're-'

Kassar cut him off with a punch to the face, a sharp jab that rocked the man's head back, crushed his skull and broke his neck. The Arbite bounced off the console, spattering its keys with blood, and crumpled to the floor.

'*Knowledge*,' said Kassar. '*Power. Let us see what we can learn.*'

* * *

The situation was dire. They cycled through vid-logs, auspex feeds and cherubim occula, vox-channels full of military exchanges and frantic, civilian chatter. They absorbed strategic information, inloaded detailed auspex maps, pillaging the Adeptus Arbites' cogitators for everything they had.

On the surface, night had fallen.

A massive superstorm was battering the outside of the hive, throwing waves hundreds of feet into the air, lighting the clouds with weird warp energies from the rift.

Lord Khordas had rammed a spacecraft into the side of the hive, his audacious assault finally winning him a beachhead. Imperial forces had responded in large numbers, and a desperate warzone had spread out through the core levels of Main Hive. The beacon remained unassailed, however, and a massive Imperial force had deployed around the primary access gate between the upper levels of Main Hive and the spire.

'Nothing is getting through there without a considerable fight,' commented Kyphas.

The Khorne worshippers were pouring in through the maglev tunnels, also. Tunnel thirteen had been the first, but it was not the last. Striking against the compromised defences around the hive's roots, more and more warbands of traitors were pouring into the Underbilge, slaughtering as they went.

'Khârn,' said Skaryth, indicating a crimson clearance rune blinking its way along a processional.

The Betrayer was on the move, cutting a bloody path up through the hive, eschewing any form of elevator or conveyor. He seemed to be shedding all the blood he could, and though the Unsung couldn't locate him in any vid feeds, eyewitness reports spoke of a billowing crimson mist building around him.

There was talk of the Cicatrix Maledictum, of empyric bleed.

Of daemons.

'There,' said Skaryth, his voice eager. 'There! Level zero-zero-seven, near the hydro-repugnor batteries one level up from point beta. It's them! Kassar, our brothers live!'

The Unsung gathered around the vid feed, several of them grinning with relief.

On the screen, a grainy image showed an area of partly swamped manufactorum, long since abandoned to rust and decay. Splashing through its shallow waters was A'khassor, Makhor at his back. The two of them were splattered in blood, firing their bolters at something out of shot.

Behind them, the others flickered into view. Haltheus, limping and towing a makeshift stretcher made from wreckage. Behind it came D'sakh, firing his bolter back into the gloom at half-seen Tsadrekhans. Sprawled upon the travois was Phaek'or, a heavy compact bound around the stump of a missing arm.

'Unbelievable,' said Skaryth. 'It actually *was* his arm.'

Kassar shot him a look.

'They're under attack,' he said. *'There's no time to lose. Kyphas, fastest route to our brothers. Skaryth, use this equipment, vox them on a secure channel, arrange a rendezvous. Bring them to this set of coordinates. We'll meet them there.'*

Skaryth glanced at the location Kassar had provided.

'A mass conveyor,' he said. *'That should take us…'*

Kassar nodded.

'All the way up.'

He basked in the Emperor's light.

It washed over him and filled him up, a gentle radiance that burned like the heart of a star.

He needed nothing. Not sleep, nor food, nor worldly goods, for he had the light and love of the Emperor, and that was all.

He had been young, when the light first came to him. A fresh recruit, his new-stamped lasgun clutched in sweating palms. A sacrifice upon the altar of battle, whose contribution would ultimately mean pitifully little.

The darkness had come, the blackening. The loss.

It had obscured the beacon by which mankind sailed the stars, and in its absence, ancient terrors had crawled from the shadows and fallen upon their worlds.

The Emperor's armies marched out like never before, to battle the horrors at their gates, and he had marched with them.

Young.

Frightened.

His life measurable in hours.

And then, on the killing fields of Dessah, amidst the acid-flats and the raging fires, the light had come upon him.

These were distant memories now, all but erased by the light within, yet still he recalled them when he could. He made himself do it, to remember where he had come from, to retain his humility, his humanity.

The medicae had rushed to him, and the priests. They had feared some weapon of the foe, some spiritual contagion, yet the light that poured from him had driven back the fiends of the pit. It had won victory that day, though he had felt his nerves burning away, his eyes seared from their sockets. Even as he had received the Emperor's gift, he had burned for it in purifying flame.

They had called it a miracle, which it was.

They had called him a prophet, or a saint, or an angel, which he was not.

He was a humble man given a godly gift.

He was hope's willing martyr.

He was Kaleb, and he was the beacon.

For time beyond time he had remained, basking in the Emperor's light. He could not sleep, must not, for it was in those dark watches that the nightmares returned. He had always to be the day, the light, the watchman's lantern that drove back the shadows.

Priests and seers had flocked about him. They had found ways to keep him ever wakeful, ever vigilant. They had found ways to keep him alive in this transcendental state but not, by their definition, sane.

None of it was any matter to him. He was Kaleb, the unremarkable boy made remarkable by the Emperor's gifts. He had prayed to the Master of Mankind for a way that he could save all of his friends in the regiment, all of his family back on Gydo's Reach, and in his beneficence the Emperor had answered.

He would not squander that unimaginable honour with selfish sleep. And besides, who could ever close their eyes upon such wonders as he saw with his eyeless gaze?

As he lay within his cradle, the Emperor looked down upon him from stained glass rendered to life by Kaleb's gifts. His eyes were kind. Fatherly. His smile was the most beautiful thing that Kaleb could ever imagine.

Around the cradle, his sanctum spread out amidst a golden haze. Its floor thronged with the souls of departed warriors, standing their own sacrificial vigil rather than take their rightful place at the Emperor's table. Perhaps it was the energies of the Great Rift that made it possible, the enemy's power turned back upon them. Perhaps it was Kaleb's light that gave them strength. Perhaps they were not real at all, but he hoped that they were. Their presence, their vigilance, made him feel safe.

Higher swept the galleries and pulpits, where his attendants laboured night and day. Every one of them wore a shimmering halo in Kaleb's sight. Sometimes he saw them framed with beautiful, flowing scripture and illuminations as though they were the characters in some holy text. At others they resembled cogs and gears of crystal, gold and light, turning smoothly in a beautiful, mechanical dance.

Most wondrous of all, though, were the Sisters of the Crimson Tear. Wherever they went about him Kaleb saw them with flowing angel's wings rising from their shoulders, burning haloes upon their brows, and the golden blades of warrior queens sheathed at their hips. Upon the stern visage of each he saw the Crimson Tears of their order, wrought in glinting firelight, and knew that they would die to defend him.

But now, she came. An angel amongst angels. A demi-goddess flown from the Emperor's side upon swift wings of determination and duty.

She came to tell him that this dream must end. That a time of testing was upon him. That hope could come only from despair, victory only from pain. Day, only from night.

He understood that her words were only for him, and he steeled himself to do his duty to the Emperor, no matter the cost to him, and to everyone he loved.

A new darkness was coming, thought Kaleb sadly. The nightmares must prevail. For without their reign, without their time, the dawn could not break again.

CHAPTER THIRTEEN

Standing atop the steps of Hive Endurance's primary teleportarium, Magos-ethericus Corphyx raised his staff and unleashed a searing bolt of energy. The blast struck a traitor square in the chest, annihilating him from the diaphragm up before he had finished materialising. The Chaos Space Marine's legs and midriff tottered and fell, splattering blood and innards across the teleportarium platform.

'Clean that away,' buzzed Corphyx to a servitor. 'It besmirches the holy dais.'

The cyborg twittered in binharic and shambled to do the magos' bidding. Corphyx had already dismissed it from his memory banks.

'Ohmdeacon Dynipsis,' he said, transmitting his vocal emissions via empasonic carrier waves. 'Are the lower platforms secure?'

The leader of Corphyx's electro-priest congregation, the ohmdeacon stood hundreds of feet below, near the base of the teleportarium shrine. He turned blinded eyes up towards his distant master as he replied. His voice crackled with motive force.

'Praise the Omnissiah, magos-ethericus, they remain sacrosanct,' he said, his reply carried by the reverberant waves of the motive force to

Corphyx's aural intake antennae. Around him, Corphyx's magnified optics could see more servitors hauling away the bodies of Khorne worshippers that had fallen to Dynipsis' acolytes. The bodies were being flung into the undernarthex for later incineration.

'That is pleasing to the lord of machines, ohmdeacon,' said Corphyx. 'Know that his myriad lenses look upon your deeds with optimal commendation.'

'Magos-ethericus!' barked a voice much closer to hand, fleshy and unaugmented.

Corphyx ignored it for the moment, plunging his quad-cortex into the noospheric data streams that flowed through the teleportarium. The sacred coronae of teleportation flares continued to flash in an acceptable – if slow – approximation of the divine sequence. He noted that rigs four, seven, twelve and eighteen had ceased to send their promethium libations.

That was displeasing, but not statistically unexpected. The invaders had been sure to interfere with the Omnissiah's holy works. Unbelievers were sent to test the faithful, and some were found wanting. Still, barrels of processed promethium continued to flash into being on most of the teleportarium platforms, to be snatched up and spirited away by sentinels.

That was pleasing.

'Magos-ethericus, please!' shouted the voice again. 'I must insist that you enact the Dysorian protocols at once!'

Feeling a flash of all-too-human irritation, Corphyx rerouted his primary perception routines to his interpersonal emulators. His optics awoke, directing a cold glare at the Tsadrekhan lieutenant before him. The man stood upon the top step below Corphyx's shrine, red-faced and frantic. Ten troopers stood behind him, clutching their lasguns, trying not to show fear beneath the monstrous guns of Corphyx's battle servitors.

Corphyx hadn't bothered to retain the lieutenant's flesh-name.

'Lieutenant,' he buzzed, 'you are asking me to sanction an act of wanton auto-desecration within a holy shrine of the Omnissiah. The technology that would be destroyed, the machine-spirits that would be exorcised, would be an irreplaceable, unforgivable loss. And the promethium would cease to flow. Also unacceptable. I will not comply with this heretical request.'

'Magos Corphyx,' said the lieutenant, his voice registering exceptional emotional stress. 'We have stockpiles of promethium to last over a year. Meanwhile, there are enemy forces gaining access to the hive via your facility. They – *you* – are compromising the safety of Hive Endurance, and thereby the beacon, and *thereby the entire Tsadrekhan Unity!*'

'Every combat-capable heretical bio-unit that has gained access to this facility has been eliminated within a maximal temporation of six-point-one-four seconds,' replied Corphyx. 'My congregation have mapped optimal extermination patterns to every dais and are running constant sensor sweeps to ensure instantaneous lethal response to any unauthorised etheric transit. The foe may appear within the teleportarium, lieutenant, but they do not live long enough to capitalise upon that fact.'

'Magos-ethericus,' pleaded the lieutenant, 'I have direct orders from Canoness Levinia herself.'

'This is the Omnissiah's house,' said Corphyx. 'The Cult Imperialis holds no sway here.'

'Be that as it may,' the lieutenant pressed on, 'my orders are to render this teleportarium inactive by any means necessary. By *any* means, magos. Do you understand what I'm saying?'

'You are attempting to convey a threat of potential violence and/ or extreme sanction, but you find the concept both emotionally distressing and distasteful, and thus are reluctant to vocalise it directly,' said Corphyx. 'I understand your subtext with clarity, lieutenant. And I can assuage your concerns in that regard. Any attempt by you or your singularly inadequate detail of soldiers to cause harm to either myself or this holy sanctum will result in your immediate terminal sanction by my servitors. I hope that I, in my turn, make myself understood.'

'I don't want to die here, fighting my own side,' said the lieutenant. 'And I don't want you to kill my boys, but I swear by the Throne itself if you don't comply right away I'll call in enough reinforcements to burn you and your precious shrine to ashes.'

Corphyx shunted a command to his servitors' neuro-receptors, preparing to trigger their extermination protocols. Before he could complete the exload, screams and gunfire echoed up from below.

Magnifying his optics, Corphyx saw a towering warrior in scorched, blood-red armour plough into the midst of his electro-priests. Jolts of motive force arced and leapt as glowing holy men hurled themselves at the figure, but with every sweep of his chainaxe he smashed them away like broken dolls.

A crimson mist billowed in the warrior's wake, and the magos-ethericus was in no doubt as to its nature. His empyric spectro-analytics confirmed it beyond a doubt.

'Reality breach,' he buzzed. 'Malefic spectral dissonance. All units retask, eliminate that warrior, pattern sanctis reductum.'

As one, Corphyx's servitors and acolyte priests turned their weapons upon the blood-wreathed Berzerker. A storm of incredible energies engulfed him, and the electro-priests he fought. Plasma, phosphor flames, lasers, voltaic blasts, all rained down upon the shrine's lowest steps until Corphyx was forced to dim his optics to avoid their receptors burning out.

'Cease,' ordered Corphyx, calculating that the target's chances of survival had dropped to zero. 'Resume targeting subroutines upon the teleportarium platforms.'

The red mist billowed upwards, coiling and churning into screaming faces and grasping, ephemeral claws. With a roar, the red-armoured warrior burst from its leading edge, scorched and smouldering but very much alive. At his heels came unnatural things, blood-fleshed terrors of the warp clutching black, smoking blades.

'Magos!' shrieked the lieutenant. 'You have to destroy the–'

A thunderous volley rang out. Corphyx's servitors chuntered as they reloaded their weapons, and the magos-ethericus dismissed the charred remains of the lieutenant and his soldiers as irrelevant.

The towering warrior was charging up the steps, closing the gap by the moment, a tide of daemons boiling into reality behind him. As they passed the teleportarium platforms, the machines' holy energies were corrupted, white lightning turning blood red and ripping inwards to tear implosive holes in the flesh of time and space. Terrible things stirred in their shadows, then surged forth to join the charge.

'Abomination!' blurted Corphyx. 'Heresy! All units, fire to repel, spread pattern sigma-rho. Keep the promethium flowing to the last. The Omnissiah demands no less.'

Confident that his shrine would operate for as long as it could, satisfied that he had done his duty to the Omnissiah first and foremost, Corphyx raised his staff and prepared to die with a binharic prayer cycling from his emitters.

So fell teleportarium shrine eight-one-seven hub beta.

It was not alone.

Captain Dysorian backed steadily down the transit tube, firing his bolt pistol as he went. He ignored the pain of his wounds, and the amber warning runes flashing in his peripheral vision. He kept shooting, picking another cultist from the howling mass, then another, then another, gunning each one down before retargeting.

At his side, the last two Intercessors of Squad Loriyan did the same, their bolt rifles roaring in the armourglass confines of the tube. The cultists came at them in a shrieking, blood-mad mob, firing pistols and brandishing knives. They trampled each other, froth spilling from their jaws as they sought to overrun the Imperial Fists.

Second by second, they gained ground.

'Tube terminates in eighty-three yards, my captain,' said Sergeant Loriyan. He'd lost his helm to a bolt impact at some point, and one side of his face was a mask of blood.

'A little further,' said Dysorian, ejecting his clip and reaching for another. Instead, he found his last frag grenade. Clamping his pistol to his thigh, Dysorian hefted the grenade.

'On my mark,' said the captain. 'Squad Ulorian, stand ready.'

The cultists surged forward, piling over the cracked armourglass of the tunnel, crushing each other against the brushed silver railings that lined the walkway.

'Now,' he said, thumbing the grenade's detonator and hurling it into the rabid cultists' midst. It vanished beneath their feet. As it did, the Intercessors raked the crowd with a burst of full-auto fire, then all three Imperial Fists turned and ran along the tunnel. Bullets chased them, ricocheting off shoulder guards and power packs. Then came the dull thump and fiery roar of the grenade's detonation, and the bullets were replaced with spinning limbs and spraying blood.

Dysorian and his brothers burst from the end of the tube onto a broad marble plaza, almost running straight into the hulking Devastator Centurions of Squad Ulorian who waited at the tube's mouth.

'Seal it,' barked Dysorian. The Centurion pilots voxed acknowledgement, stomping their heavy exo-suits into a semi-circle around the gilt-edged mouth of the transit tube. Once, it had been a beautifully appointed footway for the privileged and faithful. Now it was a potential weak spot in the hive's final defence line.

As fresh waves of cultists spilled along the tube, the Centurions opened fire. Lascannons howled and grav cannons thrummed, shattering the tunnel mouth, tearing the transit tube apart. Cultists exploded like fleshy sacs. Armourglass detonated into spinning shards, and with a terrible groan of collapsing supports the entire structure sheared away in a hundred-foot-long section. Bodies and wreckage plunged away, raining down upon the once-beautiful parkland below.

'Good,' said Dysorian. 'Now, return to the lines, brothers.'

Dismissed, the Centurions stomped away, servos and impellers whining. Meanwhile, Dysorian took in the situation with a strategist's eye.

He stood in the shadow of the Sacrosanct Arch, the place where Main Hive met the spire. Once, there had been numerous cross-over points between those two sections of Hive Endurance, but when the Great Rift opened, Canoness Levinia had ordered them all sealed barring this one.

The arch was an immense, armoured portal whose apex was several hundred feet high. The gates, which currently stood firmly shut, were gold-plated adamantium, engraved with magnificent scenes of the Emperor enthroned, surrounded by his angelic primarchs. A mighty, armoured wall stretched away to either side of the gate, forming one edge of the cavernous chamber in which it stood, studded with gun turrets and hung with the banners of the Order of the Crimson Tear.

Before the gate was the marble plaza on which Dysorian stood, its surface inlaid with mosaic patterns and dotted with armoured generator-blocks and defensive towers. A huge metal ramp, the Ascension Path, stretched down from the arch, several hundred feet across and a mile long, lined with statues of the Order's previous canonesses.

Below, the verdant parkland of the Elysial stretched out for miles, exotic plant life and magnificent fountains imported at phenomenal expense in the hive's earliest days.

Now, the marble plaza was thick with barricades and strongpoints, the parkland was torn through by earthworks and trench-lines, and Imperial soldiery thronged its approaches. Tsadrekhan infantry and tanks were present in their thousands. Battle Sisters moved amongst them, and knots of Imperial Fists stiffened the defence lines.

'Canoness Levinia has prepared the defences well,' noted Sergeant Loriyan.

'She has,' said Dysorian with gruff approval. 'Let's go and find her.'

They found Levinia and her Celestinian bodyguards at the forward command post, halfway down the access ramp. The canoness was speaking to a senior Tsadrekhan officer amidst a mass of barricades, gun emplacements and vox arrays. Levinia was a tall, spare woman, her hair cut in a short bob, steel grey on one side of her head, onyx black on the other to match her armour.

'Canoness,' said Dysorian.

'Captain Dysorian,' said Levinia, turning away from the officer. Dismissed, he made the sign of the aquila and marched away.

'The defences look sound,' said Dysorian. 'Will they be sufficient?'

'We must have faith that they shall, captain,' said Levinia. 'The Emperor protects. Enemy forces have gained access to the Elysial from nine-four-four south and nine-four-three west, but the Tsadrekhans are holding them at bay.'

Dysorian could hear gunfire echoing up from the fringes of the parkland below, and see distant fires burning amidst trees and ornamental beds.

'The Third and Sixth Tsadrekhan regiments are dug in along a double line of trenchworks, with support from their Eighteenth Tank Division,' continued Levinia. 'They have orders to fall back to the second line should the enemy mass in sufficient strength to overrun them. My Exorcist squadrons will cover their retreat, when the time comes.'

Dysorian had noted the strange tanks drawn up in large numbers near the base of the ramp. Black-and-bone Rhino hulls carried elaborate, weaponised pipe-organs upon their backs. Sisters sat at the keys behind each one, impresarios of destruction ready to unleash a rain of warheads with the battle-hymns of the Emperor.

'Do you have viable links to the lower defences?' asked Dysorian. 'The docks? The Underbilge? Our vox-channels have been sorely disrupted – I've barely been able to reach battle-brothers upon adjoining levels.'

'It's the storm, captain,' said Levinia. 'The Cicatrix Maledictum pours its poison down upon us, and whispers falsehoods in our ears. The Dark Gods seek to tempt us, or to cow us with fear. But yes, these vox-arrays have been auto-sanctified every thirteen minutes by priests of the Omnissiah and the Emperor. They hold true.'

'Good,' said Dysorian. He motioned for one of the Tsadrekhan operators to step away from his station. Eyes wide at the sight of a Space Marine captain, the man quickly complied, and Dysorian held his headset carefully to his ear. It looked flimsy and delicate in Dysorian's armoured fist.

The captain adjusted frequencies, ignoring the half-heard whispers and distant wailing that faded in and out as he did so.

'Lieutenant Lydanis,' he voxed. 'Lieutenant Lydanis, are you receiving?'

Nothing but spitting static and a suggestion of cruel, mocking laughter came back to him.

'If he was your man in the Underbilge,' said Levinia, standing at his shoulder, 'then he is most likely slain.'

'The Underbilge has fallen, then?' asked Dysorian heavily.

'There was a crash,' said Levinia. 'A maglev train carrying many foes. More enemies followed, then more still.'

'Dorn's fist,' muttered Dysorian. 'The damned tech-priests and their insistence on keeping the trains running. I warned them that the risk was unacceptable.'

Ignoring the inscrutable stares of the tech-magi who hovered nearby, Dysorian panned through his company's vox-channels.

'This is Captain Dysorian, Imperial Fists Fourth Company. If you can hear me, brothers, respond.'

Several of his warriors replied as he worked through the channels; Sergeant Oldreyan leading a force of Assault Marines and Repulsor Tanks in battle through the level eight-eight-three commercia; Chaplain Tolyon, cut off behind a raging firestorm in level seven-one-four nutri-storage, leading a last stand of brave Tsadrekhans; Techmarine Lynon, his gunship squadron still battling through the storm to strafe those invaders caught outside the city's skin.

Dysorian switched channels again.

'Captain?' came a welcome voice.

'Pavras,' said Dysorian with the ghost of a smile. 'What is your status, brother? Where are you?'

'Captain, the docks have fallen,' voxed Pavras. 'The storm tore them apart and drove us back. We were maintaining reserve positions through the maglev production manufactora, but then the heretics started pouring up from below.'

Pavras broke off for a moment, and Dysorian's mouth drew down as he heard his old friend give a retching cough.

'How badly are you hurt, Pavras?' he asked. 'We are drawing our lines at the Sacrosanct Arch. Can you reach us?'

Pavras laughed, a painful sound with no mirth in it.

'No, my captain, I don't believe that we can. I've a few battle-brothers left, a few dozen Tsadrekhans. We're barricaded within south water-lock tertius on level zero-nine-zero. We're going to blow the locks and try to cascade the blast through those on either side.'

'You're going to flood the level,' said Dysorian, closing his eyes for a moment.

'Yes,' replied Pavras, coughing again. *'I've built the cycle-pressure until the alert runes burned out, and overridden the saviour protocols. The water will tear through this level with such force, the heretics will think we detonated barrage bombs. We should be able to stem the flow of enemies from below.'*

Dysorian shrugged off his sorrow, kept his expression as unfeeling stone.

'The primarch would commend your sacrifice, brother,' he said.

'I'd like to think so,' said Pavras. *'But captain, before we do this. We've had two empyric breaches down here since we sealed ourselves in. The veil is thinning, old friend. There are daemons abroad.'*

'Thank you for the warning, Pavras,' said Dysorian, sharing a grim look with Levina. 'Your courage and sacrifice will–'

Dysorian's words were cut off by a sudden roar of gunfire at the other end of the vox, and a terrible, screeching roar.

'No time,' said Pavras. *'They're coming again, cursed unclean warpspawn! Brother Doryal, blow the charges! Now, now, now!'* A thunderclap of sound filled the vox, then was replaced by hissing static.

'Captain,' said Levina. Dysorian looked down, realising that he had crushed the headset in his fist. Disgusted, he dropped the mangled device and rose.

'How has it come to this?' he asked angrily. 'When the enemy fell upon us, we tore them from the skies. Even when Khordas smashed his ship in Endurance's flank, we contained the assault. Where is your Saint in all this? Why didn't she warn us?'

'The Saint goes where the Emperor commands,' said Levina. 'Even now she stands before the beacon with blade drawn, our last line of defence should all else fail. As to our enemies' victories, you know as well as I that this has been a desperate battle from the beginning. But the Emperor does not give his gifts to the unworthy. He is testing us, and we shall prove ourselves equal to the trial. Have faith.'

Dysorian grunted.

'Death by a thousand cuts,' he said. 'Misfortune piled atop the idiocy of blinkered priests. I fear that faith has done much to bring us to this pass, but it goes no further. They will not cross this line. They will not have the beacon. This I swear by the primarch and the Emperor.'

Levinia nodded stiffly.

'Very well, captain. Then let us prepare. I trust you do not object if I remain at this station, to coordinate our defence?'

'No, canoness,' said Dysorian. 'You know these warriors better than I. This is your city, they are your people. I will spread my battle-brothers through the key defensive positions, and gather my elites to provide a counter-strike when it is required.'

'Very good, captain,' said Levinia as a flight of Valkyries roared overhead, missiles streaking away to explode amidst the burning parkland. 'Then let us be about the Emperor's work, and may He watch over us all.'

'He and Dorn both,' said Dysorian, staring out at the sprawling firefight pushing deeper into the grounds below them. 'The enemy are at our gates.'

For over an hour, scattered warbands of Khorne worshippers had been spilling into the Elysial, breaking through its armoured gateways from the shrineplexes, high-commercia and Administratum cloisters beyond. Ragged cultist mobs, possessed Heretic Astartes and speeding bands of Khornate bikers had struck at the lines of the Tsadrekhan Third, Sixth and 18th, but each time they had been hurled back.

Now a concerted attack wave flowed in from several sundered gateways at once, spearheaded by lumbering daemon engines and howling bands of Khorne Berzerkers.

'Khordas!' they chanted, voices melding into a ragged roar. 'Khordas! Khordas!'

Seated in the troop bay of the Land Raider *Unstoppable*, re-equipped and surrounded by the Terminators of Squad Alydo, Dysorian watched the fight unfold through optic feeds and gunbox footage.

The Tsadrekhans were deployed in a long, shallow curve that stretched from one banner-hung wall of the chamber to the other. Eight thousand fighting men and women, give or take, supported by forty-two battle tanks and armoured personnel carriers.

Amongst ornamental groves of olidarne trees on the right flank, a mass of mutant cultists and writhing spawn surged into the

Tsadrekhan gunfire. Explosions hurled clods of earth and broken corpses into the air, and the nodding trees burned. Hundreds of Khorne worshippers died in minutes, annihilated by withering volleys, but still they came on until they were clambering up and over the Tsadrekhan earthworks.

On the left, Dysorian saw that the Imperial defenders were faring better. Much of the Tsadrekhan armour had massed there, amidst ornamental fountains and open contemplation gardens. Khorne Berzerkers came at them in a charging mass, only to be blown apart by whistling cannon shells. Infernal war machines spat fire at the Tsadrekhans, but lascannon beams reached out to detonate them one at a time.

'The centre,' Dysorian muttered, watching intently. 'They're going to punch right through.'

Sure enough, with both flanks engaged and the Tsadrekhan reserves moving up to support them, the Khornate hordes struck at the centre of the Imperial line. Engines gunning, red-hulled Rhinos and heretic battle tanks roared up the Sainted Road, which led from the Elysial's edge to the base of the Ascension Path. Their guns thundered, blasting holes in the Tsadrekhan barricades. Return fire flashed around the Khornate vehicles, crippling or destroying several, but the rest ploughed on, smashing aside the burning wrecks of their fellows. The tanks' guns spoke again, mowing down Tsadrekhan weapons teams and forcing the militia squads to dive for cover.

'Levinia,' voxed Dysorian.

'I know, captain,' she replied. 'I see it. Colonel Hespus is leading the reserves to reinforce the centre. Valkyries and Exorcists standing by.'

The armoured spearhead ground over the remains of the Tsadrekhan barricades. Assault ramps slammed down, yawning like the maws of beasts, and bellowing World Eaters charged out. These were elite killers, festooned with skull trophies, many bearing the stigmata of unholy mutation. Vicious talons and barbed tentacles snaked out to rip through panicked Tsadrekhans. Dysorian saw a roaring commissar stride into the fight, bolter blazing, power sword held high. A hulking champion in Terminator plate met him head on, smashing the blade from his hand then goring him with the snarling chain-tusks of his helm.

'They're going to break,' said Dysorian.

It began slowly, Tsadrekhans turning and fleeing in ones and twos. Like a dam bursting, those first trickles became a sudden flood as panic took hold. Tsadrekhans ran from the blood-drenched murderers in their midst. They screamed in terror, dropped weapons, stumbled over one another and died messily as the traitors continued their slaughter.

More Khorne worshippers were pouring into the parkland from the sundered gates, wave upon wave of renegades, cultists and madmen. Huge engines of destruction came in their midst, Titan-class daemon engines that rolled forward on tracks and spiked wheels. Rotary cannons in their maws spun up to speed, spewing streams of shells into the fracturing Imperial lines. Friend and foe alike were slaughtered as the firestorms ripped up the soil in ragged lines, chewed defences to cratered wreckage and shredded bodies in sprays of blood.

'The Tsadrekhans can't stand against that,' said Levinia. 'I'm ordering the retreat. The reserves are to pull back before they get caught amidst the rout. We'll preserve what armour we can.'

'The Tsadrekhans don't have the discipline to break off cleanly, canoness,' warned Dysorian. 'Say the word, and we will strike against the traitors' centre.'

'Not yet, captain,' replied the canoness over a background hubbub of relayed orders and voxed commands. 'The Tsadrekhans will suffer beneath the traitors' blades, but their sacrifice will not be in vain. I believe that, at the sight of our outer lines collapsing, the Arch Heretic will join the fight to lead what he believes to be the killing blow. Then shall you be the Emperor's blade, captain, to strike down the lord of the unrighteous and tear the heart from their attack.'

The Tsadrekhans tried their best to fall back in good order, but they were hardly Cadian shock troops. With their centre reduced to a bloodbath and their right flank being swiftly overrun, discipline collapsed.

Junior officers strove to coordinate the rout, but as Dysorian listened to the cacophony of conflicting orders, gabbled prayers and storm-whipped static, it became clear they were not up to the task.

On the right, reserve formations that had been about to charge to their fellows' aid were instead ordered back. Some forged ahead regardless, their blood up, and fed themselves into the carnage for little gain. Others milled, confused by contradictory commands, blocking the path of those trying to retreat in good order.

As more and more cultists poured over the breached earthworks, the Tsadrekhans found themselves beset. When packs of loping daemon engines crashed through to join the fight, discipline broke down altogether. Barely a third of the Tsadrekhan troops committed to that flank managed to disengage, and many of them came away at a panicked run.

The centre was even worse, with the World Eaters and their battle tanks driving the Tsadrekhans like cattle to the slaughter. Men fell by the dozen. Armoured personnel carriers burned by the roadside, and as the traitors mounted into their vehicles again, they roared forward over a carpet of headless corpses. Colonel Hespus' Chimera was left in their wake, just another blazing tomb full of corpses.

Only on the left did the Tsadrekhan retreat hold together, their battle tanks reversing in a staggered line, pouring shots into the oncoming foe while the infantry fell back around them. Tank commanders hung out of their vehicles' top hatches, barking orders as they strafed the enemy with storm-bolter fire. The tanks bucked on their tracks as they fired shell after shell, and one of the immense daemon engines shuddered to a halt, flames pouring from it.

'Covering elements deploy,' voxed Levinia. 'Save those you can.'

As one, the Exorcists drawn up at the foot of the Ascension Path began firing. Their operators worked the pedals and keys of their strange weapons, eyes closed and lips moving rapturously as they wrought the battle hymns of the Imperial creed. With every keystroke, another missile was primed, cycling into the organ pipes before streaking away upon trails of blessed smoke. Dozens of warheads arced up and over the fleeing Tsadrekhans, spearing down into the oncoming Khornate horde. Tanks detonated. World Eaters ripped their way out of their burning transports, only for successive volleys to blast them limb from limb.

At the same time, the Tsadrekhan Valkyries struck again. They sallied out from eyries built high in the walls above the Sacrosanct Arch, streaking low over the battle with rocket pods hissing. Explosions stippled the traitor advance.

Goaded, the Khornate horde surged forward all the faster. They poured across the burning parklands, guns thundering to knock Valkyries from the air and tear through the retreating Tsadrekhan ranks, until they neared the foot of the Ascension Path itself.

'Sisters,' voxed Levinia. 'Now.'

At her command, dozens of Rhinos and Immolators awoke. They had drawn up to either side of the ramp, shrouded in camo netting and concealed by the shadows of the Ascension Path. Now their engines roared and they churned mud beneath their tracks as they raced into battle.

'You never meant the Tsadrekhans to hold, did you, Levinia?' asked Dysorian.

'I did not, captain,' said Levinia. 'There can be no victory without suffering.'

The Order of the Crimson Tear enfolded the strung-out heretic advance from both sides. Even as the black-and-bone tanks slewed to a halt and squads of Battle Sisters leapt from within, Retributors upon the ramp set up a punishing firestorm that ripped into the Khornate ranks. Intercessors, Hellblasters and Devastators added to the fusillade. The Exorcists continued to fire, even as they retreated up the Ascension Path.

'Their assault stalls,' said Dysorian. 'Well done, canoness, your Sisters are holding them back.'

'For now,' replied Levinia. 'See, they are already spilling out around the flanks, trying to overrun them. The enemy's numbers are great, their hate greater. We shall need all our faith to endure.'

'Where's Khordas?' said Dysorian. 'Surely he must show himself soon, or lose face.'

'I believe that your prayers may be answered, captain,' said Levinia. 'Look, in the centre of the line.'

Dysorian's expression broke into a dangerous smile as he saw a mountainously huge battle-tank bulling its way through the fight with a diabolical figure enthroned atop its spiked hull.

'There he is at last.' Dysorian switched vox-channels to address his strike force. 'Brothers, Lord Khordas has shown himself. Now let us strike him down in Dorn's name, avenge our fallen, and break the spirit of these murdering scum. To the glory of the primarch!'

'To the glory of the primarch!' echoed his brothers, and the Imperial Fists' counter-attack began.

A trio of yellow-hulled Land Raiders roared down the Ascension Path. Overhead skimmed a squadron of Land Speeders, while Primaris Inceptors bounded alongside the armoured gauntlet, their heavy jump packs roaring.

They made straight for Lord Khordas' position. It was not hard to locate.

'He has a Stormlord,' said Dysorian.

'Aye, but what has he done to it?' said Sergeant Alydo.

'Profaned it, as they do everything, sergeant,' replied Dysorian grimly.

An enormous slab of armour and tracks that resembled a rolling fortress, the Stormlord was a monstrosity. Spikes sprouted from its hull, many with skulls rammed onto their points. Brass chains dangled from its flanks, and skull-fuelled braziers of black flame burned on the top. Where the vehicle's open troop compartment would normally be, there instead rose a huge brass throne, set on a mountain of brass skulls. Lord Khordas the Slaughterer sat atop this remarkable structure, bellowing at his warriors.

'Dorn's teeth, he's enthroned as though he were a god!' breathed Dysorian. 'The arrogance!'

Shrugging off heretic fire, *Unstoppable* reached the bottom of the ramp and bulled into the midst of the fight. Khorne Berzerkers vanished beneath the tank's racing tracks. A Helbrute was rammed aside, smashed onto its back like some freakish crustacean. The rest of Dysorian's strike force followed in his wake, the two Land Raiders *Resolute Defender* and *Hammer* adding their firepower to that of *Unstoppable*. Their Land Speeders raced ahead, engines flaring as they performed weaving attack runs to clear the tanks' path. Meanwhile, the Inceptors soared in huge bounds, their assault bolters thundering.

The tainted Stormlord loomed before them.

'Cripple its tracks,' ordered Dysorian. 'Force the traitor down off his throne.'

Dropping low, the Land Speeders whipped along the Stormlord's flanks. Bolt shells whined off their cowlings as they opened fire, strafing the goliath tank with multi-meltas. One of the speeders was clipped, spinning out of control and smashing into the burning trees. The other two scored palpable hits.

The Land Raiders, meanwhile, poured everything they had into their target. Lascannon beams strafed both track units, blasting and melting link after link. Smoke billowed from the Stormlord's drive units as its left track seized completely, causing it to slew sideways as it ground to a halt.

The immense Vulcan mega-bolters on the Stormlord's hull opened fire, pummelling the *Resolute Defender* until the Land Raider shuddered to a stop with flames pouring from it.

'It's halted,' voxed Dysorian. 'All squads, disembark and engage. Land Speeders, cover pattern. Inceptors, lead us in.'

Unstoppable's assault ramp whined open, and Dysorian and the Terminators of Squad Alydo advanced onto the Elysial. The super-heavy loomed above them, its guns still roaring, and Squad Alydo stepped forward to protect Dysorian with their storm shields. A lascannon blast struck one, staggering the Terminator who bore it, but doing no worse.

They began their advance, the Terminators of Squads Dethyan and Lynon to their right and left.

'Khordas is moving,' voxed Sergeant Alydo. 'Now there'll be a reckoning.'

Lord Khordas had indeed leapt up from his throne, bellowing in fury. He stormed down the mound of skulls, a towering monster of a warrior taller than a Dreadnought. His musculature was so warped and swollen that he wore no armour above his waist, save oversized shoulder guards lashed on with heavy chains. His ruddy hide was covered in scars, while his bestial features were mutated and canine. He carried two huge axes, one in each fist, their blades burning with unnatural flame, and as he leapt down from the side of his tank he pointed both weapons at Dysorian while roaring a challenge.

Berzerkers spilled from the hull of the damaged tank, only to meet a wall of fire hurled by flanking squads of Battle Sisters. With a howl of turbines, Dysorian's Inceptors soared overhead, landing before the onrushing heretics and letting fly with their assault bolters. A slew of Khorne Berzerkers were smashed from their feet before the Inceptors leapt away to safety. Most made it, but one unlucky Primaris warrior was not quick enough. Lord Khordas leapt high, even as the Inceptor lifted off, and hacked him in half at the waist.

The Khornate lord slammed down, hard enough to shake the ground. His victim's legs fell with him, the Inceptor's torso boosting away, its innards spilling in a gory wake behind it.

'You will pay for the brothers you've slain,' snarled Dysorian, and broke into a run.

His Terminators came with him, pounding the ground with their heavy footfalls. Khordas ran to meet them with fire burning in his eyes.

'Your skulls belong to Khorne,' he roared, his voice that of a monstrous beast. 'Your blood shall soak the soil!'

Dysorian opened fire, raking Khordas' chest. It was as though he had shot the hull plating of a tank.

Khordas laughed, and swept his axes down to meet the charging Terminators. His first blow hacked through one of Squad Alydo's storm shields, shearing the adamantium in half like parchment. Hellish flames leapt across the Terminator's armour and he reeled back, yelling in agony as he was burned alive. Khordas' second swing slammed into the chest of Terminator Sergeant Dethyan and hurled him through the air. Dethyan hit the front of the *Hammer* hard enough to leave a deep dent, his armour also burning.

'Caution, brothers,' barked Dysorian, ducking under the swing of Khordas' left axe. 'Beware the flames!'

'You cannot save them,' laughed Khordas, his voice so deep it reverberated through Dysorian's chest. Kicking the captain aside, Khordas waded into Dysorian's men. Another two Terminators died in as many seconds, helmed heads hacked off and bodies left burning. Brother Phylon opened fire with his assault cannon, punching a string of bloody wounds into Khordas' flank. His reward was to be split in two from the head down, his paired halves crumpling to the floor aflame.

'No!' roared Dysorian, pushing himself back to his feet. 'Brothers, fall back, get clear! Land Raiders, blast him.'

The surviving Terminators backed away, lashing out with lightning claws and thunder hammers to drive the daemonic lord back. Those with storm bolters fired them, peppering Khordas with shots. Another of the Terminators died as his legs were hacked away and his body burned to ash.

The Land Raiders fired, bright lascannon beams converging upon Khordas. One shot punched right through his torso, leaving a smoking hole. Khordas stormed forward, burying his axes in the front of *Hammer* with such force that the tank's rear end left the ground. Hellish fires leapt across the tank's hull, surging through its systems. There was a deafening boom, and the venerable *Hammer*, survivor and victor of three millennia of war, exploded from within.

'Enough!' roared Dysorian. He ran at Khordas, firing his bolt pistol into the back of the huge warrior's skull. Shells burst and exploded, ripping scads from Khordas' scalp. The daemonic lord turned with a snarl, looming over Dysorian. The captain threw himself into a dive, rolling between Khordas' armoured legs. He lashed out with his power sword as he did, and felt a bone-jarring connection.

Rolling to his feet, Dysorian spun, blade raised. Khordas tried to turn with him, and left the severed half of his right leg behind. With a roar of shock and fury, Khordas overbalanced and crashed down on his face.

He pushed himself back up as best he could. Face a mask of fury, he hacked at Dysorian. The captain threw himself backwards, almost evading the blades. One clipped him, hurling him onto his back and shattering his back carapace. He cursed as he felt the hellfire take hold, but it slowly sputtered out. Khordas was sorely wounded, and with the hymnals of the Battle Sisters swelling on all sides, his power was fading.

'Everything,' gasped Dysorian, lungs labouring. 'Fire everything.'

The world lit up as lascannon beams, heavy bolter shells and multi-melta blasts converged upon Lord Khordas. The Inceptors leapt in again, guns thundering, perforating his disintegrating body.

Levering himself up on one elbow, Dysorian levelled his bolt pistol and added his fire to the cauldron, slamming a shell right between Khordas' blazing eyes. This time the shot penetrated, as the daemon lord's powers evaporated. The shell burst within Khordas' skull, deforming his head from within and then blowing it apart in a meaty spray.

Beheaded, torso ravaged, one leg hacked off at the knee, the great Lord Khordas toppled forward and thumped into the mud, dead. A lingering scream accompanied his death, the sound of a wild beast being dragged down into the darkest hells.

'Levinia,' croaked Dysorian, spitting a mouthful of blood. 'We did it. The beast is slain.'

'Indeed!' voxed the canoness. 'A truly heroic victory, captain, and one that has torn the heart from the foe. The Emperor thanks you, as do I from the bottom of my heart. The Khornate forces are wavering. My Sisters have thinned their numbers, and with their leader so visibly slain we stand upon the cusp of victory. We shall protect the beacon yet.'

Dysorian pushed himself to his feet once more, ignoring the grinding agony in his chest. Khordas' Stormlord had been reduced to a blazing wreck, and around him Dysorian could see the Khornate forces collapsing into utter disorder. Some, the mortals, fled. Some fought on, while others fell upon one another in the hopes of seizing Khordas' mantle of leadership. One last push, he thought with grim satisfaction, and the Imperial forces would claim victory.

Then his vox clicked again, and at Levinia's words a cold weight of dread settled in Dysorian's gut.

'Emperor's mercy, Captain Dysorian. There's a crimson mist spilling across the park. Do you see it? Daemons! Holy throne, the daemons have come.'

'What is that they're chanting?' voxed a Tsadrekhan commander. *'It can't be…'*

'It is,' said Dysorian, weary beyond count. Suddenly, he felt all three hundred of his years. All the bloodshed, all the comrades slain, old and new. The desperate battle with Khordas. All for nothing. Bitterness and anger rose within him, drowning the glimmer of faith that the Saint had kindled in his heart. Dysorian's hope could not survive the horror of what was upon them.

Khârn! Khârn! Khârn!

'That is our death knell,' he voxed. 'It is defeat.'

'Captain Dysorian!' said Levinia. 'We cannot countenance defeat. The beacon is all that stands between the billions of souls we safeguard and the unclean darkness that seeks to devour them. Where is the famed stoicism of the Imperial Fists in this desperate hour? Where is your faith?'

'You shall see our stoicism, canoness,' said Dysorian angrily. 'You shall see it in the holding action that we are about to fight. You shall see it in our butchered corpses, strewn here upon this soil so that you have time to get to the beacon and evacuate it. This is Khârn the Betrayer, the greatest murderer since Angron the Red, leading the daemons of the warp down upon us. There is no victory in battle here, canoness. Only in our sacrifice, and your flight.'

Dysorian could see it now, spilling across the parkland, a terrible red fog rolling towards him. Unnatural shapes writhed in that miasmal fume, hundreds of them loping and snarling and hissing. Huge, bat-winged creatures moved overhead, their wingbeats booming like thunder. The Tsadrekhans were screaming in terror, while the prayers of the Battle Sisters rose defiantly to meet the onrushing horde. The surviving Khorne worshippers howled the praise of the red-armoured killer who ran towards them, chainaxe roaring as the crimson fog swept in his wake. They redoubled their murderous efforts, and the battle began to swing once again.

'Don't argue, canoness,' barked Dysorian, motioning his surviving warriors to form up. 'We must fight, and you must flee. Get to the Saint, and protect the beacon. In the Emperor's name, Levinia, do it now.'

'Very well,' said the canoness, the desire to stay and fight strong in her voice. 'The first through fourth chambers will remain, and stand with you to the end. The fifth shall accompany me, and see to the beacon's safety.'

'Good,' said Dysorian. 'Make this count.'

'I shall, Paetrov,' said the canoness. 'And may we meet again at the Emperor's table.'

With that, the canoness and her bodyguards began their retreat, a fifth of the Adepta Sororitas forces peeling off and following in her wake. The rest steeled themselves as the crimson fog rolled closer, drawing up shoulder to shoulder against the onrushing Khornate horde.

They would sell themselves dearly, Dysorian promised himself, and raised his blade once more. He owed his brothers that…

Then the bloody mists surged over them, drowning the artificial daylight and reducing visibility to mere feet. Hideous faces swam through the murk, cackling and shrieking before breaking into vapour clouds again. Bloodthirsty howls echoed weirdly around them, carrying clear where the gunfire and hymnals of the Battle Sisters were rendered muffled and brittle.

'Steady, brothers,' said Dysorian. 'Remember the primarch in this dark hour. Show him how his sons fight, no matter the odds.'

A huge metal flail snaked out of the blood-mists, a segmented thing of brass links the size of Space Marine helms that clattered as it uncurled. It struck the Terminator standing beside Dysorian and smashed him backwards through the murk without so much as a death cry. The weapon clattered back out of sight, then lashed out again, crushing Sergeant Alydo's helm in a spray of blood.

'Fire!' barked Dysorian, and his few remaining brothers let fly into the murk. The Inceptors bounded forward, assault bolters roaring, but a sheet of searing flame spat from the blood-fog and engulfed them. They crashed to the ground, blackened and writhing, and did not rise.

'Enough,' snarled Dysorian and, ignoring the pain of his wounds, he began to limp towards the unseen threat. Sensing his challenge, something huge moved amidst the murk. Dysorian saw dark wings spread wide, and glowing red eyes pierced him like blades. Huge hooves pounded the ground as an immense Khornate daemon surged from the murk, an axe in one fist and the long, segmented lash in the other. It loomed over him, more than thrice his height.

Without breaking stride, Dysorian shot the abomination in the face, once, twice, again. Even as his shells burst in its gnarled flesh, he broke into a lurching charge, drawing back his blade and ramming it as hard as he could into the daemon's armoured midriff.

The sword sank home, but as it did its crackling energies flickered and died. Molten ichor squirted from the wound, melting the blade and eating into the captain's armour. Before Dysorian could wrench his ravaged weapon free for another strike, the daemon drove its knee into his faceplate, staving it in and hurling the captain onto his back.

Groaning, Dysorian wrenched the wrecked helm off, ignoring the agony of the broken bones in his face. His vision swam with black spots, and his lungs filled with sulphurous smoke as the daemon loomed over him, a vast black presence with fire for eyes.

'For Dorn...' croaked Dysorian, 'and the Emperor. May you rot in the warp forever, you filthy–'

The monster's axe swung down and sank through flesh, bone and soil with a meaty thwock, cutting off Dysorian's last curse as it severed his head. Coiling its lash, the daemon reached down and lifted its trophy, breathing fire upon it in waves that crisped Dysorian's flesh and blew it away in ashen clouds. Finally, all that remained was a blackened skull, three service studs driven into its forehead and glowing with heat.

The daemon chuckled, a rumble of fell thunder, and rammed the skull onto a spike atop its axe. It spread its shadowy wings and leapt away into the blood-fog to continue its slaughter. So fell Paetrov

Dysorian, heroic captain of the Imperial Fists Fourth Company, and with him the last, faint hope for victory.

CHAPTER FOURTEEN

Choral alarms echoed through the convent prioris. Squads of Battle Sisters hastened down marble-floored corridors, their hymns echoing before them. Macabre cherub servitors winged their way through arched chambers and up spiralling stairwells, bearing gilded order-scrolls in their talons. Their incense trails hung in the air, lit like volcanic fume by strobing electro-candles. Everywhere there was a sense of controlled panic, of defiance in the face of impending doom.

All eyes were turned outwards, towards the threats encroaching upon the spire from all sides. Foes rained down from on high, breaking through the failing void shields and faltering flak batteries of the hive spire. They hammered at the Sacrosanct Arch, even as unnatural terrors scaled the convent's external walls and hacked their way in through armoured bulkheads. Few had attention to spare for the ancient and forgotten chambers that lay in the convent's deepest crypts…

The servo-lift juddered to a halt, a single bell tolling forlornly at its arrival. A cage door rattled back with a wheeze of ancient spring-coils, and a metal shutter slid up and out of sight. Inside the elevator car, Kassar and his Unsung had their bolters up and aimed, though they saw nothing before them but a dark, empty chamber.

'*Advance and secure,*' said Kassar. '*Shroud protocol paramount.*'

The Alpha Legionnaires exited the lift into the undercrypts of the convent prioris, armour whispering on half power to minimise noise. They spread out across dusty flagstones, between old tombs and stone pillars. Rusty electro-sconces provided flickers of light, illuminating scuttling salt-spiders lurking in their saline webs. A single archway led out of the chamber, electrical light spilling over the worn steps that rose beyond.

'*Looks clear,*' said Skaryth.

'*This place hasn't seen footfall in a long while,*' said A'khassor. '*The dust must be three inches thick.*'

'*Good,*' said Kassar. '*Haltheus, see if you can find an old dataport or terminal anywhere in here to set your data daemons loose. Thelgh, Skarle, cover the stairs beyond the arch. The rest of you, analysis and suggestions.*'

The Unsung gathered on their leader. Krowl loomed to one side, Phaek'or's unconscious form slung easily over one shoulder.

'*We are almost at our objective,*' said D'sakh. '*But we are in the heart of the enemy's greatest fortress. We won't succeed here through brute force alone.*'

'*Agreed,*' said Makhor. '*We need to evade the Sisters of Battle, locate the beacon, have the cultist perform his ritual, and then exfiltrate safely.*'

'*There are other factors,*' said Kyphas. '*According to Imperial vox reports, Khârn has overrun the defenders beyond the Sacrosanct Arch. He and his followers are beating at the gates. In response, the corpse worshippers are looking to evacuate the beacon and its attendant tech-priests.*'

'*If Khârn reaches the beacon before us, or the Imperials take it beyond our reach, then we've lost,*' said Kassar. '*Speed is key.*'

'*What of the exfiltration plans?*' asked Makhor. '*It was a dark miracle that we survived that crash. I've no desire to be spared a fiery death only for some Slaaneshi cataclysm to consume me when Excrucias doesn't uphold his end of the bargain.*'

'*Excrucias assured me before we deployed that his fleet would be lurking, ready to pounce the moment his sorcerers sense the ritual's completion,*' said Kassar. 'He provided me with a teleport homer, and his oath that he would send Terminators to aid in our exfiltration.'

'You trust him?' asked Makhor.

'He saw what we can do, on Bloodforge,' said Kassar. 'He'd be a fool to make enemies of us. But prior to this point, I was obliged to trust him because of the circumstances. We needed a way off Bloodforge. We couldn't board a Khornate warship in orbit, no matter what Phalk'ir believed; we possessed neither the numbers to conquer nor the leverage to bargain.'

'But now?' asked A'khassor.

'Now we are in a position to shape our own destiny,' said Kassar. He took a biomechanical device from an equipment pouch on his belt. It tingled with empyric resonance in his grip. Kassar dropped the device and crushed it under his boot. Its winking runes went out.

'No Terminators, then?' asked Haltheus as he worked at a dust-furred data-lectern.

'No,' said Kassar. 'As soon as the beacon is compromised, we make for the closest landing pad and acquire a trans-atmospheric craft. We'll return to him on our terms, not under armed guard.'

'We could still be walking into a trap,' said Makhor. 'Slaanesh worshippers aren't noted for their forgiving nature. We killed a lot of his warriors on Bloodforge.'

'True,' agreed Kassar. 'But Kyphas has bought us insurance on that front. Kyphas?'

The former spymaster was silent for a moment.

'Before we deployed,' he said eventually. 'While we were still in transit. You remember I subvocalised to those serfs, used hypnotic interrogation upon them? I also provided them with subconscious instruction.'

'Saboteurs?' asked A'khassor.

'Assuming they were not discovered, Kyphas' agents will by now have prepared a dozen acts of sabotage throughout Excrucias' ship,' said Kassar. 'Magazines mined and ready to blow. Charges laced through the warp core coolant engines. Explosives located so as to depressurise the bridge at the press of a rune.'

'And if Excrucias threatens us, or tries to renege, we trigger them,' said Kyphas.

'Then either exfiltrate in the confusion or, ideally, take Excrucias hostage and leverage passage elsewhere with his life,' said Kassar.

'Risky, but better than anything else we've got,' said Makhor.

'If it gets me access to a proper apothecarian where I can see to Phaek'or, I'll take it,' said A'khassor. 'His healing coma will help, but that wound needs proper attention, soon, or a bionic will be impossible to graft.'

'Just another reason for speed,' said Makhor. 'We should move.'

'And we will,' said Haltheus. 'In just... one... there, got it.'

The data-lectern sputtered to life, autoscripture scrolling across its glowing screen. Haltheus uncoupled the Coffer from below his backpack and set it down, running wires from the device to the lectern. He quickly removed a gauntlet and ran his knife across his bared palm, drizzling blood into the Coffer's metal slits while muttering incantations.

Crimson runes flared along the box's flanks, and sulphurous smoke seeped from within.

'Thelgh, Skarle,' said Haltheus. 'When it comes, let it pass.'

A cyber-cherub hovered down the stairway, eyes glowing the same blood-red as the runes on the Coffer.

Haltheus uncoupled the Coffer from the data-lectern, whose screen was now snowy with static and flaring, unholy runes. He mag-locked the device back in place, bearing its weight as he coiled one of its wires up and attached it to his helm.

'Brothers, our guide,' said Haltheus, sounding pleased with himself. 'The cherub will lead us to the beacon. Its optic feed is coming straight to my peripheral, so it should make an even better scout than Skaryth.'

'Brothers,' said Kyphas. 'Vox intercept confirms an Imperial fleet breaking warp over Tsadrekha, and engaging the Khorne worshippers. They've come for the beacon.'

'It isn't theirs to take,' said Kassar. 'Unsung, move with a purpose.'

While the Alpha Legionnaires spoke, Syxx had stood nearby, largely ignored. He had become used to their strange conversations, and stopped trying to make sense of them. Those without their helms gave the appearance of praising the might of the Dark Gods, boasting of enemies they had killed, and mocking the Imperium's weakness, while those who went helmed didn't appear to be speaking at all. Syxx had realised early on that it was an act or code and, after a brief and frustrating period of trying to draw sense from their exchanges, had given up.

Instead, he thought of Colla and Ganshi and the rest. It was his habit, whenever he needed to focus his determination and hate. He called to mind their faces, as they had looked in his childhood, in the days before Phelkorian Twyst came and destroyed them piece by piece. Before the sorcerer made him watch.

It had become harder, as the years went by, to recall those sorrow-lined faces, those haunted eyes that glinted with love for him, their child. The years had abraded their features as the wind and rain erode a statue, until he was left with only feelings, sense memories and echoes that sustained him through all the horrible things he had endured. All the horrible things he had done, and enjoyed.

This was for them, he thought.

And for him.

Soon, he would have his revenge upon Phelkorian. He would pervert the ritual, just as he had planned, just as the tome he had stolen showed. He would purify his soul in the beacon's burning light, and in so doing he would become a conduit for divine vengeance. That light would shine upon everything Phelkorian Twyst had ever wrought and unmake it in an instant.

Syxx felt some flicker of sympathy for the Alpha Legionnaires he accompanied, for they would no doubt suffer the repercussions of his actions. They might well be slain. If not they might find themselves wishing they had been, as he had so many times. His sympathy was reserved almost entirely for Kassar, who had at least shown him some sort of consideration. To the rest he was just irksome baggage, and they, to him, no more than a different set of Chaos-worshipping oppressors. Just because they were subtler in their ways than his masters, less obviously corrupt, did not make them any less tainted or traitorous.

Syxx glanced up as a cyber-cherub puttered into the chamber on its grav-impellers, incense wafting behind it, eyes glowing red. The Alpha Legionnaires exchanged a few more nonsensical words, then gathered and prepared to move out. Checking his last couple of ammo clips were still stuffed into his belt, shrugging off the burning itch of his rune-branded flesh, Syxx took a deep breath and joined them.

Soon, he promised himself.

Soon it would all be over.

Beyond the undercrypts, the corridors of the convent prioris echoed with alarms, shouts and distant gunfire. Every few moments there came a shuddering that caused electro-sconces to flicker and dust to trickle from their ceilings.

'What is that shaking?' asked Makhor as they made their way along a deserted colonnade.

'The enemy without?' said A'khassor. *'The storm? Orbital bombardment? Impossible to say.'*

'Perhaps the hive's primary generatora are going critical,' said Makhor, morosely.

'That's not how our judgement will be delivered,' said A'khassor confidently.

'And I suppose that was why we survived the crash, also?' asked Makhor.

'Of course,' said A'khassor.

'So it was nothing to do with the way the carriage bucked just after we'd dived back inside,' pressed Makhor. *'The way it went over on its side and slid clear of the blast? The way that those commercia stalls absorbed its impact and stopped it hitting the pipelines beyond them?'*

A'khassor glanced at his brother.

'You know that it was all of those things and so do I,' said A'khassor. *'And I know you have no patience for our judgement, but it will come when it does. The galaxy isn't done with us, Makhor. We don't escape so easily.'*

Makhor was about to reply when a vox pip silenced them both. Haltheus' scout cherub had trilled out a binharic warning. The Unsung dropped back into the shadows at the corridor's edge, crouching in the lee of statuary with their eye-lenses dimmed and their guns held ready.

Ahead, an adjoining corridor rang to the crash of booted feet and singing voices. Quick-marching in a double column, a force of Battle Sisters emerged from one side of the junction and crossed out of sight. Makhor held his breath as they passed ahead, barely twenty yards from where Haltheus and Skaryth crouched. He noticed A'khassor readying his plasma pistol. The unstable weapon itself was a talisman of the Apothecary's belief that his death would come not from some random mishap, but at its appointed time.

The last of the Sisters vanished on their way. Several heartbeats later, the vox pip rolled back down the line to proceed.

'Whether we're to be judged or not,' said Makhor, 'our arrangement stands, brother. I can't believe that we'll make it through this unscathed, not with so many enemies arrayed on every side.'

'At least we don't have to worry about Phalk'ir now,' said A'khassor as they moved on. 'From what Kassar said, that fool burned his last bridge in grand style.'

'I wonder,' said Makhor. 'Will Phaek'or see it that way? And where did Phalk'ir go, anyway? He still has our vox-channels, our cyphers, our plans... Kassar can't just let him go. He could compromise us entirely.'

'You're right,' said A'khassor. 'But one fight at a time, eh, brother? Let's deal with this beacon and get off Tsadrekha before we start worrying about hunting down Phalk'ir. If that idiot even makes it off the planet alive.'

They crossed another junction, then passed through a shadowy series of galleries that overlooked a magnificent shrine to the Emperor. Sisters Repentia scourged themselves before the idol of the Master of Mankind, their huge eviscerators lying close at hand.

'Painful and pointless,' muttered D'sakh to Kassar, distaste in his voice as they observed from the shadows.

'That is where kneeling to gods will get you,' said Kassar. 'They should fight, but instead they kneel in ritual, uttering meaningless prayers and maiming themselves while the precious moments tick away.'

'And all to catch the eye of one who is, in the end, nothing more than a rotting corpse in a golden box half a galaxy away,' said D'sakh. 'Foolishness.'

'Misplaced faith,' said Kassar. 'But let us not follow their example. Time is of the essence.'

The Alpha Legionnaires crept quietly onwards, leaving the penitents to their bloody devotions.

Beyond they found another long corridor, whose armourglass windows looked directly out onto the turbulent sky above the hive. The corridor was lit from without by bruise-coloured light that flickered weirdly through umber, crimson and angry purple, interspersed with flashes of lurid green as lightning leapt amidst the clouds. Rain slicked the thick glass and formed the suggestion of screaming faces as it ran. Beyond, Makhor could see the burning spires of the convent prioris. Gunfire spat from many of them, billowing flames from others. Battle Sisters and Tsadrekhans dashed along walkways and across parade grounds between the structures, struggling through the ferocity of the storm, while far, far below the waves crashed and boiled.

'Their shields must have failed at last,' said Haltheus. 'There's Khornate landing craft out there by the dozen. Whether we succeed or not, Tsadrekha isn't going to survive the night.'

'Agreed,' said Kassar. 'The planet's going to fall. Let's not be here when it does.'

They worked their way up through the levels of the convent prioris, climbing the inside of one of its highest spires behind their hovering guide. Kassar watched the Coffer glowing and smouldering at Haltheus' back and knew that, by now, its anger must be causing him physical pain. Yet Haltheus pressed doggedly on.

They were climbing a steep metal stairway between two huge stained-glass windows that depicted saints punishing sinners, when a ferocious shudder ran through the spire. A crack split the left-hand window with a sound like a gunshot, and shards of glass plinked against Kassar's armour as they rained from above.

'The Betrayer and his forces have breached the Sacrosanct Arch,' reported Kyphas. 'They are inside the convent prioris.'

'Not far now,' panted Haltheus in a pained voice. 'There's a corridor atop this stairway that leads along the rear of the Cathedrum Vertexis where they keep the beacon. If we're not too late, we should be able to infiltrate through the priests' quarters and hit the cathedrum from the upper galleries.'

Kassar nodded and pipped his vox for the Harrow to keep moving. If Excrucias kept his half of the bargain then all well and good. If not, Kassar swore to himself that his brothers would make it out alive, even if he did not.

At that thought, a strange numbness began to spread up his sword arm, seeming to emanate from where his hand gripped Hexling's hilt. With it came the traitorous notion that his survival was every bit as important as theirs. Perhaps more. After everything he had sacrificed for them, didn't he have a right to survival?

More, didn't he deserve a reward?

Frowning, Kassar pushed the thought from his mind and shook the numbness from his arm. He kept climbing. Outside, the storm raged on, the insidious energies of the Great Rift shining through it to taint the stained-glass saints with madness.

They moved along the corridor, past a gaggle of purposeless, idling servitors clad in electro-weave cassocks, and up another steep staircase into the shadowy priests' quarters. The Unsung passed through spartan living chambers and cramped devotional shrines, and all the while Kassar waited for their luck to run out. For all that circumstances had been against them at every turn, now at the last those same factors – the Khornate invaders, the presence of Khârn, the raging storm – all combined with the Alpha Legionnaires' natural stealth to ensure they remained unnoticed.

And so, at last, the Unsung filtered out onto a shadowy balcony high up in the Cathedrum Vertexis, and gazed down upon the Tsadrekhan beacon.

The cathedrum itself was like a vast, circular pit with a marble floor hundreds of yards across, and four huge entrance archways leading into it. Steep-sided galleries rose all around, bustling with machinery and activity. They climbed hundreds of feet to the shadowed upper gantries where the Unsung crouched, and then higher still to a magnificent, domed ceiling painted with an image of the Emperor sitting in judgement over all. A vast stained-glass window admitted light to the cathedrum, the circular disc depicting Terra at its centre, and all the spheres of human settlement radiating out from it like the cogs of some impossibly intricate machine. A candle burned on a tiny grav-impeller before each world, turning the window into a softly lit star. Yet its light was as nothing to the blinding radiance that shone from the scrawny mortal resting in a cradle of wires and machinery at the cathedrum's heart.

'That's the beacon?' asked Makhor.

'What gave it away?' asked D'sakh.

'But, that's not an It,' said Makhor. 'That's not a machine, or a... a... well... It's a He.'

'This changes nothing,' said Kassar. 'I'm more concerned with all the corpse worshippers down there protecting him.'

The beacon was surrounded by well over a hundred Battle Sisters, armoured warriors and robed Hospitallers, even scribes, artificers and novitiates in their bone-hued habits. Though they were hundreds of feet below, Kassar's enhanced eyesight could easily pick out a formidable array of weaponry amongst them. Then there were the grotesque machines that loomed amongst the Sisters' ranks. Penitent engines, bipedal monstrosities thrice the height of a Space Marine, with revving saws and hissing flamers on their arms. On the front of each, a hooded figure hung cruciform, wires and tubules pinning it cruelly in place.

Several figures oversaw a gaggle of tech-priests and Imperial clerics as they fussed around the beacon and his cradle. A tall, steely-looking Battle Sister was remonstrating with a robed adept of the Mechanicus, while a pair of Seraphim Sisters looked on dispassionately. Kassar gestured in their direction. In response, Haltheus sent his cherub winging lower until its crude aural pickups could discern what was being said. Though thin wisps of sulphurous smoke were curling from his helm where the Coffer's wire joined it, Haltheus fed the cherub's audio and optic streams direct to his brothers' vox-beads.

Kassar saw a grainy, green-tinged image of the beacon and the figures surrounding it, furred with dancing lines of infernal runes and static.

'…is taking so long,' came the Battle Sister's voice, her tone exasperated.

'The proper rituals must be observed, canoness,' replied the tech-priest, his voice a many-layered digital chorus overlaid with binharic. 'If we displease the machine-spirits of the cradle, they will not relinquish their grasp upon the mortal form of Kaleb Deciman.'

The canoness' response was frosty.

'Do the machine-spirits – or you for that matter – realise that, if they do not relinquish their grip upon the beacon swiftly, they will succeed only in killing us all and surrendering his blessings into the hands of heretics? The fleet is in orbit but the storm is worsening and they cannot wait forever.'

'Canoness Levinia,' replied the tech-priest in a tone of maddening calm. 'The blessed mysteries of the Omnissiah cannot be rushed. They do not yield to mortal concerns any more than holy metal yields to the pressure of weak, flawed flesh. My acolytes are performing the rites in the optimal fashion, and as soon as they have completed the holy uncoupling, Kaleb Deciman will be stabilised and ready for evacuation.'

Kassar frowned as the optic feed cut out for a moment, drowned by a glowing mess of the Coffer's evil-looking runes. It swam back into sight, but the image had become more occluded, and the voices were tinged with a warping echo that made them sound somehow unclean.

'Sister Chastity reports that the shuttle is ready on pad nine,' said one of the Seraphim to the canoness. 'We could simply take him now. The Emperor would forgive us this desecration if it was performed in the name of our lady.'

'Geminae Sister Kassia,' said the tech-priest. 'If you were to forcibly uncouple Kaleb Deciman before his transfer to the anointed conveyance is complete, it would result in his painful and immediate death. I calculate that neither the Emperor nor the Omnissiah would forgive you such heresy.'

Kassar saw a wheeled frame beside the beacon's cradle, a torturous-looking thing of metal bands, padded straps and strange machineries. Already, several tubes and wires had been disconnected from the cradle and hooked into this 'anointed conveyance', but it was clear that the work was not yet complete.

At that moment, Haltheus hissed a curse and ripped the wire from his helm. A squeal of feedback raced through the Harrow's vox, descending into a guttural snarl before fading to nothing. Far below, the cherub spasmed, burst into flames, and fell from the sky to hit the flagstones with a meaty slap. Several Novitiates broke ranks to investigate the servitor's sudden fall.

Haltheus decoupled the Coffer and pushed it away with his foot, leaving it to smoke and snarl.

'Sorry,' he said with a shrug. 'The Coffer became irate. If I hadn't uncoupled when I did, that could have been us, and not the cherub.'

'We learned enough,' said Kassar. 'We must stop them before they complete the decoupling.'

'How?' asked Makhor. 'Even striking suddenly from above, we would never defeat that many.'

'Cultist,' said Kassar, turning to Syxx. 'Can you perform your ritual from here? How long will it take?'

'I would need to stand within the beacon's light and recite the incantation, lord,' said Syxx, his voice tight with fear and anticipation. 'It will last perhaps a minute or two. It can't be too rushed, lest I stumble over a sentence. The results could be catastrophic.'

'Too long,' said Kassar, turning back to his brothers. 'Even if we drop explosives, surprise them and drive them back from the beacon, we couldn't maintain a cordon long enough.'

He glanced up, into the highest reaches of the cathedrum where the shadows gathered thick and heavy. Hexling crooned in his mind, a note of caution, of something out of place. Something watchful and waiting.

'Besides,' he said warily, 'I do not trust this. I've a sense that something is awry...'

'Something?' asked Makhor. 'Everything is awry. We stand upon the clinch of victory but we cannot achieve it.'

'Perhaps we can,' said Skaryth. 'If we can set our enemies at each other's throats one last time.'

'*Elaborate,*' said Kassar.

'*The Betrayer is fighting below,*' said Skaryth. '*We lure him in, bring him to the doors of the cathedrum. As the Khorne worshippers and the corpse worshippers tear each other apart, we complete our mission.*'

'*Khârn will get here himself, soon enough,*' said Makhor. '*Why risk our lives leading him?*'

'*Because everything we've seen suggests that the Betrayer is a butcher,*' replied Skaryth. '*One who kills everything in his path. By the time his rampage leads him here, it may be too late.*'

'*And what if we do get him here?*' asked Makhor. '*You've all seen what Khârn can do. What's to say that he won't rip us apart as easily as the corpse worshippers?*'

'*Nothing,*' said Kassar. '*Except the hope that they will see him as the most obvious threat, and delay him long enough for us to taint the beacon and escape. It is the best plan we have, and we don't have the time to finesse anything better.*'

'*I'll lead him here,*' said Skaryth.

'*I'll help you,*' said D'sakh. '*You won't do something this insane by yourself, brother.*'

'Send one lunatic to lure another,' said Skarle solemnly. 'Gift will burn beside you, brother.'

'*I will join you,*' said Kassar, gritting his teeth as the sharp, needling numbness flooded his arm from his sword hand again. '*The rest of you, drop to a lower gallery, get as close to ground level as you can without arousing suspicion and await our return.*'

'Kassar–' began Makhor, but Kassar cut him off.

'This is not a debate,' he said. '*Get into position, brothers. Armour to full power, all of you. And be ready.*'

Skaryth led them, unhelmed. He paused at junctions, head tilted, listening. D'sakh shot Kassar a loaded glance, but Kassar ignored it. He knew the extent of all his brothers' difficulties and gifts. He kept a bolt ready for each, should they stray too far. He had done it before, just another burden of command that he had to bear.

The scout led them along corridors and hallways, across arched gantries and through magnificent chambers. Speed was everything now, and more than once they were forced to unsheathe their blades and deal with robed Sisters unfortunate enough to stray into their path. Soon their armour and knives were spattered with fresh blood.

It wasn't long before they could all hear the clangour of battle that Skaryth was following. Emerging through an arched portal, Kassar found himself on the edge of a sprawling library. Everywhere books burned, stacks toppled and corpses sprawled. A thin line of Tsadrekhans and Battle Sisters was falling back towards him, trying desperately to stay ahead of the Khornate charge.

They were failing.

'There,' said Skaryth, dread in his voice. 'Warp save us, there's Khârn.'

The Betrayer was leading the Khornate attack, Gorechild swinging in bloody arcs as he broke through the Imperial lines and put the defenders to flight. He ripped his axe through a trio of Tsadrekhans, decapitating them all with a single swing, then shot down a Sister Repentia who came at him with her eviscerator raised high. Another Battle Sister managed to hammer Khârn with her heavy bolter, cracking his armour and spraying his blood across the burning books. In response, the Betrayer closed the gap with three quick strides and hacked the luckless woman in half at the waist.

'Get his attention,' said Kassar, shaking his head at the insanity of the order. He fired Mortis, his brothers opening fire around him. Skarle howled as he primed a fistful of incendiaries and flung them in Khârn's direction.

Their volley struck sparks from the Betrayer's breastplate and helm, and wreathed him in jade flames. Khârn looked up, and as his blank gaze fell upon them Kassar felt again a phantom pain across his chest, the sensation of his arm severed at the elbow. Gritting his teeth, he fired another cluster of shells that exploded around the Betrayer's feet. Khârn roared in fury, and ran towards them.

'Move!' barked Kassar, and he and his brothers turned and fled.

Corridors and arches rushed by. Kassar's hearts thumped in his ears, competing with his pounding footfalls and the furious roars of the murderer at his back. They ran as fast as they could, following their auspex maps back towards the pulsing icon of the cathedrum. They smashed through doorways and pounded up stairwells, pushing their enhanced bodies to the limits. Still Khârn gained on them with terrifying speed, his roars and those of his hungering chainaxe growing ever closer. He ran with unnatural swiftness, utterly inexhaustible, and a little part of Kassar envied that Khorne-given strength.

The Betrayer came for them with a psychotic, single-minded intensity and his wrathful followers boiled behind him in a tide.

'We're not going to make it,' shouted D'sakh, dashing up a set of gilded steps behind Kassar. 'He must be right behind us.'

'Just keep running,' barked Kassar. 'We're one level away.'

A bolt of plasma seared past them, close enough to peel away the paint on Kassar's shoulder guard. He sprinted, dashing down a wide corridor. Ahead lay an arched doorway, beyond it a broad ramp below a stained-glass ceiling, and atop that one of the yawning entrances to the cathedrum.

Skaryth drew level with him, legs and arms pumping as he ran. D'sakh was just behind, Skarle a few paces further back, struggling with his wounded lungs. A quick glance showed Kassar that Khârn was now less than ten yards behind, a horde of Berzerkers and baying cultists spilling in his wake. Khârn swung his axe in a roaring arc, almost clipping Skarle's backpack with its whirling teeth.

Ahead, something huge moved in the archway, and suddenly it was full of stomping metal and revving saw blades.

'Penitent engines,' yelled Kassar. 'They've taken the bait. Unsung, evade!'

As the engines lumbered into a charge, they raised their flamers and filled the ramp with leaping fire. Kassar threw himself into a dive, beneath a swinging saw arm and through the legs of the lead penitent engine. Huge metal feet crashed and stomped around him, then he was back up and running, his brothers at his back. From behind came a tumultuous crash and a furious roaring as the charging machines ploughed head-on into Khârn and his warriors.

Kassar had no time for relief, however. Behind the penitent engines came a wave of Battle Sisters, and the Unsung were forced to hurl themselves into a side corridor as their enemies opened fire. Skarle howled as a bolt shell blasted his right hand to shreds.

'Fourth cypher,' voxed Kassar, grabbing Skarle and hauling him back down the side corridor. *'Unsung, bait is taken. Khârn is here.'*

'Understood,' voxed Makhor. *'We're four galleries up. They're dispersing towards the archway, defenders thinning. What's your status?'*

Kassar and his brothers backed fast down the corridor, keeping their guns trained on its mouth. A Battle Sister appeared at the end, and was smashed off her feet by bolt shells. A penitent engine replaced her, reeling backwards, its pilot headless and jetting blood. Khârn followed, leaping and smashing the engine onto its back with a thunderous axe blow. The Betrayer vanished up the ramp and his warriors followed him. None so much as glanced down the narrow corridor.

'Extracted successfully,' voxed Kassar. *'Looking for a way to loop back to you now.'*

'Twenty feet further along the corridor,' voxed Haltheus. *'Auspex mapping shows a floor hatch leading to a maintenance crawl-way. You can follow that back into the cathedrum, but you'll want to hurry. Warp alive! The Betrayer's at the arch already. They're throwing everything at him.'*

'Understood,' said Kassar. *'We're coming to you. Be prepared to move as soon as we emerge.'*

Haltheus' reply was cut off by a sudden commotion on the other end of the vox.

'Damn it, grab him!'

'What are you doing, you little fool?'

'Syxx, *Syxx!'*

'Report!' barked Kassar.

'The damn cultist,' voxed Haltheus. *'He's gone mad. He slipped away from us somehow. Warp damn it, Kassar, he's making straight for the beacon. He's going to get himself killed!'*

Kassar looked around at his brothers, still gasping from their lethal race, armour scorched and battered, Skarle cradling his clotting, mangled wrist.

'*Come on,*' he said, wrenching open the floor hatch and revealing the dark crawlspace below. '*We need to finish this. Now.*'

CHAPTER FIFTEEN

Syxx ran. He vaulted a brass railing, dropping a hundred feet in a matter of seconds. As he did, he felt his psychic powers billow out and cushion his fall. He rolled as he hit the ground, and came up running from a fall that might have crippled a Space Marine.

'They're going to ruin it,' muttered Syxx. He shot a fearful glance up at the higher galleries, catching a fleeting glimpse of power-armoured figures pursuing him. 'Now is my moment, they can't ruin it,' he gasped, and ran.

The crash of battle was all around, deafening in its intensity. Chain-axes roared and whined as they sawed through armour. Heretics howled oaths to the Blood God, competing with the Battle Sisters' furious war hymns. Bolters boomed their own staccato war-song. Stray bolts and blasts ripped at the gallery as Syxx ran along it, filling the air with shrapnel and sparks.

He kept his head down and kept running, ignoring the madness filling the cathedrum. His rune-brands burned with power desperate to be unleashed, and he was driven to answer their call. He knew with a compulsive certainty that he *had* to reach the beacon, *had* to perform the ritual before the Khorne worshippers reached it first.

'Redemption.' The word rang through his mind like a promise. 'Justice. Revenge.'

The fighting was concentrated around the eastern arch, but already the Khorne worshippers had broken into the cathedrum, bringing slaughter with them. Syxx dodged as a Sister Superior stumbled towards him, a Berzerker hacking madly at her buckled chainsword. He weaved around them just as the Sister dropped her mangled blade and shot the Khorne worshipper through the neck. Blood sprayed, and Syxx kept running.

Bolts whipped around him and armoured figures crashed together on every side. He skidded to a halt as a penitent engine stormed across his path, then ran again, eyes glued to the beauteous radiance at the cathedrum's heart.

With every step it grew closer, and as it did so the burning in his flesh intensified, becoming a searing pain as though the brands were being applied all over again. Syxx screamed and stumbled, smoke rising from his body, but something kept his limbs moving, propelling him forward.

A chainsword swung at him from nowhere, aimed straight for his face. His mind convulsed, and the blade was smashed aside. A Khornate warrior reeled into his path, drenched in gore, one arm missing. Syxx's mind spasmed again, a sensation of delightful agony, and the Berzerker was swatted away as though hit by a wrecking ball.

The whirling tides of battle parted and there was the Beacon of Tsadrekha. Tech-priests fussed around him, uncoupling the last few wires while chanting hasty binharic. The canoness and her elite stood in a circle, a last line of defence against the powers of darkness. In their midst, barely visible through the holy light shining from his body, the beacon wore an expression of peaceful acceptance upon his gaunt face.

'Heretic!' shouted one of the Battle Sisters as she saw Syxx coming. 'Unclean!' She aimed her bolter, but with a flick of his mind Syxx snapped her neck. Three of her Sisters followed, hurled unceremoniously aside with the powers of his mind.

Exultation and agony filled him as he waded into the beacon's light. His flesh was afire, his mind full of triumph and excitement as he opened his mouth to speak the words of atonement he had waited so long to utter.

'Emperor,' he began, his speech long prepared. 'I have sinned. I have walked in darkness for so long, but now I come to atone.'

He staggered closer, his limbs becoming heavier as the light streamed around him. He felt a searing agony from the runes branded across his skin, but he didn't care. This was his moment.

'I…' The pain in his flesh redoubled, and Syxx shrieked in agony. He dropped to one knee.

'I offer… offer…' He screamed again, clutching his abdomen as he felt an awful wrenching sensation within. His head snapped up and his jaw dropped open, his eyes wild at the sensation of something else puppeting his flesh.

'N'gyakh she'ghenn'a K'gluk!' Words spilled from his mouth, but they weren't his. Syxx's eyes bulged with panic as the strange syllables wrenched themselves from him.

'Hss'trakh, Hss'trakh, N'anyuug'ul'ulakh!' His voice was monstrous, sibilant, gleeful. It boomed over the battle, and as it did the fire in his flesh intensified. Syxx was powerless, transfixed with agony and horror. His moment of redemption was being overwhelmed by some monstrous thing that welled from within him, puppeting his vocal chords and surging through his flesh like a rising tide.

The rest of the Battle Sisters had turned and started shooting, but their bolts ploughed through the air in slow motion, and flickered away to embers. Syxx had a fleeting impression of golden, half-seen ghosts flickering towards him, only to burn away in the same fashion.

'M'bathra'khajuul,' came the monstrous voice, and Syxx felt a tide of energy well inside him, bringing with it an intense, tearing agony. 'Ghaar'shlek! Yaa'khari' the words boomed out, stretching his jaw wide, cracking bone and sinew. Syxx's sanity teetered as he realised, at the last, what Phelkorian had done to him.

What he had bound within his mortal form.

'Sl'eth'kryphyr! Sl'eth'kryphyr! Sl'eth'kryphyr!'

A final surge of energy poured through Syxx, and he saw one last time the lined faces, the sorrowful, loving eyes, their vengeance lost forever. His hate for Phelkorian drove the change, and with a grotesque, fleshy surge, Syxx was no more.

Sl'eth'kryphyr rose in his place.

Kassar grabbed the maintenance hatch above his head and wrenched it downwards, tearing it from its locking bolts. A hellish din flooded the crawlspace, accompanied by searing light.

'Kassar!' voxed Haltheus from the galleries above. 'It's a daemon! The cultist was a warp-damned daemon!'

'Cover the hatch,' said Kassar. 'We're coming up.'

He grabbed the lip of the hatch and pulled himself upwards, clearing it in one smooth motion. A Berzerker loomed over him, roaring, before a shot from Thelgh's rifle blew out the warrior's helm.

As Kassar's brothers emerged behind him, he took in the scene of horror. A queen of daemons loomed above the beacon, a hellish abomination of snapping claws, sinuous limbs and perfumed flesh that stood thirty feet tall. Interwoven strands of armour twined around the thing's lithe body, hung with glowing jewels and silken strands, and its beautiful, grotesque features were twisted into an arrogant sneer.

'This is what Excrucias sent in our midst,' said Makhor. 'A Keeper of Secrets.'

'This is betrayal,' said A'khassor. 'It must be.'

Battle still raged, but those close to the daemon were lost in a bewildered haze. Battle Sisters and Berzerkers alike stared at the towering creature, weapons hanging useless in their hands. The daemon laughed, delighted, and Kassar recoiled as the sound flooded his mind with grotesque images and base urges. The sounds of battle faded around him, and his limbs weighed too much to move.

The daemon reached down with one elegant claw, seeking to caress the beacon where he lay, helpless in his cradle of restraints. Amongst the ranks of the Battle Sisters, one figure twitched and struggled, her face contorted with strain. With a furious cry, Canoness

Levinia lunged into the daemon's path, hacking her power sword double-handed through the creature's talon. Reeking filth sprayed and perfumed flesh slapped to the ground as the claw was severed. The Keeper of Secrets snatched its arm back with a shriek.

The spell broke.

Kassar snarled, and Hexling snarled with him. Enemies turned towards them, seeing the Alpha Legionnaires in their midst for the first time. Kassar and his brothers let fly, while their comrades poured covering fire down from the gallery above.

'It is betrayal,' said Kassar. 'Excrucias sent this thing to kill us even as we completed his work for him. Elegant, but he didn't foresee this mayhem.'

'What do we do?' asked D'sakh.

'We prevail,' said Kassar, gunning down a charging Berzerker. 'Unsung, rally to me. We're taking the beacon for ourselves, and then we're leaving.'

The daemon's talon hit Levinia in the chest and she felt bone shatter as her armoured corset buckled. Her feet left the ground, and she sailed through the air. She slammed down on her back a good thirty feet from her opponent, fighting to stay conscious.

The fire of her faith burned within, driving back the pain and propelling her to her feet. She spat blood, staring with righteous hatred at the abomination that had entered this most sacred place.

'Unclean thing!' she bellowed. 'You stand in the light of the Emperor of Mankind. I name thee daemon and cast you out!'

As she shouted, Levinia limped back towards the creature, firing her bolter at its chest. Several of her Sisters joined her, those who weren't desperately fending off the Khornate onslaught.

The daemon lashed angrily about itself. It swatted tech-priests away like broken toys, shrugging off the bolts that stung its flesh. The thing hissed a string of profane syllables, and two Battle Sisters to Levinia's right dropped to the ground, screaming and laughing with frantic hysteria as blood poured from their mouths.

She kept striding towards it, kept firing, and as she did so she prayed.

'Oh Emperor, Lord of Mankind,

He who sits upon the Golden Throne,
We beseech you,
Our Master,
Our Liege,
Lord of ten thousand years and more,
Drive out the unclean spirits,
Drive out the taint of Chaos,
Hear this prayer, king of our hearts,
And banish this fiend from your sight.'

Her surviving Sisters joined their voices to hers, a mantra of banishment that rang out over the madness of battle. At the same time they fired, peppering the daemon with bolts and blasts. Celestine's Geminae Superia leapt towards the daemon on tongues of flame, their bolt pistols blazing. But where was the Saint herself?

The daemon recoiled from the Sisters' prayers, then hissed out a hideous laugh.

'Perhaps,' it leered, its voice like oozing oil and bleeding flesh, 'when his light was strong. But not now, little playthings. Darkness has come, the rift yawns wide, and your lord and master is nowhere to be found.'

With a fleshy surge, the daemon's severed claw sprouted again from the stump of its wrist, now clutching a long blade of blackened bone.

Stepping over Kaleb with a single stride, it swung its sword and sent slain Sisters tumbling through the air. Its hissing incantations drove others mad, tearing at their own flesh in an orgy of wanton destruction. Levinia recoiled as Sister Eleanor and Sister Jalayne reeled past, the latter sinking her teeth hungrily into the former's face.

'No,' shouted Levinia, firing until her bolter clicked dry. 'He is with us always!'

Casting the weapon aside, the canoness charged headlong at the daemon. She ducked the swing of its blade and hacked her sword into the meat of its leg, seeking to sever the limb.

Keening in fury, the daemon recoiled, serpent-fast, and aimed a kick at her. Levinia threw herself aside, rising to her feet between Kaleb and the abomination that had come to claim him.

'You shall not have him,' said Levinia, pointing her sword at the thing towering above her.

'Slaanesh shall have him,' it hissed, leering down at her with its beautiful, hideous features. 'And you, my delicious morsel, will be mine.'

Its eyes were black pools, fathomless, fascinating. Levinia fought the thing's corrupting gaze, but it swallowed her as surely as if she had plunged headlong into a lake of oil. The sweet stink of its musk filled her senses, awakening dark, horrible longings deep in her soul.

'Emperor,' she gasped, her sword point wavering, lowering. 'Where are you?'

'He is dead…' whispered the daemon, reaching out for her.

Then, from above, the Saint struck like a thunderbolt.

The Unsung crouched in a half-circle around Kassar's position, firing into anything that came close. Their enemies were busy destroying one another, and Khârn could be heard bellowing furiously from across the chamber. The entire cathedrum shook and shuddered, candles raining down as their grav-impellers shorted out. A bloody mist was billowing through the entrance arches.

Then a winged warrior fell upon the daemon from above.

'That's an angel,' said Haltheus flatly. *'Kassar, they have an angel. This is getting ridiculous.'*

'That's the distraction we need,' replied Kassar. *'Formation Baphamet, secure then exfiltrate by the western arch. Kyphas, find me a route to landing pad nine. The beacon will be boarding his shuttle after all.'*

They rose and advanced. Skaryth and D'sakh took the lead, the former firing his bolter, the latter unsheathing the colours and slashing them through anyone too slow to clear his path. Skarle, A'khassor and Makhor followed, blazing fire into their enemies. Behind them came Kassar, Haltheus, Kyphas and Krowl, who still carried Phaek'or over one shoulder. Thelgh came last, snapping off shots at any who tried to come at the Unsung from behind.

This had been a war pitting the forces of Khorne against those of the Imperium, and no one expected to see warriors in the colours of the Alpha Legion in their midst. The Unsung used that to their advantage, capitalising upon the confusion that played across their foes' faces, gunning them down or running them through before they could react. The battle was anarchic, desperate, all shape to it lost. For Kassar and his brothers, it was perfect.

Ahead, the angel and the daemon fought furiously. The winged warrior was far smaller than her opponent, but she leapt and spun, taking to the air on metallic wings and plunging in on the attack again and again. Her blade flashed in the light of the beacon, biting through unclean flesh and spattering black, stinking ichor with every blow. Two other figures had joined the onslaught, Seraphim who fought in perfect concert with the angel and maintained a steady hail of explosive bolts.

The daemon was suffering, Kassar saw. Its perfect flesh was rent and spewing ectoplasmic slime. Its magnificent armour was buckled, its silks torn. Still it fought, hissing in fury, looming covetously over the helpless beacon. Its blade stabbed out and impaled one of the Seraphim, passing right through her midriff and bursting out between her shoulder blades.

The angel leapt high, aiming a kick at the daemon's face and staggering it, then dropping down and severing its sword arm at the elbow. It stumbled back, then shrieked in fury and unleashed a storm of kaleidoscopic warp energies. The second Seraphim dropped from the air, nothing but a blackened husk encased in smouldering armour plate. The angel was blasted backwards, metallic wings glowing, flesh flickering with flames. She gave a mighty shout, and the empyric energies were banished as she lunged at the daemon again.

'Haltheus, A'khassor, grab the beacon,' said Kassar. 'The rest of you, cover.'

They trampled the bodies of the slain as they surrounded Kaleb and his anointed conveyance. Kassar squinted against the radiant light that seemed to emanate from the man's very flesh. Mere yards away, the daemon and the angel battled on.

'There's some kind of impeller lock engaged,' said Haltheus. 'Give me a moment to profane its routines.'

'Can't we just carry the damn thing?' asked Makhor, firing his bolter into the roiling melee around them.

'*Do you see how delicate this machine is?*' asked Haltheus. '*If we start manhandling it, we're going to rip out tubes, cables, whatever else. We'll kill him.*'

'And he's no use to us dead,' said Kassar.

'Who... who's there?'

Kassar glanced down and saw the canoness, kneeling amidst the bodies near the beacon. She turned sightless eyes towards him, oily tears weeping from them, black veins radiating out from their sockets.

'Dysorian?' she asked. 'Is that... you?'

Hexling twitched, crooning at him to slay the canoness out of hand. Kassar ignored the urge. He'd seen her fight selflessly, and had been impressed. Besides, he was no Khornate butcher, and this blinded warrior was clearly no threat. Instead, he ignored the canoness and kept his bolter trained on the fight around him.

'My faith,' she said, her voice cracking. 'It failed me for... just a second... Dysorian, this is my punishment. You must bear the burden now, captain. You must take him to safety.'

Kassar glanced down at the canoness again, frowning, then looked up straight into the eyes of the beacon himself. He felt a vertiginous lurch as the holy light of the man's gaze bored into his mind, and Hexling squealed and squirmed in his grip. He felt panic threaten to choke him, and with an angry snarl he lashed out, striking Kaleb in the temple with his blade's pommel. The man convulsed, his eyes rolled up, and he slumped in his restraints.

In that instant, his radiance winked out.

'Kassar!' exclaimed A'khassor. 'What in the warp are you doing?'

'We need him alive, not conscious,' said Kassar angrily. 'Haltheus, hurry up.'

Haltheus gave a triumphant shout, and the anointed conveyance hummed as its impellers disengaged. In the same instant, there came a terrible shriek, a cry of agony and rage so piercing that Kassar's auto-senses locked out, while the stained-glass window was shattered by the soaring resonance. As its shards fell, so too did the daemon, its head struck from its shoulders with a swing of the angel's sword. Its body toppled, coming apart as black filth and scads of foaming flesh, splattering the flagstones and sizzling as it dissolved. The sweet stench of corruption was momentarily overwhelming.

'Move,' said Kassar, and his brothers responded. Haltheus and A'khassor guided the anointed conveyance, the rest of the Unsung forming a tight ring around them, guns blazing.

Kassar expected the angel to strike at any moment. Battle Sisters ran at them, frantic to stop them, but they were far too few, and as they turned their backs upon the Khorne worshippers, so they were hacked down.

Bloody mist parted before them as they ran. The arch grew closer. Shots rang from their armour, and several of the Unsung staggered, but none of them fell.

By some dark miracle, with the last of their enemies still intent on hacking one another apart amidst the rain of falling glass, they were going to escape.

Then a charging figure emerged through the bloody murk, running straight at them, armour scorched, flesh bloodied, massive chain-axe screaming.

'Blood for the Blood God!' roared Khârn.

'Oh... Throne,' said Haltheus.

They couldn't evade. They couldn't retreat. They had no gleaned secrets, no leverage, no advantage to use.

They had only one option.

'Shoot him,' barked Kassar, and he and his warriors opened fire with everything they had.

Khârn ran through the firestorm with his head down. Bolt shells fractured his armour. Thelgh put a round through his shoulder. A'khassor's plasma pistol burned a glowing crater in his gut. None of it was enough, not even close.

Skaryth was smashed aside with the flat of Khârn's axe, chest plate cracked. Skarle fired Gift one-handed, wreathing the Betrayer in flames, but Gorechild swung around, unstoppable, and Kassar cried out in anger as Skarle's head was hacked from his shoulders. The strange Alpha Legionnaire crumpled, his blood jetting over Kassar as he died.

'Mindless butcher!' roared Kassar. 'I am Alpharius, and I am your death!' He hurled himself at Khârn, swinging Hexling in an overhead cut. The Betrayer parried the blow, staggering back at its ferocity. Kassar swung again, aiming to lop off Khârn's head, but again Gorechild turned the blow aside. Then Khârn snarled in rage and swung a blow of his own that Kassar barely parried. He was propelled backwards by its force, crashing into D'sakh, and the two of them went down in a clatter of armour.

Khârn revved Gorechild and clashed the axe's haft against his chest-plate. Then he looked up, past them, and let out a long, low growl.

'The angel...' he rasped.

Celestine swept down, swinging her blade in a fiery arc of judgement. Her strike met Gorechild with a resounding clang, and Khârn was driven aside. Celestine hammered the Betrayer's guard with a blistering string of blows, darting, stabbing and hacking, driving him back step by step.

As she did, Kassar and D'sakh found their feet. A'khassor knelt over Skarle's fallen body, his reductor whining as it cracked open the fallen warrior's chestplate to extract his gene-seed.

'Do we shoot them?' asked Haltheus.

In that moment, Celestine shot a look back, over her shoulder, straight at Kassar. Her face was unreadable, but her intent was as clear to him as if she'd spoken aloud.

'No,' said Kassar. 'No. Exfiltrate.'

Leaving Skarle's fallen body, the last of the Unsung ran for the eastern arch. They passed the fight ignored; Khârn cared only about the angel he fought, and she sought only to hold his attention for as long as she could.

Bursting through a billowing crimson fog-bank, Kassar saw the arch ahead of them. A scattering of cultists stood in their way, ripping and battering at the fallen remains of a penitent engine. The Unsung fired a tight volley, blowing the mortals off their feet, and swept through the archway into the corridor beyond.

Celestine fought with speed and skill. She fought with determination, and a desire to see her enemy fall. Even though she knew that he wouldn't. Even though she knew that for her, this path, this incarnation ended here.

She was satisfied, for the Emperor's will had been done in this place, but she wept golden tears, for as the beacon's light went out, so the Tsadrekhan Unity would wither and end. Already she sensed the shadows gathering, the storm growing worse, darkness rushing in from the void to fill up the absence where light had lived. Billions were about to die, or worse.

Yet the dawn could not come without the darkness. Day could not be born anew without first vanquishing the night. She knew this as surely as she knew that the Emperor had meant to see the beacon in the hands of Kassar and his brothers, rather than let it fall to the worshippers of Khorne, or Slaanesh.

It was a grim equation, a measure of how desperate the Imperium's plight had become, but Celestine trusted her Emperor. For thousands of years, across dozens of lifetimes, he had never, ever led her wrong. He would not do so now.

She had faith.

And so, as her strength failed her, as Gorechild's ringing blows numbed her arms and drove her to her knees, she did not despair. As Khârn smashed the Ardent Blade from her hands, and ripped the beautiful wings from her back, she knew only satisfaction for her task, and sorrow for all those martyred to see it done.

And as he swung Gorechild high, and struck her head from her shoulders, Saint Celestine felt only blessed release.

The Unsung pelted through the corridors of the convent prioris at a run, guiding the anointed conveyance as fast as they dared. A terrible, sawing note rang through the air, and in every corner the shadows churned and coiled.

'In retrospect,' shouted Haltheus as they ran, 'I think knocking him out was a bad idea, Kassar.'

Kassar didn't respond. In his mind's eye he saw the final, piercing gaze of the angel, and heard again the words of the blinded canoness.

'You must bear the burden now, captain. You must take him to safety.'

'I owe them nothing,' he whispered fiercely. 'Damned corpse worshippers. They're no better than the Dark Gods. I owe them nothing!'

'Didn't catch that, captain,' said D'sakh.

'Nothing,' barked Kassar over the sounds of rumbling and moaning, explosions and screams. 'Just keep running.'

'There's a turbolift ahead,' said Kyphas. 'But I wouldn't trust it.' As if to emphasise his words, the electro-sconces along the corridor blew out as one, and red emergency lumen flickered to life. A screaming cackle echoed down the corridor, spiralling away to nothing.

'Alternative route?' asked Kassar.

'Next left,' said Kyphas. 'We take a loading ramp up three levels, then cut through the equipment hangar and straight out onto landing pad nine.'

A trio of robed Battle Sisters burst from the turning ahead, shepherding a gaggle of scribes and menials between them. Two of the Sisters carried bolters, the other a revving chainsword. They cried out and raised their weapons, but the shadows convulsed around them and a terrible wet growl filled the corridor. The scribes screamed in terror as half-seen entities swept through their midst, ripping at them with talons made from embers and dripping darkness. One of the Sisters was lifted and smashed against the ceiling with bone-breaking force. Another fell, her head wrenched around by ethereal talons, while the last was snatched up by the whirling hurricane of shadows and borne away, screaming, into the gloom.

The Unsung looked at one another.

'We really need to get off this planet,' said Makhor.

'Agreed,' said Kassar. 'Keep moving, brothers. And be ready for anything.'

Kassar led his Harrow through the dying spire. They rode out the convulsive shudders that ran through the structure, and smashed aside the few warriors that reeled into their path. Only when they reached the equipment hangar did they meet serious Imperial numbers. Battle Sisters and Tsadrekhans were spilling through the cavernous space, flowing between heaped crates and inert lifter servitors. Kassar watched them from a shadowed doorway, Hexling held to his chest.

'It's a full evacuation,' he said. 'They're carrying relics, tomes, anything they can take with them.'

'This world is doomed,' said A'khassor. 'The Dark Gods have been denied here a long while. Their vengeance will be swift and horrible, I don't doubt.'

A dull boom rang from outside, firelight spilling in through the open shutters at the hangar's far end. Khornate war cries rang out, and the Battle Sisters hastened forward, bolters up.

'Could be our chance,' said Kassar. 'Move quickly, stay to the shadows at the edge, and be ready to shoot our way out.'

The shadows thickened for a second, and a howling gale raced through the shelter. Kassar heard whispering voices upon it, hissing threats and promises.

He slipped through the doorway and into the cover of a towering equipment rack. Staying low, he ran along its length, his brothers following. Gunfire rattled and explosions boomed, getting closer by the moment.

He darted between stacks of macro-containers, then slid along the back of a decommissioned lifter, aquila-stamped tarpaulins flapping over its exposed innards. Another detonation echoed from the direction of the doors, and bloodthirsty howls rose and died away. The gunfire stopped.

Peering out, Kassar saw blazing wreckage, and corpses strewed the hangar's exit. Rain slashed down, diluting the blood and damping the flames. The Imperial evacuees milled, some fleeing back into the spire in search of another route, others crouched in cover, staring with huge eyes.

'There's something out there,' he said. 'Can't see what.'

'The shuttle should be located six hundred yards from here,' said Kyphas. 'Pad nine is the third on the right. It's a minute's run at most, even with the conveyance.'

'Ammo check,' ordered Kassar.

'*Low to minimal*,' replied Haltheus. '*We'll be down to blades if we run into anything serious.*'

'*Then blades it is*,' said Kassar. '*We're getting off this world, now, before the catastrophe overtakes it. No gods, no warlords.*'

'*For the primarchs, and the Harrow*,' said his brothers, finishing the old war mantra.

Kassar rose and led the way past the gaggles of terrified adepts and menials, ignoring their wails of fear, and out into the driving rain.

The Unsung burst from the hangar doors at a run, guns up, and out onto a wide area of ferrocrete decking and metal bridges that linked landing pads to one another above a perilous drop. The rain hit them like a wall. The wind howled around them, a screaming chorus of the damned. Burning spires rose on every side, their gothic architecture ablaze, explosions billowing as they began to come apart. The clouds whirled in insane spirals, reaching down to claw at the frothing waves with tornadoes lit red and green and black. Lurid lightning raced through the clouds, forming eight-pointed star patterns the size of cities.

Drop-ships, bulk lifters and shuttles were labouring up into that tortured sky, braving the terrors above to escape those below. Running lights winked in the darkness. Runic beacons flashed, and rocket exhausts flared.

Closer, a buckled plasteel walkway reached out over the vertiginous drop to the waves below. On either side were landing pads, supported on frameworks of girders and gothic statuary that were beginning to collapse.

Several of the pads were empty. One had canted at an insane angle, tipping a bulk hauler onto its side. Flames chewed at it hungrily. Only one, pad nine, was still occupied, an Aquila lander sitting ready amidst decoupled fuel tanks and flashing beacons.

There had been guards, Kassar saw, Battle Sisters whose bodies were now strewn in bits around the shuttle. As the Unsung ran towards the landing pad, they saw the Sisters' killers, a trio of Possessed Khornate Marines whose dead pack-mates lay amidst their enemies' bodies. The

Berzerkers' bodies were malformed horrors, bone spikes and bulging muscle showing through rents in their armour. But there were only three of them left, and they were in Kassar's way.

'Ungifted!' howled the biggest of the three, its bestial head swinging towards them.

'Kill them,' Kassar ordered, and his brothers' guns spoke one last time. Thelgh shot one, his stolen bolt rifle reducing its head to a bloody spray. The other two charged towards them, howling and screeching. Bolts ripped the second Possessed apart, while Kassar ran the leader through, driving Hexling into its chest and then shoving it backwards off the walkway. The twisted creature plunged away, rebounding from a shattered gargoyle before falling out into space and down, towards the waves below. Kassar, meanwhile, felt a surge of exhilaration and pleasure race down his arm from his sword, tasting the blood on its blade as though it dripped from his own tongue.

'So much for the gifts of the Dark Gods,' spat Kassar. 'Get aboard.'

They piled in through the Aquila's hatch, feeling the landing pad shudder beneath them. Jade lightning stabbed down, exploding against the walkway and causing runic substations to detonate.

Thelgh was last aboard. As he thumped the rune to close the lander's hatch, and A'khassor locked the anointed conveyance down as best he could, Kassar and Haltheus made for the cockpit. The hiss of the rain and roar of explosions was muffled as the hatch sealed, and atmospheric engines cycled.

In the cockpit, they found a blank-eyed pilot servitor awaiting the command to lift off.

'The Coffer?' asked Kassar.

'No,' said Haltheus. 'Still angry. I'll handle this.'

Haltheus gripped the servitor by its shoulders and tore it from its throne. Wires snapped and servos sparked as he tossed the warbling unit aside and dropped into its place.

'Everyone secure yourselves,' he voxed. 'This will not be a pleasant flight.'

Haltheus flipped switches and pressed runes, awakening the shuttle's drives and releasing its grav-anchors. Kassar gripped the back of the pilot's throne as the Aquila lifted off with a roar, and began to rise.

'We're moving,' said Haltheus. 'But where? We can't dock with Excrucias' ships, even if they're up there at all, and judging by these instruments there's a warp storm of massive magnitude closing in.'

'The Imperials are expecting this shuttle,' said Kassar, as a fiery explosion blossomed to port. 'And its cargo.'

'You're suggesting the Decaligah trick, aren't you?' asked Haltheus, then swore as he wrenched the controls to starboard, narrowly avoiding a plunging spire-top.

'We have the beacon,' said Kassar. 'They'll be terrified, panicked, desperate to leave. We have leverage.'

'And we have Kyphas,' said Haltheus, punching in coordinates and scanning the Imperial frequencies. 'Why not? It's like you keep saying, Kassar, we're about due some good fortune.'

Kassar nodded.

'Find us a likely target, then get us out of here. We're done with this world.'

Haltheus fired the shuttle's retros, and they soared away from the dying spire, into the fury of the storm. Aboard, Kassar slumped back in his throne restraints and looked around at his ten surviving brothers. D'sakh and Kyphas, both leaning back in their restraints and taking a moment with their own thoughts. A'khassor and Makhor, bracing the beacon in his conveyance, the Apothecary checking over the device's readouts and muttering. Thelgh and Krowl, with Phaek'or strapped in between them, the wounded Alpha Legionnaire braced by his brothers. Haltheus piloting. Skaryth painstakingly etching new kill tallies into a bare space on his armour's right vambrace.

It was enough. It would have to be. Through deception and leverage, they would make this ship theirs. With it, and the beacon, and the gene-seed A'khassor carried at his belt, they would begin again.

After all, he thought, with one hand on Hexling's pommel, they would need all the strength they could muster.

They had revenge to seek.

EPILOGUE

Captain Shandri gripped the armrests of his throne, gritting his teeth as the *Dutiful Blade* shuddered around him. Servitors babbled binharic alarms, and Naval ratings fought electrical fires.

'Hail them again,' he ordered.

'Lord, Navigator Tzanbindri is screaming at us to depart,' said Vox Officer Gordin. 'We cannot tarry any longer!'

'We can tarry precisely as long as the Emperor bloody well demands,' barked the captain. 'Anyone who says differently can have a swift conversation with Commissar Traeda and her bolt pistol. Understood?'

'Yes, lord,' said Gordin, turning back to his station, face pale.

Tsadrekha filled the bridge holoscreen, picked out in flickering green lines. Madness wreathed it, fleet engagement runes and malefic manifestation warnings flashing angry red.

'We are the last hope,' announced Captain Shandri, his voice booming from loudhailers along the ship's corridors. 'Understand that. Know it. With the *Mighty Colossus* and the *Seventh Saint* gone, we are the last ship of the fleet still in position to retrieve the beacon, and we will by Emperor and by dammit wait until the last possible moment to depart. We do our duty, as all must in these times, or we die for the Emperor!'

The bridge crew of the *Dutiful Blade* wrestled with their controls as empyric bleed and malefic energies fought to overtake them. The storm was minutes out at most, and Khornate and Slaaneshi fleets were tearing through the Imperial rear guard. The captain was not exaggerating when he said it was duty or death.

'Lord!' shouted Gordin, one hand clamped to his headset. 'Vox contact. Signifier reads as the *Hand of Deliverance*. It's them, lord. They're bringing the beacon out!'

'Emperor be praised,' breathed Shandri. 'Bring them up on the imager.'

The hololith flickered, Tsadrekha replaced with a vidcam image from within the Aquila lander that was battling its way out of the atmosphere towards them.

Shandri paused as he took in the huge silhouette of a Space Marine, and the colours of a Chapter he didn't recognise.

'Unknown pilot, identify yourself in the Emperor's name,' said Shandri. 'Where is Canoness Levinia?'

'Canoness Levinia fell in the beacon's defence,' rumbled a deep, powerful voice from the bridge's vox speakers. 'We were forced to intercede. We have the beacon. Requesting permission to dock.'

As Shandri listened to the Space Marine's voice, he felt the compulsion to do as he was asked, but something made him hesitate, an uncomfortable intuitive twinge that the desire to comply was not his own.

'Who am I speaking to?' he demanded.

'We are loyal warriors of the Emperor,' said the Space Marine, and again Shandri felt the desire to trust him. 'Repeat, requesting permission to dock. Do not make us ask again, captain.'

Below, in the analytics pit, robed menials chattered in alarm and sent data-packets winging their way up to his throne readout.

'My adepts claim to have identified your armour markings,' said Shandri, though he couldn't find it in himself to feel the panic he should have. 'They say you are Alpha Legion, heretics. That we should blast you from the void.'

'Captain,' said the Space Marine, his voice deep, resonant, reassuring yet menacing at the same time. 'My name is Brother Kyphas and I and my warriors are representatives of the Emperor's most holy Inquisition. The colours we wear are a false flag, a necessary deception to move amongst the traitors of the archenemy long enough to remove the beacon to safety.'

'A... deception?' Shandri's thoughts were foggy, his tongue thick in his mouth. The beacon was on its way, brought to safety by Space Marines, Inquisitorial agents no less. He should comply with them, shouldn't he?

'Of course, captain,' said the Space Marine. 'This was a war against the worshippers of Khorne, you recall? The Alpha Legion was never on Tsadrekha...'

'The Alpha Legion was never... on... Tsadrekha,' said Captain Shandri, and suddenly it all made perfect sense. What a fool he was being, questioning these brave warriors, risking execution for dereliction of duty, jeopardising their precious cargo while danger closed in from every side. Some artifice of the archenemy, perhaps? He would have to pray for forgiveness in the ship's chapel, if they survived this.

'Well?' barked Shandri at his crew. 'What are you idiots waiting for, the Emperor's personal say-so? Prep a landing bay. Weapons stand down, clear them for landing. Magos Delitrax, engage the bloody warp engines. We are leaving!'

Captain Shandri's crew dashed to follow his orders and, as the warp storm closed in to swallow the world of Tsadrekha whole, the Aquila lander swept into the *Dutiful Blade*'s third port hangar just before its empyric shutters rattled down.

On the huge hololithic screen of his ship's bridge, Lord Excrucias watched his defeat unfold. The *Herald of Pain* sliced through the Naval engagement like a blade, Excrucias' fleet spread out in a perfect spearhead behind and to both sides. Yet though the Slaaneshi warships were making short work of the battered Imperial and Khornate fleets, it was not enough.

Excrucias let out a sibilant hiss as the Imperial shuttle docked with the larger warship, bare moments before it vanished through the veil into warp space. It left behind a world whose skies danced with ghostly flame, and whose storm clouds were underlit by vast flares of leprous energy. The situation in the void was scarcely better, the darkness of space pulling apart like overstretched sinew to allow ecto-plasmic clouds and planet-sized tentacles to spill forth.

'They took the beacon,' said Phelkorian with manic glee. 'The Tsadrekhan Unity will drown in a thousand years of nightmares.'

'But they took… the beacon,' hissed Excrucias, and a thin trickle of blood ran down his mask as he pressed his tongue to its razor lips.

Excrucias' lieutenants clamoured.

'My lord,' screeched the champion Shaelbol, his tattered skin flexing over his barbed armour as he stepped forward. 'Give me the pleas-ure of leading the pursuit and–'

Shaelbol's proclamation was cut short as Excrucias' blade sliced through his throat, leaving his head to flop backwards on a thin flap of muscle and skin. The Slaaneshi champion collapsed, milky blood gushing from his neck-stump.

'Idiocy is a flaw,' snarled Excrucias, wiping the blade upon his champion's fallen body. 'The beacon was never the point, not in and of itself. It was… the act of profaning it, of dedicating its des-ecration to Slaanesh and offering up all the souls in the Unity for her alone. As you… well know, Phelkorian. That should be your head lying on the floor, if you even possess such a thing any more. Your cultist failed.'

'He was flawed, my lord, it is true,' said the sorcerer, gloved hands squirming over the grips of his staff. 'But I am useful to you still, and to the Dark Prince. My death would be wasteful, a flawed act of petulance and rage.'

'It would…' said Excrucias, breathing out and sheathing his blade. His flensing knives were foremost in his mind, and his skin itched in readiness. 'There is nothing for us here now. This war is over. The Unity falls, and I lose interest. We must depart, and begin our hunt for those who have shamed us twice. This insult will not stand, Twyst.'

'I agree, my lord,' said Phelkorian, and his many mouths leered. 'But before we make our escape, I sense something that may please you, bobbing in the ether. Lost, and prideful, and so very full of secrets.'

The sorcerer gesticulated and a shimmering spray of unclean light rose from his palm, forming a delicate sculpture in the air. A small ship amidst the void, little more than an atmospheric transport skiff. Aboard it, a single soul, full of anger and bitterness at those who had betrayed him, and hate for the galaxy that was about to snuff him so uncaringly from existence. His soul burned in skeins of green and blue, and ethereal snakes twined around him, a many-headed hydra wrought in the energies of the warp.

Excrucias stared for a moment and then, behind his mask, his scarred features twisted into a cruel smile.

'A lost son of Alpharius, making his hopeless escape,' he hissed in delight. 'Signal the ship's masters. See that he... is rescued before we leave this place. I wish to speak to him at length, Twyst. And I doubt that he will enjoy it...'